LET LOOSE *the* DOGS

THE MURDOCH MYSTERIES

MAUREEN JENNINGS

Let Loose
the Dogs

A Murdoch Mystery

MCCLELLAND & STEWART

First published by St. Martin's Press 2003
First McClelland & Stewart paperback edition 2004
This trade paperback edition 2010

LIBRARY AND ARCHIVES OF CANADA CATALOGUING IN PUBLICATION

Jennings, Maureen
Let loose the dogs / Maureen Jennings.

(A Detective Murdoch mystery)
Originally publ.: New York : T. Dunne Books, 2003
ISBN 978-0-7710-4336-9

I. Title. II. Series: Jennings, Maureen. Detective Murdoch mystery.

PS8569.E562L38 2010   C813'.54   C2009-906981-4

We acknowledge the financial support of the Government of Canada
through the Book Publishing Industry Development Program and that of
the Government of Ontario through the Ontario Media Development
Corporation's Ontario Book Initiative. We further acknowledge the
support of the Canada Council for the Arts and the Ontario Arts Council
for our publishing program.

Published simultaneously in the United States of America by
McClelland & Stewart Ltd., P.O. Box 1030, Plattsburgh, New York 12901

LIBRARY OF CONGRESS CONTROL NUMBER: 2009942547

Typeset in Caslon Book by M&S, Toronto
Printed and bound in Canada

This book is printed on paper that is 100% recycled,
ancient-forest friendly (40% post-consumer waste).

McClelland & Stewart Ltd.
75 Sherbourne Street
Toronto, Ontario
M5A 2P9

www.mcclelland.com

1 2 3 4 5   14 13 12 11 10

For Iden, as always

And Caesar's spirit, ranging for revenge,
Shall in these confines with a monarch's voice
Cry "Havoc," and let slip the dogs of war;
That this foul deed shall smell above the earth . . .

— from William Shakespeare's *Julius Caesar*

AUGUST 1895

Chapter One

HE REMEMBERED THE MATCH VIVIDLY. After that – after he had fallen by the bridge – he had no recall and only knew what had happened from the statements of witnesses at his trial. The day had been oppressively hot, the sky heavy and dark with a threatening storm. Inside the barn it was stifling, the air thick with the smell of blood and the stink of the rats. The dogs were going wild. Tripper, the innkeeper's black-and-tan bitch; the two white pugs that belonged to the Craigs; and a squat, brindle bulldog, who was there for the first time, were all tethered to the rings that ran along the wall. All of them were barking nonstop, their eyes dilated, saliva flooding from their mouths. He had shouted with the others all through the matches. They all had, even the Englishman who made such a point of being unruffled. Delaney had Flash in his arms and was having a hard time holding on to him, he was squirming so much, wanting to get back into the ring. Everybody knew this terrier had won unless Havoc got more kills. The stakes were high as they always were at Newcombe's matches, and Harry had put down a lot of money, every dime of what he'd saved over the summer. He was glad he'd drawn the last run because the later dogs were always more ferocious.

"Havoc up! Last dog. Flash the one to beat with forty kills," Lacey, the ring-keeper, called out. He released a cage of rats into the pit. They were dull brownish grey and fat from their summer feeding. At first they stayed close together, noses twitching, dazzled by the light. Lacey stirred them up with his crooked stick, then he shouted again.

"*NOW! LET LOOSE YOUR DOG.*"

Harry dropped Havoc into the ring. Immediately the terrier pounced on three rats in succession, killing each one with a single bite and a violent shake that broke their necks. The rest started to run, circling the small walled pit. Some tried in vain to climb up the smooth sides. For the next, long ten minutes the dog pursued them, biting, shaking, and dropping one after the other. The men took up the count, calling out the number of hits.

"*TWENTY-TWO . . . TWENTY-THREE . . . TWENTY-FOUR . . .*"

One of the rats twisted up and gripped the dog on the nose with its razor teeth, but Havoc wasn't deterred, running on until finally he slammed against the wall crushing the creature and it dropped to the floor. Several of the other rats tried to huddle in a corner, but Lacey banged on the side of the pit wall to get them going. The terrier killed all of them. The chant got faster, driving him on. His muzzle was crimson, his coat flecked with blood and spittle.

"*THIRTY . . . THIRTY-ONE . . .*"

Briefly, the little dog seized one of the corpses.

"Dead un! Leave it!" yelled Harry, and Havoc obeyed. The brown-and-white feist that belonged to White almost broke his leash in his attempts to get over to the ring. As if sensing what was at stake, all of the other dogs grew more frantic and shrill until it was hard to hear anything at all.

". . . *THIRTY-SIX . . .*"

The dog captured another one, almost tossing it out of the ring.

". . . *THIRTY-SEVEN.*"

Lacey was watching his big brass clock, which was on the ledge where everybody could see it. His hand was at the ready, clutching the rod to strike the gong beside him.

Suddenly the terrier stopped, panting hard. He looked toward the ring of spectators. Harry yelled.

"*Go on . . . Get 'em. Go on!*" But the dog didn't move.

"*TIME!*" Lacey sounded the gong. The match was over.

"Pick up your dog," he called out.

"It was a cheat. My dog was stopped. We could have won."

5

"Please pick up your dog now, sir," repeated Lacey.

"Don't be a sore loser, Harry. It was fair and square," said Delaney, who was across from him.

Harry turned on him in fury. "You're a cheating liar. You did something, I know it. We could have won."

He reached over into the pit and snatched up Havoc, who yelped at the roughness of his grip. Normally Harry would have felt bad at hurting the dog, but now he was too angry to care and he thrust him into the wooden carrying box.

Newcombe, who always had his eye out for trouble, who was always pouring oil on boiling water, came over to him. "Now then, don't take on so. It was a fair match. Your dog got himself distracted. It's happened to us all at some time or other."

He tried to place an arm on Harry's shoulder to placate him, but Harry would have none of it.

"It suits you to say that, Vince Newcombe." He pointed accusingly at Lacey. "I had more time due to me. He cheated. I'll wager he's getting a cut of the take."

The timekeeper shrugged but said nothing.

Again, Newcombe tried to soothe. "Walter's honest as they come and never makes a mistake. Come on, let me stand you an ale. The match was won fair and square."

"I don't believe that. Those rats looked half asleep to me. You probably smoked them."

The innkeeper wiped at his face. He was a living replica of the old-time monks, with his bald head and round belly. "Why would I do that? It's all the same to me who wins."

"Not if he gives you a cut, it isn't."

The man, Pugh, who had been running the bulldog, spoke up. He'd come on his wheel, dressed for it in a bicycle suit of brown tweed and matching cap. His beige leggings were stained with blood and dirt. His dog was useless, more afraid of the rats than they were of him. Pugh was as garrulous as a jackdaw.

"You lost, sir. Your dog balked. Nobody was cheating you. Take your lumps and stop whingeing."

Delaney started to approach his opponent. "You've got a game little lad, there, Harry. It was a good match. Why don't we shake on it like gentlemen."

He held out his hand. However, Harry turned away and spat on the dirt floor. "Hell will freeze over before I kiss the arse of liars and cheats."

For a moment, everything hung in the balance, and they all knew it. Out of the corner of his eye, Harry saw that Lacey's hand was on the handle of the water bucket ready to douse them both if need be.

"Tell me how I cheated you," said Delaney.

"You made some kind of sound. Something, I could tell the way he looked over. You've got a whistle I bet."

Delaney abruptly turned out all of his pockets, jacket and trousers. Harry thought they hung down like hounds' ears.

"Nothing, see. Will you be satisfied now?"

7

At this point, his son moved in closer. He was big like his father but smooth chinned and soft faced. For a moment, Harry thought he'd have to take on both of them, but then he saw that the boy was afraid and needed to take comfort from his father rather than defend him.

"He's not going to buff down for you, Harry," said Pugh. "Leave it now."

There were three other competitors in the barn. The Englishman, Craig, was the oldest man present. He looked ridiculously out of place in his suit of fine grey tweed, as if he should be in church rather than in a barn spattered with blood. He spoke up in an English accent as impeccable as his clothes.

"Mr. Newcombe, this has been a most exciting evening, but it is damnably hot in here. I suggest we Corinthians settle our bets and all get on home before the storm breaks."

Harry glared at him. "You're so eager to finish up here, aren't you? I wouldn't be surprised if you're not in on it as well."

Even to his own ears, his words sounded slurred. He'd lost count of how many glasses of ale he'd tossed back, although he knew Lacey was keeping a close reckoning. Craig flicked at his moustache, which was waxed to such a thin point you'd think he'd be afraid of stabbing himself.

"It might be a good idea for you to cool off outside yourself, sir."

Lacey made a slight movement, making it clear he was ready to assist if need be. James Craig stepped over, but unlike Philip Delaney, he was obviously ready to stand with his father. White wasn't saying anything and didn't look as if he would give any fight. Harry looked around at all of them, spat again, and picking up the box where he had put his dog, he left.

Outside the coming storm had overwhelmed any light still lingering. He saw the lightning flash, and from habit learned at sea, he counted until he heard a crack of thunder. The storm was nearly here. He hesitated but he was consumed with thoughts of revenge: all his money gone, stolen from him. He turned toward the end of the road and the path that led down into the ravine, Delaney's path home.

It was darker as he descended, the trees thick and lush with leaves. He was about to cross the bridge at the bottom of the path, but he misjudged his step and tripped, striking his cheek hard against the railing. Cursing, he staggered further along, but he was too full of liquor and fell to the ground. Havoc barked at being jolted, but Harry had to find a place to rest. He crawled into the dense grass that was at the side of the path and lay down.

That was all he remembered.

9

December 1895

Chapter Two

COUNTY OF YORK ASSIZES.

JUSTICE FALCONBRIDGE PRESIDING.

DECEMBER 2, 1895.

STATEMENT OF SWORN WITNESS,
PATRICK PUGH, BOOK AGENT.

MR. GREENE, Q.C.: Mr. Pugh, will you tell the gentlemen of the jury, in your own words, what happened the night of August 4, 1895.

PUGH: Yes, sir. After the ratting match, I went over to the tap-room with Mr. Newcombe, who is the publican of the Manchester tavern. I sat chinning with him until about ten o'clock when there was a pounding on the door . . .

MR. GREENE: One moment, Mr. Pugh. Even though the other witnesses will be giving their statements, it will assist the jurymen if you tell us what you recall about the movements of the other participants in the so-called match.

PUGH: Movements?

GREENE: What time did so and so leave for instance and with whom?

PUGH: Right! The first so and so to leave was the accused . . .

(laughter)

JUSTICE FALCONBRIDGE: Mr. Pugh, this is a court of law. I will not tolerate such levity. I am inclined to charge you with contempt of court.

PUGH: I beg your pardon, Your Honour, I was being literal. But as I was saying, the accused left first about half past seven or twenty minutes to eight. There was bad blood between him and the victim on account of he felt John Delaney had cheated him. In my opinion this was not the case, but he wouldn't listen. After he'd gone, we settled up our wagers. Walter Lacey had totted them up so that was soon done. I myself was only paying out, not receiving, but with the exception of me and the accused, the others won something, even Mr. White. Not that he took in much, one dollar I believe . . .

JUSTICE FALCONBRIDGE: Will you come to the point, Mr. Pugh. We don't have all day to decide this case. I would like to go home for Christmas.

(laughter)

14 PUGH: I beg your pardon, Your Honour. Mr. Greene said I should use my own words, and there always seems to be a lot of them.

(laughter)

Sorry, sir. I wasn't intending to be funny. Where was I? That's all right, Mr. Greene, I remember. After the accused left, John Delaney followed. No wait, I tell a lie. He sent his son, Philip, off home first, then he collected his winnings, put them in his leather pouch, and left. He had won almost one hundred dollars. Shortly after, the Craigs and Mr. White left together.

GREENE: How soon after Mr. Delaney was that?

PUGH: I can't say exactly because I wasn't looking at the clock, not realising it would be important four months later . . . but my guess is it was no more than ten minutes or so. There was a threat of a storm brewing, and everybody wanted to get home before it broke. We didn't realise a storm was coming, in more ways than one . . .

JUSTICE FALCONBRIDGE: Mr. Pugh!

PUGH: My apologies, Your Honour. After they had gone, Mr. Newcombe suggested we move over to the taproom where it was more comfortable, which we did, leaving Walter Lacey to clean the barn. We were together in each other's sight for the rest of the evening until young Philip Delaney arrived saying his pa had not come home.

GREENE: One moment, Mr. Pugh. You said you and Mr. Newcombe were in each other's sight the rest of the evening, by my calculation a period of about two hours. Did either of you leave the taproom at any time, however briefly, even to – excuse me, Your Honour – even to make water in the outside privy?

PUGH: I did, in fact, go out once to do just that. About nine

15

o'clock. The clock was chiming. When I went outside I mean, not while I was . . .

(laughter)

JUSTICE FALCONBRIDGE: Mr. Pugh, this is a last warning.

PUGH: Yes, sir. I was truly not trying to be funny. I am a literal man.

GREENE: So you are telling the court that except for a period of approximately ten minutes, you and Mr. Newcombe can vouch for each other?

PUGH: That is correct. He only left my sight just after I returned from the privy because Walter Lacey's wife and child had come in search of Maria. The babe was ill, and Mrs. Newcombe is well known in the neighbourhood for her nursing abilities. But Vincent was gone for only four or five minutes at the most while he made sure the situation wasn't serious, which it turned out not to be. The sick child, I mean . . .

GREENE: Please be so good as to inform the gentlemen of the jury how long it would take to go into the ravine and back.

PUGH: That depends on whether you are a tortoise or a hare sort of person. A normal man or sturdy woman, walking at a normal pace, could go down and back in about twenty minutes at the most. Down to the bridge I mean, which is where I found Delaney. You could run it faster I suppose, but the hill is steep so unless you were an Indian you would be panting pretty hard by the time you returned. What I am saying is that Mr. Newcombe was not at all breathless when he rejoined me in the taproom. We sat and chinned some more. Mostly about dogs, of which he knows a lot. The clock was chiming again, this time striking out a quarter past the hour of ten o'clock. It has a funny sort of wheeze to it so it draws attention to itself, which is why I noticed so particularly. We heard Philip at the door, as I've already told you. No offence, but he's a bit childish in his mind, and he was upset at his pa's absence. I didn't think there could be anything amiss. If we laid all the men end to end who've avoided going straight home after an afternoon at a betting match, the line would stretch down to the lake I'm sure. However, I said I'd walk back with him and take a look. I borrowed Vincent's lantern and set off. The rain had stopped, but the leaves and ground were soaked so we got wet just walking down the path. There's a little wooden bridge at the bottom of the path that spans the creek. Just past it, the path forks. One path runs up the hill to the Delaney house, the other follows the creek all the way through to Yonge Street. Philip said he was sure his father wasn't anywhere along the path to their house, so I said, "Let's take a look along here then." In the back of my mind, I thought maybe Mr. Delaney had laid down for a little kip . . .

GREENE: Had he been drinking liquor during the match?

PUGH: I wasn't paying much attention. Mr. Lacey was constantly bringing us refills, which he kept good track of, I might add. To my mind, Mr. Delaney wasn't inebriated in the same way as the accused obviously was, but he may have had enough to make him want to lie down. I expected to find him fast asleep under a tree. Well, not too far down the path, oh about one hundred yards, I'd say, the light glinted on something pale floating in the creek. It was Mr. Delaney.

17

He had got wedged in the rocks, he was on his back, and his hair and beard were flowing out like weeds all around his head. I say this because it is relevant, Your Honour. I did think at once he was dead. However, I have studied resuscitation of drowned persons, and I could but try to revive him. I put down my lantern and was about to jump down the bank into the water. At this point two things occurred. The grey terrier, Havoc, came rushing at me out of the bushes. He's small but a fierce little thing, and he grabs hold of my trousers. I'm telling Philip to take hold of the cur, and he's standing on the edge of the bank wailing that his father is dead. "No, he's not," says I. "Come and help me pull him out." But he was incapable, so I spoke to him real sharp and told him to run as fast as he could to the tavern and fetch Mr. Newcombe. He did that, but the dog was still worrying at me till I had to kick it and he ran off. I slid down the bank and managed to pull on Mr. Delaney's arm to bring him to the strip of sand that was at the verge. There I rolled him over onto his stomach preparatory to doing resuscitation, but as soon as I did, I could see terrible gashes in the back of his head. Deep, terrible gashes they were, to the point that I could see bone and brain. Turned my stomach. I thought I'd better leave him there until we could get a coroner to come take a look. I made sure he wasn't going to be pulled back into the water and climbed back up the bank. I could hear the dog yipping away from somewhere down the path and decided to see what he was going on about. To tell you the truth, Your Honour, I was already doubting that Mr. Delaney had met with an accident. There aren't any sharp rocks on the banks or even in the creek itself. Those wounds looked to me like they'd come from somebody bashing him from behind. I went to investigate the dog. I could see where the grass was flattened down a bit off to the north side of the path, and the terrier was in there. I went in only a matter of a few feet and came across the accused, who was lying on his side against a tree. The dog was barking and pawing at him, and for a minute I wondered if I was going to be encountering another corpse because he wasn't moving. But I brought the lantern up right close, and he stirred and then opened his eyes. I noticed he had an abrasion on his right cheek just below his eye. "What's a matter?" he asked, all slurred. "John Delaney's dead," I replied. I didn't say anything about an accident or how he was dead, I just said, "John Delaney's dead." That seemed to wake him up. "Well, he got what he deserved, didn't he?"

GREENE: You are sure those were his exact words?

PUGH: To the letter. "He got what he deserved."

GREENE: Did you reply?

PUGH: I did. I realise my words were not charitable or Christian, but I was shocked by how callous he was. I said, "Then I hope you, too, get what you deserve, Harry Murdoch."

END OF WITNESS STATEMENT.

Chapter Three

ALTHOUGH HE COULDN'T QUITE ADMIT to himself
that he was actually *hiding* the book from his landlady,
William Murdoch had tucked it discreetly to the back of
his small bookcase in his tiny sitting room. Mrs. Kitchen
cleaned in here once a week, and although he knew her
interest in him came from affection and concern, he felt
too shy about certain matters to reveal them even to her.
He'd found the little book titled *Our Bodily Dwelling*
in Caversham's bookshop and bought it hoping he
could gain some knowledge. So far it had yielded little.
The female author had used the metaphor of a house
to describe the various bodily functions. He'd turned
straight to the chapter called "Plumbing," hoping it was
what he needed, but it turned out to be only about the
bowels and nothing so far about private parts, although
he thought they could be considered a kind of plumbing. He skimmed through to "Questionable Guests," but

this turned out to be a long diatribe against alcohol. Murdoch sighed and flipped the pages to the next chapter. He by no means espoused temperance and saw nothing wrong with moderate imbibing. In the summer, after he'd pushed his body to the limit on one of his long bicycle rides, he liked nothing better than a pint or two of cool beer or cider. The authoress was vehemently against nicotine and smoking, so that was of no interest either. He was enjoying his pipe before retiring for the night. Frustrated, he tossed the book to the floor. He was so woefully ignorant about almost everything pertaining to intimate connections, but he really didn't know where to turn. What he'd heard from the rough-and-ready lumberjacks when he was at the camp he didn't think applied to decent women. In their all too short time together, he and Liza hadn't really talked much about it either, although he considered she was bolder than he was.

He yawned and pulled his flannel dressing gown tighter. Shortly after he'd come to live with the Kitchens, he'd asked if he could rent this room as his sitting room. He couldn't really afford to, his wages were modest to say the least, but he liked having the extra space and he knew it helped his landlady out. Because he insisted on paying for his own coal, a fire in a second grate meant still more cost, so he often didn't bother to light it. Tonight he had wanted the comfort of a fire, but it had died down and he wasn't about to build it up this close

21

to bedtime. He knocked the ashes out of his pipe on the grate, gave the embers a quick rake with the poker, and picking up his candlestick went over to the window.

The street below was moonlit, quiet, and peaceful as a painting in a Christmas card. Yesterday there had been a light snowfall. Not heavy or with staying power but a warning of what was ahead, and some snow remained on the rooftops and in the clefts of the tree branches. This was going to be his second Christmas without Liza, and he felt such a pang of loneliness he had to move to keep the pain at bay. Forget about sleep right now. He knew he'd just be tossing around for the next two or three hours. He walked over to the brass box by the fire. It was supposed to be used for firewood, but he kept his dancing shoes in it. They were fancy, two-toned black and white, with an elasticised sidepiece and soft, flexible soles. He took them out, kicked off his slippers, and pushed his bare feet into the shoes. Whenever he put them on he felt different. He fancied his back straightened, his steps got smoother, and his shyness disappeared.

Last evening when he had sat with the Kitchens in the front parlour, Mrs. Kitchen had reminded him about his dancing lessons. "You should take them up again, Mr. Murdoch. You were doing so well."

Earlier in the year, he had enrolled in dance classes at the studio of one Professor Otranto. The name was far too exotic for the vain, portly little man from

Liverpool, but he was a competent teacher and Murdoch had begun to enjoy himself. His waltz was coming along nicely, and he'd learned a two-step and something called the Palais Glide. However, he hadn't taken a lesson for a while.

Mrs. Kitchen wouldn't let the matter rest. "It's such a pleasant way to spend an evening. Better than staying here with us old pair night after night." What she meant was that it was time to get on with things. Liza had been dead for more than a year now. It was time to find himself a suitable sweetheart and stop moping. Murdoch sighed. She was right of course. Until recently, his thoughts had been definitely moving in that direction. He'd found himself strongly attracted to Mrs. Enid Jones, a young widow from Wales who was also a boarder in the house. Unfortunately, she was Baptist and he was Roman Catholic, and therein was a huge problem. He was willing to continue, but she wasn't and she had moved out.

Murdoch straightened up. The clock on the mantel-piece began to strike eleven. He'd better get a move on. He rolled back the rag rug, pushed his armchair to the wall, and took up a position in the centre of the small space he'd created. *Right arm up, shoulder level, bend the elbow, turn the palm in, placed at the midline of the lady's back. Firm but gentle command. Now, left arm raised, thumb spread out, ready to receive her gloved, dainty hand.* Whose hand? Never mind, keep going.

23

"All right. Mrs. Jones, may I have the honour of this dance?"

With a slight dip, he slid his right foot forward. Immediately, he could hear Professor Otranto's voice. "Chin up, Mr. Murdoch! This is not a boxing match!" His dance teacher was fond of declamatory expressions. "Glide! Don't stamp. You are not destroying cockroaches. Chin up, shoulders back. You are a proud soldier! Think of being a soldier!"

Forward, two, three. Back, two, three. Murdoch managed three pivots in a row. As long as his partner's skirt didn't get underfoot as it so easily could, the reverse turn was an elegant manoeuvre.

He came too close to the fender and he stumbled on a forward dip, aware he would have just tromped on his partner's slippers.

He stopped. There was somebody knocking on the front door. Who on earth could it be at this time of night? Before he could take action, he heard the sound of Mrs. Kitchen going to answer. A male voice spoke briefly, but he couldn't make out the words. Then Mrs. Kitchen started up the stairs. There was an urgency in her steps that made him hurry.

"I'm in here, Mrs. K.," he called and opened the door, taking care to keep his bare shanks out of sight.

Beatrice Kitchen came onto the landing, her candle held aloft. She had a dressing robe on over her nightgown, and her fine grey hair was in a long braid down her back.

24

"Oh, Mr. Murdoch, a constable has just come from the station." She handed him a piece of paper. "He brought this telegram for you."

Murdoch unfolded the paper, and she brought the candle closer so he could see.

To: Acting Detective William Murdoch.
Message: We regret to inform you that our beloved sister, Philomena of the Sacred Heart, has become gravely ill. We recommend that you attend her as soon as possible.

The telegram operator's handwriting wasn't very legible, and on the line that indicated the sender, he'd written something indecipherable so that, in a moment of confusion, Murdoch read only the word "Mother." It was so long since he had heard Susanna referred to by her religious name, he didn't realise at first to whom they were referring. Then he did.

"Oh dear, is it bad news, Mr. Murdoch?" Mrs. Kitchen was regarding him anxiously.

"I'm afraid it is. It seems that my sister is dying."

All three of them were in the front parlour. Mrs. Kitchen had insisted on making Murdoch a mug of warm milk and brandy, and he was sipping it gratefully. Arthur was beside him in his invalid's bath chair, drinking the scalding hot water that was one more in the long list

25

of recommended treatments for consumption that his wife was always finding.

Murdoch had sent the constable back with an answering telegraph message that he would take the nine o'clock train to Montreal the next morning. There was nothing else he could do until then, but he was glad for the company of his friends. Beatrice, who never stopped working at something, was making chains of coloured tissue paper for Christmas decorations. Arthur seemed a little better than usual tonight, and it was he who had particularly drawn Murdoch out, inviting him to talk about Susanna. The hot brandy loosened his tongue, and he found himself babbling on without reservation.

"I still remember the day she was born. In fact, her birthday is only three days from now, December twelfth. She will be thirty-one years old." He paused, conscious of all their thoughts. She might not reach that age.

"Go on," prompted Arthur. "You remember . . ."

"I was little more than three years old. My father woke me up. I still had a cot in their bedroom. He said I was going to spend the night at Mrs. Swann's house, the neighbour at the end of the lane. He picked me up, wrapped me in a shawl, and carried me downstairs. Momma was walking up and down by the window. She was making a funny gasping sound. She hardly looked at me, just said, 'Don't fuss. Be a good boy, Willie.' I was frightened out of my skin. Something was dreadfully wrong. My father was stern as usual, but I risked asking him what was the matter with Momma. 'Nothing's wrong. A little brother or sister is coming tonight.'"

Murdoch chuckled. "'Where from?' I asked him. Charlie Swann had a little brother, and Joshua Rupp had two young sisters. Was it them who were coming over?"

"What did your father answer?" asked Arthur. His wife glanced at him. This was not quite a proper conversation to be having.

"I don't remember if he said anything. He handed me over to Mrs. Swann and left. I gave that good woman a hard time as I recall. I refused to go to bed and stood at the window waiting for Poppa to come back. I was sure I saw black plumed horses coming down the lane the way they had for Mr. Tauton's funeral. I was convinced my mother would die."

Mrs. Kitchen clucked sympathetically. "Poor mite. Children do get such fancies in their heads."

"In spite of everything, I must have fallen asleep because the next I knew it was daylight, and there was my father again. He seemed happy and excited. 'Come on, we've got a surprise for you.' He picked me up again and rushed me down the lane back to our house."

Murdoch paused. His cheek had been pressed against his father's chest. Harry was wearing his thick fisherman's sweater, and the smell was strong: tobacco, fish, something sweaty and masculine. The jolting was uncomfortable, and he was unused to being carried by his father. But there was a comfort in the strength of his arms that he had never forgotten. The rare mood of happiness was sweet.

"My momma was lying in bed. One of the women from the shore was standing beside her. They were both staring down at a funny little creature in a cradle next to the bed. To me it looked like a bundle of cloth wrapped around a red face. The eyes were squeezed shut, but the mouth was moving. My mother smiled at me. 'This is your new little sister, Willie. Come and give her a kiss.' Momma seemed so happy, and I was stabbed by a terrible pang of jealousy. Right here." He indicated his solar plexus. "'Where did she come from?' I asked. 'From up above,' said my mother. She raised her eyes heavenward, and I thought she was indicating the corner of the ceiling. I couldn't understand how the newcomer had managed that and thought Momma must have meant she had come down the chimney. 'When's she going back?' I asked. They all laughed, even my father. Nobody understood how sincere I was."

"That's only natural," said Beatrice. "If the first child is a boy, he always considers himself a little prince."

There was a wistful expression on her face, and Murdoch remembered that she'd told him she had lost three children, two infants but the one boy had lived until he was two. He hesitated, not sure whether or not he should change the subject. Beatrice nodded at him. "Do go on."

"As Susanna grew up, we became the best of friends. I suppose we had our squabbles, but mostly she was my steadfast companion. I'm afraid it's true what you say, Mrs. K. She was always willing to be the ship's crew, while I was the captain."

Suddenly he felt uneasy. Was it true she had always been willing, or had he, in fact, bullied her into complying?

"She has been a nun for a long time. I believe you mentioned that."

Murdoch nodded. "She was a postulant when she was just sixteen."

He didn't want to upset Mrs. Kitchen by revealing how angry he'd been when Susanna told him what she intended to do. She had chosen a cloistered order, and he knew he would never see her again except from behind a curtained grille. No priest could talk him out of his bitterness at her being lost to him and all normal life forever.

"It is unfortunate the prioress didn't tell you the nature of your sister's illness," said Arthur. "It is not out of the question that she will recover."

Murdoch didn't reply. "Gravely ill," were the same words that the doctor had used about Liza. She had been taken ill so suddenly. He didn't know, wasn't expecting to see her until Sunday. On Friday her father

29

had sent a message to the station. "You should come at once; Elizabeth has typhoid fever." She had died that night, without good-byes or consciousness. He did not have much hope for Susanna. He sipped the warm drink, hoping his friends hadn't noticed his eyes had filled with tears.

Chapter Four

JEREMIAH BARKER LIKED THIS PERIOD of his turn of duty. The majority of prisoners were in the shops working. The few who had to remain in their cells were usually easy enough to keep an eye on. This afternoon he only had three charges. One was an old, destitute man who was too infirm to work at all. Lost in a world where time had disappeared, he lay on his cot all day, waiting to be transferred to the House of Providence. He was so scrofulous, Barker knew the cell would have to be completely disinfected when he went. More work. The other two prisoners were both on the second level. Lawson, the younger one, had received ten stripes two days ago, and he was excused from work. Barker had scant sympathy for him. He was a sly fellow with a look about him that made you never want to turn your back.

31

The third man was in the cell at the end of the row. He was a convicted murderer. He had been sentenced to hang; and as that was about to happen in a week's time, there seemed no point in training him in any of the prison workshops. For him, Barker had some compassion. He never gave any trouble and spent his days doing his sketches or just lying on his cot, staring at the ceiling. When asked what he was contemplating, he'd replied, "Just my life, sir. Nothing else but that." Usually the prisoners facing death were kept isolated in a special section of the jail that overlooked the exercise yard, but he was here because the last inhabitant of the death cell had died from typhoid and they didn't want another convict to cheat justice. The guards were not supposed to talk to the prisoners, but often loneliness on both sides overrode that rule. Since August Barker had had many a quiet chat with his charge. Initially, he'd suffered from withdrawal from liquor, but the longer his sobriety, the more he expressed regret at his previous way of life. Not that he admitted to his crime of murder. Innocent of that he was. They all said that though. Prior to his conviction, he had apparently been a lapsed Roman Catholic, but the shock of the death sentence had sent him back full speed to the fold. The priest, Fr. Healy, visited him twice a week and was happy with his progress. Jeremiah was a pious man himself, although of the Methodist persuasion, and he was always glad to see a man turn to God, even if it was the papist heresy the penitent embraced.

32

This afternoon Barker had managed to get a bit of a sit down at the table by the entrance door. His legs weren't as young as they used to be, and the constant patrolling along the iron walks, up and down the staircase, had taken its toll. He yawned and scratched a varicose vein on the back of his leg. It was a dreary afternoon, and the gloom of the cell block was deepening. The light filtering down through the central skylight was grey and sombre, threatening snow. It was only on Sundays when there was no work and the men were in their cells that the warden allowed the gas sconces to be fully lit. Otherwise, on weekdays they stayed off until after the evening meal.

Right now Jeremiah could hardly see the third-floor cells above him. He shivered and hunkered down into the collar of his thick serge tunic. There were two big woodstoves in the centre of the cell block, but like the sconces, they were kept at a low burn during the afternoon. It was all very well to say that those who had broken the law should not be coddled; nobody seemed to consider that their keepers had to suffer as well. He would be glad to finish and get back to his own room in the guards' quarters.

There was the sound of a key clanking in the lock, and Barker stood up as quickly as he could, grunting a little at the stiffness in his back and legs. Mr. Massie himself entered. He rarely came to inspect the cells at this time of day, and Barker felt a wiffle of alarm in his

33

stomach. He hoped he wasn't in trouble. The warden, however, smiled benignly.

"Afternoon, Mr. Barker. Everything correct?"

"Yes, sir."

Massie indicated an envelope he was holding. "I have a letter for one of the prisoners. It's rather an unusual situation, so I thought I'd bring it to him now rather than wait until Sunday. Can I see your book."

"Yes, sir." Barker swivelled the big roll book around to face the warden.

"Good! He's in cell six. No points lost all week, I see."

"No, sir, he's an obedient fellow."

Massie jabbed his finger on the page. "This one, Lawson? How is he behaving?"

"He's complaining quite a lot, sir. He says he should be in the infirmary."

"Ha! I don't particularly like to see a man whipped, but he deserved it if ever a man did. If he continues whining, take away one of his privileges. Maybe going without dinner for three days will develop some conscience in the man."

"Yes, sir."

"Let's go then, shall we, Mr. Barker."

The guard picked up the lamp from the table and led the way. The warden halted and peered through the bars of the old man's cell.

"Hello, Mr. Dade, how are you this afternoon?"

There was no answer. Massie waited for a moment,

then he said rather more loudly, "We'll have you out of here soon as a shake."

They moved on. "He's been most despondent, sir. Won't eat or drink anything," said the guard.

"Poor unfortunate fellow. He must be carrying at least seventy years on his back. He deserves to end his days in a little more comfort, don't you think?"

"Yes, sir," replied Jeremiah, but he was not sincere. As far as he was concerned, if you ended up a pauper, it was your own fault or your own depravity that got you there.

They climbed up the spiral metal staircase to the second floor.

As they passed by Lawson's cell, the prisoner came to the bars and reached out.

"Warden, have pity. I'm suffering real bad."

Massie scowled at him. "You should have thought of that before you assaulted that poor woman. I'm sure she suffered, too."

Jeremiah was glad he'd never been called upon to administer a whipping. He could be strict when it came to applying the rules but deliberately inflicting physical pain was another matter, and he knew he could never stomach it. He'd had to witness some of the whippings, and he hadn't liked it at all. These punishments weren't common anymore, but everybody was affected when they occurred. The prisoners were more likely to be restless and defiant, and the guards jumpy.

35

They proceeded on to the cell that was at the end of the row. The prisoner had heard them coming and was standing close to the bars, waiting.

"Good afternoon, Warden Massie . . ." His voice was civil, but his eyes were wary, afraid to hope, unable not to.

"I've brought you a letter. I know you've been anxious for a reply, so I thought I'd give it to you at once."

"Thank you, sir. I do appreciate that."

"Shall I read it for you?"

"If you please."

Massie took the letter out of the envelope and beckoned to the guard to bring the lamp closer.

Dear Sir. In reply forthwith to your letter of the second of September, '95, instance. I must first apologise for the delay in answering but it took a long time to reach us here and second we had no knowledge of the whereabouts of the man you were enquiring after. As you had said it was a matter of some urgency, I did however send a messenger to enquire of one of our former cooks who is now permanently residing in the town of Huntsville to see if he had any information. As it turns out, he did and I have forthwith included what he related. Mr. William Murdoch esquire is now to be found in the city of Toronto. According to my informant, he is employed in the capacity of a detective police officer. I do hope this is of help to you.

I am your obedient servant, sir.

      C. M. Ryan. Esquire, foreman, Apex logging
      and saw company, Huntsville, Ontario.

Harry grasped the bars with both hands. "A police officer!"

Massie regarded him curiously. "I must admit to you, sir, that I did find the irony of the situation rather rare. And clearly this is a surprise to you."

"Yes, I should say it is. I have not heard from him for many years, close on twenty-two."

"He won't be too hard to find now. I will telephone the police headquarters and see if they know which station he is attached to."

"Thank you, sir. I would most appreciate that."

The warden hesitated. "Twenty-two years is a long time. What was the reason you lost contact?"

"Him and me had a bad falling out. Both of us as hot-headed as a gingered horse. And stubborn. He wouldn't call 'hold' and neither would I."

Massie leaned in closer. "You must be careful not to raise your hopes too high. He cannot reverse the decision of the court even if he is the chief of police himself."

The other man clenched his jaw. "I am innocent, Warden. And sure as I stand here, he will prove it." There was a glint of humour in his eyes. "You have to admit, sir, there's not many prisoners who get an opportunity like this. What more can I ask? A detective and my own son."

Chapter Five

THERE WAS ONLY ONE SMALL WINDOW in the infirmary, and the December afternoon light was already weak and fading. Votive candles flickered on stands at each corner of the bed where Sister Philomena lay dying, but they could not dispel the gloom. The room was chill, the fire in the grate meagre, as coal was apportioned out carefully even in the infirmary. The order was an austere one.

The three o'clock bell sounded, and Sister Genevieve, the infirmarian, knelt and kissed the floor then touched her crucifix to her lips as she had done at this hour every day for the past fifty years. She said a brief prayer and got stiffly to her feet. Sister Philomena opened her eyes. The bell had wakened her, or perhaps she wasn't sleeping, just lying as still as she could to withstand the pain. She raised her hand, indicating she wanted the crucifix that was on the pillow beside her. Sister Genevieve picked it up and held it for her to kiss. In the infirmary the rule of silence was waived if necessary, but there was no conversation between the two nuns. In the last weeks of her illness, Sister Philomena had reverted to her own language, and she seemed to have difficulty understanding the Quebec patois of her nurse. Sister Genevieve had no English.

Sister Philomena of the Sacred Heart of Jesus had been in the infirmary for almost a month now, each day weaker. Dr. Corneille, a good pious man who ministered to the sisters, was appalled when he saw the nun's condition. It was far too late, he said in his brusque way; he should have been called months ago. Mother St. Raphael had taken the rebuke as her due. The younger nun was in her charge. However, Sister Genevieve knew all too well that Sister Philomena had hidden her illness until the tumour was starting to break through the skin. She had gone about her duties, never complaining, although she was suffering terribly. Even now, in spite of the entreaties of the infirmarian, she also refused to take morphine or opium to alleviate her pain. Her response was unchanging. "I must bear my pain as Our Lord bore His."

Sister Genevieve had asked Mother St. Raphael whether or not Sister Philomena of the Sacred Heart was perilously close to the sin of pride. However, the prioress was adamant. Their sister was withstanding the ravages of the cancer with the fortitude of the saints. They must all pray for her.

39

The infirmarian took the silver aspergillum from the bowl that was on the bedside table and sprinkled holy water on the bed. Sister Philomena opened her eyes and smiled at her.

"Thank you, Sister. I am so hot. Hell can hardly be worse than this."

Fortunately, Sister Genevieve, who lacked humour, did not understand these words. She picked up the clean linen bandages from the bedside table, preparing to change the dressing at the nun's breast. Sister Philomena could not keep back a moan of pain. As gently as she could, Sister Genevieve removed the soiled cloth, biting back her exclamation of pity. She had grown up on a farm before she entered the convent. Her father had hunted animals to provide the family with food, and she had seen these carcasses dumped on the kitchen floor. The breast of the dying nun looked as if it had been destroyed by a blast of shot.

She bathed the wound with more of the holy water. Sister Philomena was hardly breathing, holding her lips pressed tightly together to hold back her moan of pain. Finally Sister Genevieve replaced the bandage and pulled up the thin blanket. Even its light weight seemed to cause pain, and she removed it at once.

40 Sister Philomena looked up at her. "Has my brother arrived yet?"

"*Comment?*"

"My brother" – she searched for the word – "*mon frere? Est-il arrivé?*"

Sister Genevieve shook her head. This was at least the fourth time the other nun had asked this question. She seemed to have forgotten that according to his telegram, her brother was catching the first train from Toronto, and he wouldn't be arriving until early evening.

Sister Philomena was not yet of middle age, and although her face and limbs were emaciated, her brown eyes still had beauty. She was looking beseechingly at the older nun. In French, she said, "Please bring Mother St. Raphael to me." She brought her hands together on her chest. "There is something I must confess."

The nun pursed her lips. Sister Philomena had received the sacrament of Extreme Unction this morning with all of the little community present. Fr. Hiebert had heard her confession then. Surely she had not contaminated her soul in such a short space of time. Sister Genevieve did not want to fetch the prioress unnecessarily. She turned away, pretending not to understand. The other nun spoke again, her voice suddenly stronger.

"Please, I must talk to our Mother."

Genevieve was rescued from her dilemma by the entrance of the prioress herself.

Mother St. Raphael was a tall woman, rather harsh of feature, except for a mouth that outside of the cloister would have been considered sensuous. She went straight to the bedside and placed her hand on the sick woman's forehead.

"I am here, my child."

Sister Philomena licked her dry, chapped lips. "I am so thirsty, Mother."

Mother St. Raphael signalled to Sister Genevieve to hand her the sponge, and she squeezed some moisture into Sister Philomena's mouth then wiped her face gently.

She was eased a little. "When will my brother be here?"

The prioress sighed. "Monsieur Lavalle is meeting him at the train station, and he will bring him here at once. Not more than two or three hours from now." She spoke English that had only the slightest of French accent.

"Perhaps I will be in the arms of Our Lord by then."

"It is not for us to predict when we are garnered," said the prioress, but her reproof was soft.

Sister Philomena struggled to raise herself in the bed, but she couldn't and was forced to lie back.

"Shall we help you to sit up?"

"No, I cannot bear it. But there is something I must tell you. Will you come closer?"

Mother St. Raphael pulled the chair up against the bed and leaned her head toward the other nun. Sister Genevieve was busy folding the linen bandages.

"Mother, I have been wrestling with such dark thoughts. They are blotting out the light of Our Lord's face."

"These are mere scruples, my dear little sister. You have been absolved of all your sins. You are going on the journey to Our God with a soul that has been cleansed of sin." She stroked Sister Philomena's cheek.

The nun pressed the prioress's hand against her face.

"I know that my heart is still full of anger . . ."

"For whom, my child? You have been ever one of our most loving sisters. What is this anger?"

Sister Philomena became more agitated. "For the past three days, I have looked up at the corner of the room, there where the ceiling and the wall join. There, do you see it? A spider. Oh, it is so big. I asked Sister Genevieve to chase it away, but it always returns. It does not move."

Involuntarily, Mother St. Raphael glanced up at the ceiling. The wall was whitewashed; and even though the light was dim, she could see nothing.

"Does this frighten you, my child?"

"At first yes, but now I see that our Saviour has sent it to me as a sign. There is a dark place in my soul. I must cleanse it before I die."

She shifted restlessly, but the movement made her whimper. Mother St. Raphael waited patiently. When she spoke next, Sister Philomena's voice was so low she was almost inaudible.

43

"I have hidden it even from my confessor. The Lord our God commands us to love and honour our father and our mother, but I do not."

The prioress was surprised at what she heard. Sister Philomena had said so little about her life before she entered the convent as a postulant. She'd understood she had no family except for the one brother, older than she was. He had visited two times in the beginning but not for many years now.

"I led you to believe that both of my parents were dead, but that was not true." She licked at her lips. "My mother was deceased, but my father was alive when I became a postulant." She stopped. "It is he whom I reject in my heart. In spite of the words of Our Saviour, I can find no love for my father. I must not go to Our Lord's house with such uncharitable thoughts."

She was almost exhausted with the effort of talking, and Mother St. Raphael had to lean closer to hear what she said.

"What is your father's sin that you cannot honour him?"

But the nun was distracted. She glanced upward. "Perhaps the spider has come to remind me of my shame."

Mother St. Raphael stood up. "I will send for our father confessor once more if it will bring you peace. But you must not fret so. We are all only frail mortals. Our Lord sees everything and is ever merciful."

She could not tell if her words had reached Sister Philomena because she had closed her eyes again. The prioress turned to the infirmarian and spoke to her in

French. "Sister Genevieve, burn another stick of incense if you please and bring it close to the bedside. It will give her strength."

She left the room with a soft rustling of her habit on the wooden floorboards.

Sister Genevieve took a strip of the linen and carefully wiped away the moisture from Sister Philomena's forehead. She wrapped that piece in a separate strip and put it on the table. If Sister Philomena of the Sacred Heart of Jesus was truly a saint, this cloth would be a holy relic.

Chapter Six

THE INFIRMARY WAS IN A LOW, single-storey wing off
the east side of the main convent. An arched, covered
walkway ran the length of the building, the openings
small and high. In front of that was a row of hemlocks.
The snow was smooth and deep as far as the trees. No
shrubs poked up, no mark of human activity. At a different season, the courtyard might have appeared tran-
quil, but today, in the winter night, the sombre dark
stone of the convent walls seemed bleak and desolate.

At the end of the path, almost hidden by the evergreens, there was a narrow door. As Murdoch and the
driver of the sleigh that had brought him from the
station approached, it opened and a nun beckoned
them in. "Bonjour, Monsieur. I am Sister Agnes. I regret
we meet under such sorrowing circumstances."

With a tip of his cap to Murdoch, the driver tromped
off the way they had come.

"He will bring your valise," Sister Agnes said to Murdoch. She hesitated. "You may stay as long as you wish. Our accommodation is very simple but, I hope, adequate."

They were standing in an anteroom devoid of furnishings, with an uncovered flagstone floor and white-washed stone walls. The extern had a lamp but the wick was turned low, and where they were was dim and so cold he could see his own breath white on the air.

"When can I see my sister?"

The nun glanced away. "I regret that according to our rule you will not be able to see her in person."

Murdoch was well aware of the rule, but he wanted to defy it, to vent his anger on the women who applied it so rigidly.

"Surely you can make an exception in this case?"

"I regret, Monsieur, that is for our Mother to decide. However, we have arranged to have our sister brought to the infirmary parlour. She is very weak, but it is possible you can speak to her."

She turned and opened another door behind her, and he followed her into a narrow corridor, like the anteroom uncarpeted and bare. Their footsteps rang on the stone floor. She unlocked yet another door and ushered him into a small room.

"Please be seated, Mr. Murdoch. I will be but a moment."

The parlour contained only three straight-backed

47

chairs and a low table. A single candle burned in a wall sconce, underneath which was a brass crucifix that shone with a dull, ruddy gleam in the candlelight. On the other side, a text was written on the white wall: I AM THE WAY AND THE LIFE SAID THE LORD. To the left of this was what appeared to be a small window covered by a square of plain grey felt. The floor was flagstone, but a hemp carpet was a concession to comfort. There was a fire in the hearth, but it was banked down to the point almost of extinction.

Murdoch took off his hat but decided it was far to cold to remove his coat. He went over to the fireplace. There was no poker or coalbox, so he had to kick at the coal to get more of a blaze going. He warmed his hands and waited. There was absolute silence all around him.

It seemed a long time before the extern returned. There was a smell of incense on her clothes. She addressed a point over his right shoulder.

"I must tell you our sister is in a state of severe suffering," she said. "I beg you not to tire her or distress her unnecessarily."

He was on the verge of making a sarcastic retort, but he bit it back when he saw that, beneath her pious detachment, she was grieved.

"You realise, Sister, I have no knowledge of the nature of her illness."

"She has a tumour. Unfortunately, she did not inform

48

Reverend Mother that she was ill until the disease was quite advanced."

Her tone was somewhat defensive as if she expected he would hold the prioress responsible for neglect of her duty. He didn't. Susanna was always that way. Ever since he had known her, she had hidden her pain or sickness, never complaining. It frustrated him and sometimes he would tease her unmercifully. Once he twisted her finger, trying to force her to cry out. She wouldn't, and he'd stopped, thoroughly ashamed of himself.

He heard sounds of movement from the adjoining room, and there was a light tapping on the wall. Sister Agnes drew back the piece of felt. It wasn't covering a window but a metal grille about three feet square.

"You can come closer, Mr. Murdoch."

He did so and could look through the grille into the adjoining room. However, a second piece of black material was hung across the opening, and he could barely make out two shadowy figures in nun's garb. He heard, rather than saw, that the far door opened and somebody came into the room carrying an oil lamp. This light made the black curtain less opaque and he could see that a narrow bed was being wheeled into the room. He assumed the person lying in the bed was Susanna, but everything was too dim to see her face distinctly.

Sister Agnes had brought a candle with her, and she lit it from the one in the sconce and brought it close to

49

the grille. He realised this was so that, in like fashion, his sister could see his silhouette.

"You can speak to her, Mr. Murdoch. She is conscious. She has been so anxious for your presence."

He leaned forward, straining to see Susanna better through the curtain. "Cissie, it's Will. I've come to visit you."

The words were absurd, he knew, but it was all he could do to talk at all. He heard her voice, barely audible.

"Will? You are here?"

"Yes, Cissie, I came as fast as I could."

More muttering and he had to press his ear against the grille to hear better. There was another voice, speaking in French. Sister Agnes translated.

"Our infirmarian, Sister Genevieve, says that Sister Philomena regrets that you have had to come so far, and she is unable to speak to you."

"That doesn't matter."

There was another exchange between Susanna and the infirmarian. His eyes were getting accustomed to the darkness, and he could see two nuns beside the bed. He realised they were trying to prop the dying woman up on her pillow. She groaned in pain, but they raised her sufficiently for her upper body to come closer to the grille. Susanna was wearing a white bed cap, and her face was as emaciated as a skeleton's. Her eye sockets were deeply shadowed, her cheeks sunken. He wanted to weep at the sight. He could see that she smiled. "Will, it is so good to see you."

"And you, my little sprat."

"There is something . . . concern to me . . . I have tried to let go of all earthly things. . . . I can see the light of Our Lord as it beckons to me." She had to stop and one of the nuns wiped her lips with a piece of linen. "Our Poppa . . . you must speak to him, Will. He must ask for forgiveness."

He was surprised at what she said because Susanna had never joined him in his ranting about their father, never before acknowledged his many transgressions against his wife and children.

"We must cease for the moment, Mr. Murdoch," said Sister Agnes.

But Susanna whispered, "I would like it if you would stay awhile longer, Will."

"My dear, of course I won't leave."

He hadn't said, *until you die*, but that is what he meant.

It was obvious even through the impeding curtain that Susanna was in too much agony to remain sitting up, and the two nuns lowered her gently backward.

Murdoch stayed in the little austere cold parlour for the next few hours. Sister Agnes sat on a hard chair behind him and disappeared only once. She returned carrying a tray on which was a bowl of vegetable soup and a thick slice of bread. He was ravenous but his appetite vanished as soon as she placed the simple meal in front of him, and it was all he could do to swallow some of the hot broth. They had not moved the bed from the adjoining room, and twice more nuns entered and sang prayers. As far as he could tell, Susanna had fallen into unconsciousness. He didn't speak, and neither did any of the nuns. About midnight, in spite of the discomfort, he actually dozed off and was awakened by a soft tug on his sleeve.

"Monsieur Murdoch, our sister is failing rapidly. You may wish to say a prayer with us."

He stood up and peered through the grille. There were three or four nuns on the other side, and one of them was lighting votive candles at the foot of the bed, making it easier to see into the room. He could hear a harsh, gurgling kind of breathing. Susanna's mouth had fallen open. Within minutes the sound became quieter and finally ceased all together. She was dead.

Sister Agnes knelt down and crossed herself, and he could see the other two nuns were doing the same. He leaned his forehead against the cool metal grille, and the pungent scent of the incense wafted across to him. When he was a boy he had gone to his church, and at the altar, he had made a vow to protect his mother, Susanna, and Bertie. He had been very solemn about it, and although he'd couched the promise in general terms, what he really meant was that he would defend them against his father's wrath. He had failed. Then his mother had died, drowned in a shallow pool among the rocks on the beach. Bertie, always sickly, lived only six more months after this, and Susanna had turned elsewhere for her protection. His vow had been useless. He had not been able to save her when they were children, and he was helpless now to assuage her suffering.

"Monsieur Murdoch, will you join me in prayer?" asked the extern.

"Yes, Sister."

He, too, crossed himself and dropped to his knees on the hard floor.

Chapter Seven

"Good evening, Mrs. McIsaac." Walter Lacey stamped off the snow from his boots. "Where's Jessica?" He'd brought a waft of cold air into the cottage, and Mrs. McIsaac made a point of pulling her shawl up closer around her neck. She was seated in the nook by the fireside, Sally asleep in the cradle in front of her.

"She said she was tired, and she's gone up to bed." Her disapproval was obvious.

Lacey took off his hat and coat and hung them on the hook behind the door. Mrs. McIsaac was mending a shirt, and she put it aside. "You look perishing. I suppose you'll be wanting some tea?"

He blew on his cold fingers. "That would be appreciated, ma'am." He came closer to the fire and crouched down to look at his daughter. She insisted on sleeping in this crib even though she was too big for it and had to curl up to fit. He'd made the crib himself, an apple box, sanded down and painted bright yellow. Jess hadn't wanted him to. "It's unlucky to prepare too soon," she'd said, but swayed by his enthusiasm, she had finished the box, lining the sides with flannel and goose down and a cover of blue-striped cotton.

"How's my Sally been today?"

"Mardy. Nothing contents that bairn. She greets from dawn to dusk. Thank the Lord, she's gone asleep now, give me a bit of peace."

Lacey wanted to snap at the woman, but he didn't dare antagonize her. She was a dour and sour-faced Scotswoman, but she was the only person he could find at such short notice who was willing to come up to their cottage in the afternoons to "help out," as he had euphemistically called it. What this meant, in fact, was to make sure the child was looked after. Twice in the past week, he'd come home to find Jessica gone, God knows where, and Sally alone. Once she was asleep, but the other time she wasn't, just sitting in her crib bawling her eyes out. When he'd confronted Jess, she'd been remorseful but said she'd just gone out for a walk while Sally was asleep and hadn't noticed the time.

He bent down and kissed his daughter lightly on her forehead. Asleep she looked angelic, but since the incident she had become fretful, prone to night terrors, wetting her bed every night. She screamed when he had to leave her and clung to him with the tenacity of a savage animal when he returned.

55

Mrs. McIsaac hadn't yet made a move to make the tea, so Walter stood up and went to fetch the teapot from the cupboard. She watched him.

"Tea for you, ma'am?"

"No, I've got to get goin'. I have things to tend to."

Her tone was aggrieved, as if he was imposing on her, even though he paid her as much as he could afford. "Mr. Lacey, I dinna think I can come much longer. I am a charitable person and will do an honest day's work for an honest day's pay, but I see no real need to be here. Your wife is quite capable of looking after her own bairn and her own husband."

Walter busied himself with making the tea. "She caught a chill, and it makes her tired a lot. I'd prefer to take some responsibility off her shoulders until she's quite better. She's delicate, Jess is. And she's still keening over the baby."

The woman sucked on her lip as if she'd tasted something rather good. "That's as may be, but there's not a woman born who hasn't experienced some sorrow. Most of us just carry on with our duties."

"Jess has done that, Mrs. McIsaac. But it was a sad loss to both of us."

"There's no denying that and it a boy, but it's going on four months now. She should be better than this. I myself have known sorrow, as I've told you."

"Many a time," Lacey couldn't resist interrupting, but Mrs. McIsaac was oblivious.

"A husband struck down in the prime of his life, and me with nine children to raise. I buried five, Mr. Lacey, five little ones. So I know what it is to keen. But your wife is a young lass. She'll have lots more bairns, I'm sure."

She glanced over at him rather lasciviously, and he thought for a moment she was going to ask him if he was fulfilling his manly duty.

He went over to the table and sat down. Mrs. McIsaac pursed her lips. "What I don't understand is why she's had such a setback. I thought she was getting over things. She must have had some kind of shock. Did a gypsy come by? Or a beggar?"

Lacey gulped down some of the tea. "Not that I know of." He ran his fingers through his hair, making tufts stand up about his ears. "I'm sorry, Mrs. McIsaac. I know it's hard on you, too. Sally can be difficult. I'll try to give you a bit extra at the end of the week."

"Where are you going to get extra? I know what wages you're making. You havna got no extra."

"Then I'll make it up other ways. I'll bring you over some more firewood. I'll chop some first thing tomorrow."

"That'll be a help, no denying, but I'm no telling you these things so you'll do more for me. I'm telling you because you should know. She looks like she could go into a decline, and then there's no saying what would happen."

57

"It's on account of this weather. Jess never did like days like this. She used to say the grey got right under her skin and made her mind the same colour."

"Mebbe. You must be firm with her. If you're too soft, she'll just stay like this."

Lacey shook his head. "She'll come around, I tell you. She was smiling like her old self just a couple of days ago."

Mrs. McIsaac stood up. "Have it your way, but dinna say I didna warn you." She went over to the door. "I've got to be off fore it gets dark. I've put on some potatoes ready to boil, and there's the pork you can fry up when you're ready."

"Thank you, ma'am. And Mrs. McIsaac, I do truly appreciate how much you're helping me out, but if you can be back by six I'd be much obliged. I've been late getting to work. Newcombe is being kind seeing the circumstances, but I can't afford to lose my job."

Mrs. McIsaac shrugged. "I'll do my best, but I have my own family to take care of."

She pulled her shawl tight around her head and stepped out into the chill air. Lacey watched as she trudged down the path and disappeared among the trees. Then he went back to the table and sat down, his head in his hands.

Sour old tart she is, making him sweat for every inch she gives.

Sally whimpered and he held his breath, listening. But she didn't wake up, and he relaxed again. Jess had been glad when she found there was a second child on the way. She was softer, allowing him closer than before. He had even painted the name SYLVANUS on the side of the cradle. Jess had laughed. "It's too old-fashioned a name, and besides, how do you know it's going to be a boy?"

"I was told it means 'dweller in the woods,' which is where we live now. And besides, I know I've given you a son."

She'd waved her hand at him dismissively, but he could see that secretly she was pleased. The infant was, in fact, a boy, but he was born three months too soon and he had died moments after he had entered the world.

Walter stood up, took another mug from the cupboard, and poured some hot tea. There was a bottle of brandy on the shelf, and he added a splash.

"Try to get her to take a tot as often as you can," Mrs. McIsaac had said, "do her good." But for the past few days, Jess had had no appetite.

He put the mug on a tray and added a dish of arrowroot pudding that Maria Newcombe had sent down. He was always trying to tempt Jess with dainties.

Nothing had been right since the miscarriage. Jessica took it as a punishment from God. She would not allow herself to weep or show her sorrow. The hurt was pushed deep inside where it festered, the way a sliver of wood that is buried in the skin is no longer visible

59

but infects the entire body. On the surface their life proceeded more or less as it ever had. She tended to the cottage, prepared his meals, even allowed him connection with her, but he knew she had gone away from him. It was only with Sally that she showed any true emotion, grasping the child tightly to her breast several times a day until the poor mite would beg for release.

There were times when the unfairness of her behaviour filled him with rage. He shouted at her over trivialities; then overwhelmed by shame, he would leave the cottage and walk for hours down through the ravines as far as the harbour itself, until he could bear to face her again. But he thought he preferred even that half-life to the one they had been living recently. Jess had stopped even the most rudimentary care of the cottage; and even with her daughter, she was negligent.

He climbed the flight of stairs to the tiny loft where he'd made them a bedroom. The air in the room was stale. Jess hadn't been taking care of her own person either. At the moment she seemed to be sleeping.

He placed the tray on the dresser beside the bed.

"Jess? Jess, I've brought you some tea. Just the way you like it."

He turned up the wick on the lamp. She was lying on her side facing the wall.

"Are you awake, my chuck?"

She murmured something but didn't greet him or open her eyes. He touched his finger gently to her cheek. She had lost weight and the bones seemed sharp, and the lines from nose to mouth were those of an old woman.

"I've brought you some of Maria's best pudding, the kind you like."

She opened her eyes and gazed at him. "Please, Walter, I'm tired. I'll come down shortly."

He knelt down, took her inert hand in his, and held it to his lips. "Jess, you are my love, Jess. You must not leave me; I will not be able to bear it."

She didn't answer but shut her eyes again, pulled her hand away, and rolled over to face the wall.

Walter rocked back on his heels wondering whether or not he should rouse her out of her lethargy even if it meant a quarrel. Not that a barney would deter him if it brought her to life. Anger was preferable to this deadly indifference.

He stood up. Better leave it for now.

Lacey had lied to Mrs. McIsaac. He did, in fact, know all too well what had caused this relapse.

Chapter Eight

THE SERVICE OF THE MASS was so familiar that Murdoch had stopped listening. The Latin words slipped through his mind in a meaningless flow. He had been directed to the small chapel, where there were three other communicants, all women, all with black shawls covering their heads, almost indistinguishable from the nuns themselves. On the other side of the altar, out of sight, were the sisters. Susanna's coffin was on that side. He had not been allowed to see her body, and he'd had to say his final good-bye through the grille.

HOC EST ENIM CORPUS MEUM.

The priest genuflected then stood and elevated the host. At this point in the Mass, the faithful were expected to say, "My Lord and my God," but Murdoch was silent. He was close enough to the altar that the priest probably noticed, but Murdoch didn't care. The priest, Fr. Proulx, had spoken to him directly after Susanna died, but he didn't have much English and they were awkward with each other.

It was left to Sister Agnes to instruct Murdoch on the procedure of the funeral. A High Mass was to be held at seven o'clock. Susanna's body would be buried in the little cemetery behind the convent, but this, too, was enclosed, and he would not be allowed to visit the grave. "Monsieur Lavalle will take you to the station. Our Reverend Mother wishes me to extend to you her sincerest condolences. She also would like to inform you that Sister Philomena died shriven."

Murdoch bit back a retort. He wouldn't have expected anything else given she was a professed nun. God had called her and now had claimed her. He felt a momentary pinch of fear at his own thoughts, which were approaching the blasphemous.

Sometime in the early hours of the morning, the extern had ushered him into a tiny room adjoining the parlour where there was a couch. He hadn't expected to sleep, but fatigue won out and he had actually fallen into a restless sleep, disturbed by dreams of pursuit and a monster that changed its shape every time he thought he had escaped. At six-thirty the convent bells began to peal. Sister Agnes returned, bringing him a slice of bread and a cup of strong, bitter coffee. She made no attempt at conversation, but her expression was kind. Shyly she indicated that there was a commode behind a screen in the corner of the room. On the washstand

63

was a jug of tepid water and a razor and soap. When she left him alone, he felt an intense and childish pang of loneliness.

The priest had uncovered the chalice and was consecrating the wine now.

HIC EST ENIM CALIX SANGUINIS MEI NOVI ET AETERNI TESTAMENT . . .

Again Murdoch's thoughts drifted away. The chapel was austere enough, but the chalice was of an ornate gold and there was a life-sized crucifix hung above the altar. He wondered what Mrs. Enid Jones would think about such adornments. As far as he knew the Baptist Church wouldn't even allow a wooden cross in the church, and the ministers wore black suits. He sighed. It was at times like this that he had to face how far apart they were in their respective faiths. Suddenly, he heard his sister's name, her religious name that is. Fr. Proulx was reciting a prayer for the dead.

Memento etiam, Domine, famulorum tuarum. SOEUR PHILOMENA, qui nos praecesserunt cum signo fidei, et dormiunt ni somno paces. He looked in his missal, although he knew what the words meant. In spite of his anger, they gave him comfort.

Remember also, Lord, your handmaiden, who has gone before us with the sign of faith and rests in the sleep of peace.

In a brief conversation with Sister Agnes, Murdoch realised that they believed him to be the sole remaining member of the family. In fact, he hadn't heard anything

64

of his father for many years, but he assumed he was still alive. He didn't know if Susanna had deliberately chosen not to tell the nuns or if it was a misunderstanding. Neither he nor his sister had seen their father since Bertie's death. A few days after he'd gone, Murdoch and Susanna, afraid of what could happen between him and his father, had fled. He was just thirteen; she was nine. They had made their way to their only aunt, their mother's older sister, who lived forty miles away up the coast of Nova Scotia. Aunt Weldon was a spinster, a teacher who took them in because she had to – because our Lord commands us to have charity or we are as nothing. She had repeated this many times.

The priest was breaking the Host over the chalice, and the flat piece of unleavened bread made a snapping sound. Fr. Proulx was grey haired, well past middle age, and stooped. He had to peer shortsightedly at the book his server held in front of him.

The priest turned to face the communicants and held out the Host. One by one, the three women stood up and went to the communion rail. Murdoch followed them and they knelt together at the altar rail. He opened his mouth, and Fr. Proulx placed the bread on his tongue.

Corpus Domini nostri Jesus Christi custodiat animam tuam in vitam aeternam. Amen.

He then turned to the side of the altar to offer the Host to the nuns. They were all hidden from view, and

Murdoch could see only the priest as he reached forward to the invisible woman at the prie-dieu.

Murdoch went back to the pew, trying to swallow the wafer of bread, which stuck to the roof of his mouth. The nuns were singing a Miserere. He knelt down and tried to say the Paternoster.

He heard a sniffle beside him. One of the women was weeping. At what? She couldn't possibly have known Susanna. It was pure sentimental rubbish that she was crying like that. Murdoch's own eyes were dry. He was too angry to cry.

The singing ceased and the priest completed his rituals at the altar, wiping the chalice with the cloth and replacing it in the ciborium. He kissed the altar and turned to face the four of them.

Dominus vobiscum.

"And with thy spirit," replied the crying woman, her Latin somewhat indistinct.

Both priest and server made the sign of the cross, and Murdoch did the same. The mass was over. Fr. Proulx and the server disappeared into the sanctum, and the three women slipped away without any talking or acknowledgement of each other or him. He sat for a moment longer, the pungent odour of the incense tingling in his nostrils. The candles in the sconces flickered. It was daylight outside but another snow-filled grey morning, and the light in the chapel was dim.

Chapter Nine

PATRICK PUGH TILTED THE WASHSTAND MIRROR forward so he could see himself better. He separated out the front lock of his hair and daubed it with the bleach. His hair was naturally dark brown, thick, and wavy, but he'd been dyeing this one piece white for some time. He thought the flash gave a certain element of drama to his appearance, rather like a picture he'd seen of Mercury, the winged messenger. Besides, it was memorable. If anybody was talking about him, they inevitably referred to the man with the white streak in his hair. Then, if necessary, he could reverse that. Return to his normal appearance. "Have you seen a man, slim, about forty years of age, nobby dresser? He has a white lock of hair at the right temple?" "No, can't say I have." Pugh had found that, in some circumstances, it was better to be obvious than not. When you wanted to vanish, everybody was on the lookout for the flamboyant man in the tartan suit and red crusher, not the quiet, nondescript one in the plain grey overcoat and black fedora. He thought of it as a sort of magician's trick. "Look over here, at this scarf, not here where I am putting a card in my pocket." Pugh was fond of magic tricks and had learned several. On some of the lonely night watches, he practised leger-demain with a pack of cards. When he was tired of this work, he thought he would start a new career as a touring magician.

He whistled through his teeth, a jolly ballad he'd heard at the tavern. That was another thing he was good at, remembering tunes. He only needed to hear one once, and he could whistle the whole thing right through.

He scrutinised himself. That seemed good enough. He moved the mirror downward so he could get a glimpse of his naked loins. Yes, good. His stomach was as flat as a prizefighter's, and his thighs and calves firm and muscular. He could pass for a man at least ten years younger than he actually was. Finally, he stretched out his hands. Steady as rocks. The tip of his middle finger on the left hand was missing, and he never failed to experience a touch of chagrin at the sight. Even though he'd learned to take advantage of the defect, he was vain about his long, slender fingers. He'd suffered the loss when he was doing a stint as a mucker in a copper mine in Jerome, Arizona. Sheer carelessness on his part. But that was another tale to tell when he found time

68

to recount his memoirs for posterity. Keeping his voice low, he started on the ballad.

> *The wind sae could blew south and north,*
> *And blew into the floor;*
> *Quoth our goodman to our goodwife,*
> *'Gae out and bar the door.'*

He went over to the bed where he'd laid out his clothes. First, the drawers and a fleece shirt, both a mixture of silk and wool because he had sensitive skin and pure wool was irritating. Over the shirt, he pulled on a flannel chest protector lined with soft chamois. The scarlet of the flannel clashed with the burgundy stripes of his shirt, but that couldn't be helped. It was unlikely anybody would be getting a gander at his underwear today. He had his eye on a plump little tart who sang at the Derby, but she would have to wait until his job was finished. Pugh believed in discipline. While he was on a job, he never consorted with women.

Next he reached for his long socks. They were getting worn and the heels needed darning, but he had no time to do it now. He fastened the leather straps tightly, then pulled on his tweed trousers, which he'd purchased from Mr. Eaton's store only last month. Finally he put on his heavy wool jersey and checked the mirror again. Yes, he looked quite nobby. The brown sweater suited his dark complexion.

69

He picked up the imitation lamb cap, which was sitting on his dresser, and pulled it on. A snug fit. He had taken it from one of his former clients. He did not consider this stealing. The man had been less than generous with his fee, and Pugh had therefore supplemented it with the cap and a pair of decent raccoon gauntlets.

Pugh went to the wardrobe and took out the blue mackinaw. The jacket was waterproof, lined with tweed for warmth, and had a hood that gave him double protection from the weather and prying eyes. Pugh considered it was an ugly piece of apparel, but it served its purpose.

There was a silver flask in the inside pocket. He shook it. Good! Still some whiskey left. In the other pocket there was his deck of cards and his notebook and pencil. He hesitated for a moment then reached in the back of the wardrobe, pulled out a canvas bag, and undid the straps. Inside was his revolver. He took it out and stowed it in the mackinaw. He was ready. His cowhide boots were outside the door, cleaned and polished by the old man who also served as clerk to the hotel.

Pugh blew out his candle. He paid for each one he used, and he believed in being careful. He slipped out of his room and, carrying his boots, walked softly down the hall. There was only one light in the sconce, the wick turned down so low it was almost useless. He went down the stairs, paused long enough at the door to put on his boots, and stepped out into the cold night.

Then said the one unto the other,
'Here man, tak ye my knife;
Do ye tak off the auld man's beard,
And I'll kiss the goodwife.'

Pugh fastened the flap on the hood so that the lower half of his face was covered. Perhaps today he would be lucky.

Chapter Ten

MRS. KITCHEN CAME OUT OF THE PARLOUR just as Murdoch was hanging up his coat and cap. She held out her hand to him. "Please accept my condolences, Mr. Murdoch."

"Thank you, Mrs. K. You got my telegram then?"

"Constable Crabtree brought it over this afternoon. And he also wanted me to convey his regrets. The inspector has given you a leave of absence until Friday."

Murdoch shrugged. A leave of absence meant no wages, and he would have been glad of the distraction of work. However, the inspector always insisted that any of the police officers who suffered bereavement take some time off. Murdoch had decided some time ago that this had nothing to do with genuine compassion and everything to do with saving money.

He unlaced his boots and, unbidden, Mrs. Kitchen took his slippers out of the brass slipper box by the coat stand and gave them to him.

"I have some supper waiting for you."

"Thank you indeed. I forgot to book a seat in the dining car, and the sittings were full. The last acquaintance my stomach has had with any food was about five o'clock this morning. One of the nuns brought me some vegetable soup."

"For your breakfast?"

"That's what they always eat apparently."

Beatrice allowed herself a mild tut-tut of disapproval. "I've braised you a pork chop."

He followed her into the kitchen.

"How is Arthur?"

"A little better today." She smiled. "He complains dreadfully about the cream and eggs, but I am certain they are helping him. He isn't as weak and is coughing less. Don't you think so, Mr. Murdoch?"

If he were honest, he would have to say he hadn't noticed much improvement. Arthur had some days that were not as bad as others, but the progression of the illness seemed relentless.

Murdoch made a noncommittal sort of grunt. He didn't want to be the one to dash her hopes either.

"He asked if you would care to join us after your supper."

73

"Thank you, I will."

He sat down at the pine table, and Mrs. Kitchen took his plate out of the warming oven.

"I'll let you have your meal in peace."

"Please stay, Mrs. K. I would enjoy some company."

"I'd be happy to."

She perched herself in the chair opposite him. The pork chop was overcooked and dry and the potatoes lumpy, but he made enthusiastic sounds of appreciation for her sake. It didn't take long for him to consume everything. He sopped up the grease with a piece of bread.

"I was there at the end, but they wouldn't let me get close or touch her. I only saw her shadow through a grille. She is buried in the private cemetery of the convent, and I didn't see that either."

Mrs. Kitchen got up to remove his plate. She brought over a piece of apple tart and placed it in front of him. Murdoch rubbed at his eyes. He was overwhelmingly tired.

"If I may say so, Mr. Murdoch, the nuns were only doing what they ought to do. That is their vow. They call it 'enclosure,' I believe. Once in, the only people ever allowed to see them are a doctor or a priest. I know my cousin's daughter entered a cloistered order. She went down to America, but they never clapped eyes on her after she took her final vow."

"It's unnatural."

"I suppose you could say that, but it's a sacrifice they and the family make for Our Lord's sake."

Murdoch knew it was useless to argue with Mrs. Kitchen on certain matters, especially if they pertained to the church. She was as good-hearted as a woman can be, but any questioning of their mutual faith made her uneasy. She was rigid and dogmatic to the point of superstition. Besides, it was too late and he was too tired to talk much. However, as she had done so often in the past, Mrs. Kitchen surprised him.

"Frankly, if it had been up to me, Mr. Murdoch, if I was the prioress, I would have broken the rules in those circumstances. What the harm is in a man saying a final farewell to his only sister, I don't know."

He smiled at her, his irritation gone. "Thank you, Mrs. K. I cannot say I detected any softening in the nuns. Not that I saw them either. Even the funeral was conducted with them on the other side of a wall. I could hear them chanting, but that was it."

She spooned three generous spoonsful of tea leaves into the teapot and added boiling water from the kettle.

"Let it steep for a minute. But before I forget, there's a letter for you. The constable brought it over with the telegram. I'll fetch it."

She bustled off and he got up to pour his tea before it became strong enough to dissolve the enamel on his teeth. Mrs. Kitchen came back with a long envelope in her hand. There was a seal on the back with an official-looking stamp in it. Murdoch used his knife to slit open the flap.

The letterhead was that of James Massie, the warden of Don Jail.

Dear Mr. Murdoch. Will you be so good as to call at my office as soon as possible. One of our prisoners is anxious to have communication with you. A morning hour would be best at your earliest convenience.

Your servant, J. M. Massie, Warden

"Not bad news I hope," said Mrs. Kitchen.

"No, probably good news. I believe I mentioned young Adam Blake to you a couple of months ago, the lad convicted of pickpocketing? I was the one nabbed him, and I thought he might be set straight with a good talking to. He wasn't that receptive I have to admit, but I told him I'd come and visit when he saw the error of his ways. I assume a spell in jail has brought clarity to his mind."

"So it should." She reached in the pocket of her apron. "By the way, Mr. Murdoch, I took the liberty of cutting this for you."

She took out a wide strip of black silk.

"Thank you, Mrs. K."

He raised his arm and she fastened the band to his jacket sleeve where he would wear it for the next few months as a sign of mourning. He sighed. Poor little Cissie.

Chapter Eleven

CHARLES CRAIG OPENED HIS EYES and lay still for a moment, trying to determine what had awakened him. His wife, Margaret, was snoring softly beside him as she did when she had been forced to take laudanum for her pain. The room was hot and smelled of the ammonia liniment she applied nightly to her swollen joints. He listened but the only other sound was the scratch and rustle of the evergreens that grew beside the house. He slipped out of bed and, barefoot, padded over to the window. The blind was pulled down tight to the sill, and he lifted the side a crack so he could look out. Their bedchamber was at the rear of the house and below him was a large garden, smooth and white with the recent snow. Directly in front, the ground rose gently to a high fence, which demarcated the edge of their neighbour's property. Their house was hidden by a thick stand of evergreens that extended to the right and down to the road, offering perfect privacy. To the left was an open field. He thought he could detect a slight movement, a deeper shadow among the shadows of the evergreens in the upper corner, but he wasn't certain. The sky was overcast, and the moon was obscured.

He stayed motionless at the window for several minutes then, with a little groan, straightened up. Margaret muttered in her sleep, and he went back to the bed and pulled the quilt up around her shoulders. He waited a moment to make sure she had not awoken, then he went to the wardrobe and took out his trousers and a jacket. He favoured the newer style of nightwear, and he was wearing striped flannelette pyjamas. He pulled the trousers and coat on over these and crept from the room. There were no candles lit on the landing or stairwell, but his eyes were accustomed to the darkness and he made his way downstairs to the study. There was a dull slit of light showing beneath the door. He knocked, one hard tap followed by two softer ones. In a moment his son opened the door. Craig had moved out of view a few paces down the hallway and, without pause, James joined him.

"Is he out there again?" he asked.

"I'm not completely certain. Did the dogs bark just now?"

"They did a little while ago." James looked discomfited. "It didn't seem too serious," he added. "I thought it must be a squirrel or a racoon."

78

"There are occasions when you are worse than the most ignorant loafer," said Charles. He did not raise his voice or insert much inflection, but James flushed as if he had been roundly scolded.

"I'm sorry, Papa."

"Never mind." Charlie nodded in the direction of the study. "Are the curtains closed tight?"

"They are."

"Let's go in."

Craig led the way back into the room. James had been enjoying a pipe, and the air was thick and aromatic with the smoke. There was a glass of whiskey on the table beside his chair. His father walked straight over to the desk and rolled back the top.

The pug who had been keeping James company trotted over to him, waving her little curl of a tail. Craig gave her a cursory pat on the head.

"Is Tiny in the kennel?"

"Yes, of course."

Craig removed one of the inner desk drawers and reached his hand inside, turning the wooden screw that unlocked the secret compartment.

"Where is he?" asked James.

"Same place in the east upper corner." He took a small leather billy out of the hidden drawer.

"What do you want me to do?" asked James.

Craig pointed to the mantel clock, a showy walnut piece with much ormolu trim.

79

"Stay in here until that chimes the quarter. I'm going to come around through the copse. When it's time, open the curtains wide and stand in front of the window. Make a point of yawning and stretching. Then pick up Bess, get the lamp, and leave the room. Keep the lamp lit and go to the back door. Put on your boots and coat and step outside onto the patio a little ways. Make a show of getting Bess to relieve herself. Make a lot of noise about it. This is your chance to pretend you're Edmund Keane."

He put on his jacket and slipped the billy into his pocket.

"What if this fellow has a pistol?"

Craig shrugged. "You know what to do. Don't stand in the light; keep moving around. I should be close enough by then to stop him, but if I shout, get out of the way fast." Then, with a curt nod for his son, he left.

James sat down in the armchair and gulped back the rest of his whiskey. His pipe had gone out, but he didn't attempt to light it. Bess jumped up beside him, and he stroked her ears. Ten minutes dragged by, and the clock started to strike. He got up, went to the window, and flung open the curtains. He couldn't see anything outside, but knowing how visible he was made him uneasy. He did a quick yawn and stretch, snapped his fingers at Bess, and walked out of the room. At the back door he waited, listening, but everything was silent. It was almost one o'clock, and people were long in bed.

80

He put on his overcoat and slipped into his boots, picked up the dog, and stepped out onto the patio. Hearing him, Tiny popped out of her kennel and barked. James moved into the shadows, put Bess on the ground, and called out clearly, "Hurry up, Bess, don't take all night." Then he started to walk up and down, clapping his hands. Tiny continued to bark, and Bess joined in, spinning round him.

"That's enough, come on." He went over to the kennel, which was at the end of the patio, persuaded the pug to come over, and fastened her to a long leash. "Be good, you two." That done he returned to the back door, picked up his lantern, and went inside. He extinguished the light and waited in the hall. The dogs had quieted down and gone into their kennel, and it must have been only five minutes later when he heard the soft crunch of snow as somebody headed towards the door. His father entered.

"You didn't wait long out there, James."

"Sorry, Papa. Did you see him?"

"A glimpse. He was already moving away across Hernsworth's field. Either finished his job or knew we were on to him. He wasn't hurrying, so he probably swallowed your charade."

"What does he look like?"

"He's not too tall, shorter than you and me by a good foot, but he was wearing a mackintosh with the hood up, and I couldn't tell what size he was, broad or slim."

81

Craig blew on his cold hands and began to take off his outdoor clothes. "I examined the ground where he'd been standing, but there was nothing to see: no tobacco juice, no cigar butts. However long he had been there, he was a patient man."

"What do you think we should do, Papa."

"For now, nothing." For the first time, Craig grinned. "It is possible that we are making a mountain out of a molehill. He could be out there for a dozen reasons. He might be a shy suitor trying to catch a glimpse of Adelia for one thing. Or he could be a dog snatcher, looking to carry off our pride and joy." He blew on his hands again. "Or he's nosing into our business."

They had been standing in the hall, speaking in low voices. Craig tapped his son lightly on the cheek. "By the way, James, you are looking most fearful. I've told you many times, you must never show fear. Never."

"I'm sorry, I didn't realise." James summoned up his characteristic, sunny smile.

"That's better. You must take a lesson from what happened to that poor sod, Harry Murdoch. He was his own worst enemy."

"I didn't know you felt sorry for him, Papa."

Craig shrugged. "Of course I do. Not a lot but some-what. Now off to bed with you. In the morning we'll go out and have another look around. He just may have left something behind, although I doubt it. This man is experienced."

James kissed him good night and left. Craig didn't move but stood and chafed his cold hands again. He knew he wouldn't sleep yet; his blood was still racing. He needed a bit of soothing, a release. He made his way up the rear stairs, past the second-floor landing to the third. There were two chambers up here. One was used as a storage room; the other was where his sister-in-law slept. He opened the door to this room and went inside. "Carmel," he whispered. "Carmel, wake up, dear, it's me."

Jessica didn't want to go back to bed just yet. Walter was not a heavy sleeper, and it seemed that the smallest movement on her part woke him. She'd half expected him to be waiting at the door. She knew it came from love, but his solicitude was oppressing her, ultimately futile. He could not help her, could not offer any relief from her torment.

She didn't risk raking the coals even though she was chilled to the bone. Her boots were worn thin at the soles, and her stockings were damp from the snow that had leaked through. In her crib, Sally turned and cried out, "Mama, Mama." Jessica went over to her, but she was fast asleep. She looked flushed, and in a rush of alarm Jessica touched her forehead. She was warm but not overly so, and Jessica pulled back the coverlet to cool her. Then, wrapping her hands in the ends of her shawl, she began to pace around the room. A large

83

Bible was on its special stand by the window and she halted in front of it, touching the soft leather cover as if it were a live creature. She opened it at the back page where her mother had written down the family tree as she remembered it.

Evangeline Plain had married Josiah Watkins. They had seven children of whom four had lived to adulthood, Phoebe, Thomas, David, and the youngest, Jessica.

She moved her finger along the careful handwriting. Jessica had married Walter Lacey. Her mother had given her the Bible as a wedding present, and Jessica remembered how proudly and carefully she had entered the name of her firstborn, Sarah, called Sally, born October 30, 1891. There was another line underneath ready for the next entry, and Walter had written Sylvanus. The foetus had not been viable, but according to the church he had lived long enough inside her to have a soul and his christening and burial had been simultaneous. Jessica pressed her own breasts. If the infant had gone full term, he would have been suckling now.

She stood for a moment and touched the Bible reverentially. She had witnessed her mother many times gain solace from what she insisted was the word of God made manifest, and Jessica desperately needed guidance. She opened the book at Proverbs and without looking ran her finger down the page, continuing as prayerfully as she could until she felt the impulse to stop. She looked down. She had halted at chapter 30, verses 15–16.

84

The horseleach hath two daughters, crying Give, give. There are three things that are never satisfied, yea, four things say, It is not enough:
The grave; and the barren womb; the earth that is not filled with water; and the fire that saith not, It is enough.

The words became shards of glass in her throat.

Chapter Twelve

The Don Jail, an imposing grey stone building, was set back from the street on a slight rise so that it was visible to the neighbourhood. A broad gravel driveway, always neatly raked, swept up to the arched entrance as if to a manor house, although there any similarities ended. Murdoch had been here on numerous previous occasions, but he had been in through the front entrance only once before when he was in the role of a visitor. This was when he'd gone to talk to Adam Blake, the boy he'd caught pickpocketing. Normally, the boy would have been sent off to The Boy's Industrial school. However, the police magistrate, Denison, who tried the case, was notoriously unpredictable. Expressing great sympathy for the woman, he'd sentenced young Blake to sixty days in Don Jail. Murdoch thought there was intelligence in the boy and hoped that by showing some interest in him, he could help him find a better path.

However, he might as well have saved his breath. Blake was sullen and uncommunicative and not at all interested in changing his ways.

Murdoch walked up the curving stone steps to the big double doors. There was a carved stone column on either side and over the lintel was a large carving of a man's head, also fashioned out of grey stone. The hair and beard curled out like snakes, and the eyes were prominent and doleful. Murdoch thought it looked like a decapitated criminal, but he'd been told it represented Father Time, a caution to those who were foolishly wasting theirs.

He tugged on the bellpull. There was a small barred and shuttered window in the door to the right, and almost immediately, the wooden panel slid open. A man, who could have been at the mouth of Hades to judge from his forbidding expression, thrust his face into the opening. He viewed Murdoch with immediate suspicion. "What's your business? Visiting on Sunday only."

"Warden Massie sent for me. I'm Acting Detective Murdoch, Number Four Station."

The guard glanced down at something, presumably a list of some kind, and his expression changed. "You can come in." He was ushered into a tiny foyer.

"Sorry if I didn't offer you the best greeting just now, Mr. Murdoch, but we get all kinds of sob stories to get us to break the rules. Most of them a pile of horse plop." He offered Murdoch his hand. "Clarence Howe, at your service."

Murdoch shook hands.

"Sorry for your loss," said Howe, indicating Murdoch's badge of mourning. He nodded an acknowledgment but didn't feel like offering any further information.

"How is young Blake doing? Has a few weeks in the brig brought him to his senses finally?"

"Blake? You're talking about Adam Blake? Tow-headed little filch?"

"That's the one."

"Come to his senses? Not him. He's heading straight for a rope necklace, if you ask me."

Puzzled, Murdoch was about to ask if Howe knew the reason for his summons, but a door behind them opened and another guard emerged. He, too, had a military bearing with short, cropped hair and a long, waxed moustache.

"The warden says he's ready to see you, Detective. Come this way."

Mr. Massie's office was on the second floor at the rear of the building, facing the prisoners' exercise court. The new guard didn't speak as he led the way, and they marched down a dimly lit corridor, their footsteps echoing on the stone floor, the guard's keys clinking at his waist. A narrow flight of stairs led to another locked door. This opened into a short corridor, plainly decorated with rush carpeting and unadorned dark brown walls. The warden's door was at the end of the hall, and Murdoch felt as if he should

88

have snapped to attention when they halted. The guard tapped on the warden's door.

"Come."

James Massie had been standing by the window behind his desk, but he immediately came over to greet Murdoch, offering his hand. He was a short man, of middle age with a smooth, bald pate that he balanced with a trim moustache and beard. He wore gold pince-nez, which accentuated his rather scholarly look.

"Detective Murdoch, please have a seat." He waved in the direction of the leather padded chair that was in front of his desk. Murdoch sat down, removing his hat and placing it on the floor beside him.

The guard turned on his heels smartly and left the room. The warden took the chair on the other side of the wide desk. The surface was bare except for an inkwell and pen tray and a large ledger. Massie moved the ledger to one side, lining it up neatly with the edge of the desk. Murdoch wondered if he was always this uncomfortable.

"Thank you for coming so promptly, Mr. Murdoch. I, er, didn't feel I should impart my news in a letter, so I assume you do not know the reason for my sending for you?"

"I thought it might be young Blake, but I gather that is not the case."

"Ah yes, Blake. No, no, that is correct. It is not concerning him."

Massie opened the drawer on his right and took out a buff folder that was stuffed with sheets of paper. He pushed the pince-nez up his nose. The lens magnified his brown eyes.

"Well, I won't beat around the bush any longer. We have a prisoner here. His name is Henry Murdoch, known as Harry Murdoch. He claims he is your father."

Murdoch stared at him. "My father? How could he be my father?"

Massie riffled through the papers and took out one of the sheets.

"Henry Francis Murdoch, born in the city of Halifax, Nova Scotia, in the year of Our Lord, eighteen hundred and thirty-nine. He was married to Miss Mary Weldon, also of the city of Halifax, now deceased. There were three issue: a son, William, born in sixty-one; a daughter, Susanna, born in sixty-four; and a second son, Albert, also deceased." His tone was conciliatory. "I realise this must be a shock to you, sir, but we are correct, are we not? Henry Murdoch *is* your father?"

For a moment Murdoch felt as if he were gaping like a fool at the man in front of him. It had been such a long time since he had had anything to do with Harry. When he spoke, he could hear how cold his voice sounded. "It must be correct. Those are certainly the pertinent details of my father's life. What has he done this time?"

Massie pursed his lips, hesitating. "He has been convicted of murder."

90

He waited to see if there was any reaction, but Murdoch had retreated into the wooden mode of expression that gripped him in moments of great stress.

The warden looked down at his sheet of paper and read as if it were important he not include a single word not officially recorded: "On August the fourth, last, he was charged with the willful murder of one John Delaney of the county of York. He was tried before a jury of his peers and convicted on December sixth. He was sentenced to be hung, the sentence to be carried out on Monday, December sixteenth."

"What were the circumstances of the murder?" Murdoch asked, although he thought he could guess. A drunken brawl, one blow too hard. Massie turned back and indicated a large sheaf of papers that were tacked together.

"This is a copy of the complete court records, but I can summarize the case if you wish."

"If you please."

"The crime occurred on August fourth in the ravine area to the east of Yonge Street where Summerhill ends. There is a tavern at the end of the street named the Manchester . . ."

He glanced at Murdoch, who shrugged. He hadn't heard of it. "Apparently, the proprietor, Vincent Newcombe, organises terrier matches, the object being to see which dog can kill the most rats in a given length of time. Mr. Murdoch was a participant in such a match.

91

According to the witnesses, he lost heavily and became enraged, accusing almost everybody of cheating him. The man who emerged a winner was the man who was found murdered, John Delaney. Again, all witnesses agreed that Harry left the premises first. Two hours or so later, Delaney's wife became concerned when her husband had not returned home and sent her son to the tavern to enquire after him. He had apparently left not too long after Harry. One of the witnesses, a Mr. Pugh, offered to return with Delaney's son, and he discovered the body lying in the creek. He had not drowned but had suffered severe blows to the back of the head. Harry Murdoch was found lying in the grass only a few feet away. When roused and told of Mr. Delaney's death, he replied, 'He got what he deserved.' Mr. Pugh, on suspicion of culpability, bound Murdoch's hands, and when the constable arrived, Murdoch was arrested."

"Is that the sum of the evidence against him?"

"By no means. Mr. Delaney was left handed, and your father had a bruise on his right cheek, which corresponded to abrasions found on the dead man's left knuckles. There was blood on Murdoch's right sleeve and on the front of his shirt. He had no good reason to be where he was in the ravine. His boarding-house was located at the far end of Shaftesbury Avenue in the opposite direction. Finally, there was money missing from Mr. Delaney's pouch. Of course, his remark concerning the poor man's death was most damning, Mr. Delaney was held in high respect by his church and community."

"In spite of his predilection for gambling?"

"Apparently a forgivable sin."

"And Harry Murdoch had been drinking, I suppose?"

"According to the witnesses, he was quite full."

Murdoch felt a rush of bile into his mouth. The years hadn't changed his father. Massie averted his eyes, tactfully.

"I must say that since he has been here he is quite redeemed. He is learning how to read a little and has shown quite an aptitude for sketching. He cannot, of course, drink to excess even if he wished to, but he has taken the Pledge and every week he receives communion. He has returned to his faith. Roman Catholic, I believe?"

Murdoch nodded.

"The coroner's jury concluded he had lain in wait for his enemy just below the bridge. They quarrelled. Murdoch struck Delaney, probably with a piece of wood, and toppled him into the creek. Then, overcome by the exertion and still under the influence of the liquor, he lost consciousness and did not awake until he was discovered later by Mr. Pugh. Those are the bare bones of the case. You can certainly look at this report at your leisure if you wish."

"Is there any point, Warden?"

93

Massie realigned the ledger again. "That is entirely up to you."

"Did he plead guilty?"

"No, he did not. He swears he is innocent." Massie coughed politely. "But then that is quite common, isn't it?"

"Why has he asked to see me?"

"I am aware that you have not seen each other for some time. He told me himself that you had a falling out when you were a young man."

"You might call it that."

Murdoch knew his voice was bitter, but he couldn't help it. The so-called falling out was a violent quarrel that would have ended in bloodshed except that Harry was too drunk to remain upright. Murdoch, who was just thirteen years old but already growing tall, had accepted the blows his father was raining on his head and shoulders, too proud to do anything other than defend himself. When Harry had staggered and fallen to the ground, Murdoch had walked away, vowing he would never again allow his father to beat him. The last sight he'd had of his father was the man lying on his back in the middle of the living room, snoring, dribbling, and stinking.

"It's been a long time," he said out loud.

The warden rocked back in his chair. "Your father intends to ask you to prove his innocence."

Murdoch grimaced. "Does he indeed? That's why he has tracked me down then?"

94

"He was not aware until yesterday that you were with the police force. I believe he was more of the mind to see you one more time."

"A reconciliation, you mean?"

"Just so. The shadow of the gallows is a long one, Mr. Murdoch, and dark. I have seen many men repent of their sins when they are about to face that last journey." He stood up. "We have a room for visitors. The guard will take you there, and I will have Mr. Murdoch brought down. We cannot, of course, offer you complete privacy, but I will instruct the guard to leave you alone. And by the way, I have given permission for the prisoner to smoke. Under normal circumstances I do not allow any tobacco or pipes, but in this case, he may have one if he wants."

Murdoch also stood up. He could feel his heart beating faster, and his mouth felt dry. It was a long time since he and Harry had stood face to face.

Chapter Thirteen

THE GUARD, TYLER, SHOWED MURDOCH into the visitor's room. "Take any seat you like."

The room was plain, with a plank floor and one long table running down the centre. About a dozen chairs were crammed along each side, but the table was demarcated with strips of wood to indicate each place. The prisoners had to keep their hands visible within these barriers. The air was close, permanently saturated with the smell of fear and anger. Murdoch chose a chair at the end of the table and sat down. Two doors with narrow, barred windows faced each other across the room. The prisoner came in from one side and the visitor from the other. The guard walked over to the opposite door and pushed an electric button, which presumably gave a signal to the cells.

"They'll be here in a minute," he said. He eyed Murdoch curiously. "One of your nabs, is he?"

"No," said Murdoch and he deliberately began to look around the room. A row of high windows to his right let in natural light but they were too high up to give a view of the outside. It was a dull, grey morning and the wall sconces had been lit. To one side of the door facing him was a portrait of her Majesty. The Queen was depicted in her robes of state and the scarlet, ermine-trimmed train and crimson drapery behind her glowed vividly. Murdoch thought the portrait was a fine copy, better than the one that was in his cubicle at the police station. Directly behind him was a large oil painting of the chief constable, Lieutenant-Colonel Grasett. This one was in the prisoner's line of vision.

"I'll be outside the door. Holler if you need me," said the guard and left.

Murdoch took the opportunity to remove the black band from his sleeve. He wasn't ready to share the news of Susanna's death with his father. He sat back, undid his coat, and took out his watch. It was two minutes past the half hour. He knew he was trying to look at ease. It was far from the way he felt, but he'd be damned if he'd give Harry the satisfaction of knowing he was nervous.

He heard the sound of footsteps shuffling. Hurriedly he went back to the table and sat down. The door opened and in came another guard. He stood back to usher in his prisoner. This man, in grey prison uniform, was heavyset, with a pale, clean-shaven face. He was balding and what hair remained was grizzled. Relief

97

rushed through Murdoch. There was a mistake; this was not his father. He was too old, too heavy.

The prisoner moved awkwardly to the table, and suddenly he smiled.

"Hello, Willie. It's been a long time."

It was only then, in the voice, that Murdoch knew it was his father. He stood up so abruptly that the chair tilted backwards and tipped over to the ground with a crash. He flushed with embarrassment, feeling clumsy and foolish, the way he always had in his father's presence.

"Still got two left feet, I see," said Harry.

Murdoch straightened the chair and sat down, while his father eased himself into the opposite seat. He held out his hand. "Come on, son. There's been a lot of water under the bridge, but we're still the same flesh and blood. Won't you at least shake your own father's hand?"

His father's grip was firm, the palm hard and calloused the way he remembered. Harry had taken pride in that. His blows had been as damaging as a piece of wood.

The guard stepped back. "My name's Barker. I'll let you both alone, but I'll be watching through the window. Murdoch, put both your hands on the table and leave them there."

It was strange hearing somebody else referred to by his name. His father was scrutinising him, and he forced himself to meet his gaze.

"You've changed, Will, but I suppose that is to be expected. You were a lad when I saw you last. Now it's like staring into a mirror." He ran his hand across his cropped hair. "Rather, say, a reflection of the way I used to be. How old are you now? Thirty-five?"

"Thirty-four."

Murdoch was curt. He had never thought of himself as resembling his father, and it didn't sit well with him. "Warden Massie says you've been convicted of murder."

Now it was Harry who flushed. "Forget the niceties, eh, Will? Yes, that's the fact of it." He grinned again but it was like watching a dog snarl. "Unless there's a miracle, I won't be bringing in the new year." He made a grotesque gesture to indicate the hanging.

"The warden said you beat a man to death because you lost money at a betting match."

There was a sudden glint of anger in Harry's eyes, and his lips tightened. Even now, after all these years, that look sent a stab of fear through Murdoch's body. He leaned back in his chair.

"Why did you want to see me?"

Harry managed to drag up some kind of smile. "I know we didn't part on good terms, Will, and I'm sorry for that. But as you can see, I'm in desperate straits. I was hoping you might help me."

"How?"

Harry rubbed at his scalp again. "I never could talk to a man who looked as if he was about to haul off and wallop me one. Makes me nervous."

"Does it, Harry? Nothing I can do about that."

99

He had used his father's Christian name deliberately and provocatively, but Harry didn't take him up on it.

"Barker told me I can have a pipe. You wouldn't happen to have 'baccy on you, would you?"

Murdoch debated for a brief moment whether or not to deny him, but that felt too childish so he fished in his inside pocket and took out his tobacco pouch and matches, pushing them across the table towards his father. He waited while Harry opened the pouch and sniffed at the tobacco hungrily.

"Good stuff, Will."

Murdoch waited until Harry had filled the pipe, lit up, and drawn in the smoke. The motions were so familiar to him. He'd seen his father do that hundreds of times – and with the same grin of satisfaction across his face. He'd bought him a pipe once as a Christmas present. He'd had to work scrubbing the decks of the trawling fleet until he'd saved up enough money. Forty cents was a month's worth of work. Fishermen weren't able to be generous. Uncannily, Harry seemed to pick up on his thoughts.

"Remember that sweet little briar you gave me, Will? The bowl was all carved. Silver tip, too. Very swell piece."

Murdoch nodded. "You broke it a few weeks later."

Harry's face was momentarily lost in a swirl of fragrant smoke. "Did I just? Well, I'm sorry for it. It was a splendid gift." He glanced in Murdoch's direction.

"I must say, you've grown to a fine man. Have you married?"

"No."

Harry sighed. "After twenty-two years, we have a lot to catch up with, but right now I'm like a dog watching its dinner. There's not much else I can focus on."

"You said you wanted me to help you? In what way?"

Harry lowered his pipe. "I'm innocent, Will. I didn't kill that man. There wasn't any solid evidence, but the jury didn't care. Our Bertie had more brains than all of them put together. I didn't stand a chance."

It was the reference to his brother that infuriated Murdoch. Harry seemed to have entirely forgotten how he had made the boy's life a misery because he was slow.

"I understand you quarrelled with the man shortly before he was killed."

Harry sneered and, for a moment, the thin patina of benevolence slipped. "You understand, do you? How clever of you."

Murdoch's jaw felt tight and stiff as if he wouldn't be able to talk properly. Time vanished, and they were once again staring at each other across the kitchen table. Involuntarily, he steeled himself for the next move: Harry grabbing him by the front of his shirt and lifting him out of his seat. Unexpectedly, however, his father's expression softened, and his body slumped down in the chair.

"I'm sorry, Will. We're not getting off on the right foot. I want you to know I'm not the same fellow I used to be. I haven't had a drop to drink since August. The world looks different when you're sober. If I could live my life all over again, believe me I would and liquor would have no part in it."

Murdoch stared back at him. It was still a stranger's face, puffy, unhealthy-looking skin. Only the brown eyes, which he had inherited, seemed the same.

"You haven't yet said how I can help you."

Harry turned to studying the bowl of the little pipe, and he tamped down the tobacco with the end of the match. "I must admit I didn't know till now that you were a police officer. I thought you were a lumberjack. I sent off a letter. Thought maybe you could hire somebody to investigate for me, but this is even better."

"Need I point out that as far as the law is concerned, the case is closed. Shut. You've been convicted."

"I didn't do it. I swear."

"It's quite possible you just don't remember. You hit him in a drunken rage, and now you've forgotten. That's happened before."

Harry flinched as if he had been struck. "I know, Will. I know that it did, and I'd give my right arm if I could undo it but I can't. But I don't want to hang for a crime I didn't commit."

102

Murdoch shrugged. "There isn't anything I can do."

"Yes, there is. You're a detective. Talk to people again. The police had their minds made up I was guilty, and they didn't do much investigating. Somebody killed the man, but it wasn't me, I swear." Harry met his eyes. "You're the only hope I've got. No matter what's gone down between us, you are my flesh and blood. You can't deny me that." He moved his hand as if he would touch Murdoch's but stopped. "You know I'm a man don't beg easily, Will, and I'm begging you. Don't turn your back on me out of spite."

The door opened and Barker came in. "It's time for the exercise yard."

"Can't I go later?"

"You know you can't."

"I'll skip it then."

"No, you can't do that either."

"I'll come back later," said Murdoch.

Harry nodded. "Not too much later. I've learned the clocks run differently when you're in jail. An hour can seem like a week." He held up the pouch. "Can I hold on to this?"

Murdoch shrugged. "If you want to."

"Let's get a move on," said Barker, and he ushered Harry out. Agitated, Murdoch pushed back his chair, drumming his fingers on the scarred table. This was not what he had expected. He had imagined an encounter

103

with his father many times, but not like this. Not with this soft-voiced, defeated man. A man who seemed sincere. A reformed man. Murdoch put his head in his hands. Somewhere at the back of his mind, he was disappointed. He wanted to go on hating him.

Chapter Fourteen

TYLER MUST HAVE BEEN WATCHING through the other window because he came into the room immediately. "Visit go all right then?"

Murdoch looked up at him, willing himself not to take out his anger on the man.

"It depends on what you mean by all right. I didn't hit him, or he me. I suppose that means it was all right."

The guard whistled through his teeth. "Like that, is it?"

Murdoch got to his feet. "Do you think I could talk to the warden?"

"He wants to. Told me so personally. He's put off his inspection of the cells on your account."

His tone was enigmatic, and Murdoch couldn't tell if Tyler thought this was a reason for respect or resentment. He decided that in the guard's eyes, this deviation from

Warden Massie's usual routine had elevated Murdoch's status. He followed him back down the corridor.

"I must say that the prisoner is no trouble. I wish they were all like that."

Murdoch made no comment.

They were outside the warden's office. Tyler tapped and at the "Come," they both went in.

Warden Massie was behind his desk, reading from a sheaf of papers.

"Ha, good. I wonder if you would join me in some morning tea, Mr. Murdoch. Or would you prefer coffee? We have that."

"Tea if you please."

Tyler left.

"Good choice if I may say so. Our coffee here resembles weak mud. At least I imagine that is what mud would taste like." Massie glanced over the top of his pince-nez. "How was your meeting? You haven't seen each other for, what? Twenty-two years you said?"

"Yes. No contact at all. I was not sure my f–" Murdoch still couldn't get his tongue around the word "father." He continued. "I wasn't sure if he was even still alive."

"Ah, quite so."

"He's asking me to do some investigating of the case."

"I expected he would."

"What is your opinion, Warden? You followed the trial no doubt. Do you consider him guilty?"

Massie hesitated. "In cases of serious crime I attempt to be knowledgeable about the circumstances. The prisoners, naturally enough, will present their own side. I have had to write to the convicting magistrate more than once to find out the truth." He sighed. "I regret to say, Mr. Murdoch, that the longer I am in this position, exposed to such elements of society, the more hardened I become. I have almost lost my faith in the capacity of men, any men, to tell the truth. In this case I will tell you frankly, I am not certain. Since he has been here, Harry Murdoch has been sober, quiet, and industrious. He has returned to his own faith."

"That could be seen as hedging your bets, couldn't it? He *is* facing death, after all."

Murdoch realised how callous his words sounded by the puzzled expression of Massie's face. But the warden's voice was kind.

"Quite so. Unless there is a significant intervention. I have here a copy of the court records. I thought you might be interested to read it."

He pushed the papers toward Murdoch, who did not touch them.

"Mr. Massie, you have avoided answering my question. You said that the prisoner is being docile and pious, but you have not offered your opinion as to whether he is guilty as charged."

107

The warden removed the pince-nez and rubbed at the red spot on the bridge of his nose where they had marked him.

"I have twice gone through these papers. The evidence seems irrefutable. In my opinion, your father is the one who murdered John Delaney. I'm sorry. I wish I could say otherwise." He tapped the papers in front of him. "I thought perhaps it might set your mind at rest, given the circumstances."

"Those being that Harry Murdoch and I are related by blood, and that if there was an outside chance he was innocent, I would therefore seize any opportunity to prove that?"

"Quite so, but I see . . ."

Massie was saved from continuing by the return of Tyler with the tea tray.

The warden, in Murdoch's opinion, was wasted in the prison system. He should have been in the ministry. He was the most sympathetic and tactful of men. He directed the conversation to general matters about the conditions in the city. He was all for allowing the streetcars to run on Sunday, as he thought it would benefit the poorer classes. It was difficult for some families to visit the prison when they lived a distance away. And he was adamant that his charges benefited from contact with those who might arouse their more tender feelings. By the time they had finished their cups of tea, Murdoch had calmed down sufficiently to want to look at the trial records. Massie set him up in a tiny adjoining room while he went to do his daily tour of inspection. Tyler replenished the teapot, brought him some notepaper and pen and ink, and left him to it. Murdoch picked up the bound documents. They were typewritten duplicates, and for a moment they made him think of Enid, whose work often consisted of making copies of legal documents. That thought was not a happy one either.

The presiding judge was Falconbridge, a man Murdoch had encountered once or twice when he'd had to testify in court. He was a sharp-beaked old fellow, who either tried to live up to his name or had been shaped by it, and he had the reputation of being both shrewd and irascible. His concluding instructions to the jury were incisive. It was extremely unlikely they would bring in a contrary verdict if Falconbridge considered the accused to be guilty. He had obviously so considered.

The defending counsel was a solicitor named Clement, who as far as Murdoch could tell had done a competent, if uninspired, job. The prosecuting counsel was Greene, and Murdoch knew of him from reputation. Word was Greene would as soon shoot himself as lose a case. You might as well fly the pit; save yourself the time. In that respect and given that John Delaney was described as a worthy pillar of the church and a devoted family man, the odds had been against Harry. Murdoch knew how the men on the jury were wont to feel about strangers.

109

Some of them would have known Delaney personally. From their point of view, a culprit had been apprehended and why should they look further.

He took one of the sheets of paper and began to write notes.

He must have been at it for more than an hour when Massie returned. Tyler was right behind him carrying a tray.

"Mr. Murdoch, I am about to take my luncheon. I usually do so at my desk, and I wondered if you would join me?"

"I would appreciate that, sir, and if I could trespass on your time, there are some questions I'd like to ask."

Tyler, who seemed to act as much as a butler as a guard, put his tray on the desk, and began to unload plates and soup bowls. Massie sat at his desk, and Murdoch took a chair in front of him. Tyler moved over a second small table.

"Thank you, Tyler. We'll manage ourselves now."

Luncheon consisted of some kind of thin vegetable broth and slices of bread and cold mutton.

"I take my meals from the kitchen," said Massie. "I believe that the men in my care should not be indulged, neither should they be treated as vermin. They receive a plain but nourishing diet."

Murdoch sipped at the tepid broth. Plain it was. He didn't know about nourishing. It tasted like some kind of turnip.

"Please ask your questions."

Murdoch consulted his piece of paper. "What I have done is extrapolate the main points in the evidence against him. First, there was the bruise on his right cheek. He says he fell, which is plausible given he was full of liquor."

"That is true but does not account for the corresponding graze on Delaney's left hand."

"Point taken. Second, with regard to the blood on Harry's sleeve and the front of his shirt. He says his dog was bitten by the rats, and he got the blood on him when he picked him up. Did anyone examine the dog to see if it was injured?"

"Not at the time and when the case came to trial, if there had been an injury, it was long healed." Massie wiped his mouth with his napkin. At least the china and the linen were befitting his position.

"The fact that he was in the ravine at all was, of course, most suspect. It certainly suggested he had been lying in wait for Delaney, who had to go that way to get home."

"Quite so."

"I suppose there is no doubt that money was missing?"

"None at all. The hired man at the tavern has a head for figures. It was he who brought the matter to the attention of the prosecution, otherwise it might have been overlooked. Lacey kept an exact record of the wagers and what was won and lost and remembered exactly. Delaney left with almost one hundred dollars, and that was not the amount in his pouch."

"To be exact, he won ninety-four dollars and seventy-two was found in his pouch. Twenty-two dollars unaccounted for."

"Mr. Clement couldn't get Lacey to budge an inch on that."

"He tried to suggest that Delaney had taken out his money to count it, and some bills blew away. It sounded like a ludicrous proposition to me."

"It was and it lost him credibility. The jurymen actually laughed when they heard that."

"There was no search conducted at the time, I understand."

Massie waited until he had swallowed his piece of bread and could speak without his mouth full. "Not for the money. As I say, nobody knew it was missing until shortly before the trial. The constables were looking for a murder weapon, and that was soon discovered close to the place where Delaney was found."

"Mr. Greene was determined that Harry had hidden the money intending to return for it later, but if so, why didn't he take the entire pouch?"

"On that matter, Greene was most persuasive. He suggested that Harry tried to make the whole thing look like an accident by rolling Delaney into the creek. He took only a small sum of money, hoping it would not be noticed. He did not count on Lacey having such an excellent memory. Of course, jurymen are never sympathetic towards men who won't relinquish stolen goods, and it didn't help Harry's case that the money was not recovered."

"Speaking of excellent memories . . . The witness, Mr. Pugh, is another man in possession of such. Even in the midst of the shock of finding Delaney, sending the boy for help, and so on, he was able to remember exactly what the accused said."

"Ah yes. 'He got what he deserved,' wasn't it? The prosecutor could paint Harry as a remorseless and vindictive killer. According to the coroner, Delaney was killed by at least two or three severe blows to the back of the head. His torso also showed several bruises. As I recall there were clear impressions of boot tips, as if he had been brutally kicked by somebody in a rage. Harry was wearing boots. His anger was not in question."

Murdoch tried to eat some of the mutton on his plate, but it was greasy and unappetising. He stayed with the buttered bread, which had been sliced in thick pieces.

"The question of course is, if Harry Murdoch did not murder John Delaney, who did?"

"Quite so. There were no other applicants, as it were." Massie smiled at his own joke then glanced rather anxiously at Murdoch. He did not want to appear tasteless. Murdoch answered his smile.

"No, there weren't. All the other people present at the match were accounted for. The only hole here is the absent Mr. White, who seems to have disappeared. Advertisements were placed in the newspapers, I understand, asking for him to come forward and testify at the trial, but he did not appear."

"That is not necessarily a sign of culpability. He may not have seen the advertisements, and the trial itself did not receive a great deal of attention in the newspapers. He might not even be aware that a murder occurred. And the two Craig gentlemen did vouch for him. They were clear they saw him heading towards Yonge Street."

"It is not totally out of the question that Delaney encountered someone else who had not been present at the tavern, who might even have been a complete stranger to him."

Massie's expression was kind. "That is true but I'm afraid not likely. If Harry Murdoch were not so obdurate about declaring his innocence, there would be no such debate as you and I are having."

Massie reached for a small silver bell that was on his desk and gave it a brisk ring.

"I'm afraid I must be about my duties, Mr. Murdoch. I have taken all the time I can allow myself. Are you in any way satisfied?"

114

"As you say, the evidence does seem irrefutable. But I would like to speak to the prisoner again if I may."

"Of course. You can do so at any time as long as it does not interrupt the routine of the prison."

The guard entered the room. "Tyler, will you see if the prisoner, Murdoch, is available. The detective wishes to speak with him."

Tyler went to collect the luncheon plates. "And by the way, please give my compliments to the cook. A most delicious soup."

Murdoch thought the warden had been eating prison fare too long.

Chapter Fifteen

ADELIA CRAIG WAS HAVING DIFFICULTY with her recitation piece. Each student in the class was to present two verses of the popular poem "In the workhouse: Christmas Day" at the Christmas recital. Adelia had been assigned part of the first verse and the third from last, but the first wasn't giving her enough scope to use the large dramatic gestures she thought her teacher liked, and the other was so sad she kept wanting to cry.

She tried again. She straightened the strip of carpet, which she had put in front of the piano as her stage. Her teacher, Miss Hamersley, insisted that her students treat every practice as if it were a real recital. This meant the walk onto the stage, *the walk is a mirror of character*; the recitation itself, and the final bow and retreat. Adelia took a deep breath and assumed an *active chest*. She widened her eyes slightly and tried to summon a few animated thoughts. *Bright face, always a bright face, nobody wants to see a pudding.* Adelia usually had difficulty finding lively thoughts as worry was always uppermost; and even though she liked her lessons, they were another source of anxiety. She dearly valued the good opinion of Miss Hamersley, and it was always hard won.

She inhaled deeply, pushing her chest out rather like a pouter pigeon, neck stretched upwards, head gracefully balanced. Her chin tended to recede, and she had to remind herself to thrust forward slightly to compensate. She bared her teeth in a ferocious smile and walked across to the centre of the carpet. Miss Hamersley was critical of Adelia's walk, which she declared to be too timid and indecisive.

"Your audience wants to believe in you, Miss Craig. They are not going to listen to a young woman who looks as if she is about to turn tail and run out off the stage at any minute. Now, deep inspiration, assume active chest, and proceed."

First, Adelia took up position one. Her weight was on her left foot, right foot obliquely in front, heel a few inches from the other foot. She remembered to curl her hands gracefully at her sides instead of clenching them nervously as she was wont to do. She began the recitation, her right hand moving to her heart.

117

> *It is Christmas Day in the Workhouse,*
> *And the cold bare walls are bright*

Both arms extended horizontally, palms up.

> *With garlands of green and holly,*
> *And the place is a pleasant sight;*
> *For with clean-washed hands and faces,*
> *In a long and hungry line*
> *The paupers sit at the tables,*
> *For this is the hour they dine.*

She indicated the paupers as if they were lined up in front of her in a row. Her forefinger and thumb were parallel, fingers slightly cupped.

Skip to the end of the poem. The poor man was denouncing the hypocrisy of those who had denied his wife entrance to the workhouse.

> *Up to the blackened ceiling*
> *The sunken eyes were cast –*
> *I knew on those lips all bloodless*
> *My name had been the last;*

Hands clasped on "cast," head back and eyes up in supplication. She stopped. How should she move to "lips all bloodless"? Better not to overdo it. Miss Hamersley didn't like her students jumping round like acrobats, as she put it.

Adelia said the line again. "I knew on those lips all

bloodless" – a frown here. Fingers extended, slightly open and touching her lips on "bloodless."

She'd called for her absent husband . . .

Hands cupped around her mouth, head turning from side to side.

O God! Had I but known –
Had called in vain and in anguish

"Anguish" was not quite as easy to depict as one might think. Miss Hamersley liked them to be original. Finally she decided to show anguish by bringing her right hand, clenched, over her heart and sort of collapsing inward as if she had been hit by a cold wind.

Had died in that den . . . alone.

On the final line, she raised her shoulders, stretched out her arms, and slowly brought her hands together in front, pressing fingers together in prayer. She held her position for the count of three, then as the audience burst into rapturous applause, she took her bow. Right foot back into second position, bend forward slightly, bring right toe to the heel of the left foot and bend the knee, pressing firmly against the back of the left knee.

119

She was still in a bow when the door opened and her brother entered.

"Bravo, Leila, bravo."

Embarrassed, she straightened up.

"Were you practising your piece?"

She nodded.

"When am I going to see it?"

"I told you, at the Christmas recital."

"Show me now. It will be a good rehearsal."

Adelia hesitated, not at all sure if James would be a kind audience or not.

"It's not ready yet."

"Suit yourself."

He went over to the mirror and fiddled with his Windsor tie, a new green-and-red-plaid silk.

"My, aren't we a swell this afternoon," said Adelia. "A little extra macassar oil, a new cravat, and very shiny shoes. Going calling, are you? Miss Delaney, I assume?"

"Don't tease me, Adelia, I have no stomach for it today."

"I'm merely making an observation. This is your typical courting apparel."

"I would hardly say I'm courting. She is pleasant and I enjoy her company."

"So you say. On the other hand, you do seem to have a predilection for rather dull farmers' daughters."

"She's not and I don't." He frowned at her. Adelia

120

was wearing a green velvet wrapper, and her fair hair was still in a loose bedtime braid.

"It's late not to be dressed, isn't it? What if we have visitors?"

"Like whom? The only people who come here are the butcher, the baker, or the candlestick maker, and Aunt Carmel attends to them."

"I thought you said Mr. Pugh was coming this afternoon."

"He doesn't count as a visitor. He wants to sell me some books."

"The way he was attending to you last week, I had the distinct impression he had more on his mind than *Woman: Maiden, Wife, and Mother.*"

James came closer to her and whispered in her ear. "On the other hand, maybe that was exactly what he had on his mind, especially the wife part."

Adelia turned her head away irritably. "That's a stupid remark if ever I heard one."

"Leila, come on, admit it. You were quite enjoying his company. You were laughing."

"He had some clever magic tricks. They were amusing."

"Suit yourself." He planted a quick kiss on her cheek. "Well, I'd better be off. I'll leave you to your practice."

121

At the door he hesitated, looking over his shoulder at her. She looked so unhappy, he softened. "Do you want to come then? It might make things more agreeable if you do. Her mother or that lump of a brother are always lurking, and I can hardly get a moment with her alone."

"Thank you, but I do have a lot more to do."

"Are you still upset about the other day?"

"Of course I am. I hardly enjoyed testifying in a court of law."

"You shouldn't be concerned about that," he said with a grin. "You were splendid."

He switched to a girlish falsetto. "Why that old clock is so LOUD, Mamma is always complaining about it. I know for sure my father and brother came into the house at a quarter past eight o'clock exactly."

She smiled a little. "I did not sound like that. And the judge made me dreadfully nervous. I felt he could see at once I was lying."

"Of course he couldn't. Nobody could. You were cool as a cucumber. A lovely *English* cucumber, I might add. Your lessons are paying off."

"Just as I was stepping down from the witness box, I caught the eyes of the prisoner, the Murdoch fellow. He looked so afraid. I felt desperately sorry for him."

James came over and put his arm around her shoulder. "Why is it that everybody in this family is feeling sorry for the man? Save your pity. He's a murderer. And a brutal one at that."

She put her hand lightly over that of her brother. "I suppose you're right."

"Of course I'm right. But if it will make you feel better, you can go up to the police station and tell them what really happened. 'I'm afraid I didn't tell the truth. I did not see my father and my brother at all that night.' 'Oh dear, where were they then?'"

"Stop it. I know perfectly well where you were."

"I'm glad of that. For a minute I thought my own sister suspected me of knocking some poor man over the head."

"Don't be silly."

James looked at her for a moment; then he shrugged.

"I'm off. If Mrs. Delaney invites me to stay for dinner, I shall accept."

"In which case, I shall see you in the morning. I plan to go to bed early."

She waited until the door closed after him, then she stood up, moved to the centre of her improvised stage, and addressed the empty chairs in front of her.

> *There, get ye gone to your dinners,*
> *Don't mind me in the least*

For the first time, she raised her voice. The effect was so satisfactory, she did it for a second time then took her bow.

123

Chapter Sixteen

HARRY HAD GOT THERE BEFORE THEM and was sitting at the table with his hands correctly placed between the table markers. He made a worse impression on Murdoch this second time. There was a pale sunlight coming through the windows, but it yellowed his face, which Murdoch remembered as always ruddy from the weather.

Murdoch took the same chair as before, opposite him. "Do you want another pipe?"

"I'll never refuse that."

The guard was hovering expectantly close by.

"Can I offer you a bowl as well, Mr. Barker?"

"Thank you, sir."

Murdoch handed his tobacco pouch to the guard. "We'll be quite all right here. You probably could do with a change of scene." He winked.

"I could that." Barker stuffed his pipe to capacity, then passed the pouch on to Harry.

"I'll just have my smoke in the corridor outside," he said, and he left them alone. Murdoch waited while his father went through the ritual of pipe stuffing and lighting up and the deep, satisfying draw. There was a moment of awkward silence, then Harry pushed some sheets of paper toward him.

"Take a look."

They were pencil sketches, all of boats, on the beach, in heavy seas, a couple of interiors.

"Do you recognize the *Bluebell*? I was going by memory, but I spent enough time in her so she came to mind real clear."

"Yes, that one particularly. They're good." Murdoch knew his tone was grudging, but he couldn't help himself.

Harry gathered the papers together. "You've got a look on your face, Will. Hasn't changed since you were a nipper, that look. You've had a chance to read the trial report then?"

"I have."

There was a flash of anger in Harry's eyes. "Are you planning to tantalize me, Will? Keep me dangling on the line while you decide whether or not I'm a keeper?"

"It's not that at all. That's not why I was hesitating. I don't know where to start."

Harry showed his teeth in what was probably meant to be a grin. Murdoch saw that one of his side teeth was chipped, something he hadn't noticed before. "Come on then. All of it. Are you going to condemn me, too?"

"There's strong evidence against you."

Harry thumped on the table. "You've got me tight by the balls, haven't you, Will. You're just going to squeeze a little now and again just for the pleasure of seeing me wince. Well, I'm not going to do it. I know there's been bad blood between us, and you haven't forgot it. Maybe we've got to get that out of the way before we go any further. Or are you enjoying it too much? You're finally getting your own back." His eyes had darkened in a way that Murdoch was all too familiar with. He leaned forward. For all the world he looked as if he were about to challenge his son to an arm wrestle. In spite of the inactivity of the jail, he still had the broad shoulders and thick forearms of a fisherman. It was all Murdoch could do not to flinch. His heart was pounding in his chest, and he wasn't sure his legs would hold him if he stood up. He felt as if he had been deluged with scalding water, and in spite of himself he was that boy again confronted with his father's rage, an anger that had felt murderous to him then and even so now. His fear was quickly followed by his own fury.

"Why should I believe you're innocent? Answer me, Harry? Why should I? You say you don't remember anything after you left the tavern. Shall I remind you what you were like when you had tossed back a few? You liked to come out swinging. At me, Bertie, even Ma. And the next day you couldn't remember a bloody thing." He was leaning forward now, his face close to his father's, forcing him to meet his eyes. "Why should this be different?"

Surprisingly, Harry didn't respond in kind. He averted his face.

"Because it is. I'd know if I killed somebody. I'd remember that."

"Well, let's try digging into our memories, shall we? Do you recall picking up a piece of tree branch and whacking the man across the back of the head?"

"No, I do not."

"Whacking him so hard his skull split? Then maybe a recollection of kicking his body as if he was a sack of potatoes? And all because you thought he'd cheated you. Is it coming back to you now, Harry?"

"No!"

The door opened and the guard peeked in. "Everything all right, Mr. Murdoch? Do you need help?"

Startled, Murdoch realised he had been shouting. "No. Thanks. Harry and I are just getting down to brass tacks."

"Keep it down then. You sure are loud."

"Some things need to be said loud, Mr. Barker."

The guard grimaced and went back to the corridor. The interruption, however, served its purpose, and

Murdoch was able to regain some control. Harry was sitting very still, his hands in front of him. Then he spoke and his voice was taut with emotion. "Don't you think I've wondered that myself? If it is true I committed a murder, I want to know. I'd like to prepare myself to face my Maker."

Murdoch almost laughed out loud but was stopped by the expression on his father's face. He meant what he said.

"I've been thinking about little else since I've been in here. But I just don't think I could have done such violence. Even if I felt it, I was too full. I could barely walk by that time. I wouldn't have had the strength to hit him like that."

This was the only point that Murdoch had thought was in Harry's favour when he'd read the trial report. The blows that Harry threw around were easier to dodge and feebler the more drunk he was.

"What do you think I can do at this late stage?"

"I don't know. You've ended up in the police force. You'll know what to do."

His pipe had gone out, and he fiddled with the matches to get it going again. Murdoch let him have a draw first.

128   "This man, White. The one who vanished. What was your impression of him?"

"Ah, you've hit the nail on the head, Will. I begged and begged my counsel to search for him, but he always gave me tepid answers. 'We've advertised in all the newspapers,' was all he could come up with. I told him the man was a city swell, which was a mistake. That made him stop looking right away. If I'd said he was a navvy or a clerk, he'd have gone all out to find him."

He bit hard on the stem of his pipe. "Besides, I was a charity case and that slows down the enthusiasm right there. I didn't have no money to pay a lawyer, and beggars can't be choosers."

"He seemed to do a competent job, as far as I could tell."

"He was a hack. I needed somebody with spirit."

"Wishful thinking aside, do you consider White the kind of man who would kill somebody?"

Harry shrugged. "Why not? He was what I'd call a hungry bettor. They won't stop till they've won or they're broke. He didn't win nought that day. Maybe he believed Delaney was a cheat which he was. I know the Craigs said he was heading off in the other direction, but it would have been nothing to turn back and go in search of Delaney."

"What did he look like?"

"Young fellow, not thirty I'd say. Medium sized, brown hair, whiskers. It was obvious from the way he was dressed he was a swell from the city. Gold cuff links, stickpin with a diamond, the lot."

"A professional man?"

129

"Probably. I'd say a banker but could even be a doctor or a solicitor."

"Did he introduce himself? Give a Christian name?"

"Not to me. I wouldn't be surprised if White isn't his real name."

"I thought I'd try to find him. See what he has to say."

Harry reached out and placed his hand on Murdoch's. His skin was hot and dry, and it was as if a bolt of electricity shot through Murdoch's fingers. "We don't have much time. You might not believe me, Will, but I'm a better man than I was. Being in jail gives you a lot of thinking time. These last few months being cold sober has made me face up to a few things. I mean it when I say to you that I want to know truly if I have murdered a man. I'll die repentant for that if it's true. If it's not, then I'd like the opportunity to make amends for the life I've led up to now."

Murdoch wanted to sneer. This was the typical drunkard's remorse, as lasting as a piece of milkweed fluff, blown away by the next thirst. But there was sincerity, fear, and a look he could only identify as yearning. Harry wanted something from him, and it wasn't only help. He wanted his son to love him.

Chapter Seventeen

THE MANCHESTER TAVERN WAS LOCATED at the far end of Shaftesbury Avenue, and Murdoch walked back from St. Clair Avenue and Yonge Street, which was as far as the streetcar terminal. He was glad of the exercise. Within the space of four days, his life had undergone an irrevocable and cataclysmic change, and he felt the need to sort out both his thoughts and feelings. He didn't know when it would be the right time to tell his father that Susanna was dead. The recent meeting had been cut off abruptly. Tyler had come in and said Harry had to return to his cell at once. There had been some sort of barney in the exercise yard, and the warden was confining all prisoners in their cells until he sorted out what had happened. As he stood up to follow the guard, Harry called out, "Find out what's happened to my dog, will you. He's a game little fellow. Name of Havoc."

He wondered what Harry's reaction would be when he did tell him about Susanna. The new Harry, that is. The one with sensibility. When they were growing up, his father had not shown any more tenderness towards his daughter than he had to the two boys. He didn't hit her, but he did bark out orders or angry reprimands if she wasn't fast enough bringing him what he wanted. She had wept with the rest of them.

Murdoch's stomach felt tight and on the verge of queasiness. Although he didn't want to think about the expression on his father's face when he was leaving, it kept jumping back into his mind. The raw nakedness of Harry's longing was shocking. His father's physical nakedness had been easier to witness. Winter and summer, when he returned from a fishing trip, Harry would strip down in front of the fire before stepping into the tub of scalding hot water his wife had ready for him. Will had sat and watched him, and one time when he was almost ten years old, Harry had caught an expression on Will's face that had made him chuckle. He was enjoying the boy's nervous curiosity. He hadn't needed to say anything, but Will knew what it was all about and had hated the power his father held over him. After that he'd developed the ability to feign indifference.

132   He halted in front of the tavern, a long, squat building sitting alone in a patch of waste ground. In its first life it must have been a warehouse associated with the Canadian Pacific railway yards, which ran along the

south side of the street. However, the ochre-painted walls were in good repair and the black trim fresh and shiny. On either side of the double doors were two urns, empty now but no doubt filled with flowers in the summer. In the English style, there was a hanging sign on which was painted a muddy-looking picture of a little brown-and-black dog, smooth coated, with sharp, pointed ears and spindly legs. Its front paw, the claws tipped with blood, was holding down a black rat. Printed in bold red letters was THE MANCHESTER TERRIER.

There was smoke coming from the chimney and lamps lit. He could see a woman, plump and dark haired, moving about in the kitchen. A large room took up the other half of the building and was obviously the taproom, with its long tables and benches. There was a big stone hearth at one end, but there were no customers warming themselves. He assumed the tavern was closed until the evening.

He continued walking. The macadamised street ended abruptly about fifty yards on and narrowed into a dirt path that disappeared in a stand of pine trees. There were no other buildings, and the fence opposite demarcated the end of the railway property. He followed the path through the trees to the brow of the hill and stood looking down into the ravine. A blustering wind stung his face.

Beginning slightly to the south of St. Clair Avenue, the land was cut by a series of faults that ran down

133

almost as far as the lake, like gigantic sabre slashes. These ravines weren't especially long or deep, but they were rough and thickly wooded and afforded dramatic terrain in the otherwise bland landscape, a reminder of the primeval forest so recently tamed.

Murdoch paused. In the summer the trees would be thick and lush, but now they had lost most of their leaves. The spruces and other evergreens were abundant, but he could see through the branches sufficiently to glimpse a narrow wooden bridge at the bottom of the hill. He fished his watch out of his waistcoat pocket and checked it. Ten minutes past two o'clock. He began to make his way at a steady pace down the path. The ground was hard and dry, but small drifts of snow had been captured in the ruts, which made the way slippery.

"Ahh!" He lost his footing and slid down in a rush to level ground, where he lay momentarily, feeling irrationally angry at the fall as if the earth had vindictively attacked him. A black Junco lighted on a branch nearby and twittered, cocking its head to look at him.

"Haven't you seen anybody fall on their arse before?" he asked the bird in mock anger. "Humans do it all the time, you know." The blackbird darted away.

Murdoch brushed some snow off his trousers and got to his feet. Down here the wind was less fierce. It was private and protected. Even with the denuded trees, the branches were thick; in the summer he would be completely invisible. He checked the time. It had taken

134

only six minutes to descend from the top of the hill. Add four minutes from the tavern. Ten minutes more or less from there to here.

He walked onto the bridge and leaned over the railing. The creek was narrow and the banks sandy, about four or five feet high. The little river would be frozen before too long, but now there was only a thin skin of ice at the verge, the centre running freely. Just ahead, the path forked, one branch went to the left and disappeared around the bend of the hill. The other continued further along to the right then it too vanished as it wound its way up the hill. The railway bridge, the steel girders dark and slender, strode across the gap.

Murdoch took the right-hand path and walked a distance of about twenty feet. This was roughly the spot where Harry had been found lying in the thick summer grass. Delaney had been discovered in the creek further along. The banks here were higher than at the bridge but also sandy, and the rocks had been smoothed and rounded by the flowing water. He walked on a little further. The path he was on ran underneath the high railway bridge and seemed to be heading in the direction of Yonge Street. Then just around a slight bend, he came to a flight of steps, which zigzagged at steep angles up the side of the ravine. He began to climb upward.

He might have gone past the hideaway if he hadn't been on the lookout for anything out of the ordinary.

135

On the left-hand side of the path was a rocky over-hang and around it a clump of bushes, too neat and symmetrical to be quite natural. He slipped underneath the railing, clambered around the slope, and peered through the bush. He was looking into a hollowed-out cave. Branches were attached to a weather-beaten piece of wood that blocked the opening. He moved it aside and crawled inside the opening. The space was surprisingly large as the sandy wall had been hollowed deeper underneath the overhanging rock and there was just enough room to sit upright. He squatted and hugged his knees. Quite cosy really. Old moss and leaves piled on the floor made a soft cushion.

He and Susanna had had a hideaway in a cave in the cliffs that they could only reach by means of a knotted rope. He remembered the pleasure he'd experienced every time he crawled into that cold space and hauled up the rope, sealing off access. He sighed suddenly, flooded with bittersweet memories of his sister, timid, overly pious, and well behaved, but at rare times, carefree and a good companion. She'd loved to race him down to the seashore, and try as he might, he couldn't outrun her. It was probably the only way she had to triumph, and she relished it.

136

Perhaps he should have insisted on seeing her face. He could have broken through into that dark room and looked at her. He grimaced to himself. Too late now.

He turned his head in the direction of the steps, which were just visible through the protective branches. There was a rough shelf wedged into the bush roots and on it lay a heap of stiff, dried squirrel pelts and a skinning knife, quite clean. He touched the blade, which was razor sharp. Next to that was the nub of a candle and a box of lucifers. Tucked underneath the shelf was a cigar box, which was pierced with holes. He pulled it out and removed the lid. Inside was a tiny frog skeleton. Murdoch frowned. He knew what this meant. Years ago, a boy in the village had showed him something similar. He said his sister was in love with a lad who didn't want her, and she was trying to win his affections through spells. She had captured a live frog, put it in a box pierced with holes, and placed it in the middle of an ant heap. When she came back two weeks later, at the time of the full moon, the frog's flesh had been consumed by the ants and only the skeleton remained. One of the bones had the shape of a fish hook, which she had to contrive to fasten to the garment of the desired one, and he would come to her. "And did he?" Murdoch had asked. "In more ways than one," the other boy had replied with a leer. Gingerly Murdoch touched the tiny bones. The hooked piece had not yet been removed.

At that moment he heard the sound of a child crying, a grizzling kind of cry that usually tried the patience. Feeling foolish at the thought of being found

137

in the hideaway, he hurriedly replaced the box and crawled out. Above him on the hill were a man and a child. Because of the incline, they were moving carefully, the man holding the little girl by the hand. She was complaining, seemingly not wanting to be walking. They saw Murdoch and immediately the child halted, stopped whining, and shrank against the man, presumably her father. He gathered her into his arms, but Murdoch heard her wail. No words, just a frightened, high-pitched cry. The man pressed her head against his chest. He hadn't moved either, and Murdoch waved to him.

"Good afternoon," he called out.

The fellow started to descend, and Murdoch was struck by his wariness. The child had hushed, but as they approached he saw how she clung tightly to her father's coat as if she were a little wild animal.

"You startled us, sir."

"Beg your pardon, I was in pursuit of a, er . . ."

He waved vaguely. Close up, Murdoch saw the man was young, ruddy complexioned. His eyes were intelligent enough but with the same air of caution he'd observed in his movements. He was a big man, with the wide shoulders and strong thighs of a labourer.

138   "I was just out for a walk," replied Murdoch.

"Lost your way, did you?"

"Quite so. Will these steps take me to Yonge Street?"

"They don't go anywhere except up to my cottage."

Murdoch turned in the direction of the wooden bridge. "And where does that other path lead to?"

"That don't go anywhere either, except to private property." He shifted the child so she could ride more comfortably on his hip. She whimpered and tried to burrow her face deeper into his coat. "Hush, Sally."

Murdoch rubbed his hands together. "You know what, it's colder than I thought. I think I'll turn back."

"Forgo your walk, you mean?"

Murdoch grinned. "Yes, I think so. A dram of hot gin might do no harm. I passed a tavern up there on the road. Would you recommend it?"

The man's face was still grim, but he said, "I'm going that way myself. I work there. I'd say the ale is as good as the Dominion brewery can make it, and the gin's passable. But if you're peckish, what we're famous for is home-grown bacon."

Murdoch fell in beside him, and they continued on down the steps. He guessed this must be the hired man, Walter Lacey. At the trial, his description of Harry had been caustic. A man to be avoided. A swarm of wasps would be less dangerous than him when he'd been drinking.

"Haven't seen you around here before. Did you come all the way up from the city to walk in the ravine?"

Murdoch hadn't set out with any particular plan in mind, but suddenly, it came ready formed. He knew he had to ask questions and have some reason to do so,

139

but human nature being what it is, he thought it highly doubtful that he'd get much information if he revealed his true identity.

"As a matter of fact, I wasn't just out for a stroll. I am on a case."

"Is that so, sir? What kind of a case might that be?"

"I'm a detective and, er, I have a private client. He's lost his dog. That might not sound too serious to us, but he's an older gentleman and very attached to the little creature."

Murdoch wasn't comfortable lying, he never was, but he forged on, trying to sound as convincing as he could.

"He claims that he knows the name of the man who nabbed the dog. This fellow came by offering to do some handiwork; then the next thing he and the dog had gone. Pouf! He, my client that is, is offering a generous reward, and I am of course only too happy to pay for a person's time and information."

"What makes you think the dog is anywhere in this vicinity?"

"To tell you the truth, my client is a man of the Fancy. He likes to gamble. He trained the dog as a darned good ratter. He is convinced that's why this man stole it, so he could enter it in some matches. He'd heard that you could pick up a game or two at the Manchester."

"Is that so?"

"I'm not trying to fish out information from you,

believe me. I'm dead against the gambling laws. If grown men want to wager, why shouldn't they?"

Lacey shrugged. "It don't matter to me."

He was panting a little with the burden of carrying his child. He pried her away from his chest and put her on the ground, but she clung like a limpet to his trouser leg, another thin wail came out of her. She was wearing a white hooded cape of rabbit fur that looked too big for her. Murdoch crouched down and tried to meet her eyes, but he had to talk to the back of the hood.

"Hello. I'm sorry if I frightened you back there. I didn't mean to." There was no response, only a muffled whimper.

Lacey scooped her up again. "She's not afeard; she's shy. Don't get to see many strangers."

He didn't speak until they were on the path, but Murdoch's gesture seemed to have mollified him slightly.

"When did your client lose his dog?"

"A while ago. In the summer as a matter of fact. He's been out of the country and hasn't had a chance to look before. He said the man who took it gave him a name. Me, I doubt if it's his real name, but he said it was. Merton, no that's not right. Murdoch. Harry Murdoch."

He felt the shock that jolted Lacey, who frowned at him, trying to read his expression. 141

"Is the name familiar?" asked Murdoch.

"Might be. Was the dog a scrubby little grey terrier?"

"I believe it was. He named him Havoc. Have you seen it around?"

"I have that."

"With this man? He's a tall cove, middle-aged. Thinning hair, brown eyes."

"The dog was in the possession of such a person. He's not now."

"How so? Did he sell him?"

They were almost at the top of the hill.

"The man you're talking about, this Harry Murdoch, he showed up here in August, but he murdered a man and if you want to talk to him you're going to have to go to the Don Jail because he's in there. The dog is being looked after by Mr. Newcombe, the innkeeper. He'll probably be only too glad to get rid of him." Lacey seemed in a hurry to end the conversation and quickened his pace. As they approached the tavern, he said, "We don't open till five, but the missus will always find you a bite to eat. I'll let her know. You can sit in the taproom if you want. Mr. Newcombe keeps a good fire going."

He pushed open the door, and they stepped into a small, dimly lit hall. There was a delicious smell of roast pork in the air. Lacey set Sally down and pulled back her hood. Murdoch glimpsed a pretty child with dark eyes and wavy hair, but she noticed he was looking at her and she averted her eyes in fear.

"Come on, Sally. Don't be so mardy. We're going to see Maria." Lacey's voice was impatient, and Murdoch

142

saw how the child withdrew from the harshness of it. "Go through there," he said to Murdoch, indicating the door on the right. Then he hurried off down the hallway, almost dragging the little girl.

Murdoch went into the taproom, which seemed to be the entire establishment. The plank floor was covered with sawdust, which smelled newly laid. Along both walls were wooden benches with tables in front of them, and at the far end of the room was a hearth that looked big enough to roast an ox in. The fire was blazing, and he headed straight to it so he could warm his cold hands. On the mantelpiece was a fancy black marble clock with a brass plate at the bottom inscribed with lettering he couldn't make out. He pulled out his watch to compare the times.

"That's ten minutes fast, sir," said a voice behind him. "I keep it that way because my customers tend to linger."

Murdoch turned around. A stout man in a publican's leather apron was standing in the doorway. Physically he resembled a jovial Friar Tuck, but the expression in his eyes was anything but benevolent.

"I understand you're in search of a dog?"

"Yes, I am."

The innkeeper stepped closer. Lacey was behind him, and Murdoch could see that he was holding an iron poker in his hand. He wasn't smiling either.

143

Chapter Eighteen

Newcombe whistled and immediately a small dog trotted out from behind the Chinese screen that was across the corner of the room by the fireplace.

"This is Tripper," said Newcombe.

The dog was black-and-tan coloured, smooth coated, and her full dugs indicated she was suckling a new litter. There was a high-pitched chorus of squeals from behind the screen as her pups protested her absence.

"Say hello to our guest, Trip," said Newcombe.

The dog approached Murdoch and began to sniff at his trouser cuffs. He decided not to move and waited until she had finished her inspection. She walked all the way round him then came in front, sat, and offered her paw. Newcombe laughed with delight, and Murdoch saw with relief that Lacey lowered his poker.

"She's accepted you," said the innkeeper. He clicked his tongue at the dog, and she turned and jumped into his arms, licking his face as if they'd been parted for months. He held her close against his cheek, crooning to her.

"How's my girl? How's my little mother?"

The question seemed to remind her of her duties because she wriggled free, jumped down, and hurried off, disappearing behind the screen.

"D'you want to see the pups?"

Murdoch nodded. Lacey was still at the doorway, but the tension in the room had lightened considerably. Newcombe moved aside the screen sufficiently for Murdoch to see the basket where Tripper was lying on her side while four puppies rooted at her teats, sucking vigorously. She looked up at the two men, but their presence didn't seem to disturb her and she gave another polite wag of her tail.

"She's a good mother is Tripper. This is her third litter. Big one this time. These dogs don't usually have more than one or two at a time." He replaced the screen. "We'll let her get on with it. She likes you," he added, and Murdoch felt absurdly pleased.

"She's a Manchester terrier, I take it. And you've named your tavern after her."

"One and the same." He indicated the bench closest to the fire. "Come and have a seat. Would you be hungry?"

"I am indeed, and that smell makes me salivate."

The innkeeper nodded to his man. "Bring him a plate, Walter. He's all right." Lacey left and Newcombe turned back to Murdoch and held out his hand. "I'm

Vince Newcombe." He spoke in an English dialect of some sort. Not Cockney but like that.

"Williams, at your service."

"Is that your real name or one for now?"

Murdoch was taken aback. "I, er . . ."

"Come on, sir. I'm no green fool, neither is my man. You're after telling us some kind of whopper. Walter thought you was a nark, but I always trust Tripper when it comes to being a judge of character. Never fails. She can tell if a man is lying, and she can smell fear a mile off."

Aware of how he felt when the two men had first come into the room, Murdoch considered Newcombe's faith in his dog was misplaced, but he just grinned.

"Walter tells me you're a private detective and you're looking for a stolen dog, but that don't make sense. Nobody would wait four months to go looking for their dog. Besides, Harry Murdoch was here more than once with that feist. He didn't steal it." He laid his forefinger along the side of his nose, cocking his head. "I know what you are. I knew the minute I clapt eyes on you, you weren't no frog. Thems a shifty lot. I can always tell them. I bet you'd be with the newspaper. The man you mentioned, Harry Murdoch, was convicted just two days ago. The papers are probably after stories. You're a newspaper reporter."

Murdoch shook his head, preferring to keep as close to the truth as he could. "No, I'm not."

Newcombe looked as if he was prepared to argue the point. "You're sure about that?"

"Quite sure."

"There's no dog owner, I gather?"

"No."

"Didn't think so. I've got the dog myself. There wasn't anybody else to take of it. But he's a lot like his master is the pity, as mean as a snake. Bit me twice, almost killed one of the puppies when it wandered too close. I'm thinking of getting rid of it. I was just waiting to see the result of the trial."

Newcombe got up, went behind the screen, and emerged with one of the puppies. He put it on the floor, and it moved unsteadily towards him. He took a spindle of rolled paper from the mantelpiece and started to wave it under the puppy's nose. The little terrier pounced on the paper, and Newcombe jerked it out of the way just in time. "Hey, my fellow, a chip off the old block, aren't you?" He dragged the spindle again but this time he wasn't fast enough, and the pup grabbed it and tossed it into the air. Newcombe looked over his shoulder at Murdoch.

"Well, are you going to come clean? You're not a nark. You're not a reporter. What are you then?"

"I really am a detective, but I'm working in a private capacity. I've taken on a client who wants it proved conclusively one way or the other that Harry Murdoch was guilty."

147

"Ah, working for the family, are you?"

"Yes, you could say that."

"What do you want to know?"

"Anything at all that relates to the case." He grinned. "What Tripper's assessment of Harry was? What's your opinion? Anything."

Newcombe sat on the hearth bench and bent over his own round stomach to play with the pup, dragging the spindle in front of him making growling noises. Murdoch waited.

"This investigation? Are you planning to do it honest? You're not just interested in smearing somebody else's good name, I hope. Throw dirt to confuse things."

"There is no point. I just want to know conclusively if Harry Murdoch murdered John Delaney."

"The twelve good men and true who sat on the jury said he did. What are you going to find out that they didn't?"

"Perhaps nothing, but at least I'll have tried."

"For the family?" asked Newcombe, giving him a disconcertingly shrewd glance.

"Yes, for the family."

For the second time, the innkeeper offered his hand. "Shake on that. I like loyalty. What have you got if you don't have family? By the way, is your name truly Williams?"

"Close enough."

"Ask away."

"I've read the record of the trial, and I know what happened, or what was said to have happened. Like I said, I'm interested in your own opinions."

"My opinion is that the man is guilty. He got himself drunk and lost his temper. I know I shouldn't say this, seeing as I earn my living as an innkeeper, but I've seen men take their liquor in every kind of way you can imagine. Some old codgers become sweet and loving as babes when they're full. Nocky farm lads become philosophers; lawyers act like fools. Men who in daily life are affable as can be turn into savages who've forgot every Christian principle they ever knew. They'd cut your throat soon as look at you."

"Would you consider Harry one of that sort?"

"I would. When he'd got to drinking, he was ready to pick a quarrel with the good Lord Himself if He was by."

"And when he wasn't drunk?"

"Can't say he stayed sober long enough for me to tell. Quiet I suppose. But it's interesting that you say you're working for his family. We did have a long chin back in April. I like to get to know my customers. I knew he was a widower and that he'd been a fisherman out East, but he never mentioned any family."

Murdoch couldn't resist. "He didn't talk about a son? Or a daughter?"

149

"Never said a word. Acted like he was all alone in the world, but he does have relations, you say?"

"Yes."

Newcombe teased the puppy again. Murdoch let that go on for a while.

"What about John Delaney? What kind of drinker was he?"

"He never took too much that I saw."

"You don't seem to have a category for that."

Newcombe checked to see if Murdoch was making fun of him. "No, I don't."

"You'd describe him as a good man then. Without any enemies?"

Murdoch registered the second's hesitation in his host. "None that I'm aware of. He paid his debts when he had them without bellyaching. He's got a good little feist though, so he rarely lost a match."

"What was Harry's reason for killing him?"

"Surely that's obvious. He'd lost the match. He was close to winning, but his dog choked at the last minute. A brooder that man. Terrible sore loser. He started accusing everybody of cheating him. None of it true. I run those matches clean as a revival meeting. His motive? Aggrievement. It's happened a hundred times before and will happen again as long as men are men. Dogs aren't like that. You'll never find a dog holding a grudge."

Murdoch headed him back to the issue.

"As I understand it, Delaney wasn't found for almost two hours. The accused man says he was passed out all that time. Didn't come to until he was being arrested. Could somebody else have come down the ravine path, had a barney with Delaney, then scarpered off under the railway bridge to Yonge Street? It would be so dark and woody down there in August, nobody would have seen him. Or them for that matter. Doesn't have to be just one person."

Newcombe pursed his lips. "I suppose that is a possibility, but I don't know who that could be. Everybody who was here is accounted for."

"A stranger? Somebody who wasn't at the match?"

"Not likely is it? You've seen the trial record you say?"

"Yes."

"Then you must know that there was a whole pile of evidence against your man. As far as I'm concerned, he was proven guilty beyond a reasonable doubt, as they say."

He picked up the puppy, who had suddenly fallen asleep across his shoe. "Is that it then in the question department?"

"Any personal opinions about the other men, especially Mr. White, who never appeared to give witness?"

"Tripper liked all of them. Oh, she barked at Mr. Pugh at first but soon took to him after that. Mr. White struck me as a swell young man who would go to great lengths not to be mixed up with anything sordid. But I don't see him as a murderer."

"Not even in the heat of a quarrel?"

151

"In the heat of a quarrel I wouldn't swear for any man. Scratch this pup and you're not far from the wolf. We men aren't that much different."

"And the others? The Craigs? Mr. Pugh?"

"Good men one and all. Corinthians as Mr. Craig calls them."

"And none of them change character when they're full?"

But that joke had gone too far, and Newcombe frowned. "Moderate drinkers all of them. Mr. White, too. Now if you'll excuse me, I'll see what's keeping Walter with your meal."

The mantel clock began to bong out the hour. Halfway through it slowed down, wheezing like an old man. Newcombe walked over, took a key from underneath the clock, inserted it into the back of the clock and turned it a few times. With a great deal more vigour, the clock finished out its task.

"In terms of this investigation, as you call it, you don't have a lot of time, do you? The man's due to be executed on Monday morning."

Murdoch was surprised by the intensity of his own reaction. "I know," he said.

Chapter Nineteen

THE INNKEEPER SOON CAME BACK carrying a big tray. "Here you are, and I want this plate licked clean."

Murdoch wondered if he should bark a response. There was a large plate on the tray, loaded with succulent pork slices dripping gravy. The potatoes and cabbage were an afterthought. Newcombe put the plate in front of Murdoch and plopped down a mug brimming over with dark beer.

"The brew is homemade. It's on the house."

He stood to the side of the bench, arms folded across his paunch, and watched with satisfaction while Murdoch tucked into the food with many appreciative noises. Lacey was right; this was the best he'd ever eaten, even surpassing Enid's rabbit stew.

"Speaking of dogs, you might be interested in these photographs." Newcombe indicated the series of framed pictures that lined the mantelpiece. "This is

Mr. Mahogany, my all-time champion. Died just last year at the ripe old age of thirteen. I put him to Tripper time before last. He was her grandfather, and I thought they'd produce a fine litter. Only two pups though, both stillborn. I suppose the poor fellow was too old."

Murdoch regarded the photograph, a black-and-tan dog, with ears pricked, head alert, looking out to the side of the picture.

"He looks like the dog on your sign."

Newcombe was pleased. "I painted that sign myself, using Mahogany as a model. Turned out pretty good if I do say so myself. All my dogs are purebreds. I can trace Trip's lines back through five generations. Best ratters you can ever hope to find. Here, look at this."

There was a shelf running the length of the rear wall with platters, photographs, and other paraphernalia. Newcombe was indicating a box with a glass front. Inside was an enormous brown rat.

"Mahogany caught that in the barn. Exactly as big as he was, but that didn't frighten him any. One pounce and done. It was one of the last things he did. I didn't notice at first, but the rat had bit him here . . ." He opened his mouth and pointed. "Nipped him right on the roof of his mouth. It got infected and before I knew it he sickened and died. I've kept the rat just to boast about, and I was glad I did. It's my memento."

The innkeeper was clearly still upset.

"It *is* huge," said Murdoch.

154

"Biggest I ever seen." Newcombe replaced the box on the shelf.

Murdoch had got to the stage of mopping up the remaining gravy with a thick slice of fresh baked bread. "I wonder if you'd mind telling me what happened that night. I mean when Delaney was killed," he added hastily. "It's always good to hear direct from the horse's mouth."

Newcombe sat down across the table from him and launched into his story, which had the seamlessness of an oft-repeated tale. For Murdoch's benefit, he added much more dog lore, including a detailed account of each terrier's performance. However, with regard to the actual events, there was nothing substantially different from what Murdoch had already read in the trial records. He threw in one small check.

"You say that everybody had left except Mr. Pugh, and he was with you until the Delaney boy appeared. Was he in your sight the entire time? Did you go into the kitchen for instance? It doesn't take that long to run to the bottom of the ravine and back."

Newcombe chuckled. "You would have to be an Indian scout to get down there, do your evil business, and get back up here without a bead of sweat showing. It's true I went into the kitchen to fetch some grub, but he never moved. He was sitting right where you are, and I was right where I am."

"Why didn't you stay in the barn?"

"Phew. It was like a furnace in there. He wanted to come in here where it was a bit cooler, so we did."

"And your wife? Where was she?"

Newcombe stared at him. "Maria? Why do you want to know about her?"

"I'm just trying to nail down all the pieces. I noticed she wasn't called up as a witness at the trial."

"Wasn't no need. She wasn't in the barn at all. Lacey helps me serve at the matches."

Murdoch tried to find the right approach. He didn't want to risk alienating the innkeeper again. There might be a second test.

"While you and Mr. Pugh were in here, I presume your wife was in your private quarters."

Newcombe still looked suspicious. "She was. She's got enough to do during the week without spending her Sabbath day working."

"Of course" – he patted his stomach – "and if I may say so, well-deserved."

The innkeeper was mollified. "Not that she does get her day of rest all the time. There's always somebody giving birth or dying. No matter whether they're beginning or closing, they all ask for Maria. She's good with babies, and she's good with the sick."

156 Murdoch dabbed at his moustache with the damask napkin Mrs. Newcombe had provided.

"That evening was no exception. Walter's little daughter was taken ill. His wife brought her in. Quite hysterical she was, but Maria is as close to being a nurse as makes no mind. Jess, that's Walter's wife, is one of those women who's as nervous as a sparrow. Always worried little Sally is sick. She overwatches that child something fierce. She's even worse now since she lost the one she was carrying a few months back. Right after the murder it was. Some people thought it preyed on her mind like it can do with women. Maria was carrying when Mahogany died." He sighed and rubbed his hands across his bald head. "The babe came to term, but was terrible sickly and didn't live to see out the week, bless his soul."

"I'm so sorry."

"Yes, he was our only one. Couldn't seem to get any others. Perhaps that's why I love these little dogs so. They're like my children." He got to his feet. "Give me your plate. There's a raisin pudding for a sweet."

Murdoch held up his hand in protest. "I can't eat another morsel; I'll burst."

Newcombe grinned. "I'll get Maria to wrap some up for you to take with you. Her pudding is a favourite with the customers."

"Thank you, I do appreciate that. Just a point of clarification if you don't mind. Mrs. Lacey arrived after everybody had left the barn, did she?"

"That's right. There was a storm coming up and they all cleared out in a hurry except for Mr. Pugh."

"Would she have come shortly after then? A few minutes? Half an hour? An hour?"

157

Newcombe shrugged. "Can't tell you that. Jess went straight in to Maria. Like I said, everybody does." He shook his head, but it was obvious how proud he was of his wife.

"And Walter Lacey, where was he after everybody had left?"

"He stayed to clean up the barn. He's not ascared of rats, dead or alive. I'm lucky to have him. I must admit they do make me squirm. And for all the fact she's laid out more people than you can count, my Maria won't tolerate a rat within ten feet of her."

Murdoch indicated the glass box with the monstrous stuffed rat. "Can't say I blame her."

"No, none of us knew anything until young Phil came running up to the door, yelling his head off that his pa was dead. It's a wonder the whole street didn't turn out, he was yelling that loud. Maria tried to keep Jess in the back, knowing how highly strung she is, but she had her hands full with the lad, who was screaming like a stuck pig."

"I suppose Walter tended to his wife then?"

Another sharp glance from Newcombe. "He had to go and fetch the constable."

Murdoch didn't want to press him. He sat back, rather uncomfortably full. "Bad business all round."

"It was. Not that I've suffered, I must admit. Folks get a morbid curiosity about murder. I've even had people coming up from the city asking to see the bloodstains.

Anyways, let me get this plate back to Maria. I'll bring in the sweet and see if you can eat it."

He left with the now light tray, and Murdoch took the opportunity to loosen his belt a notch. He had a closer look at the stuffed rat. All was quiet from behind the screen; no puppy nightmares.

Newcombe came back into the room leading a scruffy grey terrier on a leather leash.

"Thought you might like to meet the dog that caused all the trouble. This is Havoc."

Murdoch peered at the terrier. Its brown eyes were partly hidden behind its hair, but they seemed keen and intelligent.

"Hello, little fellow. Too bad you can't talk. You could have the truth confirmed in a second."

Hearing voices had awakened the brood, and two of the puppies waddled out from their den. Immediately they came over to investigate the newcomer. Havoc lifted his lip and snarled. One of the pups halted, the other mistook this signal or foolishly decided to ignore it. He continued to approach Havoc and lifted his nose to the older dog's muzzle to sniff at him. So quickly Murdoch didn't even see what happened, the puppy was flipped onto his back and Havoc was astride him, growling into his face. The pup squealed in fright. Tripper heard and before Newcombe could take action, she came rushing from behind the screen to rescue her pup. Teeth bared, she slammed her body into Havoc,

159

knocking him off. There was a whirl of barking dogs as he retaliated or tried to get out of the way, Murdoch couldn't tell which.

Newcombe jerked on the leash, pulling Havoc up on his hind legs. "Tripper, leave it!" The bitch, feet planted, barked ferociously for a few more moments; Havoc, almost choking, answered her in kind.

"I said, leave it!"

Reluctantly, Tripper backed away, grabbed her pup, still squealing, by the scruff of its neck, and carried it back to the den.

"My Lord, he is a mean little brute," said Murdoch.

"To be fair, in this case, that little titch got what he asked for. Havoc warned him, and he wouldn't listen. Dogs are very strict on manners. But Tripper, of course, will protect her own to the death if she has to. He wouldn't have stood a chance."

"Would he have hurt the puppy?"

"It's hard to tell. Probably just wanted to scare him a bit. But you never know. Some males will kill the young ones at the blink of an eye. Here, make friends with him."

He thrust a dried piece of bacon into Murdoch's hand, who crouched down to offer the tidbit. Havoc took a cautious sniff and gulped down the bacon. Murdoch reached out his hand and tried to pat the dog's head. At once, Havoc curled back his lip, showing impressive canines. Murdoch jumped back.

160

"He is a bad-tempered cuss, isn't he?"

"It'll take time, that's all. Here, try again." He handed Murdoch another piece of bacon.

Havoc swallowed it hungrily, but Murdoch didn't make any attempt to pat him this time.

"There you go then," said Newcombe, and he handed the leather leash to Murdoch. "He's all yours."

"What do you mean?"

"I can't keep him. He's a good ratter, mind you. I've been using him in the barn. But Tripper wouldn't get along with him. As you're representing the family of his master, it makes the most sense that you take him. It would be a pity to put him down."

Murdoch was spluttering out his protest when the door opened, letting in a rush of cold air. Two men came in. One was an older man, elegantly dressed in a long, checked overcoat and brown fedora; the other man was wearing bicycling clothes. The lower half of his face was wrapped in a woollen muffler, and he had on large racoon gloves against the cold.

"Good afternoon, Mr. Newcombe," said the older man, and he tipped his hat courteously to the innkeeper and Murdoch. "Brisk out there. Very brisk."

"Come in and get yourself warm, Mr. Craig, Mr. Pugh," said the innkeeper. "Where's your lad this afternoon?"

"He's gone courting, I believe."

"Miss Delaney?"

"Yes. A very fine young woman, very fine."

He spoke with a pronounced English voice that sounded affected to Murdoch, although perhaps it was normal for the other man.

"Here you are, Newcombe. The broadsheet I said I'd do for you."

He handed the innkeeper a sheet of paper. Newcombe studied it with delight.

"Excellent piece of work, Mr. Craig. I do thank you. Look, gentlemen, what do you think of this?"

He held up the paper and Murdoch saw it was an announcement of a forthcoming "Yuletide party, complete with puddings and mulled wine. Sign up now. Only one dollar."

"Would you print up two dozen copies for me? I'll hand them out to the customers."

"I'll have them ready by tomorrow."

Newcombe took the broadsheet and fastened it to the mantelpiece by using the clock to hold it down.

"A bargain if I may say so, Mr. Newcombe," said Pugh. "I'll be here."

Both men moved closer to the hearth to warm themselves, each glancing at Murdoch with polite nods of greeting.

"It's good chance that you came just now," said Newcombe. "This gentleman and me were having a chin about the Delaney case."

"Indeed?" said the Englishman. "Is there anything else that can possibly be said?"

162

"Sentence was received day before yesterday. He'll be hung Monday morning."

"Shame that," said Pugh.

"Shame he'll be hung, do you mean?" asked Murdoch. He hadn't meant his voice to be sharp, but it was and Pugh blinked.

"I suppose I did mean that. The whole thing shouldn't have happened. Tragic. Good man lost to the world."

"You must be referring to Mr. Delaney not Harry Murdoch," said Craig. "We can certainly do without his kind."

"What kind is that, if I may ask, sir?"

Before Craig could answer, the innkeeper intervened. "Gentlemen, allow me to make introductions. Mr. Craig, Mr. Pugh, this is Mr. Williams. He is a reporter, and he's writing an article about the case."

"Indeed?"

"Indeed, sir." Murdoch was struggling to calm down. It wasn't going to help his investigation to rile these men.

Pugh took off his glove and offered his hand. "Good afternoon to you."

Murdoch retrieved his fingers from the bruising squeeze. "And you, sir. I admire your courage to take your wheel on such a day. I put up mine two weeks ago."

163

"It's not too bad if you dress warm. What do you ride?"

"A Singer."

"Good wheel. Mine's an Ideal."

"That's good, too."

He put out his hand to Craig, who accepted without much enthusiasm.

"What's your paper?" asked Pugh.

"Beg pardon?"

"Who're you writing for? The *News*? The *Globe*?"

"Er, none so important. Just a small paper."

"Which one? Try me, I know all of them. Is it the *Orange Banner*?"

Blast! thought Murdoch. He could see the man was testing him, but why he was so persistent, he didn't know. Once again, Newcombe rescued him.

"He's keeping it confidential. Less prejudicial that way. Isn't that right, Mr. Williams?"

Murdoch nodded. Pugh seemed satisfied by that answer but didn't let go of the topic.

"Have you got a slant? You don't think the fellow was innocent, do you?"

Murdoch shrugged, on safer ground. "I'm trying to keep an open mind. As for a slant, as you call it, I'm going to let that emerge."

One of the puppies decided to test the world again, and he came out from behind the screen. Havoc jumped to his feet on the ready.

"Oh, dear. Glutton for punishment, aren't you," said Newcombe, and he picked up the puppy, gave him a kiss on his nose, and popped him back at the instance

Tripper came to investigate. "You know where you are with dogs," he said. "Food, warmth, and respect is all they want. Not like men."

Craig smiled. "That sounds as if it could be the tack you need, Mr. Williams. The mysterious complexity of human nature. Tell me, Newcombe, are you raising more champions with this lot?"

"I have every expectation of so doing, sir."

Somehow the little incident released the tension in the air. Pugh sat down on the opposite bench; Craig stayed in front of the fire.

"Are you ready for your dinners?" asked Newcombe.

"I am. What about you, Mr. Pugh?"

"Wouldn't miss it. But a pint of your ale would go down smooth first off. I got up a thirst coming up the hill."

"I'll take your hats and coats, gentlemen, and I'll fetch the brews," said Newcombe. "In the meantime, please help yourself to cigars. There's a new box on the mantelpiece."

Murdoch waited until the two men were settled again. "I wonder if I could ask you gentlemen some questions as you were both present on the evening in question. Our good host here has been most forthcoming, but it always helps to verify statements."

Craig took a cigar and began the ritual of sniffing it, licking the end, and so forth. "Made a statement, did he? I thought you were just chinning with him. You make it sound like some sort of official inquiry." Behind the affable English manners, Murdoch sensed something sharper, something wary as a fox near the chicken coop.

"Figure of speech only, Mr. Craig." He didn't give the man a chance to argue further. "I understand that you, sir, left here with your son and a Mr. White, who has not been seen since. You were right on the heels of Delaney, but I assume he had already got as far as the ravine and you didn't see him – or anybody else for that matter."

Craig blew out some odiferous smoke. "It is so long ago and, frankly, was of so little moment at the time, I can hardly remember. But I do know my son and I took leave of Mr. White just in front of our house, which is on Summerhill Avenue. He was heading for Yonge Street to see if he could find a cab. He didn't have his own carriage."

"I am intrigued by this person, White. Apparently he did not reply to any advertisements to come forward as a witness. Do you know who he is?"

"Not at all. Hadn't clapped eyes on him before."

"Some swell from the city, if you want my opinion," said Pugh. "Between you and me, Vince Newcombe has a good thing going up here. Them's high wagers. Nothing to sneeze at. Delaney was the big winner of course."

"And you the gracious loser, Mr. Pugh," said Craig. "Our friend here didn't win a single bet, Mr. Williams, but he didn't complain at all. One would almost think it didn't matter to him."

Pugh flushed. "Course it mattered, but I'm not going to whinge and moan when all was fair and square, won by better dogs."

"It would be hard *not* to find a better dog than your poor beast, Mr. Pugh. I don't think he is quite suited to ratting. The rodents seemed to frighten him out of his wits."

Pugh laughed. "You're right about that. But I thought I'd give it a try."

Murdoch thought Pugh was ill at ease with this conversation, but at that moment, Newcombe returned with two tankards of beer.

"Pork'll be ready in a trice." He addressed Murdoch. "Mr. Williams, I told young Phil Delaney I'd bring up one of the pups to show him. Flash is the sire, and I already promised them they could take one of the litter if they liked. Would you like to come up with me? Maria is going to take good care of these two gentlemen."

Murdoch stood up. "Thank you, Mr. Newcombe, I'd be happy to. And may I have the pleasure of meeting Mrs. Newcombe and giving my compliments on the splendid meal in person?"

"She'd like that I'm sure. Come through here." 167

Murdoch got his coat and went to follow his host out of the taproom. At the door he stopped. "What about the dog?"

Havoc was lying down with his nose on his paws, watching him. He looked forlorn, a scrap of a dog with his dull, rough coat.

"Better leave him here for now. He won't get along with Flash."

"Best of luck with your article," Pugh called after him. "I hope you get the slant you're looking for. Remember, human complexity."

"Thank you, sir. I will keep that in mind."

Chapter Twenty

WALTER HAD SET HIS DAUGHTER DOWN on the davenport, and she'd hardly stirred since. She had her thumb in her mouth and was clutching her rag doll tight to her neck, her eyes fixed on the door. *As if she was a little dog, waiting for her master*, thought Maria Newcombe.

She sawed off a few thick slices of bread from the fresh loaf she had baked that morning; cut one of the pieces in two and dipped it into the pot of gravy that was on the stove.

"Here, Sally, would you like a taste?"

The child shook her head, although to Maria's mind she looked pinched and hungry.

"It's good."

Another shake. "All right then, I'll have to eat it myself."

She did, chewing and swallowing the bread with appropriate sounds of enjoyment. Sally watched her solemnly.

169

Maria licked her fingers and wiped them on her apron. The little girl's eyes were dark like her mother's; her expression was perpetually wary.

"Now, now, Sally," said Maria, "you're too big a girl to be sucking your thumb. That's dirty."

She made an expression of disgust and took hold of Sally's hand to pry it away from her face. The child shrank back, resisting her. Maria decided not to persist. There was something about the look Sally gave her that was unsettling.

"Very well then. I've known children who sucked their thumbs, and they all ended up with a face that was out of shape. They looked like weasel snouts. You wouldn't want that, would you? A pretty girl like you."

Sally removed her thumb from her mouth, but Maria didn't feel as if she had won a victory.

"That's a good girl. Would you like a bread dip now?"

Another head shake from Sally. Maria had to admit to herself that, try as she might, she couldn't take to the child; and she was a woman who loved children and was adored by them in return. Perhaps the problem lay with Sally's lack of response to everybody except her father. She was no chatterbox the way most children her age were; and when Maria was minding her, she mostly remained quietly on the sofa, playing with her dolly. Her mother had made it for her, and it was artfully done. The body was cut from a piece of Holland towelling and stuffed with soft bits of wool. Jess had painted a cheery face on the head and glued on dark brown wool hair that was tied into long braids. The smock was pale blue cotton with some pretty embroidery at the bodice. Sally had named it Pansy, and she sat by the hour talking quietly to herself as she played her games.

Lately Walter had been forced to bring the child to the tavern more and more when he was working. He didn't say much about it, just that Jessica was feeling poorly and he thought it better if Sally wasn't underfoot for a while.

Maria didn't really mind. She actually forgot the child was there sometimes she was such a mouse. She sighed. She couldn't really blame the poor scrap for the way she was. She was about to continue with her tasks when she was caught by the forlorn look on Sally's face. She certainly could do with some cheering up. Maria went over to the window seat and opened up the lid. In his rare leisure moments, Vince enjoyed working with his hands, and he had made some doll furniture for Sally. They had intended to give it to her at Christmas, but Maria thought the girl needed something jolly now.

"Here you go. Mr. Newcombe made these for you."

With some hesitation, Sally took the box and lifted the lid. Then her expression changed, and she smiled in pleasure.

"Do you like them?" Maria asked.

171

"Yes, ma'am." Before being prompted, she added, "Thank you very much, Mrs. Newcombe." She stood up and Maria offered her cheek for a kiss.

"They are made to fit Pansy. She can sit and have her tea like a princess."

Sally put the two wooden chairs and the table on the floor and propped the doll into one of the chairs. She fitted nicely, and Maria felt a glow of satisfaction. Making the furniture had been her idea.

"Can I play with the scrap bag?" Sally asked.

"You certainly can. You know where it is."

Sally trotted back to the window seat, and Maria returned to the stove.

The door to the kitchen opened and Lacey peered in.

"Two orders of pork and potatoes, if you please, Missus. One's for Mr. Pugh, and he wants extra crackling. The other's Mr. Craig's, and he just wants the usual, not too much gravy."

"Look, Poppa. Mrs. Newcombe gave them to me."

Sally was indicating the furniture. Lacey nodded. "That's lovely. I hope you're being a good girl."

"Yes, Poppa."

Lacey glanced at Maria questioningly.

"She's doing quite all right, Walter. Hasn't mithered once today."

He looked relieved. "Thank you, Mrs. Newcombe. I do appreciate your help." With a quick glance at his daughter, he left. Engrossed in her game, Sally didn't put up a fuss.

Maria was happy to see the success of her present. Several minutes later, she looked over at the little girl. Sally was still seated on the floor where she had placed the miniature doll's table and chairs, and she hadn't stopped her game. She was flushed, and there was an intense expression on her face that Maria couldn't quite decipher. She went over to her.

"Oh, dear, has Pansy been hurt?"

Sally nodded but immediately became sullen, not wanting the woman to intrude into her play.

"I have some ointment that will put her to rights," said Maria, and she bent down to pick up the doll. It was firmly tied to the chair, and she realised that what she had thought was an unskilfully applied bandage was, in fact, a gag that was tight around the doll's mouth.

"Sally, what in Our Lord's name are you doing?"

The door opened and Vince ushered in his new customer.

"Maria, Mr. Williams would like to offer his compliments."

Both men halted as the child suddenly scrambled toward the table, crawling on her hands and knees. Once in the shelter of the table legs, she curled into a ball, her thumb in her mouth, and began to whimper.

173

"My gracious, what's wrong with Sally?"

Maria put the toy chair with the bound and gagged doll on the table behind her.

"She's just being naughty. Don't take any notice."

She tried to muster a smile for the newcomer. She dearly hoped he hadn't seen what Sally was doing.

Chapter Twenty-one

MURDOCH AND NEWCOMBE, who had Flash's off-spring tucked into his coat, trudged down the path towards the bottom of the ravine.

"Smells like it's going to snow," remarked Newcombe.

"It does that," said Murdoch. He was glad for his old sealskin coat. It had some worn patches and gave off a fishy odour in damp weather, but it was good protection against this kind of penetrating damp cold.

Newcombe glanced over at him. "It don't sit quite right for me not to call you by your proper name. Is there anything else I can use?"

"I'd be honoured if you'd call me Will. It's the name I was christened with."

"Done. I'm Vincent. It means a conqueror. Bit fancy for a plain fellow like me, but my ma believed in giving her children names above their station. My older brother was named Lucius, bringer of light." He spat to the side of the path. "Fat chance of that. Bringer of disaster and darkness more like. The younger one is Archibald. Well, I'd never say he was bold and brave; I'd say the opposite, but at least he hasn't destroyed everything he touched."

Newcombe's voice was cheerful as he related this history, belying his words. As if Murdoch had spoken, he went on. "You may well ask why I'm casting such aspersions on my own kin, but truth is they don't mean nothing to me anymore. I came across the mighty pond to get away from them all."

"Indeed," murmured Murdoch, with some sympathy.

"I might not be a conqueror in the exact sense of the word, but I've done all right for myself. Got the tavern going good. Got a respectable name in these parts, and that means a lot to me."

Murdoch assumed Maria Newcombe had the same views, and that was why she was so discomfited when they had come into the kitchen. He'd glimpsed the doll and had wondered what Sally was playing at, but he couldn't say he was shocked. When they were children, he and Susanna had acted out many bloodthirsty adventures with the few toys they had. On the other hand, there was something unwholesome about the child. Too much fear.

176   They had reached the bridge, and Newcombe stopped and peered over the railing into the stream below. "I believe nature can teach us our lessons if only

we want to learn them. Look at this creek, for instance. Some men I've known are just like this little river. It don't appear deep, but it is. You wouldn't think it was dangerous, but it can be."

Murdoch joined him to look down at the water, which was flowing fast, swirling around the rocks. Bits of twigs and leaves dipped and danced on the surface.

"Are you speaking of any particular man?"

"No, I can't say I am."

However, Murdoch had the feeling the innkeeper was indeed referring to one person, but it was hard to know who that was. Maybe he meant Murdoch himself. He also had the sense that his companion was testing him. Throwing out a vague statement like that to see his reaction. *I'm testing myself,* he thought wryly. It was as if he were standing beside himself observing coolly. *Aha, that got to you, did it?*

They set off again. The path was deeply rutted with cart tracks.

"Delaney kept some cows. The milk gets driven down to the dairy on Summerhill twice a day. He doesn't do it himself anymore. His son, sometimes Kate, his daughter, does it." He paused as if choosing his words. "She'll be needing a husband. Young Master Craig is courting her. I hope he's not playing fast and loose, 'cos she is stuck hard on him by all accounts."

"That so?"

177

Murdoch knew that if he simply made encouraging noises, Newcombe was going to tell him all the gossip, which he could sift and sieve for nuggets of gold.

"He's a good-looking young fellow, nice manners like his pa. But for some reason, Delaney took a scunner to him. Wouldn't let him call for no price. Gave out some cock-and-bull story that Kate was too young, which she isn't. In my opinion, Delaney was just acting like a cock of the walk and would have come round, but by all accounts, there was more than one big barney up at the house, girl screaming, mother in hysterics."

"Was the Craig boy upset?"

"Hmm. Don't know if I can say that. He didn't show it to me anyways. But the lassie was. Was going into a decline, according to all accounts. That's over now, of course. The flowers weren't hardly wilting on the grave when James went back a-courting."

"How has the family been coping?" asked Murdoch.

"As well as can be expected. They've always kept to themselves. Not Delaney. He was a jolly man most of the time, but his wife is a bit of a recluse. Only ever saw her at church, and then not all the time. His older children are both married and away. There's just young Philip and his sister."

"What are they like?"

Newcombe didn't answer right away. "Kate is normal enough in her brain, but . . ."

Murdoch looked at him questioningly.

"I believe in love, don't get me wrong," continued Newcombe, "but the lass has gone to extremes. Comes from being kept too much at home probably. I heard she was sending young James presents every day. Oh, little things, a bunch of flowers, fresh eggs, a cravat; but too much of it."

Murdoch wondered who was the source of Newcombe's information, but he didn't want to shut him down so he didn't ask.

"But you said James Craig wasn't scared off. He's still her sweetheart."

"That's what I understand." He shrugged. "I mean, would you like it if a gal behaved that way around you?"

Murdoch considered the question. Liza had opened up her heart to him, but she hadn't showered him with gifts, just a special one on his birthday and at Christmastime.

"To be honest, I don't think I would. It sounds a bit on the desperate side, and I would be nervous about that being true love."

Newcombe smiled. "My thoughts exactly. I had to woo Maria for a long time before she agreed to have me. I liked that. Made me feel she didn't come too cheap."

The puppy whined and Newcombe turned him around into a more comfortable position.

"What about the young lad, Philip Delaney? What's your opinion of him?"

179

"He's a bit of a sad tale, you might say. He had a nasty accident a couple of years ago. He and his pa were bringing the milk cart down to the dairy when the horse spooked. The cart apparently hit a rut, and Phil was thrown out. Must have banged his head. He wasn't conscious for almost a week, and they thought he'd die. Unfortunately, it left him what you might call strange."

Newcombe hesitated. Murdoch prompted him. "In what way, strange?"

The other man shrugged. "It's as if he hasn't grown up, physically yes but not in his mind. And he has fits. Had one in the tavern not so long ago. Just fell on the ground twitching like a headless chicken. Good thing my wife was there. She knew what to do." He made gestures to illustrate Maria pulling Philip's tongue out of his mouth. "They can choke, you see."

The path was curving upwards around the side of the hill. The wind had blown away the snow except where it was caught in the clefts of the tree branches.

The innkeeper resumed. "Fortunately for Mrs. Delaney there was some insurance money, so she doesn't have to go begging. They rent out a cottage on the other side of the hill to my man, Lacey, so that's an income as well."

180   "Do the Laceys ever use this path?"

The innkeeper looked at him curiously, and Murdoch grimaced. "You never know what will be relevant till you start."

"I can't say I ever enquired, but this is by far the easiest way. The other's closer, but you've got to climb all those darn steps." Newcombe patted his wide girth. "If it were me, I'd take the long way round any day."

"I discovered a cosy little hideaway over near the railway bridge on the way to the Lacey cottage. I wondered who'd built it?"

"It was likely Walter made it for Sally."

To their left, about fifty yards back and almost hidden in a stand of evergreens, appeared a small house. It was plain and unpainted.

"He owned that one, too," said Newcombe, pointing. "Mrs. Bowling rents it. She works for the Delaneys."

"A widow?"

"That's right."

Newcombe had an attractive lack of guile to him, but once again Murdoch sensed something else. He wondered if the innkeeper himself wasn't one of those deeper pools he'd been going on about.

They trudged on past a sloping field where three mud-caked cows chewed dispiritedly at a stook of hay. The Delaney house was visible on the crest of the hill and the path again divided, one fork becoming the driveway to the house, the other continuing on, he presumed, to the Lacey cottage. Lamps shone in both the upstairs and downstairs windows, and a thin column of smoke drifted from the chimney.

"We'll go in the side door," said Newcombe, and he

led the way through a wooden gate down a dirt path that ran alongside the empty vegetable garden. A wreath of intertwined willow wands and bedraggled black crepe was fastened on the door, and Murdoch could see the paint, once dark green, was peeling from the windowsills and eaves. A broken pane of glass in the door panel had been patched with cardboard.

Newcombe knocked and opened the door, which led directly into the large kitchen. The smell almost made Murdoch gag, something thick and sour. An elderly woman was standing in front of the large, black range in the centre of the room, stirring an enormous pot. Murdoch assumed the repulsive odour was coming from that.

"Good afternoon to you, Mrs. Bowling," said Newcombe.

She turned around. "My, didn't expect to see you today, Vincent."

Facing them, she didn't appear at all as old as Murdoch had at first thought. Her hair was iron grey and pulled up tight in a knot on top of her head, and she was quite stooped. However, her face was still smooth enough; and when she smiled at the innkeeper, she revealed good, unspoiled teeth. She had on a stained Holland apron that looked as if it would stand on its own from the amount of grease it had absorbed.

Newcombe pinched his nostrils with his fingers. "I surmise from the pong, you are boiling up the pig food?"

182

"Bad, is it? I'm so used to it, I don't notice anymore." They could hear a dog yapping excitedly, and the puppy inside Newcombe's coat gave a short, sharp reply and wriggled to get free.

"Hold on, you titch. In a minute."

Murdoch glanced around. There was nothing homey or welcoming about the kitchen. The flagstones were uneven, and the only piece of furniture was a bare wooden table and a solitary chair. The range occupied most of the space.

"Missus is upstairs in the parlour. Mr. James and Miss Kate are playing duets. Love songs, no doubt."

She grimaced but whether that was because of the nature of the music or because the bubbling liquid in the pot spat out on her wrist, Murdoch was never to know. The door opened and a woman in the sombre clothes of close mourning entered.

"Good afternoon, Mr. Newcombe."

A small black-and-tan terrier, similar in appearance to Tripper, came dashing past her, yipping with excitement. He stopped abruptly in front of Newcombe, his head up, his little black muzzle quivering as he tried to locate the source of the new smell.

Newcombe tipped his hat to the woman. "Good afternoon, Mrs. Delaney. I've brought up Flash's whelp like I promised."

He placed the little dog on the floor. "Don't you piddle, you rascal, or you'll get me in trouble."

All four of them watched the two dogs for a moment as the pup licked at his sire's muzzle. Flash's response was quite different from Havoc's. He seemed to enjoy what the pup was doing. He sniffed in return, his tail waving.

"See, he knows it's his own flesh and blood," said Newcombe.

The woman frowned. "I don't know who's going to take care of another dog. Kate won't have anything to do with them, and I have too much to do just managing our affairs." Her tone was aggrieved.

"You don't have to keep him, Mrs. Delaney," said Newcombe. "I'd rather you didn't if it's too much. My agreement was with your husband."

She waved her hand dismissively. "We'll see. It might give Philip something to do with himself. Oh, darn that dog!"

Her remark was addressed to the little pup, who had squatted down and was rapidly making a puddle of water on the floor. Newcombe whipped him up, holding him upended.

"I'll just be a minute."

He opened the door and hurried outside. Mrs. Delaney shifted her gaze towards Murdoch. She was not an attractive woman. Her widow's bonnet and short veil were too dark and severe for her face, with its heavy brows and full chin. Long-standing discontent had etched sharp furrows on her forehead and at the corners of her mouth.

"Good afternoon, ma'am. Mr. Newcombe kindly brought me with him on his errand. I do apologise if I am intruding at this sad time."

In spite of the mourning garb, in truth Mrs. Delaney did not look in the grip of sorrow. She appeared more querulous than sad.

"We haven't had many callers lately. They flock to you when they can feed like vultures off your ruin, but when it's apparent you're not going to collapse, they disappear."

Murdoch tried a polite smile. "I understand from Mr. Newcombe you do have a steady visitor in young Mr. Craig."

He was afraid he might have gone too far, but she looked mollified by what he said. Obviously she did not share her late husband's views on the relationship between James and her daughter.

"He told you, did he? Yes, it's true. The young people are quite attached to each other, I must say." She turned to the servant. "Mrs. Bowling, I was hoping for some tea by now."

"Sorry, madam, I had my other tasks to see to. I'll get on to it right away."

"Will you join us, Mr., er, I beg your pardon, I didn't catch your name."

185

"Thank you, ma'am. It's Williams and I would appreciate some tea indeed. 'Tis fair parched I am."

An Irish accent seemed to have suddenly taken over

his tongue. He had no idea where it had come from. He was saved from further comment by Newcombe's return, the puppy tucked under his arm.

"All done."

Flash jumped up at the sight of his offspring, and the pup greeted him ecstatically as if days instead of minutes had elapsed.

"Mr. Newcombe, we're about to take tea. You can leave the dogs here with Bowling, and we'll join Kate and her beau in the parlour."

"Tell you what. I'll just watch over them for a bit longer just to make sure they're getting along; then I'll help bring up the tea things."

Mrs. Delaney considered him for a moment, as if ready to object on principle.

Flash was lying down by now, his paws outstretched in front of him. The puppy was trying to climb on his back, presumably intent on chewing his right ear. The innkeeper eyed them fondly, Mrs. Delaney with irritation. She nodded at Murdoch.

"Please come this way, sir."

He followed her into the adjoining parlour. Mrs. Bowling was right about the bad smell. After a while you didn't notice it. Only when he was in fresher air did he realise how repulsive it had been.

Mrs. Delaney led the way across to the far side of the room, negotiating her way through the heavy, old-fashioned furniture. There was a fire in the hearth, but

186

it needed building up. Only one lamp was lit, the wick turned low. She drew aside the green chenille portiere covering an archway, and they went through to a second room. The air here was a sharp contrast to both the kitchen and the sitting room. It was cold with a slight smell of mildew. There was a threadbare Aubusson carpet on the floor, but no furniture at all except for one green velvet armchair and a small side table.

"My husband liked to sit here and smoke his pipe," said Mrs. Delaney, and Murdoch wondered if it had formerly held furniture or if Delaney liked the lonely splendour of an empty room.

She sailed ahead of him to the uncurtained door on the opposite side.

"You are probably thinking we are eccentric or too countrified for your city taste, Mr. Williams, but we prefer to have our sitting room on the second floor, where there is more sunlight."

"Very sensible," said Murdoch, who had thought no such thing and wouldn't have been able to differentiate country taste from the city if his life depended on it.

The door opened onto a flight of stairs at the top of which was a short hall. He could hear the sound of singing and an off-key flute.

"In here."

The couple had their backs to him, but they were directly in front of the fireplace mirror and he could see them clearly. A young man, fair haired and clean shaven,

187

was seated at a music stand, a flute to his lips. Close beside him was a young woman, rather tall and thin, whom Murdoch presumed was Kate Delaney, she of the overwrought affections. She didn't stop singing or turn around, but Craig halted his playing and went to stand up.

"Don't stop please, James," said Mrs. Delaney, flapping her hand in his direction. "That is quite lovely. So accomplished."

He resumed his seat. Kate acknowledged their presence with a curt nod, then bent back to her music. Craig raised the flute to his lips, and his eyes met Murdoch's briefly in the mirror. Murdoch knew immediately they had met before. His name wasn't James Craig then; it was John Carey, and he was standing meekly before Colonel Denison, the police magistrate.

Chapter Twenty-two

As quickly as he realised James Craig and he had met before, Murdoch saw that the young man wasn't aware of it. He couldn't blame him for that. At the time he'd been focused on the magistrate and what sentence he was about to pronounce. Murdoch had a nab whose case was coming to trial, and he was sitting at the back of the courtroom waiting to make his statement. He might not have paid much attention to Craig/Carey except that the plaintiff was sitting directly in front of him. She was obviously a servant, and her mistress, an elderly woman, was beside her. The girl was weeping ceaselessly in spite of the frequent admonitions of her employer, who appeared to be the one who had dragged the girl to court and insisted that Carey be charged with seduction. The young servant was with child, and her mistress wanted to make sure her seducer married her at once.

Carey was a handsome fellow, with full side-whiskers and blond moustache. He had such a winning smile and a glib tongue, it was easy to understand why an unsophisticated girl would be led astray. Murdoch was mildly annoyed at Carey for having misused his charms in such a way and didn't believe his repentant manner and his promise to make good. Obviously his pessimism had been justified. Carey had fled, either changed his name or assumed his real one, and it seemed was repeating his previous behaviour, this time with Miss Kate Delaney.

She was standing beside him, leaning forward slightly so as to turn the pages of the song sheet on the stand. There was such intensity in her body, Murdoch felt a pang of longing. Not for her, but for what he no longer had for himself. He could read in her stance the intensity of her desires, how much she simply wanted an excuse to brush against the shoulder of the man in front of her.

Kate finished the verse, leaving Craig to complete a shaky trill on his flute. Mrs. Delaney applauded them with enthusiasm, and Murdoch joined in.

"Very fine, Miss Delaney, very fine indeed."

"Kate, this is Mr. Williams. He came up with Mr. Newcombe to deliver the puppy your father wanted. Mr. Williams, my daughter and her friend, Mr. Craig."

Murdoch gave her a rather fancy bow, then offered his hand to Craig. They shook hands in a firm, manly fashion, and Craig eyed him appraisingly. Murdoch

190

watched for the *haven't-I-met-you-somewhere-before* expression to dawn on his face, but it didn't.

"Newcombe tells me you've got a good little ratter yourself, Mr. Craig." There was the Irish brogue again.

Craig grinned an acknowledgement, but before he could expound on the virtues of his dog, a young man who had been slumped almost out of sight in the window seat stood up and came over to them, hand outstretched.

"Don't forget me, Ma. You are always forgetting about me."

"Don't be silly. I was just about to introduce you." Mrs. Delaney's voice was placating. "Mr. Williams, my son, Philip."

Murdoch found his hand gripped in a painful crunch.

"How do you do, sir. I'm Philip Delaney, the youngest son of the house." He pumped Murdoch's arm.

"That's sufficient," said his mother, and the young man let go. He was plump with soft, womanish features. Like his mother and sister, he was in mourning clothes, a black suit that was too tight, as if he had puffed up recently and was trying to squash himself into clothes that were far too small. His chin, clean shaven, flowed over the high white collar. Up close, Murdoch could see there was something abnormal in the young man's eyes. The pupils were almost erased in the blue of the irises, so that his eyes seemed to lack depth.

191

"I've ordered some tea to be brought up," said Mrs. Delaney. "Why don't you play another duet, Mr. Craig."

"That depends on my partner," said Craig. "Are you up for one more song, Miss Kate?"

"I'd count it an honour if you'd continue singing, Miss Delaney," said Murdoch.

Kate's sullen expression softened slightly, soothed by the wide Irish smile Murdoch was beaming at her. She turned her attention back to the song sheet. "Shall we start at the beginning, James?"

Murdoch sat down in the plush armchair by the fireside. Mrs. Delaney took the other. She picked up a fan from the side table and snapped it open. Philip wandered back to the window seat.

"Ready?" asked Craig, and he put his flute to his lips, gave Kate the note, and they resumed.

> *Oh promise me that some day you and I,*
> *Will take our love together to some sky.*
> *Where we can be alone and faith renew . . .*

The song wasn't one that Murdoch had heard before, but it was a good choice for their level of accomplishment. Her voice was thin but sweet enough; his accompaniment was rudimentary. Murdoch wondered if Craig had chosen the flute as his instrument because it meant he could cast soulful sideward glances at the singer. Murdoch thought he was grossly overdoing it, but obviously that was not Kate's opinion. He suspected Miss Delaney was not blessed with true beauty, but the intensity of her feelings had turned her into an attractive young woman. She was quite flushed, and her eyes were bright with the sheen of infatuation. She had obviously made an attempt to overcome the dullness of her mourning apparel, and her black taffeta gown had white lace trim at the neck and sleeves. She had also twined a violet-coloured ribbon in her hair, and there was a frizz of fashionable curls across her forehead.

> *. . . sing / Of love unspeakable that is to be. /*
> *Oh promise me . . .*

An intriguing line, thought Murdoch, given what seemed to be Craig's history. However, as they finished the song, he clapped enthusiastically.

"Very fine voice, Miss Delaney, very fine."

Philip added his applause, but he exclaimed loudly, "What did she do? What's she done?"

His sister glared at him with an intensity of anger that would have withered a tree. "Please be quiet, Brother. Where are your manners?"

Mrs. Delaney looked embarrassed at her daughter's outburst and fanned herself vigorously, while Craig busied himself with searching out another song from the sheets on the music stand. Fortunately, the door opened and Newcombe entered the room carrying

193

a large tray on which sat a silver tea service. Mrs. Bowling was behind him with a two-tiered cake dish. Murdoch was relieved to see that she had changed her apron and was wearing one that was relatively crisp and white. She had even added a maid's starched cap.

"You can put the tray on the sideboard, if you please," said Mrs. Delaney.

The innkeeper did so, swinging the tray with ease. Mrs. Delaney stood up and went over to the sideboard. Philip got there before her.

"Ooh, tasties," he said, and reached for one of the small cakes that were on the dish.

"Now, Mr. Philip, wait until your guests have had theirs," said Mrs. Bowling.

"I'm hungry," he said, and snatched a cake from the dish. Mrs. Bowling's reaction was fast. She slapped his hand so hard, he dropped the cake.

"Ow, ow. Momma, she hurt me."

Mrs. Delaney looked frightened. "Philip, please be a good boy and sit down . . ."

He raised his fist and Murdoch leaped out of his seat, certain Philip was going to strike his own mother. However, she jumped back and the boy pivoted toward the sideboard, grabbed the tray, and heaved it across the room. The plates and the cups and saucers flew into the air, and the heavy silver tea pot smacked into one of the lamps, sending it crashing to the floor. There was a flash as the oil caught fire.

194

"Momma, stop him!" Kate shrieked. Almost instantaneously, Philip, his eyes wild as a lunatic's, snatched up a butter knife from the sideboard and started towards his sister.

Murdoch, already on his feet, caught Philip by the wrist, while Newcombe leaped forward to stamp on the flames.

"None of that." He jerked the young man's arm downward, pulling him around and forcing him to drop the knife. At the same time, he managed to grab the other wrist, crossing Philip's arms behind him in a way that made it impossible for him to move. His mother stood where she was, petrified.

Suddenly Mrs. Bowling was at Murdoch's side. Philip was alternately grunting and roaring with rage and trying to kick out at him. Mrs. Bowling stepped in front of them and caught Philip by the lower lip, twisting it in a way that horse dealers twitch a horse they want to subdue. He quieted down at once.

"You can let him go," Mrs. Bowling said to Murdoch.

"I can't do that, ma'am, unless I have his guarantee he won't cause trouble."

"He won't."

Reluctantly, Murdoch let go of Philip's wrists. The boy made no attempt to remove the woman's hold on him but stood still, whimpering a little.

"I'm going to let you go, but you must be a good boy."

195

She released his lip.

Philip pointed at the mess on the floor, "Oo, what happened?" Newcombe had extinguished the fire, but there was a black sooty mark on the carpet and pieces of glass and china scattered around it.

"We had an accident," said Mrs. Bowling. "Come on, we'll fetch a mop and a broom and you can help me clean up."

She directed Philip out of the room, and without another word Mrs. Delaney followed them.

Kate Delaney watched them go, her face tight with anger. She turned to Craig. "Let's continue, James. I have a new sheet from McQuaig's. We can learn it together."

Craig gazed at her in disbelief. "Kate . . . what happened just now? I mean . . ." His voice trailed off.

She didn't answer but riffled through the song sheets that were on the music stand and took out a sheet. "Here it is. A piece by Mr. Gilbert and Mr. Sullivan." She thrust it onto the music stand.

"I don't think I can play anymore," said Craig.

Kate stared at the carpet. She appeared to be on the brink of tears but clenched her jaw and didn't let go. "We mustn't let him spoil everything. He always does. Never mind, though. I'll fetch some more tea."

196

She had to step over the blackened swatch of carpet as she left the room. Newcombe and Murdoch might as well have been invisible.

The three men were left in the ensuing silence like small boats bobbing in the wake of a steamer. Craig took a silk handkerchief from his waistcoat pocket and wiped his face.

"Whew. What a show that was. Worthy of the theatre, if you ask me."

"The poor fellow's batchy," said Newcombe. He tapped his own head. "Can't help himself."

"You acted with great presence of mind, if I may say so, Mr. Williams," said Craig, "grabbing him like that. One might almost think you were a professional at it."

There was a tap at the door, and Mrs. Bowling entered. She was carrying a broom and a pail.

"Master Philip is having a lie down."

Craig got to his feet. "I'll say good afternoon to you, gentlemen. I've lost my stomach for singing for today."

"Such a pity and such a sweet song." Murdoch couldn't resist. "The ladies do so want us to make promises to them, don't they?"

James Craig frowned. "I suppose they do."

He left.

Newcombe was helping Mrs. Bowling pile up some of the cakes onto the dish, which was unbroken. She was making clicking noises of disapproval.

197

"One of these days, he's going to set the house on fire, you mark my words."

Murdoch took the coal shovel from the fireplace and held it, while Newcombe swept up the glass and bits of china onto it and dumped them into the pail.

"This is going to need to be scrubbed," said Mrs. Bowling. "New carpet, too. Just bought it last month."

Murdoch realised all of the furnishings looked pristine.

"New furniture too, I see."

Mrs. Bowling frowned. "Sinful waste of money, if you ask me. The other stuff was quite good enough; but no, soon as the insurance money came in, Missus has to have everything new. But only in here, you might notice. Not where it's really needed."

"I don't know how they'd manage without you, Mrs. Bowling," said Newcombe. "You handled the lad like a lion tamer in a circus."

She cast a rather triumphant glance at Murdoch. "He's just a babe in a man's flesh. His mother's afraid of him, more's the pity, and indulges him far too much in my opinion."

Murdoch did not feel anywhere as admiring as his companion. The whole scene had brought to mind an incident that had happened some years ago when he was working at a logging camp near Huntsville. A travelling circus came to the camp one evening to entertain the loggers. One of the performers was a dwarf, who barely reached the knees of the big men around him. Near the end of the evening meal, he came into the hut with a huge brown, scruffy bear in tow. The bear lay down quietly beside him, while the dwarf sipped on a tankard of beer. One or two of the men, on the lookout for some excitement, began to yell out taunts. "What's wrong with your doggy, little man? The cat would scare him half to death by the look of him."

At first the dwarf ignored them but that only incited them to cruder remarks. "Shagged him to death have you?"

One of the loggers, more stupid and more drunk than the others, got up and swaggered over.

"Hey puss," he said and reached out his hand. Suddenly, the bear reared on its hind legs and roared, showing ferocious yellow teeth. He was almost the same height as the logger and he swiped out with his massive paw. The man came within inches of losing the side of his face. He yelled out in fear and fell backward, scrambling to get out of the way.

Calmly, the dwarf got to his feet, looked up at the animal and snapped his fingers. With a growl, the bear dropped back to the floor. Another snap of the fingers and he rolled over on his side like a huge dog and buried his massive head in his paws. The dwarf sat astride his neck. The logger was discovered to have shat in his britches, which was the joke of the camp for weeks afterward. All the men were vastly impressed by the dwarf's display of control over such a savage creature and he was showered with money. Murdoch

199

was impressed for a different reason. He happened to be sitting close by and he had seen the dwarf touch the bear with his foot moments before the logger had approached. Stuck in the toe of his boot was a long needle.

Mrs. Bowling had provided them with a show. The disconcerting thing was that Murdoch didn't know who this display was intended for.

Chapter Twenty-three

SOMEWHAT RELUCTANTLY, NEWCOMBE left the puppy in the care of Mrs. Bowling, with instructions for feeding and care. None of the Delaney family reappeared. Kate must have seen James Craig leave, and she did not make good her promise of fresh tea. Newcombe and Murdoch headed back to the tavern.

"I didn't expect anything like that to happen," said Newcombe. "The lad's been very well behaved when he's been down at the inn."

"Surely it's not the first time he's exploded in that way. Mrs. Bowling obviously knew what to do."

"She certainly did."

"I thought for a minute he was going to attack his mother."

"I doubt it would go that far but you yourself were swift off the mark, Will."

They walked on, the innkeeper unusually quiet. Finally

201

Murdoch said, "I see what you mean about Miss Kate. She has completely lost her heart to young Craig."

"Let's hope that's all she's lost. According to Mrs. Bowling, they are left alone for hours at a time. Practising they claim; but if I had a girl that age, I'd want to know exactly what they was practising at, wouldn't you?"

"Mrs. Bowling confides in you, does she?"

Newcombe stopped abruptly and faced Murdoch. The wind had reddened the tip of his nose, and his cheeks and his eyes were watery. "What do you mean by that?"

"Nothing in particular. It's just that you seem to be privy to the Delaneys' private life, and I assumed that was because their servant likes to gossip."

The innkeeper stared at Murdoch, trying to determine if he was telling the truth. He relaxed a little. "Look, Will, you seem a good sort to me. I know you've got a job to do and that means you've got to ask questions, but you're sailing a bit close to the dock. Mrs. Bowling is a decent Christian woman. She's alone and she gets lonesome. She doesn't feel comfortable coming into the tavern, as is understandable, so I take her a jug on occasion. We're friends, you might say. She chatters on like all women do. I don't pay her no mind."

Murdoch nodded sympathetically. He had touched a nerve here, but he didn't know why, and at this stage

202

he certainly didn't want to jeopardise the good feeling that had so far existed between the two of them.

At the bridge Newcombe stopped. "I need to make water."

He turned his back on Murdoch, walked over to a tree, and urinated against the trunk. When he was done, he came back, buttoning his trousers. "That's better. Nothing like a piss when you've got to do it. Do you have to go?"

"No, I'm all right, thanks," said Murdoch, although he did wonder for a moment if he shouldn't try and mark the tree to reassure his host.

He took out his watch and checked the time.

"Have you got an appointment, Will? You're forever looking at your piece, there."

"Am I? I wasn't aware of that."

In part he was timing the distance back to the bridge and from there to the tavern, but the pressure of time never left him, sitting like an ugly bird on his right shoulder ready to peck his eyes out.

You're all I've got, Will. Don't turn your back on me.

It wasn't *he* who had the appointment.

As they were approaching the top of the hill, Newcombe asked, "Are you married by chance, Will?"

"No, I've not yet had the pleasure."

"Ah. Pleasure yes." Newcombe tapped the side of his nose. "Pain, too, if you're not careful. Wives can be fierce when they're roused."

"Is that so?"

"It is and therefore I'd appreciate it if you wouldn't repeat to Maria what I just told you about Mrs. Bowling. She's the salt of the earth is my wife, but she, er, she might make more of it than there is, if you understand what I mean."

"Of course. Not every wife would be secure with their husband visiting lonely widow ladies with jugs of beer, especially if they're kept in the dark about it."

"Exactly." Newcombe let out such a sigh, Murdoch's curiosity was whetted even more. He wondered if the innkeeper's visits to Mrs. Bowling were as innocent as he claimed. He'd felt the tension between them in the kitchen. That didn't come about because Newcombe once in a while delivered some flat brew. But he was puzzled. Mrs. Bowling was plain featured, not an obvious object of illicit desire. On the other hand, his impression of Maria Newcombe was of a kind-hearted woman who, when younger, would have been round and luscious as a plum. Did desire fade as the years went by? He'd never talked about it to Liza. Their love for each other had been hot, hers as well as his, and he couldn't imagine a time when that would have waned. Apparently for some men it did.

204   "All right, are we?" asked the innkeeper. Murdoch nodded. They were at the door of the tavern now. There were two mud scrapers outside, and both he and Newcombe cleaned off their boots. Murdoch's thoughts

jumped to Enid Jones, also a widow, also lonely.

"If you scrape anymore, you're going to take off your sole," said Newcombe.

Murdoch walked all the way from the Manchester, not yet sure how Havoc would behave if they took the streetcar. The little terrier seemed to hate being picked up and snarled and snapped ferociously at the slightest indication that was going to happen. According to Newcombe, the dog would get used to him, and he'd provided some gamey pieces of meat to feed him.

Havoc so far had maintained a surly distance. Contrary to what the innkeeper had said, he showed no interest in the meat, sniffing at it and even taking a nibble but spitting it out immediately. However, he did walk well on his leash, trotting quietly at Murdoch's side. By the time they reached Queen Street, Murdoch was knackered. He was tempted to postpone his call until tomorrow, but he didn't dare.

Earlier in the year, while he was investigating the mysterious death of a young girl, Murdoch had met Samuel Quinn. The girl's frozen body had been discovered in a laneway almost directly opposite to the rooming house where Quinn lived. Murdoch had liked the young man, who was a baker with a side passion for dogs. He had a feeling that the best person to consult about the "Fancy" might be him. He turned up Sumach to St. Luke's Street where Quinn lived. The

205

houses here were tall and narrow, pressed together in tight rows of four or five dwellings. The boardinghouse was shabby, the gables peeling. Murdoch wondered if Bernadette Weston still lived here. The thought of her made him uneasy, as it always had, and he banged hard on the front door. The bellpull was broken, and there was no knocker. He thumped a second time, tried the doorknob, and found the door unlocked. He stepped into the dark hallway. There was a thin sliver of light coming from the second door; but before he had to inch his way forward in the darkness, the door opened and Quinn himself came out.

"Ahh!"

"It's all right, Sam. Detective Murdoch here."

"You almost gave me a heart seizure."

"Beg pardon. Nobody answered my knock. I've come to have a word with you."

Havoc burst into a flurry of barks, which were answered by a deeper baying from behind Quinn. A sleek hound poked its nose around his legs, saw Havoc, and barked a warning.

"Quiet, Princess. Get back in there."

The dog ignored him. Havoc was beside himself, straining at the leash to get into the fray.

Quinn grabbed Princess by her collar and hauled her into the room. In a moment he returned, carrying a candlestick this time. "Come in. I was just having my tea."

206

"What shall I do about the dog?"

Havoc was still yapping fiercely.

"I've put Princess in her box so you can bring him in."

Perversely, Havoc dragged on the leash and didn't want to move. Murdoch decided to risk it, grabbed up the dog, and carried him into the room. Princess was stowed in a homemade crate by the bed. She didn't bark at the reappearance of the terrier, just sat watching calmly. Either reassured or intimidated by the strange surroundings, Havoc stopped barking, and Murdoch put him on the floor. Just as he remembered from before, the room was uncomfortably hot, the coal fire blazing in the hearth.

Quinn stretched out his hand. "Good to see you again, Mr. Murdoch."

They shook hands. Quinn pulled forward a wooden box. "Have a seat." He glanced around the room. "Sorry, I seem to have misplaced the cushion."

"That's all right." Murdoch sat down. Quinn indicated the teapot, which was on a small japanned table beside the bed.

"Can I pour you some tea?"

"I'd like that."

Murdoch undid his coat and took off his hat and placed it on the floor beside the box. The tiny room didn't seem to have known fresh air for years. He tried to breathe shallowly. His host was dressed only in his

207

trousers and a red flannel undershirt, but even his face was shiny with sweat.

Quinn went to the bed, reached down and pulled out a cardboard box that had once contained gloves, took out a mug, and put it on the table. He poured the strong black tea and handed the mug to Murdoch.

"Finish your dinner, please," said Murdoch.

There was a plate with the remains of what looked like a pork pie.

"I'm done. Here, I'll give your dog some. What's his name?"

"Havoc."

"How long have you had him?"

"I only just inherited him."

Quinn clicked his tongue at the terrier and placed a piece of the pie on the floor in front of him. Havoc sniffed, took a bite, then gagged and spat out the food.

"Doesn't like it," said Quinn. He picked up the meat and took it over to Princess, who poked her nose out between the slats of the box and gulped down the morsel.

Quinn grinned at Murdoch. "She's like a bog; she'll swallow anything."

Murdoch sipped at the tea while Quinn perched on the bed and watched him. He looked nervous, and Murdoch hoped he had a clean conscience. He decided to put him out of his misery.

"I'm investigating another case, and it involves the Fancy. I thought you'd be a good man to talk to as you know dogs so well."

Quinn tugged at his thick moustache. "What do you want to know?"

"There was a ratting match back in the summer at the Manchester tavern up on Shaftesbury Avenue above St. Clair. Later, a man was found murdered in the ravine, presumably because of a quarrel over the win. Have you heard anything about it?"

Quinn shook his head. "Can't say I have. I'm not connected with that crowd anymore." He made a gesture with his hand. "Straight and narrow all the way, that's me. I got a better job at the Rossin."

Murdoch gave an appreciative whistle. "Swell place."

"It is. Royalty has stayed there so they tell me. I do all the cakes and tarts, just like I used to. It's more work 'cos they can put up over four hundred guests at a time. But then they're giving me more wages, so I'm not complaining. Come by any morning and I'll slip you a sample."

Murdoch drank some more of the tea. He believed Quinn when he said he hadn't heard of the Delaney case, which seemed to have passed strangely unnoticed in a city that liked its lurid details when there was a murder involved. Perhaps justice had been too swift for the newspapers to get interested.

His host picked up the teapot. "Fill up?"

"No, thanks. That's plenty for me." Murdoch could feel the tannic acid eating holes in his stomach. "What I actually wanted, Sam, was in the way of a favour. I'd like to check into all the wags who were at the match. Find out anything I can."

"Verdict in doubt, is it?"

"No, not that. The accused seems guilty all right, but I'm just tying up loose ends. There was a man at the match who didn't come forward at the trial, and I'd like to find him in particular." He used the same half-truth he had given Newcombe. "I'm working for the man's family. We want to make absolutely sure."

"Is your fellow going to hang?"

"Yes."

"Soon?"

"Yes."

"We'd better get a move on then. What's the cove's name who you want to find?"

"He went by White, but that probably isn't his real name. He's from the city, bit of a toff. Might be in banking or the legal profession. He was cagey about himself, not surprisingly."

"How'd he do at the match?"

"Didn't win or lose. Ended up fairly even. The major winner was the man who was killed, Delaney. He soaked them all. Walked away with ninety-four dollars."

It was Sam's turn to whistle. "Not too bad, that."

"One of the other players was the man now sentenced. He accused Delaney of cheating by blowing a whistle to distract his dog at a crucial moment. They had a big barney, and Delaney was found later that night in the creek with his head knocked in."

"Did your man confess?"

"No, he claims he's innocent."

Quinn poured himself some more tea and added a splash of milk and two spoonsful of sugar.

"What's his name, this cove?"

"Do you need to know that?"

"It'll be easier if I know what I'm talking about." Sam was eyeing him curiously.

"His name is Henry Murdoch. Usually gets called Harry."

"Murdoch? Are you related then?"

"He's my father."

Embarrassed, Quinn got off the bed and made a pretense of checking on the condition of the fire. He added a lump of coal to the blaze before he spoke again.

"Must be hard, that."

Murdoch shrugged. "Let's say, it's a most peculiar position to be in."

Sam straightened up and turned to face him. "I'll do what I can. Give me the names of the men and dogs." 211

"White ran a brown-and-white Parson Jack feist named Samson, bandy legged; Pugh had a bulldog by the name of Gargoyle; Charles Craig and his son,

James, both had pugs, Tiny and Bess. The innkeeper also put in his own dog, a Manchester terrier called Tripper. The dead man was the big winner, as I said, with another Manchester, Flash."

"Plucky little dogs them."

"When do you think you'd have something for me?"

"I'll start on it right this instant. There's a fellow I know down near the wharf. I'll go and have a word with him. If he don't know, nobody will."

Murdoch stood up. "I appreciate this, Sam."

Quinn dipped his head shyly. He pointed at Havoc. "This was your father's dog, I assume."

"Yes. I don't know what to do with him. He's a mean sod."

Suddenly, Sam crouched down and grabbed Havoc with one hand by the scruff of his neck. "It's all right, little fellow. I won't hurt you." Quickly he pried open the terrier's mouth. "Ha, I thought so. Look here. He's got a nasty abscess on the inside of his lip."

Murdoch peered over and saw an angry-looking pustule where Quinn was pointing.

"He got that from a rat. They give dirty bites. That's why he won't eat. Probably why he won't let you touch him. Here, hold him a minute."

Quinn took his mug and tossed the dregs of his tea into the fire. Then he scrambled underneath his bed, which seemed to act as his cupboard, and pulled out a brown bottle.

212

"Simple carbolic acid. Good for almost anything that ails you, man or dog."

He splashed some of the liquid into the mug and added water from the kettle on the hob.

"Now, Mr. Havoc, this is going to make you better, you poor mite you. Hold his head firm now."

Murdoch did so and again Quinn lifted the little dog's lip. He dipped his finger into the carbolic solution and dabbed it on the abscess. "If you can do that twice a day, he should be right as rain in a week."

Quinn sat back and they regarded the terrier as he promptly rubbed his muzzle with his paw to rid himself of the substance. Quinn went to stop him, and Havoc snapped. Sam jerked his hand away, missing the bite by an inch.

"Hey, stop that!" Murdoch said angrily to the dog.

"No sense in dinning him. That gum must hurt like hell. If he'd wanted to take a piece out of me, he would have. That was a warning. Just make sure you've got a good grip on him when you put the carbolic on, that's all. He'll be sweet tempered as a lamb before you know it."

Murdoch frowned.

"Tell you what," said Quinn. "How'd you like me to hold on to him and treat him myself? You can pick him up tomorrow."

"That would be a big relief. Thank you."

He shook hands.

213

"I'll show you out," said Quinn. He picked up the candlestick and opened the door.

"Does Ettie still live here?" Murdoch asked.

"She does. But she moved upstairs." He grinned. "She's got a new job, too. She works at Mr. Eaton's store in the sewing department. Very respectable. She doesn't do any of that old stuff."

He meant selling her sexual favours, which was how Ettie had earned most of her money when Murdoch had last known her.

"I'm happy to hear that, too. Give her my regards."

"I will. She'll be pleased to know you were by."

Murdoch nodded in the direction of the hound, who had watched all the proceedings with bright, curious eyes. "Evening, Miss Princess. Evening, Havoc."

He followed Quinn down the hall and out into the welcome cool air.

Chapter Twenty-four

On certain occasions Algernon Blackstock Jr. thought it prudent to use a name other than his real one. He'd called himself Green, Redman, and more recently White. His own family name was too well known in the city, and the last thing he wanted was for his father to get wind of his little "flutters," as he called them. Supposedly women were the ones who cared about their standing in society, but in the Blackstock household it was Algernon Sr., Q.C., to whom it mattered.

At the moment, Blackstock Senior was in his element. He was defence counsel in a well-publicised case, which he was sure to win, and he had a large audience ready to admire him. Actually, Algie felt sorry for the plaintiff, a small woman almost lost from sight in the witness box. His father was about to conduct his cross-examination. Blackstock Senior was not a tall man, but he made up for his lack of height by his commanding presence, a presence carefully cultivated. His iron grey hair and beard were neatly trimmed; his black suit and starched white collar and tabs startlingly white. He was vain about his appearance, and a barber visited him in his chambers once a week. Blackstock never lost a case. This was partly due to the fact that he only took on cases that were certainties and partly because he had a way with juries. He was able to address the men in a manner they understood and respected, even though his tone and demeanour were patrician and bespoke privilege and money. His denigration of opposing witnesses was so subtle that he never elicited sympathy on their behalf but left them lacerated with his wit and smarting from a mockery they barely understood and could not combat. Other lawyers feared him and communicated this to their witnesses so that they usually presented themselves incoherently or with belligerence. Neither attitude went over well with a jury.

To Algie's surprise, however, the plaintiff was holding her own. Perhaps because she was such an unsophisticated woman, her bewilderment was influencing the men of the jury against the defendant. He could see it. His father was aware of it too, and he began to pace in front of the witness box, a sure sign he was searching for an opening, a vulnerable spot on which to pounce.

216

"Mrs. Willfong, am I to understand then, that you, a married woman for more than three years, were not aware that the good doctor, the defendant, was having connections with you?"

"No, sir. I was tilted backwards in the examining chair so I could not see."

The courthouse was packed with spectators, mostly men, who listened with prurient attention as Mrs. Willfong whispered her testimony. The smell of winter clothes, permeated with stale tobacco smoke, was thick in the air. It was an odour Algie hated, just as he hated being a lawyer.

Judge Falconbridge scowled at the witness. "I beg you once again, madam, to please speak up. I realise this subject is most embarrassing, but it is you who have brought charges and therefore we must ensure the accused has a fair trial."

"Thank you, Your Honour," said Blackstock Senior. "I have myself no wish to press Mrs. Willfong, but this is a very serious matter before us, and my client is only too anxious to clear his good name."

He indicated Dr. Atkins, who was sitting stony faced in the prisoner's box. Blackstock had asked him to cut his usually bushy side-whiskers and trim his hair so that he was now the epitome of respectability. Mrs. Willfong, although in her best brown silk, looked plain, rather shabby. She was still a young woman, but she had no bloom of beauty to sway the hearts of the jurymen.

Algie would have considered the case a foregone conclusion if it wasn't for the clear soft voice and her air of utter sincerity. His father was going to have a difficult time discrediting her.

"Madam, as I understand from your statement, you were consulting Dr. Atkins because you wished to conceive a child and so far you were barren. Is that so?"

"Yes, sir."

The expression of pain on her face was unmistakable.

"Given this situation, it is only natural and professional for a doctor to have to conduct an intimate examination. Would you agree?"

"Yes, sir, but this was not a normal examination."

"Please answer only the questions I ask, Mrs. Willfong. It is for the jury to determine that. Try to refrain from slipping in statements that are prejudicial."

"Objection, Your Honour."

Mrs. Willfong's lawyer was a large, greasy-haired man, who looked and smelled as if he could do with a bath. Blackstock had been pleased when he saw who was representing her. "Larkins' very presence will almost take our case for us, Algie," he'd said.

Judge Falconbridge shook his head. "Objection overruled."

218   Blackstock continued, his voice a little more stern. "Mrs. Willfong, in accordance with normal procedure, Dr. Atkins introduced a medical instrument into your,

er, vagina with the purpose of determining whether or not there was a blockage. Can you say whether this instrument was stationary or not?"

"It moved backwards and forwards."

The lawyer clasped his fingers together and briefly raised his eyes to the ceiling as if in prayer.

"This next question, madam, is one of great delicacy. I do appreciate that most of the fairer sex would find it shameful to have to answer. However, it is a necessary and vital question, and I must remind you, madam, that you are under oath. You have sworn before your Maker that you will tell the truth, the whole truth, and nothing but the truth."

Algie expected that Larkins would object at any minute, but he didn't. He just sat picking at the sheaf of papers in front of him as if he had lost one of them. Mrs. Willfong braced herself. She looked over at her husband, a man also in his best clothes but with the weathered skin of a labourer. Blackstock saw the pleading look and shifted so that his body obstructed her view.

"Madam, when you felt this medical instrument inside you, moving backwards and forwards, were your passions excited?"

Unable to see her husband, she looked at Judge Falconbridge for help. There was none forthcoming.

"Answer the question, madam."

219

"You do understand my meaning, don't you, Mrs. Willfong?" asked Blackstock. "I am referring to the sensations that *some* women experience during connection."

He placed a slight emphasis on the "some."

The courtroom was utterly quiet, and Algie shifted uneasily in his chair. He had to admit the old man was good. He was only thankful it wasn't him in the box. Mrs. Willfong was on the verge of tears.

"What is your answer, madam? Under oath, would you say that during these examinations, which were repeated several times over the weeks, you became excited?"

"Yes," she whispered.

"You invariably spent?"

"Yes."

"Was this excitation something that you share with your husband during normal and legal marital connections?"

"No, I er . . ." This time Blackstock moved so that she could see her husband. Algie had never seen such abject shame on a man's face.

"Let me make this clear then, Mrs. Willfong. You returned time and again to Dr. Atkins while he treated you, as he should have, for your problem. After a three-month period, he said he could do no more and discharged you as his patient. You then turned around and brought a suit against him for medical malpractice, claiming he had forced connections on you all those several times without your being aware of it."

220

"That's right. . . . I didn't know what he was doing."

"Didn't you, Mrs. Willfong? How strange. I suppose you returned to his office again and again, like a female detective, in the attempt *to* determine exactly what he was doing."

"No, that is not true. He lay on top of me, over the chair; he was using an instrument . . ."

She was weeping uncontrollably now, her shaky composure gone. Algie studied the jury as he was supposed to do. There were thirteen men, and most of them were now regarding the woman with a mixture of contempt and pity. He knew that the most telling comment that his father had slipped in was the one about the husband. Never had her passions been excited by him, but she admitted to being spent several times with the doctor. What did it matter if he had used an instrument or his own tool, which was more likely. The case was won.

Judge Falconbridge was banging with his gavel.

"The court will be adjourned for one hour. Men of the jury, you will remain in your quarters until called for. Mrs. Willfong, you may step down. Mr. Larkins, will you kindly see to your client."

He stood up, gathered his robe about him, and left the room. Reluctantly, Larkins helped the sobbing Mrs. Willfong out of the witness box. Her husband shoved through the row of people on the bench, but turned on his heel at the aisle and left the courtroom. Blackstock beckoned to his son, and they left by the lawyer's door to the private chambers reserved for them at the back. Dr. Atkins looked pleased, but Algie didn't meet his eye.

Blackstock threw his arm around Algie's shoulders. "We've won, wouldn't you say?"

"Let's not count our chickens just yet, Father. You can never tell with juries."

"Pessimist. They're in the palm of my hand. They all see her as a randy tart."

"She's not though, is she? Seems a good sort to me."

"Never underestimate the appetite of a woman once it's awakened, my good fellow. Believe me, I know."

He didn't elaborate, and at the door of the chamber he went into the senior counsel's room. Algie went into the room for junior counsel and walked straight over to the cupboard where the lawyers kept their special bags. Quickly he fished in the bottom of his and took out a silver flask. Every day Algie filled this flask with Peruvian wine of Coco. This was supposed to be a tonic for those suffering with consumption or other blood diseases, but he found a good cap or two gave him a surge of energy and such a lift of his spirits he couldn't do without it. He took a quick gulp, then a second. His initials were engraved on the side of the flask with an inscription: FROM YOUR DEVOTED WIFE, EMMELINE. If she had ever had her passions excited during lovemaking, he was not aware of it.

"Damnation." He had dribbled some of the liquid down his white tabs. He pulled out his handkerchief and dabbed at the stain but only seemed to make matters worse. There was a tap at the door.

"Just a minute."

Hurriedly he put the flask back into the bag and took out a vial of essence of peppermint. He shook a couple of drops on his tongue, then called, "Enter!"

His clerk, Lavery, came in.

"There's somebody who wants to talk to you, Mr. Blackstock."

"Not now, I'm in the middle of a case."

"I told him that of course, sir, but he won't take no for an answer. He says he's an old chum of yours from previous days."

The clerk's eyes were bright with curiosity.

Algie scowled. "Did this old chum have his card perchance?"

"As a matter of fact, he didn't. Said he'd just run out. But he said to give you this riddle."

"What riddle? What kind of nonsense are you talking?"

"I beg your pardon, sir, I was getting to it. I am just reporting what was said to me. He is something of a joker, this fellow. 'Just for a lark,' he said. 'I've got no card,' says he, 'but Mr. Algie Blackstock likes a joke, I know he does, so let him guess who I am. The riddle

223

is as follows. My first is the opposite of woman, my second is the reverse of the back, my whole is a dog of a town.' Shall I repeat it, sir."

"No, I heard you the first time. I don't know if I like silly jokes like that, Lavery. What kind of fellow is he?"

"Clean enough; speaks well. He's sober, but he's a touch on the flashy side." Lavery paused, savouring the moment in his otherwise dull day. "If I may be so bold, sir, I do think I have solved his riddle. The opposite of woman is man; the reverse of back is front or the chest. My whole is a dog of a town." He paused to see the effect his words were having. "That is to say, Manchester. There are terriers so named, and of course there is the English town, city and dog. My brother-in-law owned one years ago. Ergo, the man's name is Manchester."

Algie stared at him. "What does he look like, this cove?"

"Medium height. Maybe thirty years or so. He's got a streak of white hair in front like a horse's blaze."

Algie laughed, but even in his own ears it sounded false.

"Ah yes, now I remember. He's just an old school pal playing some joke on me."

"Shall I show him in then?"

"Yes, yes. Of course."

"Will you be wanting some tea or coffee served?"

"No. I'll ring if I need you."

"Yes, sir."

Lavery withdrew and Algie stood up and went to the window. He leaned his forehead against the pane, and the glass felt wonderfully cool to his skin. This room was always too hot, the fire blazing in the hearth as if it was a lord's banquet.

"Damnation. Blast and damnation."

The door opened and Lavery ushered in the visitor, who went immediately to where Algie was standing.

"Hello, old chum. Good to see you again. I've had a merry dance to find you."

The clerk closed the door, and Algie turned around. He ignored the proffered hand.

"What the hell do you want?"

The man who had called himself Manchester shrugged.

"Not very much, old chum. Just a little chat really, a chin wag between friends. Why don't we sit down and make ourselves comfortable."

Algie remained where he was. "I have to be back in court shortly. Spit it out. What do you want?"

"You're looking at me like a man with a guilty conscience, Mr. White. Oh, I beg your pardon, that is your nom de plume, isn't it? I forgot."

"There's no law against using a different name as long as you're not signing any contracts or pretending to be somebody else."

"Ah, yes. And I'm certain you are most familiar with

225

the law. You must have had to rationalise to yourself disappearing like that. You do know John Delaney was murdered, don't you?"

Algie was chewing on his moustache. "I read about it. It was such an open-and-shut case I felt nothing useful would be gained by my coming forward."

"Quite so. And people are so quick to cast judgement, aren't they? They would see harm in a lawyer gentleman like yourself participating in an illegal gambling match, wouldn't they? Live and let live is my motto."

"I tell you, nothing I had to say would have been useful."

"No, I suppose not. The Craigs said the three of you left together, and you went on your way along Summerhill Avenue. You couldn't be guilty of the crime of murder, could you?"

"Why are you dinning me like this? Who the hell are you?"

"The name's Pugh, Patrick Pugh, and it is my name of baptism. However, if you'd be so good as to take a seat, I would appreciate it. I become nervous when a strapping gentleman like yourself starts to turn red and is standing over me, snorting."

Reluctantly, Algie perched on the chair behind the desk. "I told you I have to go back to court shortly."

"I see that your father is senior counsel. A fine upstand-ing man. Values his reputation and that of his family, I am sure."

226

Algie pulled open a drawer and took out a banker's chit. "So that's it. You want to be paid off, do you? Money for silence."

Pugh frowned in mock offence. "Not at all, Mr. White. Forgive me for distressing you with my comments. You obviously have reached an erroneous conclusion that I am a blackmailer. Rather the reverse. I am coming to you for help. I am the one prepared to pay."

Chapter Twenty-five

USUALLY MURDOCH WAS HAPPY TO COME HOME. In the winter Mrs. Kitchen, his landlady, always made sure a lamp was burning in the front parlour; and no matter what the hour, she would have his dinner ready for him. Not that it was always a delight to eat what she had prepared. Beatrice was an energetic and inventive woman when it came to caring for those she loved, but the art of cooking had somehow eluded her. Even if Murdoch was on time, he was often presented with dried, overcooked meat and soggy potatoes and vegetables. He didn't really mind. The friendship and mutual respect that had developed between him and the Kitchens more than compensated for unappetising meals.

Tonight, as he approached the house, however, he felt utterly glum. His mood wasn't helped by the conspicuous darkness of the second-floor room. Perhaps because of his talk with Newcombe about ardent young women, he was thinking about Mrs. Enid Jones. Since she'd abruptly packed her belongings and moved to another lodging, he'd made no attempt to get in touch with her.

"I don't want us to mistake proximity for true affection, Will," was what she'd said.

Albeit reluctantly, he had to admit there was truth in that, but he was still smarting.

Mrs. Kitchen came to meet him as soon as he entered the house. "Mr. Murdoch, I was starting to worry. I expected you would be gone for one or two hours at the most."

"So did I, Mrs. K."

She stood by while he divested himself of his coat and hat.

"I can see the young man proved very difficult."

For a moment he didn't know what she was referring to. It seemed a lifetime ago that he had set out for the jail, thinking he was going to have a heart-to-heart talk with a pickpocket.

"Adam Blake wasn't the reason for my summons. I'd like to sit down with both you and Arthur and tell you what has happened."

"I put up a cold meat plate for you. Will you have that first?"

"I'm not hungry, thank you. Just a cup of tea would be excellent. Weak, if you don't mind."

229

"Go and see Arthur and I'll bring it." She was about to go to the kitchen when she paused. "You clearly have unhappy news, so perhaps I can tell you something to cheer you up."

He smiled. "I would certainly like that."

"Mrs. Jones dropped by earlier this afternoon. I took the liberty of telling her about your sister, and she asked that I express the most sincere condolences."

His heart had given a lurch, but he wasn't about to reveal too much.

"That was kind."

"I told her you were off from the station on leave. She said that if you were not engaged tonight, she is at home and would be most pleased to see you."

"Is that so?"

Mrs. Kitchen patted his arm. "She is a good woman, most sincere. A visit might lift your spirits."

And what then? thought Murdoch. Was there any point in contemplating a courtship that couldn't be consummated.

"It's getting late, I –"

"She asked me particularly to tell you that she hoped you wouldn't mind a later hour. Half past eight would be convenient."

230   Murdoch thought that a less respectable woman would have winked. "Mrs. K., why do I get the feeling I'm being pushed out like a fledgling bird?"

She looked flustered. "Of course not. It's just that she seemed particularly anxious to see you."

"All right. I will call on her."

"Good. Please go in. Arthur was worried, too."

She went off to the kitchen. Murdoch took a moment to change from boots to slippers. She was right. In spite of everything, the news that Enid wanted to see him had lifted his spirits.

For a long time now Murdoch had got into the way of sharing the vicissitudes of his daily life with both Beatrice and Arthur Kitchen. It meant a lot to Arthur, who was housebound with his illness, to discuss cases Murdoch was dealing with. If he was well enough, their conversations often became far ranging, from the current political situation, dismal, to the finer points of Catholic theology, even more dismal. The latter point of view was never expressed in front of his wife. Murdoch waited until tea had been poured and sipped; Arthur's final egg-and-cream tonic swallowed; the fire poked and set to a blaze. He felt he should have done a drum roll first. *And the big news of the day is . . . I met my long-lost father today, and what a surprise: he is convicted of murder.*

He told them in as matter-of-fact a way as possible. After the inevitable exclamations, he settled down to tell everything that had transpired and what he knew about the case.

231

"So what do you think about all that? Any immediate opinions?"

Arthur eyed him ruefully. "Very difficult, isn't it? As you say, if not him, then who?"

"It couldn't be your father," added Beatrice, "not a murderer."

Murdoch reached over and patted her hand. He was touched by her irrational loyalty. He knew that what she meant was nobody with Murdoch blood in their veins could be a criminal.

"It would be reassuring if Mr. Quinn tracked down the mysterious Mr. White. You don't want any loop- holes to fret over."

"Exactly. First thing tomorrow I'm going to visit the doctor who performed the post mortem examination. His report was very thorough, but I'd like to talk to him face to face. And after that . . ." His voice trailed off. After that he had no more options that he could see. Neither of the Kitchens had asked him directly if he considered his father to be guilty; and he was grateful for their tact. When he had left the jail, so stirred by this unexpected reunion, he had entertained the pos- sibility that Harry was innocent. However, as the day went on and he had talked to the people who had been involved, he was reverting to his first opinion: Harry had killed a man in a fit of rage and conveniently didn't remember doing so. Justice would be served.

232

He thought of all the times he had fantasised about justice in connection with Harry. Often, he himself administered it; sometimes God did. The end was the same. Harry suffered for his sins. The knowledge that he might very well receive the ultimate punishment was not nearly as satisfying as he had thought it would be. In fact, it brought but little pleasure.

Chapter Twenty-six

WITH A GROAN SHE COULD NOT SUPPRESS, Mother St. Raphael got up from her knees. Her breath was a white smoke in the air, and she was so stiff she stood swaying for a moment as she gained her balance. Dr. Corneille had stated categorically that more warmth in her cell would alleviate the pain from her arthritis, but she refused to ask for it. Each nun had an allotment of coal and wood for her fireplace, and she was expected to only make use of it when the weather was bitter. The prioress deeply believed she must be an example to those whose spiritual life she directed. A few of the weaker sisters, in their secret hearts, wished that she might, on occasion, be less rigorous.

Mother St. Raphael had been praying for a long time, but the Lord's will was not yet clear to her. She knew that it was her own pride that was holding her back. She took great care when she selected the nuns who came as postulants. No matter what the professed ardour, she accepted only those young women whom she felt could withstand the hardship and purity of their rule. Never again to see the outside world, to live a life of prayer to which the needs of the body were subjugated, often at great cost. Only a few women were truly suitable. Sister Philomena had entered the order when she was very young. In spite of herself and the rule that forbad special friendships, Sister St. Raphael, as she was then, had become very fond of the new postulant. She saw her own struggle for perfection mirrored in the girl, and she understood the perpetual self-recrimination when that impossible struggle failed time and again.

Sister Philomena flagellated her body and her spirit but was rarely at peace with her own conscience. The prioress more than once had been forced to admonish her, albeit gently, for her scrupulosity. However, the young nun was generous with the older sisters, who became so demanding as their bodies succumbed to age and discomfort. She never complained at the most menial chores. In spite of these manifestations of her goodness, she only seemed to taste happiness when she had occasion to amuse the other sisters during the recreation hour. In the summer, like several of the other diligent nuns, she used the hour before the Grand Silence to tend to the garden they depended on. But it was throughout the dark winter months when little work could be done that Sister Philomena entertained them all with stories of the sea that she claimed to have heard in her native province of Nova Scotia. She was a

235

compelling storyteller and spun out the tales, doling out one episode at a time, leaving them all in suspense until the following day. Nobody ever questioned the veracity of these tales even though her store seemed endless. Occasionally, the prioress worried about the decidedly secular nature of the yarns, but she couldn't bear to deprive the little community of this small pleasure or quench the brightness in Sister Philomena's face as she addressed her rapt audience.

Mother St. Raphael walked over to her desk. She was not at all a worldly woman. She had entered the order when she was eighteen, the shy, youngest daughter of a genteel Montreal family. Her mother's piety was constantly besieged by the need for her daughters to marry well. The postulants whispered among themselves that Mother had become a nun when her heart was broken by the death of her fiancée. She was aware of this rumour but did nothing to dispel it. The truth was not nearly as romantic. Her mother had put great pressure on her to marry the son of a wealthy banker. She had loathed the sickly young man on sight and was certain his antipathy was the equal of hers. He had died suddenly from a lung haemorrhage, and Hermione had fled to the convent where she might be safe from the admonishments of her mother and older sisters.

236

She had been elected prioress six years ago, and under her direction life was orderly and placid. Nothing like this had ever fallen on her shoulders before. As prioress, Mother St. Raphael was responsible for monitoring all correspondence that came and went in the convent. Although the nuns were permitted to write their own letters, the envelopes were never sealed. It would have been against the rule of their order to maintain the privacy they had experienced in the outer world. Letters that were addressed to any one of the nuns were opened and read. This was not a burdensome task as communication with the outside world was restricted. At Christmas, letters could be exchanged with immediate family members to share in the joy of Our Lord's birth. On the anniversary of the nun's marriage to Christ her Saviour, the same families were expected to mark that special day both with a novena and a suitable letter. All the correspondence and small personal effects relinquished at the time of the first vows were kept in individual cardboard boxes in a special cupboard in the prioress's room. They were forwarded to the next of kin in the event of the nun's death.

Sister Philomena's box contained a child's diary, a small number of cards and letters, a garnet ring and matching ear bobs. Mother St. Raphael had been about to wrap everything and send them to William Murdoch when she found the letter. It was this that was causing her such distress.

237

On the eve of taking her final vows, Sister Philomena had written to her brother. The envelope was still sealed, indicating that the prioress at that time had not read it.

Mother St. Raphael had simply followed the rule and opened the letter.

She took it up again.

Dear Will: I do not know if you will ever read this letter or if what I am about to relate will ever be made known to you. I am leaving that in the hands of Our Lord. It is His will that be done. However, if you are reading this letter, it means I have been gathered into the arms of our beloved Saviour. I ask you to accept this with joy and not sorrow.

It is so long since we met face to face that in my mind you are forever my older brother, tall and strong but not yet a grown man, with your dark hair that you could never keep smooth, your brown eyes that would gaze on me so seriously, a smile that when it was bestowed on me gladdened my sad heart. I know you did not approve of my accepting my vocation, but being a nun has brought me as much peace of mind as I am allowed by God's mercy. Perhaps I am wrong to unburden myself in this way, but I believe that the truth shall make you free, and I long for freedom.

On the day our mother died, I was witness to a quarrel between her and our father. To say quarrel is not accurate because she never argued or defended herself, as you know. He was angry about some small and insignificant thing, and he hit her. Perhaps he did not mean to hit so hard, but she was knocked backwards and struck her head on the sharp corner of the kitchen cupboard, the one by the east window. She had to sit down and said she felt dizzy, but he was impatient and would not allow it. She got up and set off for the beach to gather shellfish. As you know, she was found drowned in one of the pools among the rocks. The coroner concluded that she had slipped and struck her head. However, I am convinced she would not have fallen if it were not for the blow she had received from Father.

All of my life, dearest brother, I have lived with the shame of doing nothing. I know that you will say I was a child and therefore absolved of responsibility, but I have never believed that. Sometimes he listened to me in particular. I could appeal to his conscience. That day, unfortunately, he was particularly vile tempered. He had run out of beer, and you know all too well what that did to him. I was sitting at the table when all this occurred, and I was so afraid I did nothing. Nothing. Perhaps she would not have died if I had begged him to let her rest. But I was silent, saving my own skin. When Mr. Markham came with the news that she had been discovered on the beach, Father behaved as if he were a grieving husband. He said nothing to me, and I truly believe that he was not aware of what I had witnessed. I dared not tell you, Will, because you were already so fiery. I knew you would challenge Father, and I feared for your safety. Dear brother, you were all we had, Bertie and I. I wrestle with my conscience every day, and perhaps by the time

239

I pass from this life I will have cleansed the anger from my heart. I pray for this.

I don't know what you will do with the information I have imparted. I am sure it will cause you great sorrow, and I pray that you will ask the Lord to guide you. I do not know if Father is alive or dead, but I hope there will come a time when I can wholeheartedly pray for his soul. You, dearest Will, are always in my prayers. May we meet in the arms of Our Lord at the judgement day.

Susanna.

For the dozenth time in the past hour, Mother St. Raphael crossed herself and asked for guidance. What good would be served if Sister Philomena's brother were to know what had happened? It was a long time ago now. According to the extern nun, Mr. Murdoch had been angry at not being allowed to see his sister's face. These past events had nothing to do with the Order, but one could never be sure with families. She had no desire to bring shameful public attention to the convent, nor would Sister Philomena have wished that.

She replaced the letter in the box and retied the black ribbon that fastened the lid.

Chapter Twenty-seven

MURDOCH HAD WALKED PAST ENID's boardinghouse once already. He had arrived at least twenty minutes before the appointed time and not wishing to appear overly eager had gone on by. The wind was biting and a sleety snow was falling, every good reason to go and knock on the door, but he forced himself to trudge on. As he went by the corner of Queen and Parliament Streets for a second time, he passed young Constable Burley on his beat, who gave him a puzzled greeting.

"Cold night to be out, sir."

Murdoch realised he had been walking as slowly as if he were enjoying a summer stroll in Allan Gardens. He raised his head and quickened his pace purposefully.

"Brisk, Constable. Good for the lungs!"

He inadvertently took in a gulp of air so cold he started to cough. Burley suppressed a grin, gave him a salute, and continued on his rounds. Murdoch walked back as far as Sackville Street where he turned, leaving the constable to his lonely job of checking the empty houses along the street to make sure no vagrants had broken in to shelter there. A few houses from where Enid was now boarding, Murdoch paused and fished out his watch from his inner pocket. Damnation, he was still ten minutes early. He didn't want to encounter the constable again, so he stayed where he was, stamping his feet and blowing into his gloves to warm his hands. He'd forgotten his muffler, and his nose started to drip from the cold air. Damnation again, he didn't have a handkerchief. He wiped the back of his hand across his nose and sniffed hard. To be visiting at this hour was quite unorthodox, and in spite of himself he was touched that Enid had issued her invitation. He'd better get inside, early or not.

The house was one half of a double and looked reasonably well cared for. There was a gaslight in the small front porch, and even though the blinds were all pulled down, bright cracks of light showed around the edges.

Murdoch walked up the flight of steps to the door. There were stained-glass panels on each side, and a soft amber light came from the hall. He gave the shiny brass bellpull a good tug and peered through the glass side panel. Almost immediately he saw Enid Jones coming down the stairs, and he jumped back and started to

242

scrape his boots on the scraper fastened to the boards of the porch. She opened the door.

"Mr. Murdoch, how wonderfully punctual you are. Please to come in out of the chill."

He took off his hat, knocked some more slush from his boots, and stepped into the hall.

"I'll take your coat from you."

He thought she was a little breathless too and was glad of the distraction of coat and hat divesting. Enid was wearing a silver grey taffeta gown that rustled as she moved. He didn't remember having seen it before. Her dark hair was fastened with tortoiseshell combs but seemed looser, less severe than the way she usually wore it.

"This is a grand house," he said, rubbing his hands together to warm them.

"So it is. I am lucky to have found such accommodations. Mrs. Barrett is a widow, and she wanted a companion more than anything." She held out her hand. "I was so sorry to hear of your sister's death, Will. It must be a great loss to you."

He shrugged. "Frankly, I felt as if she died when she was professed as a nun sixteen years ago. That was the last time I saw her, and I mourned her then."

Enid's hand was warm in his, and as he looked at her, he felt his stomach turn into something fluid. Whatever it was he communicated, she lowered her eyes quickly.

"You're quite chilled. Come and get warm. My sitting room is upstairs."

There was gaslight in the sconces, and all the way up to the landing were hung large and sober oil paintings that, as far as he could tell, were biblical in nature. Mrs. Barrett was clearly a woman of great piety. Baptist piety for certain. Enid ushered him into a room off the right of the landing. There was a cheerful fire burning in the hearth, and the lamps were turned up high. The Turkish couch and matching chairs were of rich green-and-red plush; the dark mahogany furniture gleamed. It was markedly different from the relatively simple room that she had rented from Mrs. Kitchen. He was also conscious of the fact they were alone.

She had been observing his reaction, and she smiled with pleasure. "As you can see, this is a larger room than I had before, and I have been able to add some of my own furniture. That is my table and sideboard. I brought them all the way from Wales, but when we moved into Mrs. Kitchen's house, I had to store them away."

"Very fine."

"My husband was handy. He made them."

Unconsciously she touched the surface of the sideboard as if in a caress.

244   "Please to sit down by the fire."

He did so while she went to the tea trolley, where a silver teapot was warming over a spirit lamp.

"As I remember you like plenty of sugar and milk."

"That's right."

She poured the tea and handed him the cup and saucer. He didn't want to embarrass her by constantly commenting on the fine quality of her goods and chattels, but the china was particularly delicate. He was suddenly aware that his chequered brown wool suit was shabby and his boots thick. He had never felt this before with Enid, and he didn't like it at all.

"Since you left us, the typewriting business must be going well," he said, trying for a lighthearted note. He didn't succeed, and Enid frowned.

"Mrs. Barrett has kindly let me have two rooms for the cost of one, and in return I sit with her on an evening and sometimes read to her."

"The sermons of Mr. Wesley, I assume?"

"Not at all. She is quite fond of novels. We are presently reading Mr. Scott's *Heart of Midlothian.*"

"I'd consider that rather on the pagan side, myself." He was goading her cruelly, but he couldn't stop himself.

She went over to the trolley and put one of the cakes from the two-tiered silver stand onto his plate. "It is a rousing story, and we both enjoy it."

She handed him the Eccles cake, which meant he 245 had to juggle cup and saucer in one hand and the plate in the other. That didn't help his mood. He put the cup and saucer on the small table beside him. On it was a framed studio photograph. Clearly a family portrait of Enid, a man who he presumed was her late husband, and her son, Alwyn, at a younger age. The man had the physique of a Welshman, short and stocky with thick, dark hair. He looked confident. Enid was leaning her head backwards against his shoulder, and the boy was standing between them. Murdoch had not seen this picture before, but then he realised he had never stepped inside Enid's room when she was living at the Kitchens'.

"How does Alwyn like his new digs?" he asked.

"Quite well indeed. Mrs. Barrett has let me use the old box room for his bedroom. He is very proud to be in a room of his own. He thinks he is quite grown up." She paused and took a sip of her tea. "I didn't tell him you might be coming by tonight. I wanted him to go to bed early because he seems a little feverish, and he would not have gone to bed until he saw you."

"Fear or pleasure?" Murdoch asked wryly. Enid's son had been decidedly ambivalent about him.

She looked uncomfortable. "He does like you, Will, it's just that . . ."

"It's just that he doesn't want to share his mother's attentions."

"He's still a boy."

Murdoch shrugged. No matter what he said, they seemed to end up in a place that was stiff and uncomfortable. "Quite so," he added lamely. "I can't say that I blame him for that."

Another silence that was broken by the sound of a piece of coal falling in the fire.

Murdoch got to his feet at once. "That fire needs building up," he said, and knelt down to open the coal scuttle that was beside the fender. He picked up the tongs and dropped a couple of chunks of coal into the red maw. "There you go. I'm restored to manliness. Are there any other tasks I can do for you, ma'am?"

She smiled back at him. "You can eat another cake. I made them myself this afternoon, and it is affronted I'd be if they were left untouched."

"Gladly."

He walked over to the trolley and helped himself to a marzipan square and a scone thick with currants.

"I understand from Mrs. Kitchen you are on compassionate leave for the week."

"Yes, and that has turned out to be quite convenient as I have another investigation."

He sat down by the fire while Enid looked at him curiously.

"I would be honoured if you would share the details with me. But if you have no desire to do so, I quite understand."

247

He had half decided not to say anything to her, not sure how it would reflect on him. *Oh, by the way, Mrs. Jones, not only am I a papist, my father is probably a murderer!*

However, once again, something in the kindness of her expression affected him, and he wanted to tell her the whole story.

"My long-lost father has reappeared. In fact, he is in Don Jail, where he is waiting to be hung." He raced on, glad she was controlled enough to sit and listen without exclamation while he gave her a summary of what had happened in August.

"I have agreed to do what I can," he concluded.

"What does that mean?"

"It means I am doing what I would do in any investigation. I am examining the evidence as presented. I am asking questions of the people who were there at the time, and I am trying to see if I can sniff out lies or inconsistencies or unearth new evidence pertaining to the case."

"And if you were to find such evidence, is it too late?"

"If I present a convincing-enough deposition to the prison warden, he has the power to stay the execution. If I am overwhelmingly convincing, there could be a new trial."

"You say you doubt he is innocent?"

He shrugged. "I remember all too well what he was like when he was drinking. In the morning all was forgotten. Quite possibly what happened has been erased from his mind. I am going to see if there is any new proof, one way or the other, and that's all I can do. If he goes to the gallows, so be it."

"It must have been shocking to meet with him under these circumstances. And with your sister so newly gone."

"I haven't told him about that yet."

Enid came over to him, crouching down so that they were at eye level. She touched his cheek, stroking him as if he were a child in need of comfort.

"I am sorry for you, Will."

He reached for her hand and brought it to his lips. Her skin was warm and soft, fragrant with something sweet and flowery. She didn't move away, and it was so natural to put his other arm around her and pull her close. He kissed her. She raised her arms and enclosed him, pressing against his chest. Murdoch was having trouble breathing, and the position was awkward with Enid somehow half draped across his knees. He managed to part his legs, and she slipped in between them. He wanted to moan with pleasure, and his loins were desperate to take action on their own. He wasn't sure if it was Enid or he that finally ended the kiss, but they stayed like that, clutched together, her cheek hard against his.

"You must be uncomfortable," he whispered, as he kissed her face again and again.

"I am," she said, and moved back to sit on her heels, although she was still between his knees. Her face was flushed, and her eyes shone.

"Mrs. Barrett is away at her sister's until tomorrow night."

249

He stared at her, wondering why she was telling him this right now. She laughed at him.

"We have complete privacy, Will. If you want it so, that is."

He almost yelped. "Enid!"

She stood up and took his hand. "My bedroom is adjoining. Come."

Stiffly, he got to his feet. She was in charge, and he was only too happy to surrender. If, in spite of everything, Mrs. Jones had determined they would become lovers this night, he would offer no objection. She picked up one of the lamps and pulled back the flowered velvet portieres that draped the door to the bedroom. She had lit a fire here also and already turned down the covers on the bed. The white plump pillows looked soft and welcoming. She smiled at him shyly and gave him another kiss, which lasted for a long time. Finally, she pulled away and indicated the screen in one corner.

"I'll change. You can get undressed by the fire where it's warmer."

Murdoch wasn't sure if he needed to be any warmer than he was, otherwise he'd conflagrate, but he nodded. He was glad he'd sponged down this morning and that his shirt was fresh on yesterday. Enid disappeared behind the screen, and he removed all his clothes. He hesitated at whether or not to take off his woollen combination underwear but decided it might be easier

250

if he did. Naked as a jaybird, he hurried over to the bed and jumped in, pulling up the covers.

Enid emerged. She had wrapped herself in a paisley shawl, but she didn't seem to have anything on either.

"Blow out the light, Will," she said, and he obeyed at once. The flames in the fireplace made dancing shadows on the walls. She came over to the bed, and he made room for her to climb in. He was lying on his back, and she put her arm across his chest. Her skin had gone cool.

"You're shivering," he said. "Are you cold?"

"No. But it is a long time since I have lain with a man."

He buried his face in her hair and spoke into her neck. "Enid, I must tell you I have not had connection with a woman before. I am not sure how to proceed."

She leaned back so she could see into his eyes. "There is nothing to worry about." She rolled away and pulled him on top of her. Her hand slid to his groin. "Trust this fellow; he knows what to do."

Chapter Twenty-eight

A FEW YEARS AGO MARIA NEWCOMBE had purchased an old-fashioned four-poster bed at a country auction. She had replaced the dust-laden curtains with some of claret-coloured velvet, and she liked nothing better in the winter than for her and Vince to get into bed and draw the curtains. They sacrificed some freshness of air for snugness, and she considered it a good trade. At the end of the day, the two of them climbed into bed and pressed closely side by side, discussing the business of the day, going over what needed to be done tomorrow. Maria waited until Vincent had brought up some of the things that were on his mind first. He told her what had happened at the Delaneys'.

"Mrs. Delaney appeared quite afraid. I didn't know the boy was so badly off."

"Mrs. Bowling is a strange woman, I must say. Whenever I've encountered her, she's been quite unfriendly."

Ucillus Bowling had come to live in the Delaney cottage only two years ago. Rumours had soon started about the daughter who some said had the shocking ways of a hoyden. Maria would have been a good neighbour and visited the newcomer, but Ucillus made it clear she did not welcome visitors. The gossips said that did not include male visitors. Maria knew Vincent went to see the woman sometimes, he said. Although she knew she trusted him completely, she couldn't resist jabbing at the sore place when Ucillus was mentioned.

"The problem is Delaney himself wasn't consistent in his treatment of the lad," said Vince, adroitly side-stepping the issue of Mrs. Bowling's aloofness. "You've got to leaven corrections with kindness unless you only want obedience from fear and not from respect. One minute Philip could have whatever he asked for, the next the very same demand would get him a reprimand. And then would come the temper. I witnessed it more than once."

In the darkness Maria smiled to herself. Vincent didn't see any difference between training a dog and raising a child.

"The fellow Williams kept a cool head, I must say," continued Vincent. "Good man. I wouldn't like to make an enemy of him, but I'd say he would be a steadfast friend."

They lay quietly for a while, then she said, "I was thinking I'd go and pay a visit to Jess Lacey. I can take

253

her some bread. From what Walter has said, she is very blue most days."

"Good old girl," he said, and kissed the top of her head. She could tell that he was struggling valiantly against sleep, and she murmured her own good night to release him and kissed his hand. She lay against his chest until she heard by his deepening breathing that he had dozed off, then she slipped away from under his arm and turned on her side. Her eyes were open, and she knew sleep would elude her tonight. It was in these moments when there was silence all around her that her fears began to creep to the forefront of her mind. She knew that, if asked, any of their neighbours or customers would describe her as a cheerful woman with a ready smile. She'd heard it said of her many times, but it wasn't really true. God had not seen fit to give her living children, and the lack had intensified a deep-seated, inner melancholy that only Vince had ever truly seen. She moved her foot backward until she came into contact with her husband's calf. His nightshirt had ridden up, and she was momentarily comforted by the feeling of his skin against hers. She had wanted to talk to him about the episode with Sally, which had troubled her deeply, but she had also been reluctant to say, even to him, what had happened.

254   He would probably urge her to tell Walter, but she couldn't bring herself to do so. He was already worried enough about his wife. She knew Lacey cared for his daughter, but he was such an unpredictable moody

man, and since Jess lost the babe he seemed much worse. She sometimes wondered if he would ever smile again. Not that she didn't understand the pain of losing a bairn. She did all too well. But there was a living child who needed his attention, and much of the time he behaved as if Sally wasn't there. The child was becoming more invisible by the day. Like a drift of mist in the ravine, a good wind and she would blow away.

Maria sat up, pushed aside the bed curtain, and got out of bed. The fire had died to embers, but the bedroom was still warm. She went over to the window that overlooked the rear garden. The doghouse was directly below, empty now because, since her whelping, Tripper had her box in the taproom. Vince had built the doghouse himself, and Maria had joked that it was better accommodation than many people down in the city enjoyed. She didn't really mind because she, too, loved the dogs, and his devotion to them didn't divert Vince's attention from the needs of their own home. Maria stared downwards, unable to shake off her distress.

When she was only six years old, her mother had died giving birth to her tenth child, the fifth boy, Cecil. The burden of raising the younger children had fallen on the all-too-thin shoulders of her older sisters, Fanny and Martha. To earn money, at harvest time Fanny had taken in minders, children from the village whose parents were away all day in the fields. Mostly Maria was not allowed to play with them, but one day Fanny

255

had been preoccupied with her new sweetheart and Maria had brought her doll to the kitchen where the three other children were playing. Although the two boys were giggling with excitement, she saw at once that it was the bigger girl who was the ringleader. Cecil was on the ground, and one of the boys had a hand over his mouth so he couldn't cry out. There was such terror in his eyes that Maria had screamed out loud. Fanny came running in; the girl and the two boys were slapped and pulled off. Later that night Maria heard Fanny and Martha whispering together about what had happened. She didn't completely understand what they meant except that something bad had happened to the girl that summer, and she was taking it out on Cecil. She never came back to be minded, and the incident had become a secret of such awful shame that the slightest hint of it made Maria's cheeks turn hot.

She shivered and turned away, too afraid of her own thoughts to tolerate them any longer. Vince muttered something in his sleep, but she couldn't make out the words. She went back to bed, lay down against his broad, strong back, and kissed his shoulder softly. Finally she fell asleep, and her restless dreams were full of scenes in which Cecil became Sally, who lifted her doll's smock and was poking her finger into the crotch.

256

Moving quietly so as not to wake Walter or Sally, who was in her crib by the fireside, Jess came down the stairs.

The moon was full, and there was enough of a layer of snow on the field to throw up a light through the uncurtained windows. She went over to the cupboard and took out the canvas bag where she'd hidden the clothes. Last week she had taken a pair of Walter's corduroys and cut them down to fit her. She added an old navy jersey with a deep roll collar that she knew he wouldn't miss and some heavy, well-darned wool socks. She dressed quickly and went to the door. Her own waterproof cloak was too cumbersome to bother with, and she took Walter's leather coat from the hook and put it on. Her boots and gloves were lined with rabbit fur and were warm. She had to hurry. Walter always woke about midnight so he could keep the fire built up. She knew how worried he would be if he saw her like this, but if she didn't get out of the confines of her house, she thought she would go mad. Pulling on a grey Persian lamb hood and tucking her hair out of sight, she slipped outside.

Earlier it had been sleeting heavily, but that had stopped and there was a damp snap in the air that she liked.

She struck out toward the steps, liking the feeling of being unencumbered by long skirts. She knew she must look more male than female, and the notion gave her a strange pleasure. How long had she been doing this? Two weeks, three? At first when she had awoken at the predawn hour, she had simply got up quietly so she wouldn't disturb her husband and daughter. She had

257

gone downstairs and wrapped herself in a shawl until it was a decent time to start raking out the stove. She found that moving around helped soothe her, but one time Sally had woken and she had to tend to her. It seemed better to go out of the house. Initially, she had walked around the edges of the little garden several times and then gone back inside. Now this was not enough, and every night she was going further and further afield.

At the fence line she hesitated for a moment, trying to penetrate the darkness of the dense evergreens. The wind had got up, and the trees tossed and rustled. She was about to unbolt the gate when she saw the second offering. Lying across the path on a neat bed of spruce branches was the skinned corpse of a squirrel. The tail and feet were cut off and the skullcap had been opened to expose the brains. Two days ago she had found a rabbit skin in the same place, all cleaned and laid out for her. She turned around and faced the cottage. What could he see? The kitchen window was directly behind her. With the oil lamp lit and no blinds or curtains on the windows, whoever was inside was quite visible.

Jessica's mouth went dry with fear. She picked up the squirrel by the leg and tossed it into the trees. She daren't risk continuing with her sojourn, and almost sobbing, she went back into the house.

In the hideaway the watcher crouched, waiting for her to come down the steps.

258

Chapter Twenty-nine

"WILL, WAKE UP! Wake up!"

Murdoch opened his eyes. Enid was sitting up in bed, leaning over him. Her hair was loose and rumpled, and for some reason that stirred a delightful memory.

"We both fell asleep," she whispered. "You have to go before it gets light."

He grunted, trying to gather his wits. "What time is it?"

"It's just after two."

"That's all right then, dawn won't be for many hours. There's lots of time."

"No, there isn't. Please get up, Will. You cannot risk somebody seeing you."

He pushed himself into a sitting position and rubbed his face hard. Awake now, he suddenly felt awkward. Enid had put on her nightgown, but he was still naked. The knowledge made him as shy as a schoolboy, and he pulled the sheet up to his shoulders. He wanted to talk about what had happened between them, but he felt utterly tongue-tied. Enid went to get off the bed, but he caught her by the arm.

"My sweetest girl . . . er, last night was . . ." He paused. What do you say to a woman you have just shared the most pleasurable connection with? That was sublime? The most exciting thing he had ever experienced? A relief? Some of the worry left her face, and she smiled at him.

"Oh, Will, you always need to put things into words, don't you. You should have been a poet."

This insight into his character was new to him, but her tone was fond. She gave him a quick peck on the cheek, and he made no attempt to hold her, trying to assess her mood.

She got off the bed and went over to the chair where he had draped his clothes. She brought them over to him.

"Do you want me to light the lamp?"

"No, I can see well enough."

Tactfully, she turned her back while he got out of bed and slipped into his underwear and woollen vest. He fumbled with the buttons on his trousers, his face hot with embarrassment. When he was fully clothed, he came around to where she was sitting. He took her face in both of his hands and kissed her on the mouth.

260

She didn't resist, but neither did she respond in the same way she had earlier.

"Enid, should I apologise? Did you not want me?"

"Of course you do not have to apologise, Will. Our desire was mutual, but . . ."

He finished the sentence for her. "It was a mistake."

"No. I cannot say that. But there is a promise in intimacy, and I do not know if I can keep it."

He knew what she meant, although he would like to have pretended he didn't. He stepped back, and this time she was the one who caught him by the arm.

"I've hurt you, Will, and I did not mean to. Forgive me."

She stood up and slipped her arms around his waist. "Mrs. Barrett is away with her sister tomorrow night as well. I would dearly love to have your company, Will. Say you'll come."

"Does this mean you are going to keep your promise?"

"For now. And you?"

Even if his mind had been cool enough to refuse, his body could not. "Of course."

She let him go and he tiptoed down the stairs and let himself out into the dark street. There were no lights showing in any of the houses, and he kept close to the fences where there were more shadows. He realised he was acting as guiltily as if he were a thief

261

returning from a robbery, and annoyed with himself he veered off the sidewalk and into the centre of the road. He lifted his head, letting the cold night wind blow on his face. He felt as if the delicate smell of Enid's body surrounded him, his hands, his face. If it hadn't been the middle of the night, he would have let out a whoop of sheer joy.

The bell calling her to the chapel had sounded several minutes ago and Mother St. Raphael knew the nuns would be awaiting her. She had hardly slept at all, and the pain in her knees was intense. However, she felt resolved in her actions. She went back to the desk and took out a pen and a sheet of paper. The ink in the inkwell was thickened with the cold and made it diffi-cult to write neatly. She blotted the sheet several times, signed her name, and folded the paper.

There was a light deferential tap on her door.

"Mother Prioress, are you awake? It is the time of compline."

"Yes, yes, Sister. I will be there momentarily."

She picked up Sister Philomena's letter and put it, together with the diary and her other effects, into an envelope, adding her own note. As soon as it was light, she would have the extern take them to Monsieur Lavalle to be posted to Toronto.

Thy will be done.

—

Pugh took three banknotes from his pocket and laid them flat on the dresser. He made a note on a paper wrapper, folded it around the money, and placed them in a flat leather folder. He yawned and walked over to the bed and flopped down on his back. He was so tired he couldn't be bothered to undress, not even to take off his muddy boots. Nevertheless, he knew his excitement wouldn't allow him to sleep just yet, and he did what he always did at these times. He fished a twenty-five-cent coin out of his pocket, and with his right hand raised in front of his face, he began to practise concealing it in his palm. It was a tricky manoeuvre, especially trying to do it lying down. He held the coin on the tips of his two middle fingers with his thumb, then slid it down into his palm, holding it there by pinching the muscles of his hand together. His hand was supposed to look relaxed and natural, but the effort of holding the coin made his fingers tense and spread out. The twenty-five-cent piece fell out and onto his chest. He picked it up and started again. He pushed the coin down to the palm of his hand again and squeezed it tight.

He smiled to himself. Soon it would all be over. More than a year of work about to pay off. His most persistent and pleasurable daydream was what he would do with all the money, which was more than he had ever earned in his life. He could buy himself a new wheel. A new bicycling suit to go with it. Most of

263

all of course, he would take a short holiday. He could take the train down to New York City, visit some houses of joy that he'd heard of. Cautiously, he let his fingers relax and was still able to hold on to the coin. That looked good.

The shadow at the back of his mind was kept at bay by these pleasant thoughts. He never allowed himself to think about the other people. They were all an audience to him to be tickled, played with, and ultimately gulled. The coin fell out of his hand again, but he didn't retrieve it this time. He closed his eyes. It was not his fault how the law viewed these things.

Chapter Thirty

His alarm clock was clanging, and Murdoch rolled over and pressed the lever to stop it. He would have happily gone back to sleep for a while longer, but almost immediately there was a tap on his door.

"Mr. Murdoch, here's your hot water."

"Thank you, Mrs. K. You can bring it in."

He pulled his coverlet up around his neck as his landlady opened the door.

"Shall I pour it?"

"You might as well. I'm up, at least I think I am."

He yawned so hard he thought he was going to swallow himself.

"Did you not sleep well?" Beatrice asked him, as she poured the hot water from the jug into the basin on his washstand. He glanced at her quickly, but her comment seemed without guile. As far as he knew, she had not awakened when he had come home last night, which wasn't surprising as he was floating at least two inches above the floorboards.

"Thank you, I did, Mrs. K. And yourself?"

"Soundly, thank you. And Arthur had a good night. He was asleep at ten and didn't stir until three o'clock and then he was only awake for a short while. The laudanum syrup does help him." She put a towel on the rail. "There you go. I warmed it up by the fire. Shall I light the candle?"

"Yes, please." He suppressed another yawn and waited for her to leave the room so he could get out of bed. At the door, she paused.

"Did you have a pleasant visit with Mrs. Jones?"

"Yes, indeed, very pleasant."

"I'm glad to hear that."

"She has asked me to have dinner with her tonight, so you needn't put anything up for me."

Beatrice frowned. He knew why. Although she liked Enid, the young widow was not a Roman Catholic, and Mrs. Kitchen would never be reconciled to a match between her and Murdoch. One evening's visit was acceptable; a second closely following was not.

"Breakfast in ten minutes?"

"That would suit very well. I want to go directly to the Coroner's office and see if he will give me an appointment."

"I'll let you get on then," she said, and left. Murdoch got out of bed and shuffled into his slippers. Moving hurriedly to combat the cold of the room, he tugged off his nightshirt and got dressed. The steam from the hot water was evaporating by the second. He sharpened his razor on the leather strop, dipped the shaving brush in the water, and whipped up a lather in the soap.

At one point in the night, Enid had stroked his eyes and murmured something in Welsh. "Translation please, madam," he had said, and she had kissed his lids one at a time. "There is too much weariness there."

This morning, in the gloom of the early morning and with a short night's sleep, he could see what she meant. There were dark shadows underneath his eyes, and his eyelids felt itchy and puffy. He daubed on the lather, then drew the razor down the line of his jaw and flicked off the wiped soap onto the towel. Unbidden, a memory flashed into his mind of him as a boy standing by the kitchen sink watching his father shave. The razor had made a scratchy noise as he'd scraped it down his cheeks. In the winter Harry grew a moustache and straggly beard, but in the summer he went clean shaven, more or less. If he was on a binge, he didn't wash or shave for days at a time.

"Can we think of something more uplifting," said Murdoch out loud to his own reflection. "Perhaps the delectable Mrs. Jones, for instance."

267

He cupped his hands and scooped up water, already tepid, and washed his face. Perhaps Enid had not been as disingenuous as it had at first appeared. She knew

Mrs. Barrett was away from home, and she had deliberately packed her son off to bed early. That was a big step for a respectable Baptist. He grinned to himself, not minding at all. He dried himself off and scrutinised the job he'd done shaving. Damnation. He'd nicked the underside of his chin, and there was a spot of blood on his white collar. He rubbed at it with a wet finger and only succeeded in spreading out the stain. He sighed. He didn't have a clean one; this would have to do until Mrs. Kitchen could wash one for him. Enid said there was promise in intimacy, and she was right about that. He could see himself as the most faithful of men for the rest of his life. The religious issue, the huge differences between them, didn't seem important at the moment. A small hill to climb, not an insurmountable Everest.

From downstairs, he heard the tinkle of the silver bell that Mrs. Kitchen used to summon him to breakfast. He dabbed at the nick on his chin again and hurried out of his room. At the top of the stairs, he leaned over the rail and called down.

"I'll be right there, Mrs. K. Got to do something for a minute." And he went down the hall to his sitting room. There was an old sideboard in there, where he kept odds and ends of stuff. He flung open the door and stared inside. Yes. He thought he had some notepaper and envelopes somewhere. No ink though. If he wanted that, he would have to ask his landlady. A pencil would have to do. There was a stubby one at the back of the cupboard. He blew off the dust, took a piece of paper, and sat down in his armchair to write. Damnation, he needed something to lean on. He jumped up, got a book from the bookcase, and started his letter.

Dear Enid. No, dear sweet, and darling Enid. You were in my arms last night and made me the happiest of men. I am eagerness itself to see you again.

Ugh. What sops. It was embarrassing. Suddenly a memory of Liza came into his mind. He had called her his sweet and his darling, and she had laughed at him. "You don't have to decorate your feelings with silk and bows, Will; plain and unadorned is good enough for me." But Enid had said he was a poet always searching for the right words. He tore the sheet of paper into shreds and began again.

Dear Enid. I look forward to seeing you this evening. You are so beautiful when your long, dark hair is loosened about your shoulders.

He was going to cross that out, but it looked rude as if he had changed his mind. And that was his last sheet. He left it, folded the paper, put it in an envelope, and stowed that in his pocket. As he went to replace the book on the shelf, he saw it was one that Liza had given him for a birthday present. He touched it

269

gently as if it were Liza herself. "Forgive me, dearest," he whispered.

After a rather unappetising breakfast of blood sausage and hard eggs, which he gulped down quickly, he headed out for Dr. Semple's office, which was over on Mutual Street near St. Michael's Cathedral. There was a fancy hotel at the corner of Church Street and Gerrard, and usually a boy earned a few cents by keeping the sidewalk clear of snow so that the hotel guests could have an easy walk to the streetcar when it came by. Sure enough, there was a ragged-looking urchin leaning against the wall, waiting for customers. His hair was cut short, usually a sign of lice, and he'd wrapped a woollen scarf around his head to keep himself warm. His jacket and knickerbockers were patched and grimy and looked as if they had been passed through several other owners before getting to him. There was a strip of wind-reddened skin where the knickerbockers ended and his boots began. Murdoch beckoned to him.

"You, Titch. Come over here. Do you want to do an errand for me? I'd like a letter delivered."

The boy didn't move. He had a hard-looking face, too old for his size, and his eyes were dull, a boy who had already acquired a cynical view of the world.

"Where to?"

"Over on Sackville Street."

270

"What's the dibs?"

"Five cents."

The boy turned down the corners of his mouth. "I'll get twice as much as that if I stay right here. I can do three or four ladies in the time it'll take me to get there and back."

"They're not shopping this early in the morning, so don't give me that guff. I'm making a good offer; take it or leave it. I'll find another lad in a wink."

"I ain't seen nobody else about yet, and you look like a man who's in a hurry."

"Ten cents then and not a penny more."

"All right." The boy approached him and held out his hand for the letter. He didn't have any gloves but was making do with a pair of socks pulled over his fingers like mittens. There was an angry red sore by the side of his mouth.

Murdoch had written Enid's address on the envelope. "Can you read?"

"No."

"Numbers?"

"Yes."

Murdoch pointed to the envelope. "It's number three one four on Sackville Street. The door is brown. Ask for Mrs. Jones. Got that?" Murdoch gave him a light flick on the side of his head. "If I hear you didn't deliver it, I'm going to come back and tan your hide. I'm a police officer. A detective."

The boy stowed the letter inside his jacket with elaborate care. "Is this official business then?"

"Never mind. Just go. Now!"

The arab turned and trotted off.

"Hey, Titch, wait a minute. What's your name?"

"Billy."

"From William?"

"I suppose so."

"That's my name, too, William Murdoch."

"Is it?"

There was something disconcerting in the look he gave Murdoch. There was nothing endearing about this boy.

"Go on then, young Billy. Do your job."

Murdoch watched him out of sight, then continued on his way toward Mutual Street. He was accustomed to the presence of boys who were scrabbling for money by doing what this urchin did or by selling newspapers or holding horses while the owners went visiting or shopping. The truant officers couldn't keep them in school usually because what they earned was needed by the family, almost always too large, often in the care of a woman only. He didn't know why he should be more sympathetic towards one of them today, but he was. He felt miserly that he'd only given the boy ten cents, although he knew most people would only have given him a couple of cents at a time. Murdoch looked up at the sky. The sun had struggled out, and there were blue patches in the sky. He grinned like a fool at the sight. It was amazing what a good and generous mood having loving connections with a woman put a man in.

Patrick Pugh couldn't believe his good luck. He'd been heading down Church Street to make his report when he saw the exchange between Murdoch and the street arab. He slowed his pace, keeping his hat well down over his face, and when Murdoch had continued on, he set off after the boy.

Chapter Thirty-one

Murdoch's knock was answered promptly by an elderly manservant whose manner was so gracious he could easily have been mistaken for the master of the house.

"Good morning, sir."

Murdoch handed him his card. "My name is William Murdoch, and I'm a detective at Number Four Station. I wonder if I might have a word with Dr. Semple on a professional matter."

"Do you have an appointment, sir?"

"No, I'm afraid not."

"Please step inside. I will see if he is available."

Murdoch entered. The hall was well lit with gas wall brackets and a large central chandelier.

The butler soon returned. "Dr. Semple is working in his laboratory, but he can give you a brief interview. We can go in directly. I'll take your hat and coat. Chilly morning, isn't it?"

Murdoch agreed that it was and divested himself of his long coat and his Astrakhan hat, not for the first time feeling somewhat ashamed of the shabbiness of both. Not that the butler with his impeccable manners gave any indication he was aware of this. Murdoch wondered where the man had come from.

After his apparel was duly hung on the coat tree, the butler led the way down the hall and tapped deferentially on a closed door to the right. There were no softening portieres, and the door itself might have suited a castle with its ostentatious brass doorknob and prominent keyhole. There was an unpleasant smell in the air, and for a moment Murdoch feared his sealskin coat had been reeking again. However, he realised this odour was too pungent and too close. It was also more like rotting meat than fish.

"Enter."

Murdoch was ushered into Dr. Semple's laboratory.

The stench of decay was like an assault. A tall, skinny man in a brown Holland smock was standing at a bench with his back to the door. He made a note on a pad of paper and turned to greet Murdoch.

"Good morning, Inspector. Forgive me the informality, but I'm under the gun to get some results and I can't spare you much time." In spite of the words, his tone

275

was friendly. "I won't shake hands either. I've been messing around with cadavers, and you wouldn't want that on your fingers." He waved his hand vaguely. "I suppose the place stinks to high heaven, does it? When you are in here for a while you get used to it. I thought you looked a little taken aback when you came in."

"There is a rather strong odour, I must admit."

"I'm doing a post mortem examination, that's why."

He stepped back and Murdoch saw what his body had shielded. For one brief moment, he thought he was looking at a doll, but then he realised it was an infant. The scalp was pulled down over the face like a red mask revealing the grey convolutions of the brain. The chest cavity was gaping open. The rest of the body was ash white. A male child.

"A young woman is up on a murder charge. Usual story. Silly girl got herself in the family way and was afraid to tell in case she lost her position. The baby must have come early, and she stuffed it into a valise and left it under a tree in the nearby field. She says it was stillborn, but I've got to determine that. It is possible she suffocated it as soon as it came out. There's no milk in the stomach, but the lungs do show some air. That is not necessarily conclusive of course. We know that in some circumstances an infant will breathe while still in the womb. Look, what do you think?"

There was a little heap of what looked like fresh calves' liver on the bench, and the doctor sawed off a piece and dropped it into a glass tank filled with water that was in front of him. The fragment of lung floated for a moment then slowly started to sink to the bottom of the tank. Semple reached into the water and squeezed the tissue between his thumb and forefinger. "See, no air at all. I'm inclined to think the infant didn't breathe. There is some meconium in the intestines, which is typical of stillborns." His voice had the resonance of a man accustomed to lecturing. Murdoch knew the doctor was a demonstrator at the Toronto school of medicine. He was suddenly aware that there were several glass jars on a shelf to the right of them that contained pickled embryos. Semple noticed where he was looking.

"Each of those specimens show a foetus at different stages of development in utero. My little fellow looks to be about six months, which is consistent with what the mother said and with life being unsustainable."

He leaned his knuckles on the bench, lecturer style. "Of course, some women are altogether too cunning and will kill by virtually undetectable means." He illustrated his words by pulling up his own eyelid. "A needle thrust in here will cause death at once, or here." He indicated his lower spine. "However, I see no indication that took place or any suspicion of suffocation or a broken neck."

Murdoch's feelings must have revealed themselves because Semple grinned.

"Beg your pardon. Got carried away for a moment. Too many hours in the lecture room." He cut off another piece of lung and tossed it into the water. This time the tissue hardly floated at all.

"There we go then. That's a relief. I hate being the one to condemn a woman to the gallows unless it's totally certain." He started to wipe his hands on a rag. "Not that a jury will bring in a verdict for hanging. Women get too much sympathy. Pity really," he added ambiguously.

Suddenly, he swivelled around and removed a pile of papers from a high stool.

"Take your weight off your beaters." He patted the stool.

Dr. Semple spoke with a slight Irish brogue and had the typical colouring of a Celt: fair skin, blue eyes, and black hair, which was slicked smooth across his head to hide his premature balding. His moustache was thick and in need of a trim, the ends looking as if he sucked on them in moments of contemplation. He looked about the same age as Murdoch himself.

"Now, Inspector, what can I do for you? You said you had an urgent matter."

"Not inspector, Dr. Semple, merely acting detective. I just wanted to verify a few details of a case at which you were the medical witness."

"And why is that?" asked Semple, and his voice was sharp.

"The accused denies his guilt, and I have agreed to go over the evidence again."

"Have you indeed? That's unusual, isn't it?"

"Yes, sir."

"All right, what was the case?"

"The man is named Henry or Harry Murdoch. He was charged with murder on August four of this year. He has been convicted and is sentenced to hang on Monday."

Semple frowned. "Isn't your name Murdoch, or did I get it wrong? Any relation?"

"The accused is my father, sir. I have only just discovered his situation."

"Bad luck. Not intent on proving we were all wrong, I hope. Waste of time if you are."

He wasn't hostile, just a busy man.

"I have no particular aim except to make sure that all the evidence is, as you say, conclusive." He hesitated but he liked Semple's no-nonsense manner and answered in kind. "As perhaps you can imagine, I would sleep easier if I knew I had done everything I could."

"Quite. What would you like to know from me then?"

"I was hoping you would go over the evidence again with me. Show me exactly why you reached the conclusions you did."

Semple clicked his teeth. "Very well. The Armstrong case is done really." He threw a cloth over the dead baby. "However, I do have to set up an experiment for my class this afternoon. It won't take but a moment."

Most of one wall of the laboratory consisted of long, uncurtained windows. On each side were several wicker

279

cages, which contained two or three sparrows. They weren't moving or attempting to fly around their small prisons but sat on the perches, their heads tucked down into their feathers. Semple opened a cupboard below the bench and removed a bottle labelled CHLORINE. He unscrewed the lid, and the pungent odour made Murdoch cough immediately. Semple poured a capful into an empty beaker and replaced the lid.

"As you just experienced, this gas had a considerable inflammatory effect on the air passages. Too much of it will kill. Don't worry, you only had a whiff. I myself seem to have become impervious to it. People can work in an atmosphere of chlorine with impunity and become immune. They do, however, always lose weight and remain thin. We're not quite sure why that is."

He measured out some water into another beaker, took a syringe from an open case on the bench, and drew up some of the chlorine into the needle.

"Now, I add the water to the two-hundredth part, and we're ready." He laid down the syringe and reached into one of the cages. The sparrows fluttered and chirruped, but he caught one of them and drew it out. "I have to demonstrate how the blood responds to the chlorine. Sorry, little fellow," he said to the bird, who opened its beak silently. With a practised motion, Semple injected the chlorine solution and replaced the creature carefully in the cage. He checked a large clock that was beside him and made a note in his book.

"Should take less than five minutes."

Then he walked across the room to a large metal filing cabinet and pulled open one of the drawers. Murdoch couldn't take his eyes off the sparrow, which was now obviously gasping for air. The other birds shifted along the tree branch out of the way.

"Here we are, *Regina v. Henry Murdoch*."

He turned back to Semple, who had a folder in his hands.

Murdoch heard a soft noise from the cage, and he saw that the bird had fallen to the bottom of the cage and was lying on its side, feet stretched out like a wooden toy. It was dead.

Semple came over and looked at the clock. "Hmm. That didn't take long. Let me just make a note of the time, and then we can go over your file."

Murdoch swivelled the high stool away so he could no longer see the cage.

Chapter Thirty-two

MURDOCH HAD BEEN ABLE TO SEND a telephone message from Dr. Semple's office to say he was coming to the jail, and Harry was waiting for him in the visiting room. For an instant he caught an unguarded expression on his father's face of such despair and darkness that it was like a stab into his own chest. However, Harry smiled up at him.

"Thought you'd never get here, Will."

"I came as soon as I could." He nodded at the guard. "I brought in a couple of plugs if you'd care for one, Mr. Barker."

"I won't say no to that, sir."

Murdoch handed over his little package of Jolly Tar, and the guard tipped his cap. "I'll leave you to your chin wag then. I'm right outside the door if you need me." He left.

Murdoch took another bag from his pocket and gave it to Harry. "I got Bull Durham today."

"That's a good one," Harry said. "Funny thing is, I've almost lost my craving. Never thought that would happen. I'll hold off for a bit." He pushed a piece of drawing paper across the table. "Do you know who this is?"

The pencil sketch was of a woman's head, half in profile, smiling down at a flower she was holding. She was unmistakable.

"It's Mother."

"She's young there, of course. My first sight of her. I forget what she was looking at, so I made it a flower. She was a pretty lass back then. Fair took my heart."

Murdoch had never to his knowledge heard his father make any public declaration of affection for his mother. He could not conceal his astonishment or his disgust. Harry took back the sketch.

"It's writ all over your face what you're thinking. But I did care for her, Will."

"Did you? It might have made her life happier if you had showed it."

Harry didn't react. "I know that and I'm sorry for the way I was." He rubbed at his head with the now familiar gesture. "How many times am I going to have to repeat it?"

Murdoch wanted to snap at him, *A dozen more times?*

283

A hundred? Forever? However, his temper was held in check by the sight of his father's distress.

"Let's get to the matter at hand. I'm here to give you an up-to-date report."

"I can tell it's nothing I haven't heard already."

Murdoch shrugged. "So far nothing new has come to light. I went into the ravine first to get a look around."

"Did the trees talk to you, Will?"

Harry smiled slightly to show he meant this as a joke, and suddenly Murdoch remembered how he'd been teased as a child when he was adamant that he could converse with the trees.

"I'm raising a lass, not a lad," Harry had said.

"I only wish they could. We'd know unequivocally, wouldn't we. However, there is something I'd like to ask you. I'll come back to it in a minute. I met up with Walter Lacey, the hired man . . ."

"Ah yes. He took a scunner to me. That didn't help my case at all."

"I didn't say we were related, just that I was investigating the case privately."

Harry nodded. "Better that way."

"I talked to Newcombe. He didn't add anything. While I was there Mr. Pugh arrived together with Mr. Craig. I understand his son is back to courting Miss Delaney. Newcombe said that her father had forbidden the relationship earlier."

Harry leaned forward. "I hadn't heard that."

284

"I doubt it has much significance. According to the trial report, Miss Craig swore under oath that her father and brother were at home from eight-fifteen that evening and did not leave."

"She could be lying."

"Was that your impression?"

"Frankly, I wasn't paying a whole lot of attention. I might have if I'd known James was after the Delaney girl."

"Let's not go galloping after the fox too soon. Newcombe didn't think James was too chagrined by the father's edict. Miss Delaney apparently was."

"Maybe she met up with her father and quarrelled with him. Damnation, why didn't Clement pursue this? I told you they had all passed verdict on me from the beginning."

"You forget that Mrs. Delaney was on the witness stand. She said both her son and daughter were in the house all evening. She and Miss Delaney were apparently making a quilt together. But I suppose she, too, could be lying to protect her daughter."

He could see Harry wince at his tone. "It isn't out of the question, Will. You seem able to accept that I am lying but not that these women might be."

Murdoch let that pass. "This morning I visited the doctor who conducted the post mortem. Shall we go over his evidence again? First, the bruise on your cheek, the blood on your right shirtsleeve and cuff . . ."

285

"That was from my dog."

Murdoch let that go. Semple had told him they could not distinguish between human and animal blood even with the most powerful microscopes they had. "However, we can distinguish different fibres, and we can tell human and dog hair apart. Look, I'll show you."

He was proud of his microscope, which he assured Murdoch was the best and most up-to-date money could buy. He insisted Murdoch press his eye to the lens while he inserted a slide.

"Here are three different strands of hair. This first one is from a spaniel. The second is from a horse. You can see it is much wider and coarser. The third is human hair, and the transverse lines are much finer."

At this point Semple had paused. "I consider this the most damning piece of evidence I collected. Even though he was in the water, some strands of hair were caught on Delaney's shirt and not washed away. I discovered them, dried them, and magnified them so. This hair, as you can see even with the naked eye, is dark. Henry Murdoch's hair is quite dark. Delaney's is light, grey in fact. But here, look. Under the microscope, you can see that each strand still has the root capsule attached. It suggests to me that the two men did fight and fight viciously, to the extent that Delaney pulled out some of Henry's hair by the roots."

Murdoch related this to his father, who listened quietly. "Yes, he blathered on about that. He kept saying

286

all the evidence, but what did they have when it come down to it? A bruise on my face, blood stains, bits of hair. Could be anybody's."

Harry rubbed his head as vigorously as if he had nits. Murdoch knew he must have appeared in the exact same way while he was in the court, and he could see how unprepossessing he was. It would have been hard to convince a jury he was innocent.

"He showed me the photographs he'd had taken of the dead man. The wounds seemed to indicate that the blows were coming at a downward angle. The assailant was therefore taller than Delaney."

Suddenly Harry thumped his fist on the table. "No, Will, goddamn it! I'm not a total fool. My counsel nailed him on that matter, and he admitted that Delaney might have been pushed to the ground. If he was even on one knee, the blows would have come at that kind of angle. His killer didn't have to be bigger than him. Semple agreed. Did he tell you that, or have you chosen to ignore it?"

In fact, the doctor had told Murdoch of all the possibilities.

He pushed back his chair, walked down the length of the table, and studied the photograph of Her Majesty. With his back to Harry, he said, "As we say in the police world, give me opportunity and motivation and I will show you the criminal. You had both, it seems."

287

"I admit I was in a temper with Delaney, but that doesn't mean you go out and kill the man. We wouldn't have much of a population left if that were the case."

Murdoch came back to his seat. "You have asked me to do everything I can to help you, but how can I?" He met his father's eyes. "You are still lying. Unless you tell me the absolute truth, I will have to put a stop to any further investigations."

"I . . ."

"Of course you had a fight with Delaney. You purposely went into the ravine to wait for him. You had no other reason to be there. When he came along the path, you had an argument during which he struck you on the cheek and quite possibly grabbed you by the hair."

Harry flushed. "That's it then. You think I'm guilty as charged?"

"I didn't say that. I am just asking for some honesty here. Did you or did you not have a fight with Delaney?"

"I don't know!" Harry yelled. He glared at Murdoch for a moment then quickly looked away. "Lately I have had vague recollections. I've thought so much I can hardly tell if they're dreams or real, but I can see his face, him standing over me. I assume he had clobbered me one. After that, it's totally blank. I sort of remember crawling off into the bushes, but that's all. Then there's a man leaning over me telling me Delaney is dead.

288

They made a lot of what I said, but I thought there'd been an accident. I was still in a bad skin. What I said didn't mean anything."

"And this has just come back to you?"

Another pause while Harry considered what to say. "Not just now. I did know it when I was tried, but I'd already denied any fight so I thought it wiser to say nothing." He shrugged. "Didn't seem to make a difference one way or the other."

Murdoch reached for the piece of drawing paper. "Do you mind if I use this?"

"Go ahead."

He took out his fountain pen, reversed the paper, and did a quick sketch.

"Here's the bridge at the bottom of the ravine. Here's the creek and the path that goes to the right. You were found here, Delaney's body was in the water, just there, a few feet up from you. Why was he on that path? His house is the other way. I assume you would have been lying in wait for him at the bridge."

Harry studied the drawing. "I wish I could say I remember, but I don't any more than I just said. We might have been moving and shoving each other, but I don't know."

"There are some other things I'd like to clarify. You accused Delaney of distracting your dog during the match by whistling at him. But he didn't have a whistle on him. He emptied his pockets."

289

"Ah, that one I am clear about. There are special dog whistles called mouth whistles. They use them for sheepdogs in Scotland. They're made of bone, triangular shaped, quite small. Real easy to conceal. I know he distracted Havoc."

"Could it have been one of the others?"

"Not likely. Flash was the one to beat. One more rat and we would have won the match. That's when he did it."

"All right. We'll let that go for now. Did you let Havoc out of his box when you went into the ravine?"

"What?"

"Newcombe says you put the dog in a box and left the tavern. But Mr. Pugh said Havoc was on the loose and barking at him, which was how he discovered you."

"I have no recollection. Sometimes Havoc has got out. He's a cunning little fellow. Is it important?"

"Probably not. Just another loose end I'm trying to tie up."

Harry actually glanced with admiration at his son. "You're thorough, Will. I thought you would be. You take after me in that regard. Did you locate the dog, by the way?"

"Yes, Newcombe was looking after him. He's currently with somebody I know. A dog fancier."

"I'm glad to hear it."

Harry looked as if he was about to discuss the dog's future. Murdoch didn't want to get into what might possibly happen to Havoc, and he moved on quickly.

"The money that was gone from Delaney's pouch. Any more vague recollections about that you haven't mentioned?"

"None."

"You're sure you didn't take back what you considered your rightful money?"

"If I did, where is it?" Harry gave a wry smile. "Even full to the gills, I can't see myself taking money then letting it blow away in the wind."

"You could have hidden it."

"I don't believe I was capable of that much effort. But I was thinking about that, too. What's to say Delaney didn't hand over some of his bills before he met up with me?"

"Nobody came forward."

"They wouldn't, would they, if they was the one who killed him?"

"In which case the encounter would have occurred after yours."

Harry rubbed his head again. "Right. I'm not thinking straight. But say this unknown somebody felt cheated like I did. He confronts Delaney and demands money. Delaney hands over something but not enough. More argument and this person clobbers him, then rolls his body into the creek."

"Any candidates? You were the one at the match. Who was the sore loser? Other than you?"

291

"Nobody lost too much, except me and Pugh. He coughed up the most. He wasn't complaining, mind, but he could have been hiding it."

"He has a solid alibi. He was with Newcombe the entire time."

Harry sighed. "We're going round in circles."

"I have put somebody on the man White's track. As you know, he too has an alibi. He went with the Craigs."

"I heard that, but what's to say he didn't double back and follow Delaney?"

"Why would he? He didn't lose money."

"He didn't win either. Maybe he had grand expectations. I wasn't the only one tossing back brew. If he was all hotted up, he could have gone after Delaney. Especially if he believed me that Delaney was a cheat."

"We'll know better when we find him. If we do."

Harry reached for the bag of tobacco and began to stuff the bowl of his pipe. Murdoch waited while he lit up and drew. When he spoke his voice was neutral, but Murdoch knew that was an effort.

"You sound as if you've given up."

"That implies I ever started. I don't know if that is the case."

292

Harry put his pipe on the table and pushed back his chair. "I can't just sit here while you gloat over me, Will. If you want to come back, I'd be glad. If you don't . . ." He didn't finish, but he stood up ready to go to the door.

Murdoch could feel his face going hot. It was true what his father said. He'd been relishing this strange experience of power over the man who had created so much terror around him. But he was also ashamed of himself. It was like fighting a cripple. Harry could not retaliate. His only hope lay with his son.

"Wait!"

Harry turned around.

"I apologise. I realise you have been relying on me."

"Indeed I have."

"Frankly, I don't know what the truth is, but I promise you I will do what I can to find out."

Harry returned to the table, reached over, and squeezed Murdoch's shoulder.

"I'm grateful, Will. I don't know anybody I'd trust more than you."

Briefly, Murdoch patted his father's hand. He felt almost unbearably awkward with this new softness.

The guard entered. "We've got to go to the yard, Harry."

"I'll come back as soon as I can," said Murdoch.

Barker took Harry's arm and led him out of the room. Murdoch remained where he was.

Chapter Thirty-three

MURDOCH MADE HIS WAY HOME in what could only be described as a trance. He was half aware that the wind was cutting and there weren't many people abroad, but as he was turning onto Ontario Street he realised he had no recollection of getting there. He was like an old horse who follows the same route back to the stable without need of guidance.

"Mr. Murdoch! Mr. Murdoch, wait up a minute!"

The voice was behind him, and he turned to see Samuel Quinn hurrying down the street. He had two dogs on leashes trotting beside him. Havoc gave no sign of recognition, but Princess was flamboyantly happy to see him, letting out her high-pitched yips. Murdoch stopped to allow them to catch up to him and held out his hand to the hound who was straining at her leash in her eagerness.

"Hello, Princess, hello."

She showered soppy kisses on his face.

"Enough, old girl. I'm going to drown." He pushed her away and managed to reach Havoc. He was able to give him a quick scratch on the head before the dog ducked away. There was the lifting of the lip and a growl, but to Murdoch it looked more perfunctory than before.

"How's he doing?" he asked Quinn.

"Good. The abscess is healing nicely. Princess is teaching him some manners, and he's the better for it. Aren't you, boyo?"

He bent down and playfully tapped the dog on the nose. Havoc wagged his tail with pleasure.

"Hey. He doesn't do that with me," said Murdoch.

"He will. He just has to get to know you. He likes to play."

Quinn pulled out the remnants of a leather glove from his pocket and dangled it in front of Havoc's face. The dog pounced on it, and they had a little tugging match.

"Out!" said Quinn, and Havoc dropped his end of the glove at once. His eyes were bright, and his tail wagged wildly. Princess, in the meantime, had seized the opportunity to give Murdoch's boots and trouser bottoms a minute inspection. Quinn put the glove back in his pocket. "I'm glad to have caught you, Mr. Murdoch. I have some interesting information for you."

295

In spite of himself, Murdoch felt a surge of excitement.

"Come on in then."

Dogs in tow, Quinn followed him into the house. Mrs. Kitchen came bustling out of the kitchen to greet them.

"My, my, what sweet dogs."

"Mrs. Kitchen, this is Mr. Quinn. You've heard me mention him."

"How do you do, ma'am," said Quinn, with an old-fashioned bow that obviously won Beatrice over immediately.

"This wicked hound is the famous Princess, and the piece of hearth rug is Havoc," Murdoch continued.

"Say hello," said Quinn to his dog, and Princess sat obediently and held out her paw. Mrs. Kitchen laughed and shook it.

"Could I impose on you for a pot of tea, Mrs. K.? And some biscuits, if you have any."

It might have been his imagination, but Samuel looked peckish. His pockmarked face was reddened by the cold, giving him a rather ferocious expression that was quite at odds with his cheerful nature.

"You can go into the parlour," said Mrs. Kitchen. "You both look perished, if you don't mind my saying so. Why don't I take the dogs to the kitchen and give them a biscuit."

"Thank you, ma'am, but I do warn you, Princess here is a bottomless pit."

The hound wagged her tail on hearing her name but seemed to recognise a benefactor when she saw one and trotted after Mrs. K. down the hall. Havoc went with her.

"Give me your coat and hat, Mr. Quinn," said Murdoch.

Quinn unwrapped his long muffler and unthinkingly wiped his nose on his jacket sleeve.

"Cold out there."

Murdoch ushered him into the parlour, which was cheery with the fire and lit lamps. Quinn perched on the nearest chair and launched into his report.

"I asked around like you said, Mr. Murdoch, and I hit gold, wood, and you might say, tin."

"Hold on a minute, let me write this down." Murdoch took out his notebook and fountain pen. "Go on, if you please."

"Wood first. That is to say, the plain unvarnished." He ticked off on his fingers as he spoke. "First, the grey pugs belong to an English gentleman and his son. They haven't been here too long, but they play when they can. Good dogs, nothing special. Sometimes they win; sometimes they don't. Owners never wager too high. Steady is the word. No whispers about them so far. The Manchesters, Flash and Tripper, are high dogs. Everybody who's in the know wants a whelp from them. Newcombe is well known in the Fancy, and is trusted by them that don't trust many."

297

"What's the tittle-tattle on John Delaney? Was he likely to cheat? Distract a dog that was about to win the match?"

Quinn considered the question carefully, an important one in the gaming circuit.

"His feist was so damn good, he never needed to duck. Then sometimes that brings its own trouble; no man likes to be knocked off his perch. Mr. Murdoch, your, er, your father, was recent here, too. Good dog but . . ."

He hesitated.

"Go on, you won't offend me. What did he say about Harry?"

"Bad loser. Wagered too high a lot of the time, but his dog is a game feist and he did get money back often enough."

Mrs. Kitchen entered at that moment with a tea tray, and he waited while she busied herself putting out the cups and saucers and tea paraphernalia.

"The scones just came out of the oven. Let me know if you need anything else," she said, and left them alone.

Quinn bit into one of the hot cakes that she had brought. Murdoch had been right, he was hungry, but first he tasted the cake with professional interest.

"A little heavy on the baking soda," he said, but nevertheless crammed the cake into his mouth. Murdoch waited until he had room to continue and sipped at his own cup of tea, welcoming the strong, sweet brew. He felt as if a chunk of ice was sitting in his stomach.

"Good, Sam. Please go on."

"Tin next then. A little disappointing, I'm afraid. This Mr. White. My chum knew of him at once. Game little feist, he runs. He's a swell for sure, from the city, and my friend says he'd lay odds of two to one he's in the law profession. Odds of four to one, he's a physician, and odds of ten to one, he's a banker. He uses various names, White, Green, Brown." Quinn grinned. "Not too imaginative, is he? According to my pal, he's a gambling man bar none. He'd wager on anything, horses, dogs, fleas, if they were running." Quinn flicked crumbs off his moustache and reached for another cake. "He's not canny though and loses a lot of money. Doesn't seem to stop him, so he must be born in the silver. Unfortunately, my chum didn't know what his real name is or where he can be found."

"Nothing more than that?"

"'Fraid not." Quinn frowned, trying to come up with something else, but there wasn't anything. "Sorry."

"That's all right. It gives me something to go on. I can check registries. So what was the gold?"

Quinn leaned forward, his hands on his knees.

"My chum has a brother who is a breeder. Not big, just two bitches and one male. Bulldogs. According to brother, in the summer this cull approached him. Said that he was a writer for a newspaper in America, and he was writing an article about bulldogs. He wanted to see how they reacted to rats, for instance, and could he

299

hire his dog. 'Oh no,' says brother, 'you're not having my prize dog to get all bit up and infected by no rats.' 'Oh no,' says the man. 'First, he's no prize.' Too true, Mr. Murdoch. 'Second, I'll pay for any damages that might be incurred, plus a good sum for taking him for the day.' And it was a good sum; brother couldn't turn it down. So off they go and the dog – Gargoyle is his name, ugly beast – is returned safe and sound to brother, but the next day not as promised. 'Got delayed,' says the cove, and coughed up more dosh. 'Did you get what you wanted?' asks brother. 'Unfortunately, I did not,' says the cove. 'Well, I told you right off he wasn't a fighter,' says brother. 'Give him a bear and he'll go to the death, but he ain't interested in rodents.' The cove didn't answer to that. 'Won't you be writing your article now?' asked brother. 'No, I won't' is the reply, 'but here's an extra dollar for your troubles and one more if you keep all this under your hat. Pride, don't you know.' Brother didn't see what was shameful about taking in a dog that wouldn't do his stuff, but it takes all sorts to make a stew, as we say."

"Did this man give a name?"

"He did and he didn't. Brother has found it wiser to forget any information given out to him in certain circumstances."

"In other words, he wouldn't say what the man's name was."

"That's it."

Murdoch tapped the tips of his fingers together. "When did all this hiring and returning take place?"

"Last summer. Early August. Don't know which day exactly, but I did go and speak to brother myself and near as he could remember it was the first Sunday in the month."

"Could he describe this man? Or is that also something he won't do?"

"He didn't mind that. Said he was a nondescript sort of fellow. Not too tall, quite stout, maybe just past thirty. Said it was hard to tell if he was a workingman or not. Softish hands but his clothes were quite decent."

"He didn't mention a streak of white hair in front?"

"No. As I said, he was hard put to describe the man at all. 'Bland as blancmange' was the very words he used. Except for one thing . . . he had the tip of his middle finger missing. Left hand. Said he'd got it caught in a rat trap."

Murdoch frowned. "Did Pugh get somebody to negotiate for him, I wonder? He definitely told Newcombe the dog was his. He said he'd had him two weeks."

"Well, that's a nailer. Brother would never part with that cur. Not for any price. Hire him out, yes; sell, no." Quinn gulped down his tea. "I'll tell you what I think, Mr. Murdoch. If you would like my opinion, that is."

"I would indeed."

"There's always some silly culls who want to be one of the Fancy no matter what, but they don't really care to do the work: the breeding and the training. It's not just

301

instinct, you know. You have to get the dogs moving faster than they would normally, and they have to ignore the rats they've killed. That's not natural to a terrier. Fellows like this one, they're the kind who'd enter a donkey in the Queen's Plate with the Thoroughbreds just so they could say they've done it. Anyway, that's my view."

"You're probably right. He certainly didn't seem to mind that he lost every round. I suppose his story to your friend could also be true."

"Actually, brother didn't believe that at all. He said he'd lay even money that was just thrown out to give the whore a hat."

"Beg pardon?"

"Sorry, Mr. Murdoch. I meant, to make things look more respectable than they are." He wiped his lips with his fingers and replaced the cup and saucer on the trolley. "I've got to get going. I'm due in at noontime."

"Thank you very much, Sam. I much appreciate your help."

"Nothing to it. A raisin, we might say, in the cake. I owe you my life, don't forget. What do you think you'll do now?"

"I'm not a gambling man, but I'm going to go with the best odds. If your friend thinks Mr. White is in the legal profession, I'll start there. And I assume the best place to find a lawyer is in a court of law."

Quinn slapped himself on the leg. "The Rossin is not too far from the courthouse. Come by and see me.

If you want to splurge and have a meal, make sure you ask for Joseph for your waiter. I'll tip him off. He owes me a few favours. He'll keep the cost down."

"Thank you, Sam. I think what I'll do is ask Vince Newcombe of the Manchester if he'll accompany me. He knows what White looks like."

"That is savvy thinking." Quinn got to his feet. "Time waits for no man, least of all a baker. No, stay where you are. I'll let myself out. I'll just collect the dogs. Don't worry about Havoc. You've got enough on your plate, and it's not cakes, if you don't mind my joke. I'll bring him back when he's better. You can call on me at any time for consultation if you need to."

He shook hands heartily and left. Murdoch sat for a moment staring into the fire, watching the flames dip and dance around the coals. He felt as if he was not making progress at all. The information about Pugh and the hired dog didn't seem relevant. On the other hand, he knew that in any investigation, one of the best ways to proceed was to follow the lies, the way a hound follows spoor. You were bound to end up with some kind of prize.

He stood up, fighting off a feeling of desperation. He didn't have too much to go on. One way or the other, he wanted to know for certain if his father was John Delaney's killer. No, "wanted" was too pallid a word. He *had* to know.

303

Chapter Thirty-four

THEY WERE ALL GROUPED AROUND Margaret's bedside as if it were her deathbed. She was propped up on her cushions, her eyes closed. Adelia looked at the gaunt face, the distorted hands that were resting on the hot water bottle lying on the quilt. How she wished her father would stop maintaining the fiction that Margaret was an active participant in family affairs. For many years now she had increasingly retreated into a world of her own, driven by unremitting pain and the dependency she had developed on her opiates. She was very different from the pretty, vivacious woman that Adelia remembered from her childhood.

On the bedside table there was a delicate, painted porcelain lamp, which had started to smoke badly. Charles stopped in mid-sentence to stare at it.

"The chimney needs a good wash, Carmel," he said in a mild voice.

"So I see," replied his sister-in-law. She didn't add a complaint about how much work she had to do, but the reproach was clearly there in her voice. She was seated on the other side of the bed, across from Adelia, who avoided looking at her as much as possible. Carmel was Margaret's younger sister by six years. She was inclined to be stout, and her light brown hair was turning mouse grey. Whatever resemblance there may have once been between the sisters was long vanished, except in the colour of their eyes, which were a peculiar green-blue. Adelia thought that her aunt had been complimented far too often on her fine eyes when she was younger because she still frequently and inappropriately cast flirtatious glances at any person in trousers who came to call. As she was so fond of saying, she could have had her choice of several suitors but had sacrificed the pleasures of matrimony for the duty of family loyalty. When Margaret had become debilitated by severe arthritis when she was less than forty years old, Carmel had come to nurse her and take care of her poor children and husband. She had stayed ever since.

"Perhaps you could take charge of cleaning the lamps, Adelia. It would help lighten your aunt's burden," said Charles.

"No, Brother-in-law, I wouldn't dream of it. My niece has plenty to do, and she is always willing to help me if I ask."

305

Adelia flushed. It was not true what her aunt said. She hated doing housework and never helped out with a good grace. She preferred to spend her days practising her recitation pieces. Besides, she knew Aunt Carmel was kind only in front of her father.

"Very well, then let us recap the situation and discuss the various choices that are before us," said Charles.

Still stirred by the previous remarks, Adelia spoke with unusual directness. "I thought you told us we had no choices, Papa."

He waved his hand impatiently. He didn't like to be interrupted in his judiciary.

"We'll see, we'll see. Now, James, recount your tale again."

Craig Junior had brought in a dish of oysters and his after-lunch glass of port. He took a gulp before he answered.

"I was in the music room, as Mrs. Delaney insists on calling it, accompanying Miss Kate on my flute when he came in. He said he was with Newcombe and had come to see the dog, but I knew him right away." James looked slightly discomfited. "He was in court at the same time I was. He's not a man you forget easily."

306   "Oh, James, what trouble you caused us," said Adelia.

Her father held up a warning finger. "Enough has been said on that topic. I believe James learned his lesson."

Adelia's assertiveness disappeared, as short lived as a struck match.

"You are certain this officer didn't recognise you?" asked Carmel.

James hesitated. "I can't be absolutely sure. He acted as if he didn't, but I thought there was something there when he first saw me."

"And you gave no indication yourself?"

James grinned. "Not a wink. Mr. Irving himself could not have done better."

"If he was not passing by innocently as he claims, why was he there?" asked Adelia, her voice low.

"I wish you would speak up, Addie," said her brother with considerable irritation. "We have to strain to hear you all the time. It's most aggravating."

"Adelia's question is most pertinent," interrupted Charles. "In fact, it is *the* question. Why indeed is a policeman paying a visit to the Delaneys at this late date?"

Margaret opened her eyes. "Charles, do we have to move again?"

"I am not sure, dearest. We are discussing the matter at this moment."

She turned her head, wincing at the pain of the movement. "If so, I would like to go where it is warm."

"I know, my sweeting. We will, of course, take that into account."

307

Craig continued, his voice measured and pensive as if he were contemplating a fine point of philosophy as he had done when he was a student at Oxford.

"The answer to the question is that we do not know at present why he was there. Does he have Newcombe under observation? A trifling matter of keeping a gaming house? Or is it more sinister? Does it involve us?"

"We can't assume that, Papa," said Adelia. "Surely he cannot know. I beg you not to make us move again. I have been preparing for my Christmas recital. I really cannot bear the thought of leaving right now." Her voice was shaky with held back tears, and Craig frowned.

"You must not be selfish, Adelia. There are others to consider. Your mother would benefit from being in a warm climate, Florida perhaps. Moreover, we cannot risk that, in fact, this officer is on our trail. Do you agree, James?"

"I think we must. If it is a false alarm, we can always return."

"Carmel?"

"I suppose so. We really have no choice as I see it."

"Precisely."

Charles leaned over and patted his daughter's arm.

"Don't fret, child. We won't go all at once. That would look very strange. I am suggesting that James and I leave immediately. We will announce that my mother is very ill. Margaret, I'm afraid you will have to stay here until we know how the land lies. But I do promise you at the very least a long holiday in the sun in the new year."

"Thank you," murmured his wife. She appeared to be drifting into sleep.

"You can't go alone," said Carmel. "You are both as helpless as newborn lambs when it comes to looking after yourselves. I will come with you. Adelia is quite accustomed to taking care of her mother."

Craig beamed at his sister-in-law. "How generous of you, Carmel. That would certainly be the best arrangement. Margaret won't have to be disturbed at this time, and Adelia can go to her recital. Is that agreeable with you, child?"

Adelia's hands were clasped tightly in her lap, but she had had too many years of training to reveal what she felt, how resentful she actually was, and underneath that how hurt.

"I'm sorry you won't see me perform," she said.

Craig stood up and bent over her to place a kiss on the top of her head.

"And I know I am speaking for all of us when I say that we, too, are sorry. You must give us a private demonstration."

"Yes, Papa."

"That's settled then. James, will you go down to the railway station at once and make arrangements."

309

"Yes, Papa."

Adelia looked up at her brother. "And what will you say to poor Kate Delaney? She had already gone into one decline because of you. Will you send her to her grave now?"

James laughed. "Don't be so melodramatic, Addie. I will write her a tender note informing her that my beloved grandmother in America is desperately ill, and I am accompanying my father to her bedside. Shortly, dear grandmother will recover some of her health but be precarious. I will write letters of increasing scarcity, but eventually I will inform Kate that another has won my heart and that will be the end of that."

"No, you won't," said Craig, his voice sharp. "One letter to say we are leaving, and that's it. Letters can be traced."

"Yes, of course. Sorry, Papa."

"How can you be so callous, James?" Adelia burst out. "You break their hearts like a boy smashes robins' eggs just to see what's inside."

"My, my, don't tell me you have become attached to somebody, Leila? Is that really why you are riding me so? Has Mr. Pugh won your heart? He has, I see. Look how she blushes, Papa."

Craig scrutinised his daughter. "Is that the case, Adelia? Is that why you are being so obdurate?"

"No, Papa. I am upset that my brother has developed the morals of a tom cat."

James burst out laughing, rather pleased with her words. "She's fibbing, Papa. She is in an amour with the cheeky Mr. Pugh."

Adelia didn't respond, but her knuckles had turned white with the pressure of her grip.

Craig spoke soothingly. "We really don't have a choice, Adelia. It is not impossible that this officer recognised your brother. What if he pursued the matter? What would happen to your mother if we were ever to be discovered and prosecuted? How could she face years of her beloved husband and son incarcerated? And don't forget, my child, disagreeable as it is to your nunlike soul, you also are implicated. You don't want to be in the Mercer, I assume, with women who are of the very foulest kind."

He always used this elaborate language, and Adelia thought it was like gold braid on a filthy coat. She stared at her own thin, pale fingers and hated him with all her heart.

"Very well then. James and I will go on the first train. We will head to Chicago and will send you a telegram to the post office, the usual code."

"Are you going to leave the plates here?" asked Adelia.

"Of course. Given that this policeman might be on to us, it would be most foolish for James or I to carry them with us."

"What if they demand to search the premises?" 311

"They are well hidden in the usual place and will never be found. In the highly unlikely event that they are, you all will plead complete ignorance. Not a hint;

not the slightest deviation. Do I make myself quite clear, Adelia?"

She nodded, sullenly.

"I will send you word when it is safe to move them."

"Do we have enough money to live on?" asked Carmel.

"For a while." Craig sipped again on his wine. "But I am thinking it is time one of my children made an advantageous match. A wealthy American heiress, for instance. What do you say to that, James?"

His son shrugged. "All the same to me. As long as she's pretty and not a bore, I'll marry her. The problem is we haven't stayed long enough in any one place for me to court anybody."

"I haven't noticed that to hinder you, James. You seem capable of cementing a friendship with quite amazing rapidity as far as I can tell." He looked over at his daughter. "We won't talk about it now, Adelia, but you must start to consider your duty to your own flesh and blood. You are an attractive girl when you want to be. Next year I want you going out in society much more than you do. As the poet says, why be 'a violet born to blush unseen . . . on the desert air'?"

"What about Aunt Carmel?" burst out Adelia. "She's still single. She could marry a rich widower."

"Don't be silly, child. Carmel has long given up such notions. Isn't that so, Sister-in-law?"

312

"Long ago, Brother Charles. I have no other wish but to tend to my sister and her children until the time I am no longer needed."

The lie sat in the air, thick and cloying as the smoke from the oil lamp. Adelia felt as if she was choking.

Chapter Thirty-five

ALMOST AT A TROT, Murdoch headed over to Church Street where he could catch a northbound streetcar. He was also anxious to talk to young Billy. The lad was at the same spot, and when he saw Murdoch he called out.

"More letters for me, Mister?"

"No. I just want to make sure you delivered the one I gave you."

"I did. No gammon. I did exactly what you asked." He grinned cheekily. "If I told you how she was, will you give me another nickel?"

"Maybe. Depends if it's worth it. But the truth only. No fibbing. Was she pleased?"

"She was and she wasn't. When I said the letter was from you, she looked alarmed. You know, as if you was going to write something bad that she didn't want to hear. Then she stood there and read it and she looked happy; then she looked sad again."

Billy was suiting his facial expressions to his words so that the contortions made Murdoch laugh even though he didn't like it that Enid had looked sad.

"Did she say anything?"

"She thanked me kindly for bringing the letter. She talks in a funny way, doesn't she? Like she's singing. 'Thank you, young man. I am obliged to you.'" He gave such a perfect imitation of Enid's Welsh accent that Murdoch laughed again.

"Hey, mind your manners, fellow."

The arab was studying him shrewdly. "I should tell you, Mr. Murdoch, you've got a rival, a masher."

"What are you talking about?"

"'S true. He must have seen you give me the note. I hardly got round the corner there when he was on me. He offered me twenty-five cents if I'd tell him who you were."

"And did you?"

"Not me. 'Why do you want to know?' I asks." He squinted up at Murdoch. "Shall I tell you what he says?"

"You'd better!"

"All right, you don't need to blow. He says, 'Because I have reason to believe that man is of a suspicious character, and if you are carrying a letter for him it could get you in trouble with the law.'"

315

"What! Who the hell was this fellow?"

"I told you, he's trying to shove you out with your lady. That was just guff he was giving me about suspicious character."

Murdoch frowned. "Did you tell him my name?"

"'Course I did. I says, 'You've got it all wrong, Mister. He's the law himself. He's a Detective, name of Murdoch.'"

The boy was grinning at Murdoch triumphantly.

"Get on with it, Billy, for the Lord's sake."

"That stops him right in his tracks. 'Can I have a peek at the note?' he asks, which was when I knew he was trying to move in on your lady. 'Not a chance,' says me. 'This is private for her eyes only.' 'Very well,' he says, 'I am mistook in my suspicions,' and off he goes."

Murdoch stared at the boy, who immediately shifted his glance.

"You're a little liar. You showed him the letter, didn't you?"

Billy flinched away from the raised hand. "No, I didn't. I swear, Mister."

Murdoch stepped back, ashamed of his sudden temper.

"Can you describe him to me?"

"He wasn't anything special. Not as tall as you. Brown moustache. He had on one of those waterproofs with a cape. He wasn't no swell, but he didn't look hard up either. Spoke sort of soft." The boy regarded Murdoch anxiously. "That's all I noticed, honest."

"You were probably staring at his money, that's why."

Billy flushed and once again, Murdoch felt ashamed of himself. He cuffed the boy lightly on his arm.

"It's all right. I'd be the same if I was in your shoes."

"I just remembered something," Billy said. "He took off his glove to pay me, and he had the top of his finger missing. This one."

He held up the middle finger of his left hand. Murdoch stared at the boy.

"You're not having me on, are you?"

"No, sir. I swear that's what I saw. This finger."

"All right, I believe you. If he comes and talks to you again, let me know at once. You can come to the station. They'll take down a message. Don't look so nervous. If you've got a clean conscience, nothing will happen to you." Murdoch fished another couple of pennies out of his pocket. "Here. Add that to your haul."

At that moment a carriage stopped at the kerb, and an elderly man leaned out of the window, snapping his fingers at the lad to clear a path to the hotel door.

"Yes, sir. Here we go."

Billy jumped to the command, and Murdoch left him to it and continued on his way. Unless there had been an epidemic of amputations of middle fingers in the city, he assumed this man was the same one who had negotiated hiring Gargoyle for Mr. Pugh. Sam Quinn must have let it leak out why he was inquiring. Trying to stop gossip among the Fancy was as impossible as trying to stop fleas hopping from dog to dog.

He wondered how the man had tracked him down. It was also embarrassing to think of another man reading his tenderest thoughts, but there was little doubt the boy had shown him the letter. How could he resist such an offer when it meant a night's lodging to him? On the other hand, maybe it was strictly a coincidence about the dogs, and this man was truly a rival. As far as he knew, Enid had had no callers all the while she lived at the Kitchens', and it seemed unlikely. So either the "bland as blancmange" stranger was interested in knowing about Murdoch because he was Enid's suitor or because he was investigating the Delaney case. Both possibilities troubled him.

Chapter Thirty-six

THE COURTHOUSE FOYER was full of hazy blue smoke as many of the spectators were taking advantage of an adjournment to have a pipe or cigar.

"Let's look at the notice board," said Newcombe, and he forged a path through the crowd to one of the massive concrete pillars in the centre of the foyer where the boards were fixed. In spite of his attempt to honour the gravity of the situation, the innkeeper was enjoying himself. He had accepted Murdoch's invitation with alacrity, declaring it was not often he got to go down to the city.

"There's a case in courtroom A, which is that one to the right. We might as well start there."

They shoved through the mass of people and went into the courtroom.

"Over here. There's space in the third row, next to the prisoner's box."

Murdoch followed close behind, and they slid into the bench. Murdoch looked around. The room could not in any way be termed majestic with its unadorned walls and plain wooden benches. The best feature was the tall windows that faced onto Adelaide Street on the north side and Toronto Street on the west. There was a new electric light hanging from the ceiling, but it was pale against the sunlight that was coming through the windows. The winter sun was putting in an appearance.

"Oi, them's our seats," boomed somebody behind them. Two men, one of them big and wide-shouldered, were glaring at them. Newcombe was not in the least intimidated. "Finders keepers," he said, cheerily. The man who had the weather-beaten face of a teamster looked as if he was about to make an issue of it, but fortunately, at that moment a woman on the end of the row stood up and relinquished her place.

"You can sit here. I'm leaving."

"You haven't heard the verdict yet," said another spectator.

She shrugged. "He'll get off. They always do."

With a little angry swish of her skirts, she left.

"Anybody want to take odds on it? Two to one, Not Guilty," said one of the men, a sharp-nosed fellow who looked as if he'd make a wager on his own mother's death hour if somebody would take him up on it.

"Done," said another man in front of him. There were no other takers, but a lot of reluctant shuffling as the row made room for the large man who had challenged Newcombe.

Murdoch was squashed between a stout, rosy-cheeked woman on his left and Newcombe on his right. The woman's hat was so wide it was virtually brushing his cheek, and he felt sorry for the man seated behind her who, he could see, was bobbing back and forth to peer around her.

Murdoch had appeared as a witness on a few occasions in the court; and because he knew there was a risk of being recognised, he'd taken the precaution of wearing his brown fedora instead of his Astrakhan cap, and he had it pulled well down over his forehead. His muffler was up around his cheeks. He knew that many of the spectators were regular visitors, especially if the case was sensational, as he gathered this one was. All around him was the same air of anticipation and excitement you'd find at a music hall show just before the curtain went up. Nobody dared spit or break open nuts because of the court constable observing them, but they would have if they could.

Murdoch pulled off his gloves and wiped his forehead under the brim of his hat. He was already sweating. The courtroom was heated by a large woodstove, and with so many people in their winter clothes, all jammed together, it was stifling. He wasn't sure he could maintain his cover much longer.

Newcombe nudged him. "We're starting," he said.

The door at the far end of the room opened, and the clerk of the court entered, a tiny, bespectacled man in sombre black. A tall, shambling sort of man in the black suit and white collar and tie of a barrister followed him.

"My, oh, my," exclaimed Newcombe. "Look who it isn't." He nodded in the direction of the lawyer. "It's Mr. Clement himself. He was Harry Murdoch's counsel."

Murdoch's heart thumped, and he stretched to get a better look at the man. Harry had spoken of him with some contempt, and Murdoch could understand why. Clement's appearance was not impressive. He was beardless but his side whiskers were long and wispy, and the hair that was dragged across the crown of his head in a futile attempt to hide his baldness was greasy. His black gown didn't fit him well, as if it were on loan from a shorter man. He took his seat at the lawyers' table, which faced the jury section, and began to riffle through the papers.

Unobtrusively, a man came down the centre aisle from the back of the courtroom and stepped into the prisoner's box, which was next to them. Murdoch assumed this was the accused in the case. He must have been granted bail and was therefore under his own recognisance to show up for his trial. He was a trim-looking man, well-dressed in a dark grey morning suit and sober cravat. In contrast to his counsel, his hair and beard were neat. He was close enough for Murdoch to get a whiff of his pomade.

The stout woman prodded Murdoch in the ribs with her elbow. "That's the complainer. The woman in the brown cape."

She indicated the bench behind Mr. Clement. The woman was clearly under a strain, fiddling with her hair, repetitiously tucking strands up beneath her wide-brimmed hat. It was rather hard to place her, not quite respectable with a too lavishly beribboned hat, but her clothes were decent enough.

The door facing them opened yet again and in strode two more barristers. Newcombe thumped Murdoch in his excitement.

"Bull's-eye, first time out. It's him. The one in front. It's our man White."

The teamster heard this of course, and he snorted with the contempt of those in the know for the ignorant.

"No, it's not. That's Mr. Blackstock. He's the junior defending counsel."

Murdoch glanced at Newcombe for confirmation, and the innkeeper nodded. "That's the one we want all right. No matter what he's calling himself, there's no mistake." The men were seated at the same table.

"Are he and Clement partners then?"

The teamster answered for Newcombe. "Yes they are, although Mr. Blackstock senior is the one who does most of the questioning. Sharp as a tack he is. Clement seems half asleep."

323

Newcombe shook his 'head. "Very strange. There wasn't a whisker to be seen of Mr. Blackstock cum White at the trial."

"What trial are you talking about?" interrupted his neighbour. "I've seen most of them. I can't work because I hurt my back. I come here whenever I can; gives me something to do."

Murdoch thought he'd throw some bread on the water and see where it floated.

"Did you see the case of *Regina v. Henry Murdoch*? He was charged with the murder of John Delaney up in the Shaftesbury Road ravine this past August. Mr. Clement was his defence counsel."

"Murdoch? Is he a tall scrawny fellow, no hair on his head to speak of? Glum looking?"

"Yes, I suppose that would describe him," said Murdoch.

"I did watch that case." He stared at the innkeeper. "Hey, now that I take a closer gander at you, you were one of the witnesses. You're a publican." He tapped the side of his nose with his forefinger. "I never forget a face."

"Yes, that's me, Vincent Newcombe. And who are you?"

"George Rogerson, at your service. And who's your friend?"

"Williams," answered Murdoch.

"Have we met before? You look familiar as well. Were you a witness?"

"No, I don't think we've met. I hear that all the time. I must have a common sort of mug."

They shook hands all round.

"Why were you asking after the Murdoch case?"

"Just curious. I understand there was doubt as to whether he was guilty or not."

Rogerson shrugged. "Don't know where you get that from. Open and shut. I prefer a case that's got a bit of drama to it. You know, is this poor man wrongfully accused? Yes he is, no he isn't, well make up your mind because there's a rope necklace to be fitted. But that fellow was a goner from the start. Got himself drunk as a lord then bashed the man he thought had cheated him. Mark my words, it happens all the time. He should have pleaded manslaughter. He'd have got a lighter sentence."

Murdoch felt an unreasonable desire to knock the knowing look off Mr. Rogerson's face.

"Did Mr. Clement do a good job, would you say?"

"Not bad considering he didn't have much to work with. But the prosecutor was better. A Mr. Greene. He'll go far, that young man. Hungry as a shark for advancement. And jurors respect him. Don't talk down to them or get too familiar. Mr. Clement mumbles, which in my opinion is bad for a barrister. Makes you think he doesn't know what he's talking about."

325

Mr. Blackstock alias White was at the prisoner's box talking to his client. He was medium height, young to be a barrister, with dark, full hair and a luxuriant moustache. He ignored the spectators as if they didn't exist, shook hands with the defendant, and sat down beside Mr. Clement. Murdoch knew Newcombe was not mistaken. Blackstock fitted the description Harry had given him. He could not mask his own air of confidence and privilege. He was a swell, there was no doubt about it.

Suddenly, responding to some signal Murdoch could not detect, the clerk of the court picked up a bell from the table and rang it with vigour.

"Oyez, oyez, oyez. All rise. The court is now in session, His Honour, Mr. Justice Falconbridge, presiding."

With much shuffling, the spectators got to their feet as in swept the judge, an imposing figure in his long, black robe. He mounted the steps to the judge's bench, which was on a raised platform. Here he paused, surveyed the courtroom, nodded, and sat down.

The clerk called out. "You may be seated."

More shuffling as everybody sat down; Murdoch was squashed even more against his neighbour as the spectators on his bench seized their opportunity to make more room for themselves. The judge indicated to the clerk that he could call the jury, and they soon filed in, thirteen men. All of them were neatly turned out, and Murdoch surmised they were predominantly merchants, one or two might even have been professional men. The counsel for the defence had done well by himself with this jury. They took their places in the jury section,

326

which was on Falconbridge's left-hand side at right angles to the spectators.

The clerk had the commanding manner of the officious. "Foreman of the jury, please stand. Have you collectively reached a verdict?"

"We have."

"And will you therefore speak for your fellow jurors. What is that verdict? Do you find the accused guilty or not guilty of the crime of rape?"

The foreman smiled. "We find the accused to be not guilty."

There was an outburst of chatter in the court, which the judge immediately suppressed by hammering with his gavel. From the noise, however, Murdoch assumed this was a popular verdict. The man in the prisoner's box actually gave a little wave of his hand in acknowledgement. However, Murdoch saw how the woman responded as if she had been slapped. Then she stood up slowly. There was a man in the first row of onlookers, and he came forward and took her arm. He did not comfort her, nor did she ask for comfort. She looked over at her own barrister, who said something to her then turned back to gather up his papers. She began to walk down the aisle toward the rear doors. Murdoch had the impression that if it was not a court of law, many of the men watching would have been jeering and shouting at her.

327

"What was she charging him with?" he asked Rogerson.

"Carnal knowledge. He's a doctor and she says he fiddled with her when she was being examined."

"And?"

The man tugged at the ends of his moustache. "Mebbe he did, but why's she bringing it out in public I want to know? If she was my wife, I wouldn't countenance it. Disgrace to the family. And look what happened. He got off. You can't charge a doctor and expect it to stick. She was worse than foolish to even try."

There was quite a crowd around the doctor congratulating him, but Murdoch saw the younger Blackstock was walking towards the rear door.

"Come on, Vincent, let's go and have a word with Mr. White."

"I told you, his name's Blackstock," said their neighbour.

Chapter Thirty-seven

MURDOCH WASN'T SURE HOW he was going to be granted access to Blackstock without admitting to the court clerk, and therefore to Newcombe, who he really was. Fortunately, a well-wisher was delaying the barrister in the courtroom, and by ruthlessly shoving through the crowd Murdoch was able to get close, Newcombe right behind him.

"Mr. Blackstock, a word if you please."

The young man halted. He looked at Murdoch politely enough, ready for more congratulations, but then he saw Newcombe and an expression of utter alarm flitted across his face. Murdoch seized his chance and stuck out his hand.

"My name is Williams." He nodded over his shoulder. "I believe you already know Mr. Newcombe. I wondered if we could have a word in private."

Blackstock returned his handshake reluctantly and

329

gave Newcombe a brief acknowledgement. The transparency of his thoughts was almost laughable. He was considering denying all knowledge of the innkeeper, refusing an audience to them, and vanishing into his chambers. This was swiftly followed by the realisation that Newcombe must know who he was and was seeking him out for a reason. Not a benign reason, if his nervousness was any indication.

"Yes, of course. Come this way to my chambers. Thank you, sir. Thank you very much."

This last remark was to one more well-wisher. They were acting as if the Blackstocks had won a championship of some kind instead of the dubious victory of prejudice over truth. Murdoch was happy to follow him through the door into the calm of the adjoining hall.

"I'm in here," he said, indicating the door to the right. They followed him into the room.

Mr. Clement either had a different chamber or was still being detained in the courtroom because, to Murdoch's relief, he wasn't present. Like the courtroom itself, the chamber was plain. No fancy panelling or lush curtains here. The floor was planked, the fireplace small and meagre, and the window was covered with a beige Holland blind. A single table sat in the corner, and a weather-beaten bookcase, crammed with papers, was beside the door. There were two armchairs, both in worse condition than the one Murdoch had in his own cubicle at the station.

330

Blackstock took refuge behind the table, waving at them to sit down. He opened a wooden box and took out a cigar. As an afterthought, he offered the box to the two men.

"No, thank you," said Murdoch, but Newcombe accepted eagerly.

"What can I do for you, Mr., er, Williams?" He didn't look at Murdoch but busied himself with the ritual of clipping his cigar and lighting it. Newcombe did the same, and the air quickly filled with aromatic smoke.

"I understand you were present at a ratting match after which one of the participants, John Delaney, was found dead in the creek."

"Oh, you do so understand, do you? And who told you that?" Even now he could not totally forsake his barrister's attitudes.

"I did, sir," interjected Newcombe. "We came here to find a Mr. White, and we found a Mr. Blackstock. But you are one and the same, unless you perchance have a double."

He chuckled and Blackstock smiled nervously. "No, not that I know of."

Suddenly, he pulled out a red silk handkerchief from his inner pocket and wiped his forehead. "As you see, I am one and the same."

"Why did you not come forward, sir?" asked Murdoch. "The police put out advertisements for you. A man was charged with the murder."

331

"Right. As a matter of fact I never saw any such advertisements. I did read about the murder, shocking thing that, but the murderer was apprehended immediately so I saw no reason why I would be needed."

"It was a criminal case, Mr. Blackstock."

"I do realise that, but as I say, it seemed no concern of mine."

Again there was the hurried mopping of the forehead, and Murdoch saw it was no mere ritual. Blackstock was sweating profusely. Suddenly he seemed to realise what Murdoch was doing, and he scowled. "Why are you here? By what authority do you ask me such questions?"

Murdoch hesitated but Newcombe gave him a reprieve. "Mr. Williams has been hired by the family of the accused man to do a further investigation – to make absolutely certain that justice has been served."

"What are you talking about? There wasn't a shadow of a doubt. I, myself, saw the bad feelings between Harry Murdoch and John Delaney."

Murdoch interjected. "You're a man of the law, Mr. Blackstock, yet you deliberately ignore a plea for your witness in a murder case. I find that reprehensible."

"I told you, I didn't know anything about it."

"And yet your own partner was the defending counsel. According to Harry Murdoch, he offered to take on the case, pro bono. I should say that normally you would only take a case that pays well, like the doctor today.

332

Why did you agree to defend somebody who had no money at all?"

"Clement and I don't discuss everything. We work independently. If he wants to work for charity, it's up to him."

Blackstock was sitting very still staring at Murdoch, a lamb watching the wolf circling.

"Isn't it more likely that you instructed him to take the case so you could keep close tabs on what was happening? Clement is not a particularly good lawyer. Is that why you had him take the case? So that the accused man would *not* get off?"

Blackstock pushed his chair away from the desk, as far from Murdoch as he could.

"That is preposterous. I really do insist you leave, sir. This entire harangue is an insult."

"An insult doesn't measure up to the damage of a hanging, Mr. Blackstock. You can feel as indignant as you want, but you are not the one who will be dead before the week is out, insulted or not."

Murdoch could feel his own anger was barely in check. He'd actually spat, and there was a glistening dot of spittle on Blackstock's chin. Newcombe intervened.

"Gentlemen, I think we need to discuss this matter more calmly. Perhaps Mr. White, I mean, Mr. Blackstock, knowing the gravity and urgency of the matter, would be willing to make a statement, in confidence as it were."

333

Perhaps because he saw the innkeeper as his inferior, Blackstock managed to find some dignity again. He wiped his chin.

"I repeat, I have nothing to add that would at all change the verdict of the case."

"Unless it was a confession," said Murdoch.

"What on earth do you mean?"

"Exactly that. You yourself could easily have murdered Delaney."

"What utter nonsense." Blackstock picked up a silver bell that was on his desk. "I'm not going to listen to this. I shall have you removed at once, sir."

Before he could shake the bell, if that was really his intention, Murdoch leaned over and grabbed his hand.

"We haven't finished our conversation to my satisfaction."

"Are you threatening me, sir?"

"If you like. And I will go further if necessary. Mr. Newcombe, will you lock the door, please?"

Although he looked uneasy at this turn of events, the innkeeper obeyed and remained by the door. Murdoch released Blackstock's wrist.

"All I require are the answers to some simple questions. If you have a clean conscience, you need have no fear."

"Of course I have a clean conscience. Why shouldn't I?"

"Why indeed? Now then. I understand you left the tavern at the same time as Mr. Craig and his son?"

"Yes. And they have confirmed that under oath."

334

"They merely stated that they went into their house and left you apparently walking towards Yonge Street. However, it would have been easy for you to turn back and go into the ravine. You weren't that far behind Delaney. What's to say you didn't catch up with him? There's nothing easier than to get hot about a cheater when there are high stakes. You challenge him, you lose your temper, and as he turns away from you, you hit him with a piece of wood. He falls to the ground. You get out of there as fast as you can. And wait to see if somebody else will take the blame."

Blackstock gaped at Murdoch. "Are you insane? I did no such thing."

"It's not that far-fetched; don't pretend it is. You are a respectable professional man, but you're also a gambler. You were drinking that afternoon. Perhaps your judgement was affected. Maybe you didn't even realise Delaney was dead when you fled."

"Don't be ridiculous."

Murdoch picked up the bell. "Would you like to come forward and make a statement?"

"There is no point. The case is closed. As far as I am concerned, the guilty party has been apprehended. Any testimony I could have made would not have affected the verdict at all."

335

Murdoch stared into Blackstock's eyes. He believed him. The other man sensed his change of attitude and relaxed a little.

He got up and went to a cupboard underneath the window behind him. "Excuse me, gentlemen. I have to take a tonic for my health."

He poured himself a full glass from the bottle, and gulped it back. Dabbing at his mouth, he returned to his chair.

"You say you are conducting an investigation on behalf of the family of the convicted man?"

"That's right."

"You must be working for Murdoch's son then. He listed one daughter, who is in a convent, and a son, who was last known to be a lumberjack."

Murdoch fenced the question. "So you admit to being conversant with the case?"

There was silence for a moment, and he saw the conflict on the barrister's face. Blackstock mopped up again. "To tell you the truth, I wouldn't mind making a clean breast of the whole thing."

Murdoch sat back in his chair. "Please do."

"When I read about the murder and the detaining of the Murdoch man, I thought the least I could do was to ensure he had a fair trial. No, wait, sir. It is not at all what you were imputing just now. I did not want it known to the public that I had been present at your establishment, Mr. Newcombe, but that is the extent of my prevarications. I suggested to Clement to take on the case. He is not a showy fellow, but contrary to what you believe, he

336

is competent. I assisted him to the best of my ability when he needed it. However, I have to assure you, Mr. Williams, it was not complicated. I don't think it would have mattered very much who represented Mr. Murdoch."

Blackstock picked up a frame photograph from his desk and held it out to Murdoch.

"I do realise I must seem like a shabby sort of chap, but I have more than just myself to consider. That beautiful woman is my wife, Emmeline. The little infant is my son, Algernon the third."

Murdoch took the picture. It was a studio portrait. An impeccable Blackstock was standing beside his wife, who was seated, an infant in christening robes and bonnet in her arms. She was very young, perhaps not more than twenty, with fair hair, elaborately coiffed, and she was elegantly and fashionably dressed.

"As you can imagine, Mr. Williams, I . . ."

He didn't get a chance to finish his sentence. There was a sharp knock on the door.

"Algie, open up."

Newcombe unlocked the door, and Emmeline Blackstock herself swept in.

"Why have you got the door locked, Algie?" She stopped when she saw her husband's visitors, but Murdoch thought it was a calculated hesitation, a brief concession to social etiquette. "I beg your pardon, I didn't realise you were busy."

337

Blackstock hurried over to her and took her hand. "We'll be finished in a moment, dearest. I'll join you in the carriage."

But the lovely Mrs. Blackstock was not going to be fobbed off so easily. She knew who was important and who wasn't. "Little Nonny is wailing like a banshee. He so wants to see his poppa."

She turned to bestow a pretty smile on Murdoch. He could see Newcombe was ready to bolt out of the door, but something about Madame Emmeline infuriated him. She could not be considered an exceptionally pretty woman, but he had never before seen anyone so gorgeously dressed. Lush ostrich feathers bobbed at the crown of her pert hat, and her walking suit was a soft golden velvet with a trimming of dark fur at the hem and waist. There was an insert at the bosom of ivory-coloured leather, which looked as if it was sewn with small precious stones. That piece of apparel alone would have cost more than Murdoch earned in three months, and that was a conservative estimate.

"I'm afraid Nonny will have to cry a little longer, madam," he said. "Our business is not yet concluded."

One might have thought from her shocked expression that he had suddenly started to unbutton his trousers. Blackstock, on the other hand, suddenly reacted like a cornered fox. He positively jumped into action.

"Mr. Williams is quite right, my dearest. Please wait for me in the carriage, and I will be there momentarily."

He was almost shoving her out of the room, and in the upheaval she dropped the dainty fur muff she was carrying. Murdoch picked it up and handed it to her. She looked into his eyes for a moment. Whatever she saw there seemed to alarm her, and she made no more resistance. Blackstock closed the door behind her and pulled out his handkerchief. At first Murdoch didn't realise that it was not only sweat Blackstock was wiping away, but also his tears. He glanced over at Newcombe, who gave a little shrug of embarrassment. However, Murdoch wanted Blackstock to squirm some more so he said nothing else, just sat waiting for him to recover his composure.

"You were saying, sir? As I can imagine . . ."

"I, er, well, you saw her . . ."

"I saw that your wife is accustomed to luxury. I assume she would not approve of any habits that would jeopardise her style of life. Is that what you wanted to say?"

"Yes," whispered Blackstock.

Chapter Thirty-eight

Fr. LeBel clutched at his wide-brimmed hat, which was in danger of sailing off his head in the gusting wind. He regretted now that he hadn't caught a streetcar along King Street, but he practised little economies whenever he could. His parish was small and not a wealthy one, consisting largely of French Canadian tanners who had formed a community in the vicinity of the church. They didn't even have their own building yet but were using the former Methodist Church that was on that spot and which had been abandoned for the more splendid cathedral on Church Street. This never ceased to disturb Fr. LeBel, who said to anybody who would listen he felt like a cuckoo, who he understood were too lazy to build their own nests but simply borrowed those of other birds to lay their eggs. His congregation listened to his homilies on this subject with impassivity. They were struggling *mettre le pain sur la table*, and for the moment they were content to worship in the old church, especially as the bishop had come down from Montreal to bless the site.

After putting in a brief appearance, the sun had retreated and the afternoon had turned grey and cold. There were fewer pedestrians than usual. Nobody was out for a stroll the way they were when the weather permitted, admiring the shop windows of the fancy stores that lined the lower end of King Street. However, there were two or three carriages waiting on the street. Fr. LeBel frowned in disapproval. The horses were glossy and well fed, but they stamped and blew air from their nostrils that was white as smoke. In his opinion it was far too cold to keep the poor beasts standing still like that while their mistresses were pampered and fawned over by sales clerks. The coachmen were muffled from top to toe with heavy fur coverings, but it was the horses he pitied. He decided to make it the point of his homily this Sunday, even though there was not one of his parishioners wealthy enough to keep a horse and carriage. He could extrapolate into the sin of vanity he supposed, although he had dealt with that recently.

As he approached the corner of Church Street, he had to wait for a moment, clutching his hat with one hand and trying to pull his cloak tighter to his body with the other. The wind bit at him savagely. On his right was St. James Cathedral, its soaring copper spire dulled in the gloom. Fr. LeBel said a brief prayer for

341

the souls of the unbaptised who worshipped there. This church disturbed him with what he considered its flagrant imitation of a Roman Catholic edifice. The devil often took a pleasing shape to tempt the faithful into sin. He hurried on.

Every two or three days, it was his task to go to the general post office on Toronto Street to collect mail. Many of the people of the parish used his church as an address because it was easy for their relatives to remember. Also, they didn't have to worry about losing precious letters or parcels at the lodging houses where so many of them lived.

The priest had his head bent so low, he couldn't see where he was going, and suddenly he almost collided with a woman who was coming out of one of the shops. She had a long, silver fur stole wrapped around her face, the little fox head sitting on her shoulder.

"*Pardonnez moi, madame,*" he said, but he was not oblivious to her expression of dismay. With his long, black cloak and wide-brimmed hat he knew, as far as she was concerned, he was a bizarre figure.

The shop from which she had emerged was known as the Golden Lion. Beautiful tall glass windows faced onto King Street, and above the arch of the doorway was a crouching lion cast in brass. Two floors were above that and on top of the pediment was another huge lion striding confidently into air. It was gilded and in summer the sun burnished it like gold. Fr. LeBel could not understand why a lion should be chosen as a symbol for a dry goods store, and he didn't approve of this either. However, the height of the upper lion meant it could be seen from afar, and it drew many customers. Visitors to the city were usually taken to the store so this magnificent example of Toronto affluence could be boasted about.

He continued on his way with the uncomfortable awareness that the woman with whom he had almost collided had pulled the fur close around her chin as if to protect herself against a pestilence. Fr. LeBel said another prayer to protect himself from the malevolent thoughts of those outside the true faith.

He turned north on Toronto Street heading toward the post office, which was at the end of the street. In spite of the cold journey, the priest enjoyed collecting the mail. The post office never failed to remind him of his Parisian birthplace with its tall, paired columns, recessed windows, and ecclesiastical dome. The fine stone carving over the lintel was the English Royal Arms, so he avoided looking at that. To the left was a wide canopy shading a side door. When he had first arrived in Toronto a year ago, he had inadvertently entered by that door only to find it was intended for the ladies and opened onto a private room where they would not be disturbed. Amidst smiles tinged with contempt he had withdrawn hastily, gathering his soutane in his hand to lift the skirt above the mud.

343

Today he went in the main entrance, glad to be in the warmth. He hurried over to the wicket, where a postal worker sat waiting for customers. The priest was relieved to see it was Mr. Langley on duty, a man he knew.

"I would like to 'ave the poste for the church, if you please," he said, careful to pronounce his words clearly so as not to give offence.

The other man checked one of the cubby holes behind him. "You have a package today, Father, from Montreal."

Fr. LeBel accepted the small number of letters and signed the chit.

"Somebody will be happy," said Mr. Langley.

Chapter Thirty-nine

QUINN'S FRIEND JOSEPH TURNED OUT TO BE A TALL, straight-backed waiter with the gravity of an undertaker. He was dressed in a black jacket with a neat white bow tie and black trousers. Murdoch took him to one side and, out of Newcombe's hearing, explained who he was. The waiter nodded.

"I've been expecting you, sir. I will do the best I can."

He led them to a table by the window and pulled out a chair for Murdoch to sit, then walked around and did the same for Newcombe. Then, with an almost inaudible murmur of "I will bring menus," he sidled off and disappeared behind the protecting screens at the far end of the room.

"The man could pass for a lawyer if he took off his apron," said Murdoch. The innkeeper grinned at that and relaxed a little.

Murdoch had overridden Newcombe's protests and insisted on taking him to the Rossin House Hotel, which was at the corner of York Street and King.

"It'll cost a week's wages," said Vince.

"I don't care. Let's see how the swells live for once. My money's as good as theirs. Besides, I've been promised a discount. It should only be three days' wages."

Reluctantly, Newcombe complied, but added a sly comment about always wanting to taste the pork cutlets he'd heard about to see if they were as good as Maria's roast pig.

At the moment Murdoch was having to battle his own discomfort. The Rossin House Hotel was one of the finest the city had to offer. The dining room was long and full of light from the tall windows along one wall. Cleverly, the opposite wall was hung with equally tall mirrors, which doubled the feeling of size and brightness. The polished oak floor gleamed in the gaslight. Murdoch glanced over at the mirror and grimaced. They had been relieved of hats and coats at the door, but his brown suit looked old and he knew there was a stain on his collar by the chin. Newcombe, however, had dressed in his best clothes for his trip to the city; and although he would never have been mistaken for a swell, he was respectable in a navy suit and striped silk four-in-hand.

"This is the most nobby place I've been in," Vince whispered, as if they were in church.

Murdoch looked around. Underneath each mirror was a marble shelf on which stood a blue Chinese vase filled with rushes. Each table was covered with a white damask cloth, and the cruet set looked as if it was solid silver. The dining room was quite full, the soft murmur of voices interwoven with the sound of a small string quartet. He had no idea where the musicians were. Perhaps behind the screen.

I'm going to bring Enid here, he thought to himself, although he suspected she would be even harder to persuade than Vincent had been.

Joseph returned carrying what seemed to be municipal declarations, leather bound with a tasselled marker of gold silk. He opened each one and handed it to Murdoch and Newcombe, respectively. Then discreetly he disappeared.

Newcombe stared at the menu. "Are we expected to eat all this?"

"I don't think so. We can choose what we want from each section."

The first course was SOUP AND FISH.

"I like fish. I think I'll have the mock turtle soup to start off with."

Newcombe laughed. "It's not made from fish stock. Heaven knows why it's called mock turtle. It's made from stewed calf's head. Can be tasty if it's done properly."

347

"Hmm. In that case I'll go for the salmon trout and oyster sauce."

Newcombe chose the same. Next listed was BOILED AND ROAST followed by ENTREES. Murdoch settled for the leg of mutton with caper sauce, and Newcombe took the corned beef and cabbage. Unfortunately, to his disappointment, pork wasn't offered, and they each decided on fillet of venison larded with wine sauce.

"I'm starting to feel like a lord of the manor," whispered Newcombe. "I'm going to throw the bones to the peasants."

"To the peasants!" exclaimed Murdoch.

They both laughed, incurring the curious glances of a man and woman who were seated nearby. Murdoch had read that the Rossin House Hotel was frequented by the wealthier class of American tourists. Well then, they were now having an opportunity to observe two of the poorer class of natives.

"Come on, Vince. We haven't got halfway through yet. What ornamental do you want?"

"I don't know. What's buffalo tongue *décoré au verdure*?"

"Tongue that's gone mouldy, but they're fancying it up. You'd better take the game pie à la surprise."

"I hope it's a pleasant surprise."

Joseph returned.

"May I recommend the wild turkey with parsnips and boiled potatoes?"

348

"You may and we accept," said Murdoch, and he relayed their other choices. Joseph collected the menus and went off again.

"I was hoping I could keep mine," said Newcombe. "I wanted to show it to Maria."

Murdoch expected they would have to wait for a long time for the meal, but that was not the case. Joseph soon came back carrying a large tray, which he set on a carved wooden table against the wall. Then he leaned over Murdoch and removed the heavy damask table napkin from the water goblet where it had been elegantly folded. With a movement worthy of a matador, he draped it across Murdoch's knees. He was about to go around the table and do the same for Newcombe, but the innkeeper forestalled him and snatched the napkin from the glass and dropped it in his lap. Murdoch hid his grin.

The trout was cooked perfectly, flaking away to the touch. They both ate it quickly.

Joseph must have had a spy hole in that rear screen because Murdoch had hardly put down his fork when the man was at his side. He put fresh plates in front of them.

"Fillet of venison," he murmured reverentially.

They tucked in, but this course was not as delicious.

"Needs onions, that's the problem," said Newcombe.

"Those damn peasants must have been chasing it too long. It's tough," added Murdoch.

The entire meal must have lasted close to an hour. By an unspoken but mutual agreement, they didn't talk about the meeting with Blackstock. They needed more

349

privacy and the waiter was never too far away. They ate their way through to the turkey and parsnips . . .

At this point Newcombe discreetly undid the buttons of his waistcoat.

"I don't think I can eat another morsel," he said to Murdoch.

"You've got to. The entire meal comes with puddings and pastry, and my friend would never forgive me if I didn't sample one of his cakes."

At that moment the waiter returned wheeling a trolley on which was an exotic selection of sweets. Boiled tapioca with wine sauce; lemon cream pie, Christmas plum pudding with brandy sauce, and three varieties of fruit tarts.

Murdoch chose the raspberry tart, which was the lightest one he could see. Newcombe decided he had to taste the Christmas pudding as Maria's was the best in the county and he wanted to be able to tell her so.

"The problem is that after this I'm going to want to have a cigar," he said to Murdoch.

The waiter overheard. "We do have a gentlemen's smoking room just off the dining hall, sir. I would be more than happy to bring you a cigar and a dark sherry if you desire."

350 Murdoch knew the man's deference was purchased, but the waiter was far too well trained to show any signs of discrimination at what were so obviously less-than-affluent customers. And there was a glint of self-

irony that he liked, well hidden as it was.

"Shall we go and be gentlemen, Newcombe?"

"Indeed."

Slightly staggering, they followed the waiter out of the dining hall. Murdoch noticed many pairs of eyes followed them, several women in wide, bedecked hats and expensive-looking walking suits were dining together. No men in sight, so he assumed it was some kind of delegation.

The smoking lounge was empty, and they were able to take armchairs by the fire. As promised their waiter brought them a box of choice Cuban cigars, assisted them to snip and light up, then withdrew.

Murdoch waited until they had luxuriously savoured the fragrant smoke.

"I was wondering what you thought of Blackstock's story," he asked.

"To tell the truth it was much as I expected. The man was scared witless that he'd be found out for a gambler. I suppose he could have turned back and followed Delaney, but I don't think he did."

Murdoch agreed. It was hard to believe that the loss of a few wagers would provoke Blackstock to murder. Men of his type let money run through their fingers like fine sand. They always had confidence there was plenty more. And it did seem that the young barrister had made an attempt to appease his conscience by paying for his partner, Clement, to defend Harry.

351

—

"I suppose, by the same token, one or both of the Craigs could have doubled back into the ravine. Perhaps young James was upset that Delaney had forbidden his courtship of Kate."

Newcombe shook his head. "Craig's daughter testified under oath that they were in the house by a quarter past eight."

Murdoch didn't want to disabuse the innkeeper of his faith in the female half of the population, so he made no comment. Besides, he was making smoke rings.

"What do you intend to do now?" Newcombe asked.

Murdoch shrugged. "I'll come back with you and have another gander around the ravine. You never know if something new will strike me."

He actually wanted to talk to Mrs. Bowling, but he thought it wiser not to reveal everything even to a man as apparently honourable as Newcombe.

He had been staring into the dancing flames in the wide hearth while he was ruminating.

Newcombe looked over at him. "I hope you don't mind my bringing this up, Will, but I think it's better said than not said. You have been weaving me a bit of a story, haven't you? You're not investigating on behalf of the family. You *are* the family, aren't you. You're Harry Murdoch's son."

352

His broad, ruddy face was gleaming with a light patina of sweat from the warmth of the room and the rich food they had eaten. Murdoch realised how much he had come to like Newcombe. He smiled ruefully.

"Yes, I am. Sorry I told you a tale, but I thought it might be easier to get answers that way."

"Absolutely. People would have shut up like clams if they knew who you really were. But I must say, you've been doing a bloody good job so far. Wish it had better results."

"I should do a good job, I'm a detective, well actually an acting detective, Number Four Station."

Vincent slapped his own knee in delight. "I knew it! Must say, you're one of the pleasantest frogs I've met to date."

He held out his hand, and they shook on it. Both of them, Murdoch realised, were feeling the effects of the rich port they had been drinking for the past half hour.

Newcombe leaned closer. "How could I have missed it? It was nagging at the back of my mind, but I just couldn't place you. Now that I look, you do resemble your father. Here, around the eyes, and maybe the mouth a bit. Yes, there's Harry in there all right."

Murdoch looked away. He wasn't sure if he was happy to know that or not.

There was a polite tap on the door, and Joseph came in with a fresh decanter of port.

"Another glass, gentlemen?"

Murdoch waved him away. "Not for me. I'll never leave here upright."

353

"I'll take one more splash, if that's all right with you, Will."

"Of course." But Murdoch was starting to feel a little worried about how big a bill he was going to have. Before he had left the house, he had taken money from the tin where he kept his cash. Not quite a week's wages but almost.

Joseph slipped a piece of paper on the side table. "Mr. Quinn sends his compliments, sir. He is sorry he cannot come out to see you, but he is rushed off his feet at the moment."

"Please tell him the tart was extraordinary."

"I will. And I do hope your companion will feel better soon."

Both Murdoch and Newcombe stared at the waiter who, still with solemn face, winked so quickly they could have imagined it.

"He quite lost his appetite, I see."

Murdoch grinned, blessing Quinn. "That is true."

Joseph left and Murdoch peeked at the bill. Even being charged for just one person was four dollars and fifty cents. Add a gratuity and it came to almost as much as he earned in four days.

"Savour every drop, Vincent."

354   "I intend to lick the glass, old chap," said the innkeeper, and he did.

Chapter Forty

NEWCOMBE DECIDED TO STAY A LITTLE LONGER in the city and take the opportunity to buy a Christmas present for Maria. Promising to meet him later at the tavern, Murdoch headed back to Shaftesbury Avenue.

He was really not too sanguine about unearthing new evidence, but in spite of that he was curiously happy. He didn't know if his father had, in fact, killed Delaney in a drunken rage or even if it would ever be known for certain one way or the other. Nevertheless, there had been affection between them. He had long given up hope of ever having what he considered to be normal filial feelings. To know that he might be capable of loving his father was an increasing source of joy. Added to that was the anticipation of being with Enid Jones in a few short hours.

When he was on the streetcar, however, lurching and clanking up the gradual incline towards St. Clair, his mood changed again. Harry's predicament was serious indeed. Go over it again, Murdoch said to himself, but this time think as if Harry was telling the truth. That everything had happened the way he said it did. Possibly, a quarrel with Delaney, a blow, and him crawling into the bushes where he lay until Pugh found him. By the time Dr. Semple conducted his examination, Delaney had been dead for some time. The best he could determine from the progress of rigor mortis was that the man had died somewhere between eight-thirty and nine-thirty. It was possible he had died very shortly before his body was discovered, although Semple admitted it was difficult to pin the time down because Delaney was in the water. Logically there were two possibilities. One, that somebody had been right at his heels and killed him directly after he had the short bout with Harry. Two, that Delaney had continued on his way, wherever he was going, and met his murderer on the way back. Had he followed the path as far as Yonge Street? To what purpose? Convinced they had the right man, the police at Number Seven Station had not pursued an extensive enquiry except for advertising in the newspaper. If Delaney had an assignation, no one was admitting it. And even if he had, it didn't mean there was anything nefarious about it, or that it had anything to do with his death. But here again, assuming Harry had told the absolute truth, how could money have disappeared? The fact that only part of his winnings had gone

356

suggested a payment of some kind. On the other hand, Murdoch was even starting to wonder if the hideout he'd discovered on the way to the Lacey cottage was one used by Delaney. He had assumed a young person, but the hole itself was big enough to accommodate an adult. Had John Delaney been lovesick? Casting spells with frogs? If so, about whom? Jessica Lacey had made no acknowledgement of seeing Delaney that night, so Murdoch assumed the man had not gone as far as the cottage, unless he was a Peeping Tom and had gone to spy on her. That couldn't totally be ruled out. However, for the sake of argument, say he did go to the hideout. On the way back, he could have met somebody who hated him enough to bash him on the head. And that person had been behind him because either Delaney didn't see him coming and was taken unawares or he had turned his back not expecting to be hit, which meant he did not fear his assailant. Murdoch sighed. He didn't feel any clearer.

"You shouldn't sigh like that, young man."

Startled, he looked over at the seat opposite, where an elderly woman in the demure black bonnet of a widow was regarding him with some concern.

"I beg your pardon, ma'am?"

"Every time a person sighs, they lose a drop of blood. You've sighed more than once while you've been sitting there."

"Oh dear, I wasn't aware of that."

357

Unexpectedly, she smiled at him, a sweet smile that crinkled the fine skin around her eyes. "Are you having problems with your wife?"

"Er, no. I have not had the good fortune to be married."

She actually leaned forward a little to scrutinise him more closely. "I must say, I cannot understand that. You certainly have most agreeable features."

"Thank you, ma'am."

"But then that's not important really in a gentleman, is it? Not so much as with we ladies. With the gentlemen, it's character that counts."

He didn't quite know how to reply to that and was afraid his bachelor state might indicate a serious flaw in his personality.

"Character and money in the bank, don't you think, ma'am?"

She shook her head. "No, I don't. My late husband was as poor as a church mouse when we first married, but he was very hard-working and when the good Lord saw fit to take him, I was left comfortably off."

There was a glisten of tears in her pale blue eyes, and Murdoch felt a twinge of guilt that he had been guying her on with his comment.

358

"I'm glad to hear that," he said with sincerity, and was rewarded by the sweet smile.

At that moment the conductor called out, "St. Clair Avenue next stop. End of the line. All out."

The old lady stood up, swaying slightly at the movement of the streetcar. Murdoch jumped to his feet to steady her. As they came to a halt, he escorted her down to the rear of the car where she could alight. He got off first and helped her down.

"Thank you very much, young man. Promise me no more sighing." She patted his cheek lightly with her hand. She was wearing pale fawn kid gloves, but they looked a little on the worn side. Perhaps her claim to being comfortably off was exaggerated, thought Murdoch. Or perhaps it was a matter of degree.

"I'll try not to." He watched as she walked slowly away, almost wanting to run after her and continue the acquaintance. He had never met any of his grandparents, who had died long before he was born. His father had no living relatives, and his mother's only sister, Aunt Weldon, had never married. There were no cousins. Now his brother and sister were gone and only his father left. In spite of the old lady's warning, he sighed so deeply, he must have lost half a pint of blood.

He quickened his pace. The short winter evening was closing in fast, and he was concerned that it would get too dark to go into the ravine.

The path leading down to the creek wasn't as icy as he'd feared, and he was able to move at a good trot to the bridge. Here the air was damper and thin shreds of mist were drifting over the path. To the west, silhouetting

359

the treetops, the sky was flushed salmon pink against the darkening night.

He continued on along the right-hand path and once again started to climb the steps to the Lacey cottage. Halfway up, he stopped to examine the hideout. The box containing the frog skeleton was no longer there.

The final flight of steps was the steepest, and he was panting when he reached the top of the hill. Here there was a low wooden fence built close to the edge of the ravine in order to squeeze out as much space as possible for the cottage property. He pushed open the gate and walked through. The vegetable garden was bare now but showed evidence of being well-tended. From where he stood, he could see into the cottage. A lamp was lit and the curtains weren't drawn. A young woman he presumed to be Jessica Lacey was clearly visible in the kitchen. He paused, not wanting to spy on an unsuspecting woman but curious about her. She had not herself testified at the trial. A physician had stated she was in too fragile a state of health, but he had presented her testimony which was uncomplicated. Mrs. Lacey had neither heard nor seen anything on the night of the murder. Her child was taken ill, and she had taken her down to Maria Newcombe. She had remained at the Manchester until next morning, given that the police were coming and going in the ravine.

Jessica was moving slowly like a woman in pain. She took a pot from a hook on the wall, pumped in some water, and placed it on the stove. Murdoch didn't quite know how to warn her of his presence, but he couldn't just stand here at the gate and have her catch him. That would really frighten her. He called out, "Hello, Mrs. Lacey, hello," and proceeded to walk down the path, waving his hand in as friendly a manner as he could. She heard him and turned and stared out of the window. There was still sufficient light for her to make him out, and he continued to smile and wave at her. Her fear was palpable, but there wasn't anything he could do to mitigate it other than what he was doing.

"Do you mind if I come in?" he shouted, not sure if she could hear him but not wanting to move out of sight of her. She came over to the window and pushed it open a crack. Close up, he could see even more clearly the terror in her face. She was young and probably, in usual circumstances, a bonny woman with abundant dark hair and rather refined features. Her eyes were blue, and he could see how shadowed they were with ill health.

He smiled as reassuringly as he could and tipped his hat. "Mrs. Lacey, my name is Williams. I'm sorry if I startled you, but I wonder if I could have a word?"

"What about?"

"I met your husband, Walter, yesterday at the Manchester. And your daughter, whom I must say takes after you for prettiness."

361

The flattery was blatant, but he was doing everything he could to calm her. He was not succeeding.

"Did he mention me?" he asked.

"No."

"I am conducting an investigation into the Delaney case. I was hoping I could talk to you for a moment or two."

If anything she looked even more afraid.

"What sort of investigation?"

Murdoch was beginning to feel ridiculous talking to the woman through the window, but he knew she was not going to let him in.

"I've been, er, hired by the family of the man who is accused of the crime. They want to make sure that there is no miscarriage of justice, that he is guilty as charged."

"He has been tried and convicted."

"That is true. I am simply trying to put everybody's mind at rest once and for all."

"How can I be of help? I already gave a statement to the constable."

"I know, ma'am, and I do apologise again for disturbing you. Do you mind if I ask you one or two questions?"

"What are they?"

"I understand you and your husband rent this cottage from Mr. Delaney, that is, I should say now, from Mrs. Delaney."

"Yes, we do."

"Have you lived here long?"

"Since March."

"Before that?"

362

"In Alberta, but I fail to see the relevance of the question."

In fact, Murdoch was circling, trying to get her to reveal more about herself.

"Did you know Mr. Delaney well?"

"No, I dealt with Mrs. Delaney."

"In your opinion, ma'am, was he a man who might make enemies?"

"What do you mean?"

"I am trying to determine if there was, in fact, any person other than the man now convicted who might be motivated to kill Mr. Delaney."

She was steadier now, more sure of herself. "I cannot say. He had an enormous funeral by all accounts. He must have been well liked."

"You yourself did not attend the funeral?"

Even in the gloom he could see the flush that swept into her face and neck.

"I was not able to. I was unwell."

He remembered that she had miscarried a child shortly after the time of the murder, and he regretted his question.

"I am getting cold, sir."

"One more question then, Mrs. Lacey. Did you hear anything at all on that night? A cry? A dog barking? Anything?"

363

"I have said I did not. My child was taken ill. That is all that was of concern to me."

"Did you take notice of the time when you went down to the Manchester?"

"No, I did not."

He stepped back. "Thank you very much, ma'am. I do appreciate your talking to me."

She had closed the window before he finished, and she pulled down the blind, leaving him staring at a blank window. That hadn't got him very far.

He walked around the cottage and began to follow the path that ran along the top of the ravine.

The Delaney house soon came in sight, just on the other side of the rise. Here were no uncurtained windows to look into. All the blinds were drawn, with cracks of light from the upstairs windows. He could just make out the sound of somebody singing, and he assumed Miss Kate was practising. There was no flute accompaniment. He walked on, hitting a pong of pig food floating on the air.

Chapter Forty-one

Just as he was approaching Mrs. Bowling's cottage, he heard the sound of crying. It was odd, not loud, not quite a child's cry, or even one that was expressing pain. It was more rhythmic and repetitious, as if the weeper had lost faith some time ago in ever being heard. He could see now that there was a girl standing outside the Bowling cottage. She banged on the door and wailed again, the crying he had just been hearing.

"Hello there," he called out, and she whirled around. She had a drab brown shawl over her head but no overcoat or gloves, and he could see her arms had reddened with the cold. It was hard to tell her age, maybe fifteen or sixteen.

"Hello," he said again. "Did you get yourself locked out?"

She grinned at him and now that he was closer he

realised there was something odd about her: her eyes were blank, her lips slack.

"I'm here to see Mrs. Bowling," he went on, and she nodded vigorously.

"She's in the back feeding chickens." The words were slow and careful, as if she had been coached with pain to articulate properly.

"How did you get locked out?" Murdoch asked.

The girl shrugged. "It's time for my tea. Momma must have forgot." Suddenly, with a shock, Murdoch saw that she was tethered like a dog to a post near the door. There was a leather collar around her ankle with a rope attached. She saw his stare and lifted up her skirt as far as her knees. She had on boots but no stockings.

"Do you want to see some more?" she asked, and he couldn't tell if it was the question of an innocent child or a seasoned whore. He was saved from answering by Mrs. Bowling, who came around the side of the house.

"Nan, stop that at once."

The girl dropped her skirt and whimpered in fear. Mrs. Bowling addressed Murdoch.

"What can I do for you?"

"Good afternoon, ma'am, we met yesterday. I came up with Mr. Newcombe."

366   "Oh yes, I recognise you now."

"I was wondering if I could have a word with you, ma'am."

"I'm just about to feed the chickens. You'll have to come around to the back."

She actually started to head in that direction. "Mrs. Bowling, this young woman has got herself locked out. I assume she is your daughter?"

Mrs. Bowling turned, looked as if she was about to ignore what he'd said, thought better of it, and came back to the porch.

"Yes, this is Nan, my cross and burden in life. As you can see. You might think it cruel that I've tied her up like this, but if I don't she's liable to go wandering off and get herself into trouble. I can't afford to have somebody watch her every minute of the day, and I work as you saw."

"She's cold. She should be inside."

"Fresh air's good for her," said Mrs. Bowling sullenly, but she unbuckled the collar from the girl's leg, opened the door, and directed Nan inside. The girl went obediently, casting one glance at Murdoch. There was no intelligence in those eyes. Nan should be in an institution where he was certain she would receive better care. As if she had read his mind, Mrs. Bowling said, "People are always telling me I should put her in the asylum, but the poor child is so attached to her own flesh and blood she would pine away. So I put up with her sly ways and do my best. The Lord will give me my reward in heaven."

367

Murdoch bit back his own anger. "From what I witnessed yesterday, I'd say you share similar burdens with Mrs. Delaney."

"It isn't the same at all. Her son was quite normal until his accident. And he is so most of the time now. She doesn't know how to handle him."

"Unlike you, ma'am."

She gave him a sharp glance, trying to assess the implications of what he'd said. He kept his face neutral.

She shrugged. "Necessity is a good teacher."

She started off for the rear of the cottage, and he went after her. Nan was watching them from the window, and he smiled and waved at her. To his astonishment, she stuck out her tongue and ran her forefinger around her nipple.

There were a half-dozen scrawny chickens scratching and pecking in the hard, mud-crusted ground by the chicken shed. Mrs. Bowling picked up a bucket and poured mashed grain into the trough, and the hens ran over clucking in excitement. A big rooster with glistening green-gold plumage and bright red dewlaps pushed his way through them to get closer to the source of the food. Mrs. Bowling scooped some of the seed and held out her cupped hand.

368

"Here, Chanty."

The cockerel pecked from her hand, and she beamed at him as if he were a pet dog. "There's my clever boy. Are you going to make Momma some good eggs?"

At that moment Murdoch noticed one of the hens, which was on the fringe of the group, had red streaks down her chest.

"What happened to that one?" he asked, pointing.

"She got herself pecked. She was lucky I happened by else they've had killed her. They see blood, and they go for it. Nocky bird. She just stood there letting them do it."

"Good Lord, why do they do that? It's one of their own."

Mrs. Bowling was stroking the rooster's coxcomb. He actually seemed to like what she was doing and didn't move away.

"They sense weakness and it sends them into a blood frenzy." She sniffed. "Dogs are the same. And so are people, if you ask me. They sense a soft spot, any kind of weakness, and they'll go for it. To destroy. Especially men."

Her tone was so bitter and cynical that Murdoch bristled.

"Not everybody is like that surely, Mrs. Bowling?"

"Aren't they? God expelled Adam and Eve from Paradise because of our base nature, and we've been disobeying Him ever since."

Suddenly one of the hens rushed over to the injured chicken and pecked it hard on the chest. A gout of blood spurted out. A second hen joined the first and within seconds they were both stabbing at the other

369

chicken, drawing blood. It stood transfixed, not running away. Mrs. Bowling didn't move.

"Shoo!" shouted Murdoch, and he ran at the attackers clapping his hands. He was almost on top of them before they took any heed. He grabbed up the injured bird.

"Won't do any good," said Mrs. Bowling. "Not unless you want to take her home with you. They've got a taste now, and they'll go after her again till she's dead."

"Can't you separate her until she heals? She must be worth something to you."

"She won't be wasted. She'll be a good stew."

"I'll take her then."

"You'll have to pay."

"That doesn't matter."

The poor chicken was bleeding all down his coat, but he didn't care. He managed to fish in his pocket and found a dollar.

"Here."

"That's not enough for a good layer."

"And a pot of stew is fifty cents, so you're making a profit."

Whatever it was, she looked pleased, as if she had enjoyed the skirmish. She put the money in the pocket of her apron.

370 "I doubt you came all the way up here to rescue my birds. What do you want?"

The hen struggled feebly in his hands. "Can you do anything here?" he asked.

"Isn't worth it. One of them got through to its heart. Look."

Murdoch could see a deep puncture wound that was pulsing blood. He knew he was being sentimental about this poor creature, but he couldn't help himself.

"Do you have a cloth I can bandage her with? Anything?"

Mrs. Bowling wiped her hands down the sides of her coat, which was a long, man-sized check overcoat.

"We might as well go in. It's frigid out here."

She turned on her heel, leaving Murdoch to hurry after her. The chicken's long neck drooped over his elbow, and the beak was gaping.

At the back door, his reluctant hostess took a key from her pocket and went inside. Murdoch followed and almost gagged on the fetid air in the room, a sour smell overlaid with acrid smoke from the woodstove. Nan was sitting on a chair that she had pulled close to the stove in the corner of the room. There was only one small lamp that had been lit, and the wick was turned down low.

"What happened to the chook?" She got up and came toward them, but her mother shooed her away with an angry gesture.

"Nan, leave it alone. Go and sit on the couch until I tell you."

The girl scurried over to a bed sofa that was against the far wall. In size and shape this cottage seemed

371

identical to what he had glimpsed of the Lacey one, but whereas that had appeared neat and pretty, this room was dirty with broken mismatched chairs. There was a beige-coloured drugget on the floor that looked so dusty he almost sneezed at the mere sight of it.

"Bring the wretched thing over to the sink," said Mrs. Bowling. She took a grubby strip of cloth from a hook and wrapped it tightly around the bird's chest. The wing fluttered briefly but that was all the response.

"Will it live?" Murdoch asked.

"Probably not. But you said as you wanted me to do something."

She laid the stricken hen on the draining board beside the sink, and for a minute he thought she was going to reach for a chopping knife and take off its head. However, she took down a teapot from the window ledge.

"I could do with a cup of tea; I suppose you could too?"

Not exactly gracious, good society manners, but he accepted, hoping he wouldn't catch some dirt-engendered disease. There was a steaming kettle on the stove, and she poured some hot water into the pot, swished it around, then emptied it. Then she added three large scoops of black tea leaves from a tin caddy and made the tea. Murdoch noticed that the pot was a good china and realised he'd seen that same pattern in the Delaney house. As he glanced around the room, he saw there were two lush green velvet throws on the couch and the chair. They looked new.

Nan was watching him and her mother. When she met his eyes she smiled, and for a moment Murdoch quailed, wondering what would follow. However, this time the smile was that of a child, rather shy and sweet.

Mrs. Bowling poured tea into a china cup and handed it to him without the saucer.

"We don't have any milk, and the sugar's low. I hope you can drink it like this."

"Of course. Thank you."

She hadn't asked him to sit down, but he went to the table and sat in the wooden chair. He sipped the tea. In spite of the fact that he usually liked his brew sweet and milky, it tasted good. Fresh and strong.

"I see you share the same pattern as Mrs. Delaney," he said, tapping the cup.

"A gift."

"You have a generous employer," he said, pointing. "I assume she gave you those handsome covers as well."

Mrs. Bowling frowned. "As a matter of fact, she did. I get my due. That's a big house to take care of. And Mrs. Delaney understands the cross I have to bear." She remained where she was, leaning against the sink. "Well, what do you want? What's the reason I'm honoured with a visitor? You're not on the lookout for a dog, I hope. I don't know nothing about them. You'll have to talk to Vincent."

373

There it was again, the sly suggestion that there was a special relationship between her and the innkeeper.

"I'm doing a further investigation into Mr. Delaney's death."

She regarded him over the top of her cup. Her eyes were shrewd.

"What do you mean a further investigation? I thought everything was finished. The Murdoch fellow is going to hang soon, isn't he?"

"I'm tying up loose ends, as it were, just in case. We wouldn't want an innocent man to die, would we?"

She frowned. "The Lord is the great Judge, not us. On the day of judgement we will all know as we shall be known." She took a noisy gulp of tea. "Who are you then? By what authority are you acting?"

"I'm a detective and I'm acting in a private capacity for the family."

"Are you?" Again she looked at him shrewdly. "What's it to do with me?"

"I'd like to ask you some questions. I noticed you didn't testify at the trial."

"I wasn't asked. The constable talked to me once but decided I had nothing of importance to say."

"Was that true?"

"I suppose so."

374

Murdoch could see that the cloth around the chicken's breast was stained a bright crimson, but it was still breathing.

"Do you mind repeating to me what you told the constable?"

"He asked me if I had heard anything that night and where I was."

She paused maddeningly and Murdoch tried to keep back his impatience.

"And what did you tell him, Mrs. Bowling?"

"I was here in my own house. I didn't hear anything except the wind and the birds in the trees."

"When did you know that Mr. Delaney had been killed?"

"Oh, I heard that ruckus all right. That was later when they came to tell the missus. She carried on like a scalded cat."

"And what time was that?"

"I couldn't say. Me and Nan go to sleep when it's dark. Saves on candles. It could have been the middle of the night as far as I know."

Murdoch put his mug down on the table, unbuttoned his coat, and pulled his watch out of his vest pocket.

"Speaking of time, I mustn't linger. What does your clock say, Mrs. Bowling?"

His ruse seemed transparent to him, but she shrugged. "I don't have a clock. No need. Chanty wakes us up every morning, rain or shine, and as I said we go to bed when we've had supper."

Murdoch guessed she had never learned to tell the time. He replaced his watch.

"I understand that Mrs. Lacey came past your house with her little daughter about nine o'clock that night. The child was unwell, and she was taking her down to the Manchester tavern where her husband works."

"She might have. I didn't hear or see her."

Nan interrupted her. "No, Momma. Sally was crying." Nan imitated the sound of a child crying, startlingly loud. "She went down the path."

"Don't be foolish, Nan. That must have been a different time."

"No, Momma, I remember. It was the same night Philip's poppa died. I do remember."

She was proud of herself for having such important information.

Murdoch looked over at Mrs. Bowling. "Do you mind if I ask Nan the same questions?"

"Yes, I do mind. You can see how handicapped she is. She won't understand you, and she'll get upset."

Nan spoke out in an excited voice. "I can answer, Momma. Let me answer a question. Please, Momma, let me."

"No, it has nothing to do with you, and what are you doing, sitting there listening to what doesn't concern you. Get off upstairs."

Nan looked as if she was going to burst into tears. Murdoch reached into his pocket again.

"My client would be glad of any information relating to the case, Mrs. Bowling. I understand this is

376

inconvenient for you, and I hope I can compensate for your time."

He laid a dollar bill on the table. He didn't like the feeling at all. It was as if she were a procuress.

"Besides, Nan is obviously going to be more upset if I don't say anything."

Mrs. Bowling didn't touch the money. He dipped into his pocket again and added two twenty-five-cent pieces.

"Do what you like, then," she said, "but I warn you she's got no sense."

Murdoch walked over to the girl and squatted in front of her.

"Nan, do you remember what happened to Mr. Delaney?"

She nodded her head with great vigour. "Oh, yes. He had his neck wrung until he was dead."

Murdoch ignored the guffaw from behind him. "Do you know when that occurred? What time of the year it was?"

She put her head to one side and brought her forefinger to her chin in a grotesque imitation of a coy, genteel young woman.

"It was hot. When it's hot, it means it is summertime."

"Could you name the month?"

She scrunched up her face to concentrate. "April, I think."

377

"Oh, Nan, what a stupid girl you are," said her mother from behind Murdoch.

He smiled at the girl. "I've known it to be very hot in April. But what I am more interested in is the night when Mr. Delaney died. Is there anything you can tell me about that night? Your momma says there was a lot of noise after you had both gone to bed that woke you up. Do you remember that?"

"Mrs. Delaney was crying because Mr. Delaney had his neck wrung. Momma went up to see what was the matter, but I stayed here out of the way. I didn't mind though because I had Flash to play with. Have you seen Flash? He's Philip's dog, but he likes me best."

"Don't tell lies, Nan," snapped her mother. "You didn't have no dog here. You were fast asleep like the piece of wood you are."

Nan looked confused. "I did see Flash, Momma. And the other dog. Philip brought them to play with me. I couldn't sleep because it was so hot. We played for a long, long time because Philip was sad and needed a bolster. His poppa swatted him, and he fell out of the wagon and hurt his head."

"Nan!"

Murdoch tried to ignore Mrs. Bowling. "When did that happen, Nan?"

"Last week."

"See, what did I tell you?" interjected her mother.

"Philip's poppa has passed away. I don't think it could have been last week, Nan."

"I know that. It was a long, long time ago. Philip has a sweetheart, but his poppa was very cross and swatted him."

Without turning around, Murdoch took another twenty-five-cent piece from his pocket and held it up. Mrs. Bowling managed to hold her tongue.

"His poppa swatted him because he had a sweetheart?"

Nan shook her head vigorously. "Oh no! Not for that. He doesn't know. Philip is my brother, and he tells me."

"He's lucky to have somebody to talk to. I had a sister, but she has gone to heaven."

Nan leaned forward and planted a wet kiss on his cheek. "You must be sad. Philip was very sad when he come, but I bolstered him again and we played with the dogs. The other dog wasn't as nice as Flash."

"What dog was that, Nan?"

"I forget his name, but he wanted to bite me."

Mrs. Bowling couldn't hold back any longer, and she approached the two of them. "I told you, she don't have any sense."

"It's not true then? Philip Delaney wasn't here that night?"

379

"Of course he wasn't. He does come over on occasion. He's as much a child as she is. They are good companions. Nan thinks that makes them brother and sister. She likes the dog, and they play together. But she's got it mixed up. She does that."

To prove her point, she leaned toward her daughter. "Nan, tell the gentleman what day this is?"

Happy for the attention, the girl grinned. "It is March tenth. In seven days' time it will be the birthday of the Lord Jesus, which took place on December fifth more than twenty years ago."

"And did Philip bring Flash over to see you this week?"

"He came yesterday."

Mrs. Bowling shook her head. "He hasn't been here for a while."

Nan looked over at her mother, and her expression was sly. "You didn't see him, Momma. You were asleep. He did come yesterday. He brought a puppy, a baby dog. We played tag, and Flash fetched every one of the sticks I threw for him."

"That must have been fun," said Murdoch. "I've met Flash, and he likes to run. But it wasn't this puppy you saw in the summer, was it?"

"No."

"What colour was the other little dog Philip brought? The nasty one?"

"She doesn't know," interjected Mrs. Bowling.

"I do, Momma. It looked like ashes. I called it Ashes, but that wasn't its real name." She looked solemnly at

Murdoch. "Momma won't let me play in the woods anymore. She says I'm too big. I used to play all day long. I got sweeties."

Whatever she'd said made her mother angry. "There she goes, lying again. I've never let her play on her own. She needs watching all the time. What sort of mother would let a big girl with no sense like her go wandering off?"

The girl was shrinking back on the couch, watching her mother intently. Murdoch stood up. He didn't think he was going to get any more information, and he didn't want to make Nan's life more difficult than it already was.

"Thank you for answering my questions, Nan. You have been very helpful. Thank you, Mrs. Bowling."

He walked back to the sink, noticing that the money was no longer on the table.

The wounded chicken was gasping, and gently, he picked it up. Both Mrs. Bowling and Nan were watching him. He touched the brim of his hat in acknowledgement and left.

By the time he got to the bottom of the hill, the bird was dead, and he buried it under a mound of ice-rimmed leaves.

Chapter Forty-two

ALTHOUGH THE MANCHESTER HAD JUST OPENED, the taproom was already almost full. Unlike the Bowling cottage, the smell in here was salubrious, wood smoke mixing with roasting pork. The wall sconces blazed with light, and a fire was crackling in the fireplace. Murdoch stood for a moment at the threshold, but Vince Newcombe, who was at the serving window, saw him and shouted out a greeting.

"Will, come on in."

There was a smattering of applause, which momentarily disconcerted him until he realised it wasn't for him but for Mr. Patrick Pugh, who was standing by the hearth. There was a small circle of space around him, and several customers were watching. Apparently, he had just completed some kind of magic trick.

Newcombe indicated Murdoch should go to one of the fireside benches and he did so, making his way through the cluster of topers, who at this point were friendly and thirsty. The innkeeper drew a tankard of ale and brought it over.

"Mr. Clarry, move your rear end in a few inches and let Mr. Williams sit down."

The elderly man, whose face was completely obscured with a full, old-fashioned beard and bushy side-whiskers, slid over good-humouredly, and Murdoch squeezed himself in beside him.

"Good evening to you," he said.

"Likewise," replied the old man.

Newcombe placed the tankard in front of Murdoch. "You look like you could use this." He nodded in the direction of the man by the fireplace. "Mr. Pugh is honouring us with some entertainment."

Pugh heard him and grinned an acknowledgement. The streak of white hair at his temples was particularly vivid in the firelight.

He approached Murdoch's neighbour. "Mr. Clarry, I heard you complaining yesterday that you didn't have two quarters to rub together. Is that right?"

"Certainly is. I'm not as young as I used to be. Can't work."

In spite of these words there was something complacent in the old man's voice that belied what he was saying.

"You're giving us a nailer, Mr. Clarry. I'd say you are a rich man indeed."

383

Pugh reached forward and under the man's full beard. He pulled out a shiny silver dollar. "My, my, a strange place to put your savings . . . and what's this?"

Another coin appeared magically from behind Clarry's right ear. "Good gracious, you've got at least two dollars tucked in here," said Pugh, and removed another coin. To everybody's amusement, Clarry reached up and pulled at his ear lobe as if it was a teat full of silver. "Ah, here's another," said Pugh, and he removed a fourth coin from Clarry's left ear. He addressed his audience. "I'd say Mr. Clarry could easily pay for a round, don't you?"

A chorus of yeahs and whistles was the answer. "Give me the money then," said the old man. "I'll be glad to treat."

"Sorry, can't do that. Finders keepers. But I tell you what, if you can find those coins, they are yours."

It looked as if Pugh had dropped the silver into his pocket, they had heard each coin clink as he did so, but he turned his pockets inside out and they were empty. Clarry stood up. "I'm going to pat you down then. Here let me out." This remark was addressed to Murdoch, and he shoved him a little. Murdoch knew that Mr. Clarry wasn't too happy at being tricked.

384   Pugh stepped back. "Tell you what. Winner take all on this next trick. You win, I pay. I win, you pay. Agreed?"

"What is it?"

"I am going to bet that I can cut right through your

wrists, through flesh and bone, using only a silk hand-kerchief. Let's see them."

Clarry held up his hands. His knuckles were knobby, the skin leathery, and his wrists thick. Pugh turned over his right hand to look at the palm. "A farmer, I see."

"That's right."

"Are you game then?"

"Just as long as you leave my goolies intact. My wife wouldn't like it if anything happened to them."

There was a loud jeering from the other customers. "Whooee. You're dreaming, Jonah. She hasn't seen them in years," cried out one of the men, almost a twin of Clarry with his beard and rough farmer's complexion.

"Come on, men. Give him a chance," called out Newcombe, ever the host. "Let's see the trick."

Pugh spun around. "Does anybody have a silk hand-kerchief they can lend me? I'd prefer a clean one. You, sir. Yours will do."

A younger man was seated at the opposite bench. He was wearing a corduroy jacket and trousers and a black slouch hat. Around his neck was knotted a bright blue-and-yellow handkerchief. He shrank back. "What are you going to do with it? I just bought it."

"Fear not. It will be returned to you intact, sir, or I myself will pay twice the cost."

Pugh wasn't to be denied, and the man undid the handkerchief and handed it over. Underneath he revealed a red flannel collarless shirt.

"What did this cost you? Twelve cents?" asked Pugh.

"No! Twenty-five."

Pugh ran the handkerchief through his fingers. "You were robbed, sir. But never mind. It will do. Now where's my vict– I mean my helper. Mr. Clarry, show me your wrist. Either one will do."

Clarry held out his right arm and pushed back his sleeve so that his wrist was exposed. Pugh twisted the handkerchief into a rope and began to wrap it around Clarry's wrist.

"I must tell you gentlemen I have performed this trick for the best English society. Prince Albert himself assisted me."

The men watching him groaned and banged on the table to express their disbelief.

"Tell us another, Pugh. You're as full of wind and piss as a whore's belly," said one man.

Pugh worked fast and knotted the handkerchief tightly.

"Clasp your two hands together if you please, sir, so there can be no doubt of my authenticity."

Clarry did so and the rest of the men went quiet. Pugh's voice was commanding.

"I am now going to draw up this handkerchief by means of magic right through the flesh. Keep your hands tight together, sir."

Pugh took one end of the handkerchief in each hand. "One, two . . . no wait, this is a particularly difficult trick to do. I wouldn't mind a little assistance. Count with me. ONE. TWO." The men joined in and on a loud "THREE," Pugh pulled the handkerchief, still knotted, up through Clarry's wrist. "Ha!" He waved it in the air, while they all clapped; then he tossed it over to its original owner.

Clarry was examining his wrist. "How the devil did he do that?"

Murdoch didn't respond. During the trick, he saw for the first time that the clever Mr. Pugh was missing the tip of his middle finger on the left hand! He took a drink of beer. What the hell did that mean? He couldn't believe there were two men in his sphere, both of whom were identically maimed. But Billy had sworn that the man spying on Murdoch was pale and nondescript, rather fat, with a moustache. Quinn's dog procurer was described in the same way. He stared at Pugh, who was slaking his thirst from one of the mugs now offered to him by his admiring audience. He was clean shaven, slim in his brown guernsey and dark trousers. But a false moustache was an easy disguise to assume, as was padding. It had to be the same man. But what the hell was he doing? Why all the subterfuge?

Suddenly, Pugh looked over at him, and their eyes met. For a moment Murdoch feared he could even read minds.

387

"Listen up, you topers. One more entertainment. For the round. Brain versus brawn. Mr. Newcombe, may I avail myself of your good broom?"

"Of course. Help yourself."

Pugh picked up the corn broom that was leaning against the mantelpiece. "I am going to show you an amazing feat. As you can see, I can never be called a big man. Five feet, three inches in my boots is all I can claim. But I am going to ask the assistance of a much taller and stronger man to see if he can push me over using this broom. You, sir, next to Mr. Clarry. Mr. Williams, isn't it? You look like a fit man. Will you come up and participate in a little fun?"

"Why not," said Murdoch, and he got to his feet. He was trying to be nonchalant, but he felt tense and angry. The little rat wasn't going to get the better of him if he could help it.

Wagers immediately began to be placed, coins and dollar bills slapped down on the tables. Murdoch heard them call out.

"Three to one on the conjurer. I'll give you five against."

Murdoch had a hazy sense that he was not getting a lot of favour.

"Hold this broom horizontally like so across your chest. Now, I am going to make things easier for you. I will oppose you using only my one thumb, like so."

Pugh placed his thumb lightly on the broom handle. "Now, Mr. Williams, push me over. If you can!"

Murdoch pushed hard on the broom. He knew there had to be a catch in it, but he didn't care. He'd enjoy

388

seeing the cocky rooster sprawling on the floor. That didn't happen. Pugh remained upright, his thumb touching the broom. "Harder, Mr. Williams. A young lady could do better."

Murdoch felt himself flush, and he pushed again. There was a strong resistance on the other side of the broom. Pugh started to whistle merrily, his position unchanged. Murdoch tried again. He was proud of his strong legs and back. With a grunt, he put his back into it, but the resistance was even stronger.

The men called out, "Get on! Shove him over! Go!"

Finally, Murdoch had to stop he was so out of breath. He stepped back, panting.

"Do you concede the match?" asked Pugh.

"No. One more try."

"Very well. I will make it even easier. I will stand on one foot." He did so, tucking his left foot across his right calf. "Now go."

Murdoch took a deep breath and pushed as hard as he could. Nothing happened. Pugh didn't move an inch. The men were cat-calling. He had to stop.

"Concede?"

"No!"

At that moment Newcombe stepped forward. "This is a man who won't give up until the Other place freezes. Come on, Mr. Williams, you've been fairly beat. Or unfairly. It was good entertainment, and the next round is on the house."

389

He indicated Walter Lacey, who had been leaning through the bar window watching.

"Walt here will fill up your mugs. Once only, so don't think you can gulp 'em down and get seconds."

There was a surge as the men closest to the pumps went for their refills. Newcombe patted Murdoch on the shoulder. "I've seen him do it before. It's a trick, but devil take me if I know how he does it. He's withstood men even heavier than you."

Pugh had tossed back a glass of whiskey, and he wiped his hand across his mouth. He grinned at Murdoch. "They may have been bigger but none as stubborn. Shake on it, sir."

He held out his hand. Murdoch went as if to accept the handshake, but instead he caught Pugh by the other wrist and twisted his hand around palm side up. "You've had an accident I see, sir."

"Ah yes. Not serious, thank goodness."

He pulled his hand away and held up the truncated finger. "A snake bit me when I was a boy. I got between him and my infant sister, who was cooing on the grass."

"Ha!" exclaimed one of the topers, who was nearby. "I thought you told us last week that you was stamped on by a wild buffalo. You was caught in a stampede, and you was rescuing a little puppy dog at the time. He said that, didn't he, Vince?"

Pugh didn't give him a chance to reply. "Both are

true, my dear sir. I have lost the tip of my finger on two separate occasions."

"Carry on like that and you won't have anything left."

More laughter and Pugh bowed in acknowledgement. Murdoch felt completely at a loss, and he struggled to control himself. He didn't know how to break through the man's composure, and he was burning to do so. If he had an excuse, he would have happily asked him to step outside, but he knew he was being unreasonable. The crowd broke up into smaller groups, and Murdoch took his seat on the bench. Pugh sat on the other end next to Mr. Clarry. Newcombe brought three foaming tankards.

"On the house."

"Where's Mr. Craig tonight?" asked Pugh, wiping foam from his lip with the back of his hand.

"Haven't seen him yet. Or James. They're late."

"Oh, didn't you hear?" said another man nearby. "I was by there this afternoon with my delivery. Mr. Craig's mother's been taken poorly. She lives in America somewhere, and he and his lad have had to go off to see her." His voice dropped. "She might not live to see Saturday."

"Have they all gone? The entire family?" asked Pugh, and Murdoch could feel the sudden tension.

"No, just Mr. Craig and his son and the aunt who lives with them. Missus isn't that well either, and Miss Adelia is staying to look after her." The man looked over at Pugh, slyly. "If that's what's worrying you."

391

Pugh shrugged. "Well, she is a mighty pretty lady."

He stood up and fished some coins, regular fashion, from his pocket. "In fact, I think I should go and pay her a call. Offer my sympathies."

Grabbing his hat from one of the hooks by the door, he left.

The baker winked at the other men. "I'd say he's a smitten man, wouldn't you? That was one of the fastest exits I've seen since my dog got the scent of the bitch down the road. Mr. Pugh's tool was practically dragging on the ground."

"Watch your tongue, Driscoll," interjected Newcombe. "I won't have decent women talked about in that fashion."

"Hold on, Vince. No aspersions on the young lady. I was referring only to our fast friend."

"That's as may be, but I won't tolerate coarse language in here and you know it. What if my Maria was to come in and hear you?"

Driscoll shrugged, unperturbed. It was obvious that he considered overhearing vulgarities went with the territory, and if they were going to run a tavern they must know that.

Murdoch gulped down some of the sharp-tasting ale. Was Pugh upset at the thought that Miss Craig might have left? If he was courting her, surely he wasn't also chasing Enid Jones? Damn. He didn't know if he should go after him. But if he did, then what?

Suddenly his eyes met those of Walter Lacey, who was leaning in the open window to the bar. The barkeeper had been scrutinising him, he realised. Murdoch considered himself to be adept at reading unspoken thoughts on other men's faces, but he couldn't quite fathom Lacey's expression. Not malevolent exactly, but as intense as a wolf watching its prey. He felt a stab of anger at being the object of this stare, and he tipped his finger to his forehead. Lacey looked away, quickly wiping some nonexistent spilled beer from the counter.

Murdoch got up and went over to the farther table, where Newcombe was collecting empty mugs.

"Vince, can I have a word with you in private?"

"This minute?"

"I'd appreciate it." He looked at him. "It's concerning Mrs. Bowling and her daughter."

"Right! I'll hand these glasses over to Walter. We can go to the parlour."

Newcombe was no good at dissembling, and Murdoch saw how nervous his request had made him.

Chapter Forty-three

THE INNKEEPER FOLLOWED MURDOCH into the parlour then turned the key in the lock.

"People wander around," he said, nodding in the direction of the taproom. "Please have a seat."

There was no question that there were plenty of chairs to choose from, the problem was negotiating a path through the furniture to any one of them. The room was filled with small tables, and on each one of them was a glass case under which was either a stuffed member of the dog family or representatives of their prey. He didn't dare get Newcombe launched on a history of each piece, so he got straight to the point and remained standing.

"Vince, I just came from talking to Mrs. Bowling, and I met her daughter. Nan said some troubling things, but I couldn't quite determine if they were true or not."

"Not true, I'm sure. Poor girl isn't right in the head as you could see."

"She certainly seemed muddled but not completely in unreality."

Newcombe regarded him uneasily. "What did she say?"

"That Philip Delaney was at their cottage the night his father died. However, according to his testimony and that of his mother, after the match he went directly from here to his own house, where he stayed until she sent him to look for his father."

It was obvious this wasn't what Newcombe had been expecting him to say, and Murdoch thought he was relieved.

"Philip does visit Nan to play with the dog. She probably got the days mixed up."

"She said Philip brought two dogs with him, Flash and a grey dog that, by the sound of it, could only have been Havoc."

"No, Will, no. I do appreciate the peculiarity of your circumstances, but you're clutching at straws. Nan mixes up times when events take place. Don't forget, the terrier was on the loose when Mr. Pugh found Delaney. Maybe the little cur wandered up to the Bowling cottage and Nan saw him, then in her mind added him to a visit Philip had made on another occasion."

"She didn't sound that confused, Vince. Not about this."

Newcombe went and sat in the armchair by the hearth. "Forgive me saying so, Will, but I know the

395

girl better than you do. You can't rely on anything she says. And besides, even if by a remote stretch of the imagination she did get it right and Philip came to visit her that night, what does it prove?"

"That the boy was lying. He wasn't at home."

Newcombe rubbed at his head as if he were polishing it. "Well now, Philip Delaney isn't quite accountable either. His memory isn't the best."

"Nan said he has a sweetheart. Does he?"

"Not that I know of. He's a boy in a man's body, don't forget. I don't think any proper young woman would encourage him."

"By the same token, Nan is a girl in a woman's body, but I doubt we men are always as scrupulous."

Newcombe flinched like somebody whose sore tooth had just been probed by a dentist. He reached up and straightened one of the half-dozen photographs that hung in a line on the wall.

"Bad business," he said ambiguously.

"Vince, listen to me. I don't have time for niceties. There's too much at stake. Why is it that I keep getting the impression you want to hide something? And I don't mean about your charity act with Mrs. Bowling's ale." He caught Newcombe by the arm, forcing him to keep still. "Are you poking Nan? Is that the real reason you're visiting the cottage? Is that why you don't want your wife to know?"

Newcombe stared at him, appalled. "My God, no. How could you think that?"

"Because I saw the girl. She's got the wiles of a whore. Some men find that appealing."

"Not me. I promise you, I don't."

"Is it her mother then? Is the surly Mrs. Bowling your mistress?"

Newcombe shook off his hand. "No, she is not. You wouldn't even say such a thing if you knew me better. And if you knew my Maria."

"What is going on then? Tell me, because I know there's something between you and Mrs. Bowling."

The innkeeper moved away from him and perched on the edge of one of the armchairs. "You're right but I swear it's not on my part. Ucillus acts cosy like that all the time."

"Why do you keep visiting her then?"

"I told you, I feel sorry for her. The girl is a handful."

"I don't believe you, Vince."

"Whether you do or not isn't the point. Besides it has nothing to do with your father's case."

"Let me be the judge of that."

Newcombe stared at him, then he slumped back in the chair. "Will you promise not to repeat what I tell you?"

397

"That depends on what you tell me. If it is not, in fact, relevant, I'll forget it."

Newcombe picked up a smaller glass case and absent-mindedly rotated it to get the best view. There was a stuffed weasel inside.

"My Tripper got this one when she was only one year old."

"Vince, not now, please."

"All right, all right." He returned the weasel to its place. "I knew Ucillus Bowling many years ago. Fifteen to be precise. I had just arrived in Canada. I went to Peterborough first of all. Maria and me were engaged, but she was still in England . . . I'm ashamed of myself and will be forever, but it's a common story. I was lonely. I met Ucillus, who was eager to show me how welcoming Canadian girls could be. I succumbed. The whole affair lasted no more than a fortnight at most, and I told her I couldn't continue. I moved away to Toronto and got work in a hotel. She hadn't seemed to be bothered much by me going, and I never expected to see her again. Then she showed up here just over a year ago. She had a daughter in tow." He nodded at Murdoch. "I can see you're expecting what comes next. She said Nan was mine. She'd never married, and there's no doubt in my mind she'd many another man in her bed. But what could I do? She didn't want much from me, just some money every now and again. I didn't want to tell Maria I'd been unfaithful to her, and I wanted to do the best I could by the girl." He held out his hands in a gesture of

398

supplication. "There you have it. I told you it wasn't relevant to your situation."

Murdoch studied Vince's face for a moment. "Has Nan been in the habit of wandering about in the woods?"

Newcombe looked away and again Murdoch caught the uneasy expression in his eyes. He was not a difficult man to read, and he suspected Maria knew more than Vince gave her credit for.

He moved closer. "Why is it, Vince, that every time we get near the topic of this girl, you look like a poacher caught with a brace of pheasants in your hands? No, don't gammon me. I believe what you've told me already. . . ."

"Thank goodness. . . ."

"But you haven't said everything there is to say, have you? What are you hiding?"

"Nothing. . . . I, er . . ."

"Will you please answer my question. Her mother had the girl tied up like a dog. Why?"

Newcombe's shoulders slumped. "Nan did start slipping out of the house. Ucillus likes her drink, and the girl can be cunning. She'd go when her mother was asleep. I started to hear gossip, real covert, mostly when the men were in their cups; but it seemed she had picked up ways more becoming to a woman of the night than a young girl. Thank God nobody, as far as I knew, was prepared to take advantage of her; although I made it clear there would be no funny business from the men or they would hear from me. But I was sure it was only a matter of time before somebody trespassed. I warned her mother, and I myself try to keep a good lookout."

"Was Delaney one of those men? He would have seen her often enough. Was he titillated by the girl?"

Newcombe sighed. "Yes, he was. I was on my way to visit Ucillus one afternoon in the spring. I came across him and Nan. He tried to deny it, but I thought he was on the verge of taking her. I warned him off."

"I'd say it's a good thing you have an alibi for the time of his murder, Vince."

"Good Lord, you don't think I . . . I'm not that sort of a fellow. I might give him a good talking to or even a swat but never like that . . ."

"All right, all right. As I said, you are covered. Unless you and Mr. Pugh are shielding each other."

Newcombe looked so appalled that Murdoch couldn't keep him in his misery much longer.

"I'm talking like a policeman, Vince. There are moments when you suspect everybody. Nevertheless, what you're telling me might not be as irrelevant as you think. Damnation, this should have come out at the trial."

400   "Will, it doesn't change anything."

"The jury might not have been as antagonistic towards Harry if they knew this about Delaney. Not quite such an upstanding Christian after all."

Newcombe's voice was kind. "They did know. They live here and there's always been talk about him. But I must emphasize, I only found him with Nan one time. If that had come out, all it would have accomplished is several lives being dragged through the mud."

"And as it stands, only one man's life is getting all dirty. But a man who they didn't know. How convenient."

"Come on, Will. I can understand you being bitter, but so far you haven't convinced me somebody other than your father killed John Delaney."

There was a rap on the door and Lacey called. "Mr. Newcombe, are you done? Mr. Clarry wants to settle his bill."

"I'll be right there, Walter." Newcombe turned. "I'd better get back." He pressed Murdoch's arm. "Sorry about all of this."

He went to the door, unlocked it, and ushered Murdoch out into the hall. Lacey was waiting for them.

"Everything all right, Mr. Newcombe?"

"Yes, thank you, Walter. I was showing Mr. Williams the collection."

Chapter Forty-four

Enid had not extinguished the bedside candle, and the soft light ruddied her bare shoulders and arms. She was lying on her back, her eyes closed, he on his side facing her. He could never have imagined a woman's body was so soft. This time making love with Enid was, if possible, even more sensual. He wasn't as afraid he wouldn't know what to do or, worse, be incapable of intimacy. When he was working at the logging camp, the end of the day talk frequently turned to sexual matters. Full of the strong beer brewed at the camp, the men boasted, piss proud of their sexual exploits. Murdoch was only eighteen, uninitiated into the mysteries, but he would never have dared to admit that, as he knew the hazing would have been relentless. So he pretended, saying little, getting the reputation of being closemouthed. He was capable of showing a hot temper and didn't hesitate to follow up with his fists if need be. However, at the end of the day the only place to be was in the dining hut, so whether he liked it or not, he got a certain kind of education. He'd had no idea how many ways it was possible for men and women to copulate and how many expressions existed to describe these positions. "Knee tremblers" up against the back walls of taverns; "taking flyers" with women, fully clothed. The loggers liked what they called "willing tits," the rare ones who were as eager for connections as the men. A lot of them had contracted Venus's curse, but this was another occasion to boast as if it were a mark of manhood rather than a sin, not to mention a painful condition. What Murdoch soon discovered was that the men feared the unwanted by-blow much less than they feared impotency; and their hatred for sodomites, those who used the windward passage, was corrosive. Fortunately for Murdoch, he had made friends with a married man who seemed to love and honour his wife. Once in a while they talked about the mystery of sexual relations, and Ned's point of view was a relief, a sweet salve on the rapacious appetites the other loggers revealed.

Murdoch left the camp and moved to Toronto, where he met and fell in love with Elizabeth Milner. She had soon softened his views of women and begun what she laughingly called his new education. She was a fervent

403

New Woman, as they were referred to, sometimes with a scorn that masked fear. Although Eliza insisted on remaining chaste until her marriage day, she made no attempt to hide her own desires. "We will be partners in this, William Murdoch," she had said many times. He sighed. He never failed to feel the pain of her loss. He shifted to better study Enid's face. She was darker complexioned than Eliza, her jaw wider, her lips fuller, an attractive face but not beautiful.

Enid opened her eyes and looked directly at him. "You're very silent, William Murdoch. What is it you're thinking about?"

He glanced away, feeling guilty that he was lying naked beside this woman and pining over another. "I'm sorry, Enid. I was wool-gathering."

She hardly ever mentioned her dead husband, and he wondered at this moment if she had been making her own mental comparisons between him and Murdoch.

"Thank you for a delicious meal, Enid."

She smiled. "I assume you do mean the fish cakes."

He felt himself blush and was glad she wasn't looking at him. He laughed, realising his own double entendre. "Yes, of course."

In fact, he had found it difficult to finish the dinner she had ready for him. He was so hot with desire, he felt as if he had a fever. He was afraid she would see in his flushed cheeks and eager eyes what was on his mind and be repulsed. However, she remained

404

affectionate and welcoming. He'd tried to concentrate on eating the mashed potatoes and thought he'd choke.

She'd made a lemon pudding that was too tart for him, but which he pretended to eat with gusto. Then the meal was over, and it was only eight o'clock. Conversation had seemed strained to him, and he blamed himself. Early on, to get it out of the way, he asked her if she was acquainted with a man named Pugh. He gave both versions of Mr. Pugh's appearance and his aptitude for magic, but she denied any knowledge of him. He was glad to believe her. He asked her about her work, and she responded with animation. Her reputation as a fast and efficient typewriter was growing, and she had been getting steady employment. She then asked him to talk about Susanna. "I wish I had known her," she said, and he marvelled that she could say that about a nun. He didn't respond in kind. He wasn't sure if he was eager to meet a family of Baptist, hymn-singing Welshmen. She enquired as to how his investigation was coming along, but it was the last thing he wanted to talk about. "Not well. I'm stumped," was all he could say, and she didn't press him. The clock finally struck nine, the gong dying away on the air, echoing in the silence that had fallen between them. He got up and moved to the couch where she was sitting and took her in his arms, kissing her slowly at first then not so slowly. Finally, she moved back from him.

405

"I think we should go to my room where we will be more comfortable," she whispered against his cheek. And they had, she accepting his ardour. Even remembering it made him stir.

Now she was the one who was doing the scrutinising.

"What? Am I that strange a country, so different from Wales?"

"Yes, sometimes. Your eyes are very dark, and I can no more see into them than I could see the bottom of the mountain caches. When we were children we were allowed to swim in them, and the surface was sun warmed; but just below the surface, it was icy cold."

"Oh dear, that is not a flattering image."

"All the water needed was a longer time in the sunshine."

· He kissed her then, tracing the line of her neck lightly with his fingertips, just above the swell of her full breasts. "Your skin is so smooth and soft, as if you have been dipped in velvet."

With a sigh of pleasure, she closed her eyes again. He continued his exploration, moving his fingers downwards. He felt like a sculptor determining the skeletal underpinnings of the flesh. Here the bony front breastplate; here the curve of the ribs. He had to press a little harder to feel them through the covering of flesh, but he was careful to avoid the pendulous breasts. He was saving them for later. He retraced his path back to her neck, proceeding along the right collarbone to the shoulder joint.

406

"What are you doing, exactly?" she murmured. They were both speaking quietly, mindful of Alwyn who was asleep in his box room.

"I am getting to know your body. What if all the candles were blown out, and I had to find you among all the other bodies . . ."

She opened her eyes. "What other bodies? Is it in a seraglio, we are?"

"Heavens no. Much too crowded."

"Continue then."

Before he could do so, the door opened. "Momma!"

Alwyn, eyes wide with total dismay, stood in the doorway staring at them.

Murdoch rolled onto his back immediately, pulling up the sheet. Enid said something in Welsh to the boy, who responded with a spate of words that Murdoch didn't understand but whose import he sensed unequivocally.

Enid spoke again, and Alwyn reluctantly turned his back to them. She jumped out of bed and put on her dressing robe.

"He isn't feeling well," she said to Murdoch.

She went over to the boy and put her hand on his forehead. "You're hot," she said in English. He replied in Welsh. Enid shook her head.

"Mr. Murdoch was tired, and I offered him a bed for the night. Now remember your manners and come and say hello to him."

407

Sullenly, Alwyn allowed his mother to lead him to the bed.

"Hello, young man," said Murdoch, who was having a difficult time suppressing his laughter.

"Good evening, Mr. Murdoch. I am not feeling well."

"I'm sorry to hear that."

"Come, Alwyn. Back to your bed."

His eyes filled with tears and he started to wail, again talking to his mother in their own language, effectively excluding Murdoch. Enid took the boy in her arms and comforted him.

"I'm afraid he's too upset. He does feel a little feverish," she said to Murdoch.

"Does that mean he is not going to go back to his own room?"

She looked abashed. "When he has these fevers, he doesn't sleep."

"Which means in this bed and not his."

"I'm sorry, Will. It is just that he is used to having me all to himself."

Alwyn was watching Murdoch through tear-laden eyes. His distress was genuine, and Murdoch was torn between feeling completely aggravated at the boy and understanding how threatened he must feel.

408   "It was time for me to leave anyway. Alwyn, bring me my trousers from the chair."

The boy did so, Enid hovering anxiously nearby. She

handed Murdoch his other clothes, indicating he should get dressed behind the screen.

When he emerged, Alwyn was already in the bed, sitting high on the pillows while his mother stroked his head. Murdoch grimaced. He had the sense he was not the first man in history to witness the bond that exists between mother and son and to feel excluded by it.

Chapter Forty-five

THE STREET WAS DESERTED, and the pavement was black and slick in the light of the street lamps. On impulse, Murdoch headed up to Gerrard Street to the jail. He'd gone there earlier from the Manchester, but the guard had refused to admit him.

"No visiting after six." Murdoch hadn't met this guard before. He contemplated making a fuss but decided against it. Frankly, he didn't know what he could bring to tell Harry. That Delaney wasn't such a saintly fellow? That wouldn't surprise Harry. His own encounter with Mrs. Bowling and the innkeeper's confession were still to be assessed in his mind. At this stage he didn't want to reveal anything to Harry that would raise unjustified hopes.

The two cell wings were in darkness and only a single gas sconce sputtered in the entranceway. He wondered if his father was lying awake on the hard cot, afraid to lose what little time was left to him.

Murdoch wasn't sure how long he stood outside the jail, but suddenly he realised his teeth were starting to chatter. He turned away and headed for home. He wasn't quite as lighthearted as he'd been yesterday, the boy's interruption had seen to that, but there was still a glow of warmth around his heart that made him impervious to the biting cold wind that was soughing in the trees. He'd been carrying on about the major impediment between him and Enid being their different faiths, but now he was beginning to wonder if it wouldn't rest more in the presence of an intensely jealous boy. Murdoch smiled to himself. Poor Sprat. He could hardly blame him. He vowed he'd try to do more to win him over. Every lad needed a father. And that thought brought with it such a pang it was as if he had breathed the cold air into his soul.

He was hurrying along Wilton Street as if he were going to work. He was late because he hadn't been able to find his collar. Hastily, he wrapped a scarf around his bare neck, hoping that the inspector wouldn't notice. Suddenly, directly in front of him, he saw Eliza. She was moving slowly, looking into shop windows in a way that she never did in real life. He was filled with intense joy, and he ran up to her, calling out, "How could you not tell me you hadn't died?" She shrugged with an indifference that stabbed him to the heart. "I've met somebody else," she said,

411

and there was suddenly a man at her side. She had her arm linked through his. He smirked at Murdoch with all the smugness of assured possession. Murdoch's happiness that Eliza was alive turned immediately to a hot rage. "No!" he yelled, but the sound wouldn't come out, and she and her escort turned away and continued their walk. "No!" he screamed, but the cries were still so choked they could not be heard.

Murdoch woke up. He couldn't tell if he had been actually shouting out loud or not. A pale strip of daylight was showing beneath his window blind. He looked at his alarm clock. Ten minutes past seven. He was surprised he had slept as long as he had. He listened. From the back room downstairs, he heard Arthur coughing, and he gauged the severity of the sound. Bad. The cold, damp air was hard on him. He could hear Beatrice talking. Her voice was, as usual, calm and reassuring. She never for a moment conveyed despair, and ever since Murdoch had been living with them, she had not given up hope of finding some treatment that would bring about a cure. He thought Arthur would have died many months ago if she had not been ministering to him.

His room had grown cold in the night; and although he was warm underneath the quilt, he wanted to get away from the misery of his dream. He got out of bed and dressed as fast as he could, wondering if Enid was awake and, if she was, what was she doing?

412

He went downstairs and headed for the kitchen. Beatrice came out carrying a tray. There was a delicious smell of frying bacon in the air.

"Good morning, Mr. Murdoch. I've just started your breakfast."

"Thank you. Here let me take that."

She relinquished the tray. The jug of cream and a bowl of eggs was Arthur's breakfast. This was a reputed cure that he had been taking for some time now. Six fresh eggs stirred into a glass of milk with its heavy cream. Beatrice indicated a small brown bottle.

"We're going to try this as well. It's iodine I got from the chemist. Mrs. O'Grady said she's heard it works wonders."

She opened the door to what was essentially both bedroom and sitting room for the Kitchens. The front small parlour was converted into a dining room for her lodgers. Once again, that meant only Murdoch now that Mrs. Jones had moved out. He knew that most nights Beatrice made up a cot in the kitchen for herself, but by morning it had been tidied away.

The smell from the disinfectant bucket filled the room, which was very cold. The window was kept open so that Arthur could get fresh air.

He was propped up in his Bath chair, wrapped in a blanket. He wore a nightcap and today gloves against the cold.

"Ah, good morning, Will. Welcome to Siberia."

413

"What? It's positively sweltering in here."

It was a feeble attempt at humour, but he was rewarded by Arthur's grin.

"You must be burning up yourself then if you think that. There's something going about called Welsh fever. Quite debilitating. You'd better watch out." He glanced at Murdoch with a sly look.

"Now, Arthur! Don't tease," said Beatrice, but she, too, smiled expectantly.

"If there is such a thing, I must say, it has not affected Mrs. Jones, who is in excellent health."

"I'm glad of that. Here you go, Arthur."

She poured out the cream, added the raw eggs, then dripped some of the iodine into the glass.

Arthur drank the mixture down in a few big gulps. It was the only way to do it.

His face was grey this morning, and the skin was stretched tightly across his cheekbones. The receding flesh was making his teeth prominent, and the shape of his skull was coming through more and more visibly. He coughed uncontrollably, and Beatrice reached for a fresh strip of linen from the bedside table. He spat into it and she quickly dropped the bloodied cloth into the bucket.

414 Arthur lay back on his pillow. His chest was heaving as he tried to breathe. Beatrice calmly took his hand in hers.

"I'm just going to start Mr. Murdoch's breakfast.

I'll . . ." She was interrupted by the sound of knocking at the front door. "That's probably the bread man. He's coming earlier and earlier."

"I'll see to it," said Murdoch.

The truth was that he was only too glad to get out of the room. Sometimes he found the sight of Arthur's struggle almost unbearable. It was like being forced to watch a man drown while you were a mere two feet away on the shore but unable to do anything about it.

The rapping sounded again, and he opened the door with some irritation. On the threshold was standing a constable, whose enormous bulk filled the doorway. It was his fellow officer, George Crabtree.

"George! What are you doing here at this hour?"

"Good morning, Mr. Murdoch. I'm sorry to intrude at a time like this and so early in the morning, but Inspector Brackenreid would like you to come down to the station on a rather urgent matter."

"What urgent matter?"

"I'm afraid he didn't say, sir. He just asked me to fetch you right away."

"Do I have time for my breakfast?"

"I rather doubt that, Mr. Murdoch. He said he wanted to see you in his office in fifteen minutes."

"Well, we'd better hurry then. I'd hate to disappoint our good inspector. He clearly has a high opinion of our abilities to get from the station and back in that amount of time. Let me tell Mrs. Kitchen."

415

Murdoch turned around but his landlady had come out into the hall, and he explained the summons.

"No lodger of mine is going out on a cold morning like this without a bite of breakfast in his stomach. You can wait for one minute at least."

She went back to the kitchen.

Murdoch, in the meantime, started to put on his coat and hat. "Any guesses as to what he wants, George?"

"Apparently he had an early visitor. I was in the back room and didn't see him arrive, but he was in the office when I went up to answer the bell. The inspector didn't say who he was or why you were being summoned at this sorrowful time, but the man must have something to do with it."

Mrs. Kitchen returned with a sandwich wrapped in grease-proof paper and handed it to Murdoch.

He thanked her, put it in his pocket, and left with Crabtree. Once outside, they started a fast jogging trot up the street.

"What did the fellow look like?"

"I didn't really get a look at him. He was standing with his back to me and was looking out of the window."

"Tall? Short? Fat?"

"Sorry, Mr. Murdoch, it was such a glimpse. I'd say he was quite slim and on the short side."

"By ordinary standards, George, or compared to you?"

Crabtree grinned. "Ordinary standards."

416

They were at the station. The lamps shone into the grey morning, and Murdoch felt the familiar pleasurable response to the sight. He realised he would be glad to get back to work.

"Just a minute, George. Let me get my breath. I don't want the inspector to have the satisfaction of seeing me panting. He might get an inflated sense of his own importance."

He would have liked to have taken a bite of his sandwich, but he knew it was going to be greasy, and he didn't want to see Brackenreid with bacon fat smeared all over his face.

"All right, Constable Crabtree. Let us face Caesar."

They went into the station where Sergeant Seymour, the soberfaced desk sergeant, greeted him. "He's waiting for you," he said with a grimace, indicating Brackenreid was in a mood. Not unusual, but depending on its severity, there was always the hazard that the station would be rocked back on its heels with his unreasonable demands and the laying out of fines and charges for petty misdemeanours.

"Give me your sandwich, I'll keep it warm, and I'll mash some tea," said Crabtree. "Come and have some when you're done."

"Hold on a minute. There's a package come for you," said Seymour. He reached under his desk. "Strange fellow brought it in. A priest of some kind; couldn't even speak English properly."

417

Curious, Murdoch examined the parcel. On the front was the convent's insignia.

"Hold on to it for me. If I don't return, I've willed all my effects to my landlady."

He hung his coat and hat on one of the hooks on the wall and went upstairs to the inspector's second-floor office. There was a serviceable rush carpet on the stairs, but outside the door there was a strip of luxurious Axminster carpet. Even though the station was in need of repairs, Brackenreid refused to acknowledge it and spent money on furnishings that enhanced his own position.

Murdoch knocked on the door. He could feel his pulse was faster. What the hell was the reason for this urgency?

"Come!"

He entered the room. Brackenreid was seated behind his desk, and his visitor was seated in the sole easy chair in front of him. In what seemed to Murdoch a staged effect, the man was holding a newspaper in front of his face. The air was blue and pungent with cigar smoke. It could have been a gentleman's club rather than a police inspector's office.

"You asked to see me, sir," said Murdoch.

418 Brackenreid drew on his cigar before answering. He waved his hand in the direction of the other man.

"You know Mr. Pugh, I understand."

Chapter Forty-six

MURDOCH COULDN'T SAY he was really surprised. Once he was confident that Pugh was not Enid's suitor, he suspected the man was also doing a little investigating of his own. He assumed he was a genuine reporter getting ready to write something sensational when Harry was hung.

"Good morning to you, Mr. Murdoch. No hard feelings, I hope?"

"About what?" asked Brackenreid.

"A little contest that Mr. Murdoch and I engaged in. I assure you, sir, the secret is all a matter of physics. I use your weight against you by actually pushing downward on the stick."

419

"I for one have no idea what you're talking about, Mr. Pugh, but let's get to the matter at hand, shall we?" He scowled at Murdoch as if he were the one meandering. Scowling at Murdoch, however, was his typical expression.

"I sent for you because Mr. Pugh here has brought a most grave matter to my attention." He brushed some ash from the front of his jacket. "I realise that you are, er, under some duress as it were, but I felt nevertheless it was imperative we clarify some things. You have been trespassing, Murdoch, and I'd like to know why."

"I do not know what you are referring to, Inspector."

Whether it was Murdoch's tone of voice or memories of previous encounters, Brackenreid seemed to think it prudent to turn toward Pugh.

"Perhaps you could explain."

"Certainly. Mr. Murdoch, I have to confess I have not been altogether honest with you." He grinned. "But then we were both masquerading under false pretenses, weren't we, Mr. Williams?"

Murdoch nodded, waiting. Pugh cleared his throat. "Yes, well, the point is, you see, that I am not a book salesman as I have been pretending to be. Like you, I am a detective, a private one with the Hoskin Agency. You may have heard of us?"

"Yes, I have."

Murdoch did not add that much of what he had heard had not enhanced the agency's reputation.

Pugh took a leather folder from his jacket pocket and removed two bills.

"Mr. Murdoch, take a look at these two-dollar notes.

One is genuine; one is counterfeit. Can you tell me which is which?" He held them in front of him, ever the showman.

Murdoch moved closer. The bills both had portraits of the Marquis and Marchioness of Lansdowne on the front, and both were creased and grubby. He chose the dirtier one.

"This one is counterfeit."

Pugh couldn't quite hide his chagrin. "Yes, well done. But you must admit you had to study them carefully. It was not immediately obvious that it is a forgery. In the normal business of commerce, it would pass unnoticed. They are the work of truly expert engravers." He replaced the notes in the folder. "For the past year, I have been employed by Mr. Cockburn of the Dominion Bank. They have become aware of a steady increase of counterfeit money, all two-dollar bills, circulating in the city. As you can imagine, it is a very difficult task to trace the source of queer money as it can pass through literally a dozen hands before being detected. However, I have finally discovered what I believe has been a primary source of distribution. In other words the engravers themselves. I was on the verge of making an arrest when my birds were flushed. Phit! Scared away by a wily fox who was poaching on my land, as it were. All my work for nought."

Again he paused, his cigar held aloft. Murdoch shrugged.

"Mr. Pugh, you are an excellent magician, but perhaps it has affected your ability to be direct. I do not know what in Hades you are talking about."

Pugh smiled, not offended by these hot words. "Quite right, Mr. Murdoch. Circumlocution becomes ingrained. To the point then. What I want to say is that this summer past I had narrowed down my search. I won't bore you with the details of how I followed my trail; suffice it to say I ended up at the Manchester tavern. . . ."

"That's ridiculous."

"Why so, Mr. Murdoch?"

"Vince Newcombe is no queer pusher."

"I must admit he does appear to be a jolly, well-meaning sort of fellow, but come sir, as a police officer you know how money can tempt the most honourable men to mischief."

"Where would he print them? Unless it's remarkably well hidden, he doesn't have a press."

"You race ahead of me, sir."

Brackenreid interrupted. "Let him tell his story, Murdoch. You'd do well to listen closely."

Murdoch would have liked to have sat down. While the other two were seated, he felt like a naughty school-boy being reprimanded. Pugh must have become aware of this discomfort because he stood up and walked over to the window. Leaning against the sill, he drew on his cigar.

"I will admit for a while I did not know if the bills

422

were coming from his tavern because of the turnover of money that takes place there, or if he was more directly responsible. Mr. Newcombe, as you are aware, on occasion runs betting matches. He pretends they are friendly contests for sport only, but of course that is not the case. Money is wagered, and therefore many notes are passed among the Fancy. In August I got myself a dog so I could participate in the match, and I made a careful record of what money was passed along by what person. As it turned out, my suspicions were quite justified. Delaney had in his possession eleven two-dollar bills of which eight were queer."

He turned around but his back was to the light, throwing him into shadow so that his expression was inscrutable.

"Not counting myself, only two other people had passed along bills of two-dollar denomination. I had marked all the money I myself exchanged, so it was a simple matter to determine where the false currency had come from."

He couldn't resist a short pause before his denouement. Murdoch did not accommodate him and kept his expression indifferent.

Pugh continued. "In a word, James Craig contributed five bills and his father three. All were counterfeit. As you may know, the Craigs make their living publishing pamphlets and broadsheets. They therefore had access to a printing press. I kept them under close observation

423

from that time on and soon determined that the appearance of queer money seemed to coincide with father and son working late hours in their printing shed. Yes, Mr. Murdoch, I know what you are going to say. Not proof enough by any means. I needed to catch them red-handed with the engraving plates in their possession. Then I could make an arrest. A big feather in my cap, as I'm sure you can understand. However, before I could proceed any further, they were scared off. Poof! Gone! Miss Craig will not or cannot give any indication of their whereabouts."

He returned to his seat. "I discovered that you, sir, were neither a reporter nor another private detective but an officer from this station. My guess is that the Craigs also got wind that you were a police detective and went into hiding because they assumed you were onto them."

"What the hell have you been doing, Murdoch?" interjected Brackenreid. "You are supposed to be on compassionate leave, not chasing around the country, poaching."

"I was not poaching, as you call it, sir. I have had no inkling of what Mr. Pugh is pursuing. I did accidentally encounter the Craig lad, however. He has been up before the magistrate before. He called himself Carey then and he was in court on a charge of seduction. I was in the courtroom that day. I didn't think he recognised me, but he must have."

"How unfortunate. Actually, Murdoch, Mr. Pugh here is offering to do us, this station, a favour. He feels he is not ready to make an arrest, and he does not want to reveal his incognito." He turned to Pugh. "You believe that Miss Craig is becoming quite attached to you, and you wish to cultivate that friendship, isn't that so?"

Pugh nodded, rather shamefaced.

"He has done all the hard work, and we can just capitalise on it. Suit both of us. We'll get some much-needed public approval, and Mr. Pugh here will receive his just wages."

"I am not sure what you are implying, sir," said Murdoch.

"Quite simple. Mr. Pugh is proposing we search the Craig house. If we find the engraving plates, we take credit. If we don't, Mr. Pugh is still not unmasked and can go on with his investigation."

Brackenreid opened his drawer and took out some notepaper. "I'm going to draw up an order. The sooner you get on to it the better."

He started to scrawl on the page. Pugh remained at the window.

"By the way, Murdoch," said the inspector, "if you weren't barging in where you shouldn't, what *were* you doing? Why did you give out a false name? Mr. Pugh said you were pretending to be some kind of reporter."

Before Murdoch could answer, Pugh jumped in. The mood between them had changed quite suddenly. Pugh was no longer behaving as if they were competitors in the race for the golden apples thrown down by the Dominion Bank. In fact, he now seemed anxious to end the interview.

"Inspector Brackenreid, I am quite satisfied that Mr. Murdoch was not following the same trail after all. I can quite understand his circumstances. We can let it rest."

Murdoch sensed how fidgety the other man had become, and with a sense of shock, he realised why. He actually took a step in Pugh's direction.

"You took money off Delaney's body, didn't you?"

"I beg pardon, sir."

"There was money missing, part of his winnings: twenty-two dollars. You took them when you found his body."

"Murdoch, what's the matter with you? What are you blethering about?" spluttered Brackenreid.

Murdoch whirled around. "You asked what I was up to, sir. Well, I was conducting an investigation of my own. I wanted to make absolutely sure that my father was guilty of the crime he is to hang for."

"Good Lord, Murdoch. Have you lost your mind? What are you talking about?"

"Didn't Mr. Pugh tell you? My father, Harry Murdoch, was convicted of killing John Delaney directly after the betting match Pugh referred to. He is due to be hung in two days' time." He turned round to face Pugh, who backed off a few steps. "The fact that money was missing

426

was used to support the guilty charge against Harry. It was assumed he had stolen it. Yet another nail in his coffin. Why didn't you come forward and say that was not the case? That you had taken it?"

Pugh looked down at his boots. "It wasn't relevant."

"I'm tired of people saying that. Isn't a jury supposed to decide what is or is not relevant? Isn't that what our bloody justice system is all about?"

"Now, now, Murdoch," said Brackenreid, "calm yourself. Please realise this is the first time I have heard of your situation. It is most unusual to say the least."

"I realise that, sir. But this man here actually withheld information that might have made a difference to the outcome of the trial."

Brackenreid could be an irascible Napoleon of a man, but he retained some pride in his job as a police officer. He frowned now at Pugh.

"Is this true, sir? What Mr. Murdoch is accusing you of?"

"I assure you, I answered honestly the questions put to me at the trial." Pugh tried to meet Murdoch's eyes with only partial success. "I am sorry for your situation, but your father bashed Delaney and that's the truth."

"Is it? Are you God, Mr. Pugh, as well as a magician? Can you see into his heart with such certainty?"

427

"Please contain yourself, Murdoch. Mr. Pugh, is it true that you removed money from the body of this Mr. Delaney?"

Pugh shrugged and, for the first time, his jovial entertainer's mask slipped. "Inspector, I have been pursuing this investigation for more than a year. I have spent untold hours on this case. I needed to check on those bills. I had no idea that it would come up at the trial."

"But when it did, you said nothing."

"Mr. Murdoch is understandably overwrought, but I tell you sincerely the matter of the missing money was small compared to the rest of the evidence, which was quite conclusive."

"Nevertheless, we must in conscience bring this to the attention of the court."

"If you do, we stand to lose every advantage we have."

Brackenreid leaned back in his chair. "I believe you mean that you yourself will lose the advantage."

"Will you deny me the search then?"

"Counterfeiting is a serious crime. I have every intention of following up on the information you have given me. However, this other matter must take precedence."

Murdoch could hardly believe what he was hearing. If he'd had a different relationship with his inspector, he would have jumped forward at that moment and shaken his hand.

428   Brackenreid actually gave him a kind look. "Mr. Murdoch, I suggest you go at once and apprise the warden of this meeting. I will myself come over directly and speak to him in person. Mr. Pugh, if you would be

so good as to remain here, I would like to hear from you the events of that evening. I will write it down."

Pugh looked as if he were contemplating doing a bunk, but he thought better of it. He reached into his pocket and casually brought out a silver dollar and began to twist it through his fingers.

"Of course, Inspector."

"Thank you, sir," said Murdoch, and not trusting himself to stay near Pugh any longer, he left and hurried down to the station hall.

Seymour saw the expression on his face. "Will, what happened? You're white as a ghost."

Murdoch could hear himself panting as if he'd run a long distance. "I can't tell you right now."

He started to head for the door when the sergeant called to him.

"Hold on a minute. You've forgotten your package."

He hurried around the desk and handed it over to Murdoch.

"Will . . . ," he started to say, but Murdoch took the parcel, grabbed his coat from the rack, and practically ran. With a desperation he could hardly bear, he knew he needed to speak to his father.

Chapter Forty-seven

Jessica put her two copper pots in the wooden crate; then she took the top one out again. She'd need it to heat up milk for Sally. The child loved to have her "possy," a mug of hot milk sweetened with honey. Jessica glanced over to the hearth where the child was seated on the floor. She had placed her favourite doll, Min-min, in a box for her bed. She was talking quietly to herself, but Jessica heard her say, "Go to sleep like a good girl. Don't bother Momma. Momma has a heartache."

Last week Sally had asked her mother what was wrong, why she lay in bed sleeping all the time. "Momma has a heartache," Jess had replied, and now Sally said that all the time. She had bound a piece of cloth about the doll's head, confusing head and heartaches. Jessica wanted to go to her and hug her tightly, but she felt as if she could hardly move, as if her limbs were too heavy. She simply stood and watched for a moment; then she went back to her task. She had packed the three valises, which was all Walter would allow.

"Only what we can carry, Jess. Put everything else you'll need later in the trunks. I'll get some crates, and you can put the dishes and your pots in them."

She blinked. She had been standing at the sink staring through the window but seeing nothing. How long? There was a plate in her hand that she had been in the process of wrapping in the strips of Holland cloth that Walter had cut for her. These dishes had come to her from her own mother when she'd died. Her older sister, Catherine, had been angry at that, considering it was more her right as she had nursed their mother in the last days of her illness. "You can have them," Jessica had said, but her sister had pouted and retreated into martyrdom. "No, if that was her wish, you must have them," but after that the feelings between them were even less cordial than they had been. Jessica knew that she had been her mother's favourite child, the last born, the youngest daughter. She hadn't wanted to move away, but Walter was always restless and, she suspected, all too anxious to move her far from her family, where he'd have her all to himself. So they had moved to Ontario and taken this cottage in which she had once taken such delight.

She couldn't return to Alberta, not with Catherine's coldness and constant reproach, and yesterday, when Walter had suggested they move further east, she had agreed. Not with enthusiasm or even fear; she had no

431

strong feelings anymore. They were soaked up like ink on blotting paper by her prevailing lethargy, her indifference to any event around her, even her own child.

The door opened and Walter came in, bringing a waft of cold air. He couldn't hide his dismay when he saw her.

"Jess! Not done yet? We don't have much more time."

She looked around, saw the half-empty crate, the pots on the floor. The stack of dishes, already wrapped, were still on the table.

"Here, I can help now," he said.

Sally jumped up and ran over to him. She was sucking her thumb, the doll tucked under her arm.

"Arh. That's dirty," he said, and pulled the thumb away from her mouth. She started to whine.

"Leave her alone, Walter. She'll just get upset again, and she's been playing nicely."

Sally was winding up for a full crying jag. Jessica picked up a dish where a honeycomb sat in a sticky mess. Flies never completely died off, and one or two were crawling around the dish. Jessica knocked them away, broke off a piece of the comb, and handed it to Sally. The child quieted immediately, stuffing the sweet morsel into her mouth.

"Go and play with Min-min for a bit longer, there's my girl."

432

Sally cast a sullen look mixed with some triumph at her father, and he sighed in exasperation.

He began to place the dishes in the crate, where he'd put wood shavings.

"Maria has agreed to keep an eye on things until I have a chance to come back for our belongings."

"Did she have anything to say?"

"No, not really." He hesitated for a moment. "I told her your sister had invited you to come and live with her for a while until you felt more like yourself."

"Catherine has virtually disowned me."

"Maria doesn't know that, Jess." He tried to keep the impatience out of his voice, but she felt it and turned away from him. She looked out of the window.

"It's starting to snow," she said.

"Yes, it's gone very cold. It will be warmer where we're going," he answered, struggling to inject jollity into his tone.

She didn't turn around, and her voice was so low he almost didn't catch what she said.

"Are you certain we are doing the right thing, Walter?"

He stood up and came over to her and put his arms around her, burying his head in her shoulder. "Of course we are, my chuck. We'll have a new start. No bad memories. You'll see. Before you know it you'll be feeling right as rain."

Briefly she rested her cheek against the top of his head. "Will I? Sometimes I feel as if I will never be happy again. Not as long as I live."

433

"Jess, come on. You have Sally. We'll have sons, seven of them if I have anything to do with it."

He moved his hands to her breasts, caressing them through her gown. She flinched and he could feel her body stiffen. He let her go and stepped back.

"I'd better get on with this packing. Are you going to help or not?"

Without looking at him, she walked over to the door and reached for her shawl. "I'm feeling so tired. I think some air will wake me up."

"Jess . . ."

"Watch Sally, will you. I won't be long."

"Momma!" Seeing what her mother was doing, Sally let out a wail and ran toward her. Walter caught hold of her.

"Sally, stop it. Momma will be back. She's going for a walk. You can help me."

"No! I want to go, too. Me, too."

Jessica closed the door behind her, almost running toward the gate. She could hear the frightened screams of her little daughter, but she pulled the shawl tighter about her head to shut out the sound. She didn't know where she was going, only that she couldn't bear to be in his presence. The pretence between them was like acid in her gut. It wasn't only the loss of her unborn son that was destroying her life energy, it was the circumstances that had caused the miscarriage, circumstances they had never referred to again so that she thought she would go mad, as if she had swallowed poison that she must vomit up if she were to live.

She was sliding down the hill now, the snow and mud over her boots cold against her bare legs. She came to a halt by catching hold of one of the trees. She clung to it, pressing her cheek against the rough bark. She began to cry out over and over. "You lied to me. I know you did. You lied."

The skin on her face began to bleed.

Chapter Forty-eight

THE GUARD UNLOCKED THE DOOR and let him into the hall.

"Is the warden available? I need to talk to him on a matter of some urgency."

"He's not here. He's gone over to Central Prison to talk to the warden there, see if he can get some tips on how to run a jail."

He grinned, inviting Murdoch to share the joke. However, he was in no mood for humour.

"When will he be back?"

"Shouldn't be much more than an hour." He regarded Murdoch with curiosity. "Do you want to see the prisoner today?"

Murdoch nodded.

"He's with the priest, confessing or whatever it is they do. Be about half an hour. Do you want me to fetch him anyway?"

"No, that's all right. I'll wait."

He followed the guard into the waiting room.

"Here you go. Make yourself comfortable. Warden Massie's given orders you can stay as long as you like, seeing it's . . ."

His voice tailed off. He meant seeing it might be the last time Murdoch would see his father alive.

Tyler went out through the opposite door that led to the cells, and Murdoch sat down at the table. The clock on the wall gave an asthmatic whirr. It wasn't yet eleven o'clock. He propped his elbows on the table and leaned his head in his hands. He was almost surprised to find his forehead was cool. When he was about ten years old, Murdoch had come down with scarlet fever. He had a vivid memory of being sent home from school and how odd everything round him had seemed; colours were stronger, sounds louder. There had been a bad storm the day before, and as he walked along the shore to his house, he saw that the landscape had altered. A dock had been knocked askew and sand had buried some rocks and been blown away from others. In his feverish state, he tried to make himself understand this, but he couldn't. All he knew was a feeling of dislocation and strangeness.

Even though he had no actual physical illness right at this moment, he had the same peculiar sense of abnormality. The words "relevant" and "irrelevant" were buzzing in his brain like flies in a jar. It wasn't that

437

good men didn't get murdered, they did. However, Newcombe's revelations about John Delaney's character could change the picture. Murdoch grimaced. Suddenly the circle of suspects had widened. There was really quite a queue if he looked at it like that. What if Delaney's wife had taken exception to his behaviour? Or his son or his daughter? Or Mrs. Bowling? Or somebody he didn't even know about yet who had been affected by Delaney's lasciviousness. The news about the Craigs and their sideline also muddied the pond considerably. What if Delaney had found out and was trying a spot of blackmail or even righteously was about to report them? Easy to get a daughter to lie in court, and give them an alibi, especially as she, too, would be affected by the discovery. *Relevant? Irrelevant?* Buzz, buzz.

The problem was one of time. He needed much more time to pursue these possibilities, and he had no certainty he would get it. For Massie to postpone the execution, he would have to be convinced there was sufficient doubt concerning Harry's culpability now being raised. Was there?

The waiting room was hot, the oil heater blasting out warm air, and he removed his coat. He'd almost forgotten about the package Sergeant Seymour had handed to him. More for something to do than anything else, he took it out of his pocket and tore open the brown paper wrapping. Inside was a diary. He smiled, recognising it, a birthday present he'd given to his sister when they were

438

young. He opened up the cover, which was lavishly embossed with gold flowers on a background of red velvet. He'd agonised over the choice, he remembered, finally settling on this showy book.

Printed in a big, childish hand that tended to slope off the page, was the first entry. She hadn't got enough command of her penmanship yet, and this one entry took up three pages. He had helped her with the spelling, but it seemed as if he hadn't been that good either.

December 12 the year of Our Lord 1872
Today I am eight years old. I got this writing tablet from William Murdoch, my brother. I have a brother named Albert. He is one year yunger than me and he is simpul. My mamma gave me a blue riban for my hair.

Murdoch touched the page with his fingertips. Susanna had loved pretty things, not that she received many.

He continued reading.

January 10 in the year of Our Lord 1873
My poppa wos angry with Bertie. He is also angry with Will. He is not as angry with me because I am a girl but momma loves us all more.
Sunday. We all went to mass and Father Maloney blessed us. Poppa did not go. Bertie was a good boy.

439

He turned the page and there was one solitary entry on the next page that stopped his heart for a moment.

March 12
Momma has gone to heaven.

He had been helping Mr. Mitchell in his dry goods store that afternoon. He'd been laying down fresh sawdust on the floor, and for years after, he couldn't smell that odour without remembering that day. There were only two short entries in the following pages, both about going to church again. Then another laborious record.

November 28. 1873
Bertie, my brother, has been taken by Jesus. His hart was broken.

Again Murdoch touched the page. After their mother's death, Bertie had withdrawn into a world of his own. He didn't laugh, and no matter what he and Susanna tried, he wouldn't play with them anymore. That particular morning he had complained of hurting in his chest, but nobody had taken him seriously because he was always moaning about some kind of ache or pain, which they dismissed as his bid for attention. Harry had gone off to his boat, Will to school, and Susanna was left to tend to the house and get the evening meal. When Will came home, the neighbour from down the road was in the living room, sitting beside the couch bathing Bertie's face. Susanna had fetched her because Bertie had collapsed, and she couldn't rouse him. Murdoch had taken over the ministrations, but they had been futile. Eventually, the doctor came from the village, but he said Bertie had suffered a heart seizure. It was common for children like him to have bad hearts, he'd said, in a hateful pedantic voice. "There wasn't anything anyone could do," he said, and Bertie obliged by dying at that moment in front of all of them. A little gasp, a sigh, and he was gone.

The memory was still painful. Murdoch had loved his brother even though he was often exasperated with him when he couldn't do what seemed like simple ordinary tasks. However, his father seemed to hate him from the moment it became apparent Bertie was not normal, as if that reflected on his prowess as a man. He never acknowledged him as his son and frequently beat him unmercifully for small mistakes. Murdoch intervened as often as he could and got the brunt of the anger drawn onto himself.

The clock wheezed again. Quarter past eleven. He wondered if he should read the rest of the diary later. The memories it was stirring were hot. He didn't particularly want to colour these last moments with his father, especially after what had happened at their last

441

visit. Perhaps he should let sleeping dogs lie. However, he couldn't resist, and he continued to read.

December 1873

Will and me are now living with our Aunt Emily Weldon who is momma's sister. She is strict. Her house is pretty. We have been here one week. After Bertie was taken to Jesus, Poppa was angry a lot. He was cruel to Will. Then Will got me up in the middle of the night. It was very dark. It took us a long time to walk to the station. Will had to tell a white lie to the ticket man but he let us buy a ticket. He was kind and gave me a sticky bun with currants in it. Aunt Weldon was surprised to see us. I was afraid she would send us to a Home but Will talked to her. He had to show her his arm which is bad where Poppa hit him. He has promised to work hard. I will lern to sew.

Murdoch touched his left forearm. The scar that ran from his elbow to wrist was jagged and long. The next entry one year later showed much improved handwriting and didn't take up as much space.

December 12, 1874

I am ten years old today. Aunt gave me a picture of Jesus who is my Savyour. Will gave me a new nib for my pen.

They had stayed with their aunt for the next four years. Those were not especially happy times. His aunt was a schoolteacher at the one-room schoolhouse just outside St. John's. She had not wanted two young children to look after. She was poorly paid, and it must have been a hardship for her to raise them. A few months after they arrived, she had received a letter from their father enquiring as to their whereabouts. She had decided then that she would not send them back, and that moment was one of the few times of warmth he had experienced from her. Now he could see that she had loved them both as much as she was capable of, but then he didn't feel it, only constant criticism and carping. Harry had not pursued the matter, and Murdoch had not seen him again or heard anything from him until now.

He began to skim through the pages. Susanna wasn't diligent in her diary and only managed one or two entries a year, mostly birthday times. He stopped at the entry for 1878 when Susanna had gone away to the convent school when she was fourteen. Her writing was now very neat, a result of many a knuckle rapping by their aunt.

September 7 '78

I have begun school with the Sisters of St. Ann. I am sharing my room with five other girls. We are all the same age but Emilie is the oldest. She is almost fifteen. I cried when Will left. Aunt Weldon did not come as she was too ill to make the journey. I would have gladly stayed home and taken care of her but she and Will thought this was best as the sisters have a good name. JMJ.

She had drawn a little cross at the top of the page. More scattered entries all about school or references to letters from Will or her aunt. Desperate for some freedom, Murdoch had left their aunt's home and made his way west. He'd had to do odd jobs along the way to earn money for food, and it was a rough, difficult time when he often went hungry. However, he remembered being happy. He was independent for the first time, beginning to feel his own power as a man. He'd grown tall, and the labouring work had filled out his chest and broadened his shoulders.

The last entry was written on the eve of Susanna becoming a postulant at the Holy Name convent.

Tomorrow I will say goodbye to the world and enter into the haven of this convent. May I be worthy.

He closed the book. He hadn't noticed at first the envelope that was tucked at the back of the diary, addressed to him. He opened it. There were two letters, one a short one from Mother St. Raphael.

Dear Mr. Murdoch. I am sending you these last effects of your sister Susanna Murdoch, known to us in God as Sister Philomena. I cannot express my deep distress and sorrow at the contents of her letter, and I have prayed for many long hours as to whether or not I should send it to you. Obviously my decision was to do so, and the letter is enclosed. I do, however, beg you to keep your heart open to the mercy of Our Lord in whom lies all justice and retribution. If you have a desire to consult with me further, I will make myself available.

Yours in God,

Mother St. Raphael

Curious, Murdoch unfolded the second piece of paper.

Chapter Forty-nine

WALTER STOOD STARING OUT OF THE WINDOW, Sally clinging to his leg, whining. Jess had been gone at least an hour. He'd tried to continue packing up some of the household utensils, but it was as if he had been infected by her lethargy, and he moved slowly although they had to catch the train at seven o'clock. He leaned his head against the cold windowpane. The trouble was, it wasn't they who needed to vanish, it was more that they needed to lose the past. He had little confidence the move would make that much difference, but he didn't know what else to do. He hoped that without constant reminders of what had happened, Jess would recover her spirits, that she would come back to him.

446   "Sally, stop whingeing. You're getting on my nerves."

Of course, his harsh tone only made the child cry louder, and in remorse, he swept her up into his arms.

"All right. It's all right. There, there."

"Where's Momma?"

Walter used his sleeve to wipe the child's tear-stained face.

"Let's go find her, shall we? Maybe she's just playing hide-and-seek with us."

Sally looked doubtful, but he gave her no chance to start up again. He put her back down and went to get her cloak. He really didn't know where Jess could have gone, but it felt better to move than to stay here wondering.

"Go get your boots, Sally."

He spoke to his child in a cheery voice and tried to smile at her, but his stomach was tight with fear. He didn't want to face his own forebodings.

"The frigging bastard." Murdoch smashed his fist on the table. "The rotten frigging bastard."

He hit the table over and over, bruising his hand. Suddenly the door from the cells opened and Barker came in, leading his father.

"What's the matter?" the guard asked.

Murdoch didn't answer him, but he reached in his pocket and took out all the money he had. It wasn't much, less than two dollars. He stood up and walked over to him. Harry was eyeing him warily, but he didn't say anything and went and sat down at the table. Murdoch handed the money to Barker.

447

"I need to speak in absolute privacy. Will you leave us alone? This is our last chance."

"You're not going to try to spring him, are you?"

"Not at all. You don't have to worry about that."

Barker stared into Murdoch's face, puzzled by what he saw there but not quite understanding.

"All right. Ten minutes but then I have to come and check on you."

Murdoch remembered he had another dollar in his inside pocket, and he fished that out and pushed it into the guard's hand.

"If you make that twenty minutes, I will appreciate it."

"I'll come back then."

He left, closing and locking the door behind him.

Harry looked up at Murdoch.

"There's hatred in your face, son. What has happened?"

Murdoch thrust the letter under his nose. "This is from Susanna. She's dead, by the way. I haven't told you yet. She wrote this. Read it."

Harry didn't touch the paper. "When did she die?"

"This last Tuesday. She had a tumour that she wasn't telling anybody about. She wrote me a letter before she took her final vows, and I have just received it from the prioress. Read it."

Harry shrugged. "You've forgotten I don't know how."

448

Murdoch grabbed the letter. "Then I'll read it to you . . ."

"No! I don't want to hear it. What's done is done and forgotten."

"It's not. It never will be as far as I'm concerned."

Suddenly, Harry got to his feet. "You're just aching for a fight, aren't you?"

"I learned from a master."

"Then you shall have it."

Murdoch saw the blow coming and deflected it with his left forearm. With his right fist he hit his father hard, so that Harry jerked backwards.

"You frigging bastard," said Murdoch, and he hit him again, knocking him to the floor.

Harry lay back. His nose was dribbling blood and snot.

Murdoch came around the table and stood over the fallen man. "Did that jolt your memory? If it didn't, maybe we can continue until it does."

He stared down at his father. So many times he had imagined such a confrontation, but now that it had happened, the triumph was no more than ashes.

Harry took a long time to get to his feet. Murdoch braced himself for the retaliation and he was ready for it, would have welcomed it, but his father merely leaned against the wall, wiping his nose with the back of his sleeve. There was a red mark already appearing on his cheekbone. His flare of anger had evaporated, and he looked defeated.

449

"I assume you felt you had a good reason to do that."

"I do indeed."

"Tell me what your sister wrote. I'd like to know."

"Is that so?"

Murdoch's mouth felt sour to him, and he was ashamed of himself for losing his temper like that. He walked around to the other side of the table.

Harry righted the chair and sat down. "I've already told you I'm sorry for my ways. I'd give my right arm if I could go back and change the way I was to all of you, but I can't."

His voice was steady and sincere, but to Murdoch it was like pouring kerosene on a fire.

"Sorry isn't enough, Harry! You can say 'I'm sorry' now that you're about to be strung up, but sorry isn't going to wipe out what you did."

Murdoch's voice was loud, and he glimpsed the curious face of the guard peering through the window, but Barker didn't intervene and went back down the hall.

"Susanna says she was present the afternoon our mother died."

He stared at his father, hoping for some sign of uneasiness, some flash of guilty recognition, but there was none.

Harry leaned forward, his hands on the chair as if his back was sore.

"Why don't you make your point, Will."

"My point! This is not a debate we're having where

I make a point and you can make a rebuttal. . . . Susanna says she saw you hit Momma, and she fell and struck her head on the stove. She was dizzy. You insisted she go to the shore because you couldn't do without your goddamn whelks. Is it coming back to you now, Harry? You do remember how fond you were of your whelks, don't you?"

Harry's nose had stopped bleeding, and he was leaning on his elbows, his head in his hands.

"Well? Is it coming back to you now? She should have gone and lain down, probably should have gone to see Dr. Curtis, but you wouldn't let her. You wanted your dinner nice and fresh."

He saw that Harry was weeping, but he couldn't stop himself.

"Mother didn't have any fight left in her. She obeyed as she always did. She went to the shore, and she slipped on the rocks because she was dizzy – because you had slapped her across the head. What do you have to say to that, Harry? I'd say that was tantamount to murder, wouldn't you?"

This time there was a reaction from Harry. He drew in his breath sharply. "I . . . I would like to deny that ever happened, but if Susanna says that is what she saw then I believe it did. If I could give my right arm to bring Mary back, to beg her forgiveness, I would."

451

"You've already given your right arm, I'm afraid," jeered Murdoch. "You'd better say your left. And then maybe your legs because in my books Bertie was also a casualty. He died because Momma was gone, and he knew you hated him. He had nothing to live for. Poor, sad, sad Bertie. You should add him to your list of regrets. You didn't directly put a knife in their hearts, but you might as well have."

Harry gave a groan and shook his head for all the world like a tormented bear.

Murdoch went on. "You don't remember, eh? How convenient for you. Just like you don't recall killing John Delaney."

His father's face was twisted with grief. "Maybe this is retribution for what I did do, but surely that is for Our God to decide, not you or even me. I will face Him at the day of judgement, and He will decide if I am worthy of forgiveness or not. Or would you rather take that decision into your own hands?"

Suddenly, Harry seemed grey and frail, as if all of his life force had been drained away. Murdoch felt as if he himself were being torn in two. His own anger subsided, leaving not forgiveness, that was too far away, but a wrenching, unbearable sorrow. His father could weep and regret to the bottom of his soul what he had done, but it would not change what had happened. Both his mother's and brother's lives had been shortened because of this man. He had blighted them while they were alive, and nothing would make up for that.

The door behind him opened, and the warden entered. He saw Harry's bloodied face.

"Goodness me, what's happened here?"

Harry answered him quickly. "I fell and banged my head, sir."

"Fell how?"

Murdoch interrupted. "The truth is we were fighting. I hit him."

"You were fighting with your own father?"

"Yes, sir. I regret to say I was. I regret, not because we are related by blood, but because I am younger and fitter and it was an unequal fight."

Massie looked from one to the other and then at the opposite door. "Where is Barker?"

As if on cue, the guard's face peered in through the window. Seeing the warden, he came into the room immediately.

"Mr. Barker, please take Mr. Murdoch back to his cell. And tend to that bruise on his cheek. I don't want the clergy to think we are the cause. When you've finished your shift, I'll speak to you in my office."

"Yes, sir."

Barker put his hand on Harry's shoulder. He didn't resist but stood up like a man sleepwalking. At the door he turned and looked at Murdoch. "I thank you for what you've already done for me, Will. I believe I'm ready to face my Maker. But I tell you, the punishment for my sins, my most grievous sins, is not for you to decide."

453

Barker led him out. Murdoch felt as if his legs might not hold him up any longer. He could hardly breathe, as if there were a scream trapped in his chest that was holding all the air in his body.

"Why don't you sit down for a moment, Mr. Murdoch." He became aware that Massie was standing close beside him.

"Why you, a police officer, were fighting with a prisoner under my care is something I will get you to explain at a later date. However, there is an urgent matter you must know about."

Murdoch stared at him, unable to comprehend what he was saying.

"I did not want to say this in front of your father because it might cruelly raise his hopes. We have received a message over the telephone from Number Seven Station. Apparently, Walter Lacey's wife has attempted to take her own life, and she has confessed to killing John Delaney."

Chapter Fifty

MASSIE PUT HIS HAND ON MURDOCH'S SHOULDER. "The woman is still alive. Her husband found her just in time and carried her to the tavern. It was the publican who insisted you be sent for. I assume he is aware of your relationship with Harry."

"Yes, he is."

"Mr. Murdoch, I have been a warden for a long time, and I have perhaps seen all there is to see of human depravity and human foolishness. Unfortunately, I have encountered many instances of such confessions, which always prove to be spurious. It might be very tempting for you to clutch at this as a last hope of proving your father's innocence. But I do not advise it."

Murdoch pressed his fingertips against his temples. He had developed a stabbing headache.

"Mr. Murdoch? What would you like to do?"

He looked up. "I have to find out what this is all about. I'll go right away."

"Ah, I rather thought that would be your decision. I have made my carriage available to you. It is ready in the driveway."

"Warden Massie, if this is in fact a true confession, how shall I proceed?"

"Not to be facetious, but I'd advise, with the utmost speed. If you bring me credible proof that she was the one who killed Delaney, then I will be able to stay the execution. However" – he grimaced – "apparently her life hangs by a thread. It is highly likely she will have gone to Her Maker before you get to her."

Spontaneously, in spite of the warden's presence, Murdoch crossed himself.

"Dear Lord, preserve her soul."

"Amen to that," added Massie.

"And if she is already dead?"

"I cannot answer that question until I have heard all of the circumstances. God speed."

The warden's horse was young and well cared for so the coachman was able to hold a canter from the jail to the Manchester tavern, and they were there in less than thirty minutes. Murdoch replayed the confrontation with Harry over and over in his mind. The expression, *to be at the boiling point*, was virtually a literal truth about the way his body felt. The news about Jessica Lacey was a surprise. He'd gone through his list of local people in answer to "If not Harry, then who?" but he hadn't seriously considered her a suspect. "A spurious confession" was the term the warden had used. Momentarily, Murdoch wasn't sure if he wanted it to be genuine or not; but even in his anger, he couldn't stomach Harry hanging for a crime he didn't commit.

The coachman was pulling up his steaming horse in front of the tavern. They came to a halt, and he jumped down from his seat and opened the door of the carriage as smartly as if Murdoch were the warden himself.

"Shall I wait for you, sir?"

"Yes, for now."

As Murdoch got out, the front door opened and Newcombe waved at him.

"I heard the carriage," he said. "Come this way."

Murdoch followed him inside. "How is she?"

"Very weak. She lost a lot of blood."

"Will she recover?"

"The doctor is optimistic." He ushered Murdoch into the hall. "She's in the parlour. Walter carried her up from the ravine, and we put her in here."

"Can I talk to her?"

"The doctor said nobody should go in, but given the circumstances, he might relent."

"I have to, Vince. You know that."

457

Murdoch was on the verge of going into the parlour no matter what the opposition, but the doctor himself emerged.

"Dr. Moore, this is Detective Murdoch. I spoke to you about him."

The physician was a tall, thin man with what turned out to be an implacably cheerful bedside manner. He thrust out his hand and greeted Murdoch energetically.

"Yes, yes, no need to explain your astonishing circumstances; I heard the entire story, and I quite understand you will want to talk to the young woman. And so you shall, but not for too long. I have written down everything she said to me, as is the law, and she has even been able to sign the paper herself so you need not worry on that account."

Murdoch couldn't get a word in edgewise and had to wave his hand in a dumb show of wanting to go into the parlour.

"Give me ten more minutes, and then you can come in. She'll be quite all right," he continued, and he popped back into the room. Vince touched Murdoch's sleeve.

"Why don't you speak to Walter in the meantime? He's in the taproom with the constable."

"Vince, does Lacey know who I am?"

"Yes, I had to say it out. The sergeant wouldn't have sent for you otherwise." He hesitated. "Do you want to hear what happened first?"

"Yes, I would."

458

"Let's go into the kitchen then. We'll leave the door open, so we can see if the doctor comes out."

They went in.

"Tch, tch!" exclaimed Newcombe, and he quickly opened up the stove and pulled out a pan of meat. "Completely forgot about it in all the excitement."

He put the pan on the table and without being asked picked up the teapot and poured two mugs of tea. The tea had steeped so long, it almost walked into the mug, but Murdoch was glad to drink it.

"All right, tell me what happened."

Newcombe sat down at the table. "Maria and me were having our dinner, right here, when we heard Walter calling from outside the window. I looked out and there he was with Jess in his arms. He'd carried her all the way up from the ravine. She'd cut both her wrists, and she looked nigh to death's door. Well, we both ran out to help him, and he told us he'd found her in some hideaway near the cottage. Thank God he'd had the presence of mind to tear up his shirt and apply a tourniquet on both arms. And thank God for my Maria. She took right over. I brought Jess straight through into the parlour." He pointed at the floor. "Look, you can see the blood spots. It was pumping out of her. Maria snatched up her towels and bound up the wrists tight. Walter looked like he was going to fall down himself, but Maria shook him into some sense and sent him back for the child, who was tagging behind him. We could hear her bawling from here. I ran off fast as I could to fetch Dr. Moore, who's just around the corner, thank the Lord. I thought I'd see the lass dead when

459

I got back, but she was still breathing and looking a bit better. Maria had got some brandy down her throat. Dr. Moore took over, but really Maria had done as much as could be done. He stitched up the wounds but it's prayer now and waiting."

"At what point did Jessica say she had killed Delaney?"

"About an hour ago. She recovered consciousness sufficiently to speak, and the doctor of course asked her why she had done such a dreadful thing to herself. She said it was because she had killed John Delaney, and an innocent man was going to be hung for it." He patted Murdoch's arm.

"Go on. I'm all right."

"She said she wanted to talk to Maria alone, but my good wife was too sensible to be the sole witness. She got some paper and made the doctor write down what Jess said. Maria asked her why had she killed Delaney if 'twere true? 'Because he tried to force himself upon me. I pushed him over the fence,' Jess said." Newcombe wiped his face with the back of his shirt sleeve. "All this time Walter was like a tethered wild horse. He just about burst. 'You did not kill him. I told you that.' Poor girl got mighty distressed at that and looked as if she was going to give up the ghost right there and then. The doctor said no more talking. He got Jess to sign the paper with what she had said; then he told me to take Walter into the other room. Which I did, although

460

he didn't come easy. I felt as if I was swimming in waters that was too deep for me, so I didn't ask him any more. Dr. Moore came out and said he had to fetch his nurse, and he would go to the station and get a constable to come. I told him to have them find you and get you up here. I sat with Walter." Newcombe screwed up his face. "I must tell you, Will, that was one of the longest hours I've ever spent. Neither of us spoke a word. I didn't think it wise. I was only too happy to hand him over to Constable Stanworth. Ready?"

Murdoch nodded. They both drained the mugs of tea and went down the hall to the taproom.

Walter Lacey was seated in the ingle seat close to the fire, huddled in his chair. There was a blanket draped over his shoulders, and he was dressed only in his undershirt and trousers. He looked like a man who had been washed ashore after a shipwreck. Constable Stanworth was standing at the window. He saluted and he and Murdoch exchanged introductions.

Murdoch went over to Walter and sat down across from him in the ingle.

"Mr. Lacey. I know this is a most difficult time for you, but it is imperative I ask you some questions. I believe Mr. Newcombe has told you who I am."

"Let me make this clear. My Jess didn't kill that devil, although she had damn good reason to. God himself wouldn't pass judgement on her. She just thinks she did, and it's weighed terrible on her conscience."

461

"Please tell me what happened."

Lacey blinked. "I suppose it was about nine o'clock. Everybody but Mr. Pugh had left. I was out back washing down the pit when Jess comes running in. She's carrying our daughter and she's white as paint. Sally's screeching like she's been stabbed. I couldn't understand Jess at first; she's trembling so much, she could hardly talk. Then I realise what she's telling me . . . that Delaney had come up to the cottage and tried to force himself on her. She says he's had his eye on her for some time, which she'd never revealed to me before." He clenched his fists and his eyes were so hot with rage, Murdoch could understand why his wife had kept her secret.

"Please continue, Mr. Lacey."

"Delaney used the dog as a pretext. I knew he'd been bringing it around more frequently lately, but I thought it was so as Sally could play with it. But it was Jess he was after." Again he stopped to regain some control. Newcombe and the constable hovered uneasily nearby. "She wouldn't even tell me every which thing, but Sally witnessed it all. Delaney says he's going to harm the child if Jess doesn't give in. He makes like he's going to tie Sally to the chair. But she manages to snatch her up and run outside. He follows after her, playing like a fox with a rabbit. Next thing she knew, he grabs her by the hair. But she's got spirit, has my Jess, and she gives him a fight. She was too quick, and she got free. They had both got turned

462

around somehow, so that he's backed up against the rear fence. She gives him a shove as hard as she can, and he falls backward and rolls down the hill." Lacey was starting to breathe hard as if he had been fighting himself. "According to Jess, he hit one of the trees. She hardly took notice she was so needing to escape, but she says he lay still and she thought his neck was broken. She took Sally and fast as she could ran down the other path to the tavern. I told her we had to get Maria, but that really set her off again. She didn't want anybody to know, not even Maria. I said I'd look after everything. I ran back down to the ravine. There wasn't a sign of the bastard, living or dead. I came back and told her that. That he must have been able to get up and walk so his neck wasn't close to being broken, more's the pity. She starts to calm down but makes me promise I won't say anything or try to get revenge on Delaney. She says she would die from the shame of it. I tell you frankly, I'm beside myself but thought it best to wait and see what falls out. Maria is fetched and tends to both of them." He paused and looked over at Newcombe. "I'm as parched as a desert, Vince. Could you pour me a drop of spirit?"

The innkeeper hurried over to the counter and poured out a shot of whiskey. Murdoch waited as patiently as he could while Lacey drank some of the liquor, shuddering as men do who haven't had the fire in their belly for some time.

463

"She's just starting to get some colour back in her cheeks when along comes Philip Delaney a-looking for his pa, and well, you know the rest of it. He and Mr. Pugh found Delaney in the creek. He was dead, may he burn in hell. One bastard killed by another."

"Meaning Harry Murdoch?"

"That's right. I'd be lying if I said I was sorry. Justice was done. But Jess, she . . . she let it plague her to the point where she's not stable. She lost the babe she was carrying right the next day. She's not been right since. Then she hears as the verdict is in, Harry Murdoch is convicted, and that was the last straw."

Murdoch crouched down so he could look into the other man's face. "Mr. Lacey, is your wife aware that the coroner himself said Delaney was killed near where he was found? He walked on his own legs down to the path. And even if that weren't the case, even if Delaney had broken his neck in a fall, no jury in the world would blame Jess for trying to defend herself."

"She wasn't up to attending the trial, but I told her and told her she wasn't responsible. She just moiled on it. Wouldn't believe me."

"Why didn't you, yourself, bring this forward at the trial?" asked Murdoch.

464

"Are you married?"

"No, I'm not."

"Then you can't understand."

"I know what it's like to love a woman. Married men don't have the prerogative on that."

"It's different when it's your wife. Getting her to talk about what happened was like taking a bandage off somebody who's been in a forest fire. I couldn't do that to her again and in public. It was obvious who the real killer was; there was no sense in destroying Jess and Sally any more than they'd already been destroyed."

Murdoch took a deep breath. "Mr. Lacey, I think you are a liar. That you are a yellow coward, and that for all your professions of love, you are, in fact, intent only on saving your own skin. That you would allow an innocent man to die for a crime he didn't commit and you would even allow your beloved wife to take her own life because she thinks she is the one responsible."

Lacey leaped to his feet, and it was only because Newcombe got in front of him in time that he wasn't at Murdoch's throat. The constable had to help force him back to the bench.

"Calm down, Walter," said Newcombe. "We're all under pressure here."

"He's not. It's not his wife who might die!"

"No, it's not!" Murdoch shouted back. "But Harry Murdoch is my father, and there is no doubt he will die – this Monday morning at seven o'clock to be precise – unless I find out the truth."

"What truth? He did in Delaney."

465

"Did he? Or was it you?"

"Horsecrap!"

"Is it? I think you were the one who encountered Delaney when you ran back into the ravine. You were enraged at what he had done to your wife. You smashed him over the head then rolled his body into the creek, hoping it would look as if he had drowned by accident . . ."

"No!"

"You told your wife you didn't see any sign of Delaney, but it's my guess she knows you're trying to protect her. She is an honourable woman, and she cannot bear the thought of an innocent man dying for something she did. But you don't care, do you? You'll let both of them die as long as *you* are alive. Isn't that the truth, Mr. Lacey?"

Tears were streaming down Lacey's face, and he could hardly speak for his sobs. Murdoch felt like a torturer.

"Look, Mister, if you think I would do that to Jess, you have another think coming. I would die on the rack before I saved myself and not her . . ."

"Tell me the truth then. Did you or did you not kill John Delaney?"

"I swear I did not. I never saw him alive after he left this tavern."

"Will you take an oath on a Bible?"

"Yes."

466

Lacey caught Murdoch by the wrist. "And you? Do you swear to me that there is no possibility that Jess was responsible for the bastard's death?"

"I am sure of it."

"Then I will tell you the truth."

Murdoch looked over his shoulder at Newcombe. "Can you fetch us a Bible right away?"

Chapter Fifty-one

NEWCOMBE WENT TO THE BAR COUNTER, reached underneath, and removed a small Bible. Murdoch handed the book to Lacey.

"Hold this in your right hand. . . . Do you swear that the evidence you are about to give touching the death of John Delaney shall be the truth, the whole truth, and nothing but the truth, so help you God."

"I do."

"Mr. Newcombe and Constable Stanworth, take note of what Mr. Lacey says, commit it to memory. I, myself, will write it down. Please go on, sir."

Lacey slid the Bible onto the bench beside him. "What I have to say isn't that much different from what I've already told you. If the man had been in front of me, I would cheerfully have killed him with my bare hands. But he wasn't and I didn't."

"What did you do?"

"Like I said, as soon as I'd got the story out of Jess, I ran down into the ravine. I expected to find Delaney's body, and I did. He was lying across the path just up along from the bridge. I could see he was dead. I thought she had killed him. How was I to know any different given what she'd told me? I didn't have no clear plan, but I rolled him into the creek, like you said, thinking it would look like he'd slipped in accidentally."

"Did you kick the body? Remember, you're under oath."

Lacey stared at the Bible beside him as if it would jump up and bite him. Reluctantly, he said, "Yes. I put the boots to him. I was only sorry he couldn't feel it."

"What then?"

"I ran straight back here. Jess was in such a desperate state I knew right there and then I wasn't going to tell her he was dead. So I said I hadn't seen hide nor hair of him. I didn't expect that Harry Murdoch would be found nearby, and that him and Delaney had had a fight." He wiped his wet face with the back of his wrist. "She couldn't have said anything that night; she was too upset. The next day she miscarried . . . our first son. By the time she'd got over that sufficient to talk about what had happened, I'd heard enough to convince her that Harry Murdoch was the culprit, and it wouldn't matter if she gave evidence or not. She hadn't killed Delaney, Harry had. She was terrible low after she lost the child, but I thought she was

469

coming out of it. But the trial last week was too much, as you see."

Murdoch turned a fresh page in his notebook. "How much time elapsed from when your wife came into the barn till you found Delaney?"

"I can't be too sure. Everything seemed to speed up. But I ran there and back, and that's about ten minutes or so each way."

"A few minutes to roll the body into the creek. Roughly twenty-five minutes. Add to that at least ten minutes or more for Mrs. Lacey to get here. She must have talked to you for another ten minutes at the minimum. All told that would give us about forty-five minutes from the time Delaney fell over the fence railing to when you found him. Did you touch him? Was the body still warm?"

"I don't know. I didn't think. He was dead, that's all I can say."

"Let's suppose he was hardly even stunned by that first fall. He gets to his feet and proceeds to walk down the steps. He must have seen Mrs. Lacey going by way of the other path. Who knows, perhaps he intended to catch her at the bridge? However, when he gets to the bottom of the hill, he meets up with somebody else. That person hits him from behind, at least two blows and so hard the skull is fractured. That person disappears."

Lacey scowled. "He didn't go far. He was in the bushes. That person's been convicted."

"I don't need to remind you, Mr. Lacey, that the

verdict was reached without all the evidence being brought before the jury."

"Don't change the picture that much."

"It might! Besides, that's what our bloody justice system is all about, isn't it? We let the jurymen hear everything, and they decide."

Newcombe edged a little closer and Murdoch tried to calm down.

"Will the case be reopened?" asked Lacey.

"We'll see when I take all this new information to the warden."

"If there is a new trial, Jess will have to go on the witness stand, won't she?"

"Yes, I'm afraid so."

Lacey's face was contorted with grief. "She would have spoke up if I'd insisted. But I couldn't bear to put her through the ordeal . . ."

He was interrupted by Maria Newcombe entering the room. "Excuse me, gentlemen, but Jess is asking to speak to Walter."

He jumped up. "How is she?"

Maria smiled a little. "I do believe she will recover. Now only a minute with her. I think she is worried about Sally."

Lacey followed Maria from the room, the blanket clutched about his shoulders.

Murdoch let out a long, deep breath. "What do you think, Vince? Is this man telling the truth?"

471

"I do believe he is, Will."

"Constable Stanworth?"

The young man blushed a little with pleasure that Murdoch was consulting him.

"I found him convincing, sir."

Suddenly, there was a soft whimper from behind the screen. Tripper appeared, a puppy dangling by its scruff from her mouth. Newcombe went over to her. "You get back in there." His voice was fond. He picked up both dogs and replaced them in the whelping box. "Ever since we took the puppy up to the Delaney house, she keeps wanting to move the remaining litter to another place. I don't want her to lose him. I might have to chain her up."

Murdoch had been in the process of looking over the notes he had just taken, and he only half heard. However, at that moment, there was a shift in his mind rather as if a stereoscope card had come into focus. He went over to Newcombe and grabbed him by both arms.

"Vince, what did you just say?"

"About Tripper? Just that she's trying to move the pups . . ."

"And you might have to chain her up?"

"Yes . . ."

Murdoch let him go. "Goddamn it, my own anger has closed my mind like one of your traps. From the beginning I assumed Harry was lying or simply did not remember. That he was guilty as charged. But what if it happened just as he said it did? He goes to the bridge, falls and hits his cheek. A bit of bad coincidence for him that Delaney clouted somebody as well. Let's say for now, a different person. Then Harry staggers further along the path, passes out. He admitted to me that he had a hazy memory of Delaney standing over him. We assumed they'd had a barney. Harry is accustomed to barneys that he doesn't recollect. But what if that wasn't the case? That Delaney came across him, either on his way to the Lacey cottage or afterward. Nothing else happened. The only credence I have been able to give to my father is that he might have been too drunk to be capable of a fight. So let's say Delaney left him where he was. Then he returned to the path, and here he encountered his murderer. Probably this is where Delaney got his scraped knuckles. However, that person picked up a heavy piece of wood and, when Delaney turned his back, hit him hard. The coroner said the blows came at a downward angle and concluded they were delivered by a tall man, hence Harry, but that doesn't have to be the case. If I shoved you to your knees, then hit you, the blows would come from above your head. Am I right?"

Newcombe was regarding him doubtfully. "Yes, I suppose so."

473

"And, Vince, all this while, Havoc was still in his box."

"Is that important?"

"I'm beginning to think it is crucial. You see, I've also assumed the girl is too confused to say the truth or to know what happens. But what if that's not the case? What if she was telling me exactly what took place."

"Do you mean Nan?"

"I do. I can't explain at the moment, Vince, it would take too long. Come on, I've got to talk to Mrs. Lacey."

Murdoch beckoned to the constable. "There is a carriage waiting outside. I want you to go to Warden Massie at the Don Jail. Tell him you have a message from me that there is new evidence, no, say absolute evidence, that there must be a new trial. I will meet him as soon as I can. Make sure you see him eye to eye. Even if he's in his own quarters, you must find him. Can you do that?"

"Yes, sir."

Murdoch led the way on the double out of the taproom.

Chapter Fifty-two

MURDOCH COULDN'T RECALL SEEING ANYONE as pale who was still among the quick. Jessica Lacey was lying on the couch, her wrists heavily bandaged. Her dark hair had come unpinned and was loose on the pillow, accentuating the whiteness of her face. However, her eyes were open, and she looked directly at him when he came over to her. Dr. Moore had sent Walter to his daughter, and Maria Newcombe was now sitting on a stool beside Jessica.

"Two minutes and no more, Mr. Murdoch," said the doctor.

Maria indicated the empty chair next to her, and Murdoch sat down.

"Mrs. Lacey, I am a police officer. . . . Your husband has told me what happened the night of Delaney's death." He paused because she had flinched as if he had touched her with something white hot. "I must emphasise that you are entirely free from culpability in the murder. Entirely so. Mrs. Lacey, it now seems possible that Harry Murdoch is not guilty of this crime. I am trying to uncover evidence that was not disclosed at the trial." Again he saw the flinching, not as pronounced but there. "Please do not think for a moment that your husband was responsible. I am certain he was not. However, he *did* lie to you. He did come across Delaney's body on the path, and it was Walter who rolled the body into the creek. He was afraid to tell you, and when you became ill, decided not to rescind his story, convinced Harry Murdoch was the killer."

Jessica closed her eyes, and Maria sat forward in alarm. However, Jess seemed only to be gathering her strength because she spoke, her voice light and brittle as a dried leaf.

"What do you want?"

"I am so sorry I have to speak of the dreadful events of that night, but I must. You don't have to talk if that is too much for you. A nod will suffice."

"When Delaney came to your cottage that night, did he bring his dog with him?"

She nodded and whispered, "He had come before. Flash was his introduction. Sally liked him."

"What did he do with the dog? Was it in the house?"

Murdoch could see Maria frowning at him, not comprehending the relevance of the questions. Jessica licked her lips.

476

"No. It was raining and I had washed the floor. I asked him to leave the dog outside. He tied him to the fence."

"And when you took Sally and ran down the other path, was the dog still tied up?"

"I'm not sure . . . yes, yes, he was. He was barking."

Gently, Murdoch placed his hand over hers. "Thank you, Mrs. Lacey. There is only one more thing I have to ask you. Has Philip Delaney been paying his attentions to you?"

This time she didn't answer, and her nod was almost imperceptible.

Murdoch stood up. "That is all I wanted to know. Please set your mind at rest now."

Dr. Moore approached the couch. "I'm going to give her a sedative powder. Mrs. Newcombe, help me raise her, will you?"

Murdoch left them to their ministrations and went out into the hall. Vince was waiting for him. "What can I do to help?"

Murdoch had contemplated asking Newcombe to come with him but decided against it. His case felt as delicately balanced as a house of cards, and he couldn't risk anything that might bring it tumbling down.

"Nothing at the moment. I'm going to talk to Mrs. Bowling again." He smiled. "If I don't come back before nightfall, come and find me."

Once outside, he set off as fast as he could into the ravine. He didn't know if anybody else knew about

Jessica's suicide attempt, and he couldn't risk losing even a few minutes.

The cows watched him with indifference as he hurried by. The short winter afternoon was drawing in, and the candle shining in the front window of the cottage winked brightly in the gloom. Nan was sitting there, her face pressed against the glass. She saw him approaching and waved a greeting, a child's happy greeting at seeing anybody who might relieve the tedium of the day.

He smiled and indicated she should open the door. She looked worried and shook her head. He tried again but it was obvious she wasn't going to let him in. He went up the steps and banged hard on the door.

"Open up, Mrs. Bowling, I'm a police officer. Open up!"

He heard the bolt slide, and the door opened a crack. It wasn't Mrs. Bowling but Nan, who peeked out.

"Nan, I must speak to your mother."

"She's resting."

"Will you wake her up then? Tell her it's urgent."

He almost considered pushing his way into the house, but he didn't want to frighten the girl. Fortunately, Mrs. Bowling woke up.

"Who's making all that din?" came her querulous voice.

This time Murdoch did push.

478   "Excuse me, Nan, I must come in." She stepped back. The cottage was cold and dark, the only candle the one in the window. Mrs. Bowling was sprawled in the

armchair. She half sat up when she saw him and pulled a grimy quilt up around her chest.

"What do you want?"

"Mrs. Bowling, I'm a police officer."

"What? I thought you said you were a reporter."

"I did say that, but in fact I'm a detective, and I am investigating the Delaney murder."

"What? It's over with."

"It's not. There is new evidence in the case."

"What?"

"I have just come from the Manchester tavern. Earlier today, Jessica Lacey tried to take her own life."

He paused to see her reaction.

"Poor desperate woman. I'm not a bit surprised. Miscarries take some women that way."

"The reason she gave is that she says she is the one responsible for Delaney's death."

Nan had understood what he said, and she touched his sleeve.

"Has Mrs. Lacey gone to heaven?"

"No, she hasn't, Nan. She is going to be all right."

"Philip will be glad."

"He likes Mrs. Lacey, does he?"

She grinned. "She is his sweetheart. He gives her squirrels."

"Don't listen to her," her mother cried out. "She doesn't have a proper mind."

479

Murdoch went over to the armchair and crouched in front of Mrs. Bowling so that he was a few inches from her face. Her breath was ripe with the smell of wine.

"I'll listen to you then. On the night Delaney died, you were here in the cottage. Nan said Philip came to the house with two dogs. One was Flash, the other was a little grey dog the colour of ashes. It belonged to Harry Murdoch. Nan couldn't have made that up."

"Yes, she could, but why does it matter?"

"One of them was in a box, the other was tied to a fence. Why did Philip have these dogs?"

"I didn't see him with any dogs."

"Yes, Momma, two dogs. Philip was crying, but I cheered him."

"Be quiet, you minx," said her mother. "You've got it wrong. It wasn't that night at all. Mister, she can't even tell you what day it is let alone what happened last August. Look. Nan, tell him what today is. Go on, tell him."

"It's Tuesday," said Nan with a grin.

"See."

"Yes, you've gone to great lengths to prove to me that Nan gets confused."

Mrs. Bowling shrugged. "She does. You can't count on anything."

He wanted to grab her by the neck and shake her.

"I notice that you have some fine gifts from Mrs. Delaney."

"What of it?"

"Did she give you them to buy silence? So you wouldn't talk?"

"About what? I have nothing to say."

He leaned closer. "So you don't care that a man is about to be hung for a crime he didn't commit? You know he is innocent. You've known all along he is innocent."

"If you mean, did I know about Jessica Lacey, no I did not. Besides, any confession from her isn't likely to be true. She's not of sound mind. She's been unhinged ever since she lost the babe she was carrying."

"Do you know what was the most likely cause of that miscarriage, Mrs. Bowling?"

"Of course I don't."

"John Delaney, respected citizen and family man, tried to rape her. He had been after her for some time. It was not the first time he'd shown such tendencies. He was a man of lust, Mrs. Bowling." She tried to back away from him but there was nowhere to go.

"He never showed that to me."

"Oh, don't give me that rubbish. Vince Newcombe found Delaney with Nan. Delaney would have had her if Vince hadn't shown up. The helpless ones are destroyed. You told me that yourself."

"I was talking about chickens."

481

Murdoch looked over at Nan, who had sat in her chair and was rocking back and forth. She had draped her leg over the arm of the chair so that her drawers were visible. She caught his glance and smiled, and he saw again the disconcerting precocious sexuality.

Mrs. Bowling saw what her daughter was doing. "Nan, sit properly and pull your skirt down."

Murdoch moved back. "I don't have the good fortune to have a daughter, Mrs. Bowling, but if I had and she were like Nan, I would want to protect her with every last drop of my blood and I would want to kill any man who used her that way."

The room was too dark for him to see her expression clearly, but he sensed that what he said had made an impact.

"From the sound of it, you think I killed John Delaney. As if I could!"

"I saw you hauling a heavy pot around. You're no weakling."

She looked over at Nan. "Light some candles, there's a good girl."

The girl got off the chair eagerly. Mrs. Bowling watched her for a moment as she clumsily struck a match. "My daughter is simple-minded as you see, and there's always some wicked enough to take advantage. She's just a baby, but she's learned what will get her sweets."

"I'm sorry."

"She is my cross to bear."

Nan lit one of the candles then a second. She carried one over to the side table near Murdoch. For

482

a moment she studied him in the way that very young children do.

"Is your poppa dead, too?"

"No, no, he's not, Nan."

"Philip is my dear friend," she said.

Her mother sighed. "Yes, he is. Thanks be to Jesus that she does have one friend in the world."

Murdoch felt the mood in the room shift again. The momentary softness was gone. Mrs. Bowling was as wary as a stalking cat.

"Philip has his troubles, too," she continued. "Perhaps that is why they have become like brother and sister. My Nan relies on him, and when I am gone, God forbid, he will take care of her."

"I see."

"Philip's poppa hit him on the head," said Nan. "So he wrung his neck till he was dead."

"That's enough. Nobody wants to hear from you."

Murdoch went a little closer to the girl but carefully, not wanting to frighten her.

"Nan, when Philip came here with the two dogs, did he tell you he had wrung his father's neck?"

She nodded her head with delight. "He had a fit, and his poppa went straight up to heaven in a carriage."

Mrs. Bowling jumped out of her chair and rushed at her daughter, her arm raised to strike. "Hold your tongue, you silly girl."

483

Murdoch caught her in time. "Leave her alone. I have the authority to arrest you for interfering with a police investigation and believe me I will have no hesitation in doing so."

"You can't believe anything the child says."

"Can't I? Let's see."

Nan was looking increasingly anxious as the tension built in her mother, and he spoke to her gently.

"What did you mean, Nan, when you said Philip had a fit? What did he do?"

"He wrung his poppa's neck."

"Why did he do that?"

"His poppa was hurting Philip's sweetheart. He was in the hideaway. We built it together, and when Momma let me play in the woods I used to stay in there for weeks and years."

"I've seen it, Nan, and it is quite splendid. But how do you know Philip killed his poppa, Nan? Did he tell you?"

"Yes. He came to the door . . ."

"Nan, for goodness . . ."

"Mrs. Bowling, I warned you. I shall continue this at the police station if you don't let her continue."

But Nan was rapidly losing her interest in the conversation, and he could see she was afraid of her mother.

"What else?" he prompted her.

She got up and went over to the dresser that was underneath the window, pulled open a drawer, and removed something. She held out her hand, palm up. In it was resting a small triangular-shaped piece of bone.

"Philip gave it to me," she said, and she popped it into her mouth. With her lips lightly closed she blew out and emitted a thin, high whistling sound. Pleased with his response, she blew again.

"Can I see that?" he asked.

She removed the whistle from her mouth and handed it to him.

"The dogs hear it better than us. Flash was killing hundreds of rats, but Philip's poppa stopped him." She looked at Murdoch. "Are you going to take Philip to a dungeon because he did a bad thing?"

Her eyes had filled with tears, and her lower lip was trembling. She seemed so lost, he wanted to take her in his arms and comfort her, but he knew he couldn't.

"I have to go and talk to him, Nan. If Philip has done something wrong, you wouldn't want somebody else to be punished by mistake, would you?"

This was too complicated for her, however, and she began to weep in earnest.

The noise of her crying masked the creak of the door, and Murdoch wasn't aware that anybody was behind him until he felt a violent shove that knocked him to the ground. Instinctively, he rolled over to his side.

485

The brass head of the walking stick that Philip Delaney was holding came down inches from his arm.

Chapter Fifty-three

"LEAVE HER ALONE!" Philip screamed and swung the walking stick again, Murdoch barely had time to deflect the blow so that it landed on his upper arm. He was at a severe disadvantage, half on his hands and knees, and all he could do was scrabble backwards and try to shield himself. Philip's face was that of a madman. Murdoch was aware of Mrs. Bowling standing behind them not uttering a word. It was Nan who saved him. She started to cry.

"Philip, he's nice. Don't hit him anymore. He's my friend."

Philip actually stopped in midswing.

Mrs. Bowling said, "He was trying to hurt Nan."

Philip dropped the stick, giving Murdoch time to stand up. He was still off balance, however, and before he could defend himself, Philip grabbed him by the throat. Murdoch was pushed back with the force, and he gripped his attacker's wrists to pull them off him.

But Delaney had the furious strength of a lunatic, and Murdoch could feel the air being squeezed out of him. Nan was squealing while the two men shuffled in a grotesque dance. Murdoch let go and at the same time dropped his weight suddenly downwards. Taken by surprise at the lack of resistance, Philip relaxed his grip for a moment. Murdoch brought his arms up and outward breaking the hold on his throat. At the same time, he lunged forward with his head in a savage butt to the chin. Blood spurted from Philip's mouth. He howled and dropped to his knees. Murdoch was on top of him in a moment, grabbing his arm and twisting it behind his back. Philip fell forward, his face pressed into the floor. He began to cry like a child.

"I'm sorry, Poppa. Don't hurt me anymore."

"Put your other arm behind your back."

Philip did so and Murdoch was able to hold both wrists.

"Mrs. Bowling, hand me that scarf." His voice was harsh and raspy.

"He won't cause any more trouble. You can let him go."

"Hand me the scarf. If you disobey or create any more disturbance, I promise you I will see that you end up in jail."

Sullenly, she picked up Philip's muffler, which had fallen to the floor, and handed it to Murdoch. He tied it tightly around Philip's wrists then cautiously he got

487

off his back. Nan crept over and dropped to her knees, patting Philip's head to comfort him.

He reached down and pulled at Delaney's bound arms. "Stand up. You are under arrest for assaulting a police officer. If you try to resist in any way, it will go badly for you. Do you understand me?"

Philip's chin was covered in blood from his bitten lip, and his nose was running. Awkwardly, he got to his feet, Nan dancing around him nervously. The heat from the life-or-death struggle that had flooded Murdoch's body began to subside. He reached in his pocket, took out his handkerchief, and wiped away the blood and mucous from Philip's face. The fellow had minutes ago been intent on murdering him, but as he looked at him standing with his head bowed, his coat bloodstained, and tears rolling down his face, Murdoch felt his own anger dissipating.

"Your poppa hurt you, did he?"

"You don't have to tell him anything," called out Mrs. Bowling, but he didn't seem to hear her.

"He was hurting Mrs. Lacey. She's my sweetheart."

"Did you see him?"

He nodded. "I was in my hideaway. I heard her crying."

"What did you do then?"

"Don't answer that. He has no right to ask questions."

Murdoch turned to face her. "Mrs. Bowling, I have already warned you about interfering."

488

"What about him? What will my Nan do if anything happens to Philip?"

"All I want is the truth. The law protects innocents."

More blood was seeping from Philip's lip, and he licked it away.

Murdoch dabbed at it. "Philip, if I untie you, will you promise me to sit in that chair and not move until I give you permission?"

"Yes."

"Mrs. Bowling, sit over there beside Nan where I can see you. If you try to incite him in any way, it will be the worse for him."

He waited while she did as he said; then he untied the muffler from Philip's wrists and gave him the handkerchief. Nan was back swinging her legs, singing quietly to herself.

"Now, Philip, it would help me if you'd answer my question. After you heard your father hurting Mrs. Lacey, what did you do?"

"I stayed in the hideaway." He sniffed. "I was afraid. Then it was quiet except for Sally, who was crying. And Flash was barking, too."

"Did you go and get Flash?"

He looked confused. "I thought I'd better wait, but then Poppa came down the steps. He was really angry at me when he saw I was in the hideaway." He rubbed the side of his head. "He gave me such a stotter, see right here."

489

"That must have hurt a lot."

"Yes, it did."

"What happened after that? Did you lose your temper just like you did now?"

Philip grinned at him shamefacedly. "I don't remember."

"Try. He hit you hard. What did you do?"

"I went and got Flash."

"Before that. Did you pick up a stick and hit your poppa?"

Philip thought for a moment. "I forget."

Epilogue

FOR THE NEXT TWO WEEKS, Murdoch looked and sounded like a pugilist. The capillaries under his eyes had burst from the constriction on his throat and were now black shadows. His vocal cords were bruised. Mrs. Kitchen immediately bought the Christmas goose, cooked it, and used the grease to rub on his neck. She also stood over him while he swallowed big spoonfuls of the oily mess. He was obliged to take more sick leave from duty, which he couldn't afford but which he was enjoying.

Massie had immediately cancelled the hanging, and after hearing Murdoch's report he had agreed there were grounds for a retrial, which was to take place early in the new year. Murdoch consulted Sam Quinn, who recommended a barrister he referred to as a sly fox who could be hired for a reasonable sum.

However, Murdoch couldn't face a meeting with his father. For one thing, it was painful to talk, for another Murdoch wasn't yet reconciled to him. Instead, he wrote a letter outlining what he thought had happened the night of the betting match. After Jessica Lacey had fled, Delaney had got to his feet and walked down the steps to the path. Partway down, he was confronted by his son, who was distraught about what he had overheard. He must have challenged his father, and Delaney struck him. At this point Philip lost his temper, probably shoved his father to the ground and hit him on the back of the head, killing him. The lad had then gone up and released Flash. Either he saw Harry and let Havoc out of his box, or the terrier had already got free. Regardless, Philip had taken both dogs and gone to see Nan. All this time Harry was lying unconscious in the long grass, just as he said. Lacey's actions had overlaid what happened but there was little doubt Harry would still have been accused. Whether or not a jury would believe this was what actually happened remained to be seen. Neither Philip nor Nan would be credible witnesses, and Mrs. Bowling was going to do everything she could to deny Philip's presence at her house. However, Mr. Quinn's "sly fox" thought he had a good case.

Tonight, Murdoch was trying to switch his thoughts onto a different track. Mrs. Kitchen had invited Enid and Alwyn to dinner. They had all feasted on the goose

492

and stuffed themselves on the dark, rich plum pudding that Mrs. Kitchen had been preparing for weeks. Now the table and chairs had been pushed against the wall to make a bit of room, and they were all gathered close to the Christmas tree. Mrs. Kitchen had fixed tiny candles on the branches, which were also hung with gingerbread men and sugar candy sticks. At the base of the tree was a satisfying pile of boxes and parcels that Alwyn was assessing with great concentration. Havoc, greatly improved in health and temperament, was at his feet. The terrier had come to stay, and he and the boy were immediate friends.

"Mr. Murdoch, I believe you are going to act as Father Christmas's representative," said Mrs. Kitchen. Arthur was at the far side of the circle, and Murdoch felt a pang when he saw how his friend was struggling not to cough.

"I am indeed," he said, and jumped up. He picked up a beribboned parcel. "This is addressed to Master Alwyn Jones."

"That's me," said Alwyn. Excited, Havoc yipped.

Alwyn tore open his package and lifted out a brand-new board game called A TRIP TO MARS. Murdoch was highly gratified to see the boy's pleasure. He had stewed over what to buy him for days.

Enid spoke to her son in Welsh.

"Thank you, Mr. Murdoch," he said, and walked over and gave him a kiss on the cheek.

493

Murdoch tapped him lightly on the side of the head. "We'll have a game soon."

The boy sat down again, ready for the next present.

"For Mrs. Kitchen," Murdoch said. The box was a large one, and Beatrice looked appropriately mystified. "This is from Father Christmas himself," said Murdoch. In fact, he and Arthur had joined in to buy her a special present. With maddening slowness she unwrapped her box.

"Oh my," she whispered. Nestled in soft red tissue paper was a caperine of grey seal. She lifted it out, stroking the sleek fur. "Oh my," she said again, as she saw the matching winter hat. Murdoch grinned at Arthur. The short cape was Enid's idea, and the two men had willingly agreed to it.

Murdoch returned to his tasks. Mrs. Kitchen surprised him by her gift of a book by Mr. Oliver Wendell Holmes who, as far as he knew, was not a Roman Catholic. He'd guessed that Enid would give him hand-monogrammed handkerchiefs, which she had. That deserved a kiss, albeit chaste, out of deference to his landlady. Enid seemed delighted with the cut-glass bottle of perfume he gave her, and that garnered another kiss. She had bought the Kitchens a stereoscope and a dozen cards, all pictures of Egypt. This was an excellent choice as Arthur found reading taxing these days but still had a lively curiosity about the world.

When all the parcels were opened, there was a

494

sudden rather awkward silence. In previous years, after the ritual of gift giving, Beatrice had suggested the three of them say a rosary together, and Murdoch was afraid she might do so again. However, with great tact, she didn't, only murmuring what a splendid Christmas they were having. It was Havoc who distracted everyone by seizing a piece of paper and proceeding to tear it to pieces. Murdoch snatched him up.

"Enough of that, you imp." The dog touched Murdoch's chin with his cold nose. "Give me a kiss then," said Murdoch.

Havoc nipped him instead.

Everybody burst out laughing, as Murdoch dropped the terrier to the floor.

"Come here, you naughty dog," said Mrs. Kitchen.

"Don't be nice to him, Mrs. K., he's wicked," said Murdoch, dabbing at his bleeding chin.

But Havoc, like all dogs, had an unerring instinct for a soft touch, and he trotted over to Beatrice and licked her outstretched hand.

"See, he didn't mean to hurt you," she said.

"Oh, but he did," interjected Alwyn. "He doesn't like him."

Murdoch sighed.

Author's Note

I strive to be as accurate as possible with my historical details concerning Victorian Toronto. However, in one instance I have changed the facts to suit the fiction. J. M. Massie was the warden of the Central Prison, not the Don Jail, as I have it in the book. I made this change for two reasons: The Don Jail still exists and you can go and have a look at it if you want to (the outside only). The Central Prison, which was on Strachan Street, was torn down. Secondly, Mr. Massie left behind correspondence and a fascinating journal, which I was able to read. Some of the things I have him say in the book are his own words, and the views he expresses are certainly his.

Acknowledgements

Especially when writing historical fiction, there are always so many questions to ask, and I am most grateful to the people who passed on their expertise to me and lent me their valuable books.

Thanks to Sharon McKenna and Jan Oddie for trusting me with their precious possessions.

Maurice Farge always answers my questions about the Catholic Church with patience, no matter when I call him.

Cheryl Freedman has again taken time to read the manuscript and offer me excellent and invaluable feedback.

As always, my editor, Ruth Cavin, is astute, kind, and improves everything.

EXCEPT THE DYING

In the cold winter of 1895, the naked body of a servant girl is found frozen in a deserted laneway. The young victim was pregnant when she died. Detective William Murdoch soon discovers that many of those connected with the girl's life have secrets to hide. Was her death an attempt to cover up a scandal in one of the city's influential families?

"Terrific . . . the best historical mystery of the year."
– MYSTERY COLLECTOR'S BOOKLINE

Trade Paperback
978-0-7710-4331-4

UNDER THE DRAGON'S TAIL

Dolly Merishaw is an abortionist in Victorian Toronto, but her contempt for her clients leaves every one of them resentful. So it's no surprise when this malicious woman is murdered. But when a young boy is found dead in Dolly's squalid kitchen a week later, Detective Murdoch doesn't know if he's hunting one murderer – or two.

"Late-19th-century Toronto comes startlingly alive in Jennings's second gripping tale."
– PUBLISHERS WEEKLY

Trade Paperback
978-0-7710-4335-2

POOR TOM IS COLD

In the third Murdoch mystery, the detective is not convinced that Constable Oliver Wicken's death was suicide. When he begins to suspect the involvement of Wicken's neighbours, the Eakin family, Mrs. Eakin is committed to a lunatic asylum. Is she really insane, he wonders, or has she been deliberately driven over the edge?

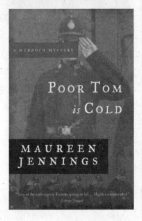

"Jennings has a wonderful feel for the places and tasks that give life and context to a character."
– NEW YORK TIMES BOOK REVIEW

Trade Paperback
978-0-7710-4337-6

NIGHT'S CHILD

After thirteen-year-old Agnes Fisher faints at school, her teacher is shocked to discover in the girl's desk two stereoscopic photographs. One is of a dead baby in its cradle and the other is of Agnes in a lewd pose, captioned "What Mr. Newly Wed Really Wants." The photographs are brought to Detective Murdoch, who sets out to find the photographer – and to put him behind bars.

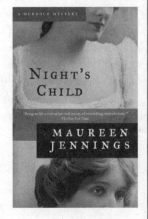

"[Night's Child] *brings to life a violent but vital society of astonishing contradictions.*"
– NEW YORK TIMES

Trade Paperback
978-0-7710-4334-5

VICES OF MY BLOOD

The Reverend Charles Howard sat in judgment on the poor, assessing their applications for the workhouse. But now he is dead, stabbed and brutally beaten in his office. Has some poor beggar he turned down taken his vengeance? Murdoch's investigation takes him into the world of the destitute who had nowhere to turn when they knocked on the Reverend Howard's door.

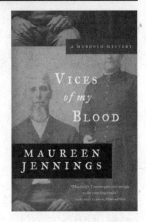

"Jennings opens a window on the realities of a late-Victorian city. . . . Let Jennings be your guide. There's really none better."
– OTTAWA CITIZEN

Trade Paperback
978-0-7710-4332-1

A JOURNEYMAN TO GRIEF

In 1858, a young woman is abducted and taken across the border from Canada and sold into slavery. Thirty-eight years later, the owner of one of Toronto's livery stables is found dead. Then a second man is murdered, his body strangely tied as if he were a rebellious slave. Detective Murdoch has to find out whether Toronto's small "coloured" community has a vicious killer in its midst – an investigation that puts his own life in danger.

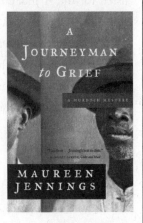

"A Journeyman to Grief is Maureen Jennings's best to date."
– MARGARET CANNON, GLOBE AND MAIL

Trade Paperback
978-0-7710-4340-6

Iden Ford

MAUREEN JENNINGS's first novel in the Detective Murdoch series, *Except the Dying*, was published to rave reviews and shortlisted for both the Arthur Ellis and the Anthony first novel awards. The influential *Drood Review* picked *Poor Tom Is Cold* as one of its favourite mysteries of 2001. *Let Loose the Dogs* was shortlisted for the 2004 Anthony Award for best historical mystery. *Night's Child* was shortlisted for the Arthur Ellis Award, the Bruce Alexander Historical Mystery Award, the Barry Award, and the Macavity Historical Mystery Award. And *A Journeyman to Grief* was nominated for the Arthur Ellis Award. Three of the Detective Murdoch novels have been adapted for television, and a Granada International television series, *The Murdoch Mysteries*, based on the characters from the novels, is shown on CityTV and UKTV.